KEEPER
OF THE
LOST CITIES
EVERBLAZE

Also by Shannon Messenger

KEEPER
OF THE
LOST CITIES
EVERBLAZE

SHANNON MESSENGER

SIMON & SCHUSTER

First published in Great Britain in 2020 by Simon & Schuster UK Ltd
A CBS COMPANY

First published in the USA in 2014 by Aladdin, an imprint of
Simon & Schuster Children's Publishing Division

1 3 5 7 9 10 8 6 4 2

Simon & Schuster UK Ltd
1st Floor, 222 Gray's Inn Road
London WC1X 8HB

www.simonandschuster.co.uk
www.simonandschuster.com.au
www.simonandschuster.co.in

Simon & Schuster Australia, Sydney
Simon & Schuster India, New Delhi

A CIP catalogue record for this book is available from the British Library.

PB ISBN 978-1-4711-8941-8
eBook ISBN 978-1-4711-8942-5

Printed and bound by CPI Group (UK) Ltd, Croydon, CR0 4YY

MIX
Paper from
responsible sources
FSC® C020471

For Faith,
Because I would be lost
without my Book Babe

PREFACE

THE MIRROR SLIPPED FROM SOPHIE'S hands, landing on the petal-covered carpet with the softest thud.

Both sides of the glass survived the crash without cracking. But inside, Sophie shattered.

She kept a smile plastered across her lips as she listened to the rest of the story, searching for the tiniest detail or clue that would rule out the terrifying possibility.

But by the end she knew.

All this time.

All these wasted, hopeless days.

Her kidnapper had been right in front of her.

Watching.

Waiting.

Hiding in plain sight.

All the signs had been there. She'd just been too blind to see them.

And now, it was too late.

ONE

WHAT ARE YOU WAITING FOR?"
Keefe shouted over the howling wind
and the roaring sea. "Don't tell me
the great Sophie Foster is afraid."

"I'm just trying to concentrate!" Sophie shouted back, wishing her voice didn't sound so shaky.

Not that she could fool him.

As an Empath, Keefe could feel the terror coursing through her veins like a herd of stampeding mastodons. All she could do was tug out an itchy eyelash—her nervous habit—and try not to think about how very far down the ocean was.

"You *should* be afraid," Sandor told her in his strange, squeaky voice. He placed a gray gobliny hand on Sophie's shoulder and pulled her back from the edge of the cliff. "There has to be a safer way to teleport."

"There isn't."

Most of the time Sophie was grateful to have the constant protection of a burly bodyguard—especially since her kidnappers had proven they could find her anytime, anywhere.

But sometimes she had to take risks.

She shrugged off Sandor's hand—which took quite a lot of effort, considering he was seven feet tall with biceps like giant boulders—and inched forward, reminding herself that she liked teleporting better than light leaping. Despite the nexuses she had clamped on each wrist, or the force fields they created to hold her body together during a leap, she'd faded too many times to truly feel safe.

Still, she wished free-falling wasn't an essential part of teleporting.

"Want me to push you?" Keefe offered, laughing as Sophie jerked away from him. "Come on, it'll be fun—for me, at least."

Dex snorted behind them. "And *he* gets to go with you today."

"Uh, more like *she* gets to go with *me*," Keefe corrected, flashing his trademark smirk. "Go on, tell Dex who the Council contacted first."

"Only because your dad's in charge of arranging visits to the Sanctuary now," Sophie reminded him.

"Eh, firsties is still firsties. Just admit it, Foster. You need me."

Sophie wished she could argue, but unfortunately the

Council *did* want Keefe to go with her. Apparently Silveny was having some sort of trouble at her new home in the elves' special animal preserve, and since Sophie and Keefe each had a connection with the precious alicorn, the Council had asked *both* of them to head to the Sanctuary immediately.

The Councillors had to be pretty concerned if they were willing to rely on Keefe. . . .

"I'm sorry, Dex," Sophie said, trying not to worry. "You know I'd bring you if I could."

Dex smiled—but not enough to show his dimples—as he went back to playing with the lock she'd asked him to open.

Sophie hadn't wanted to tell him she was going with Keefe, afraid it would make Dex feel left out again. But with Grady off on a classified assignment, and Edaline helping rescue a verminion—a rottweiler-size, purple, hamsteresque creature—before humans found it, Sophie needed a Technopath to get past the Cliffside gate.

"If it makes you feel better, Sandor's not allowed to come either," she added, regretting the words as Sandor reeled on them.

"Yes, and it's completely absurd! I'm supposed to be protecting you—not banned from entering because of arbitrary new rules!'"

"Hey, even my dad's not allowed to go with us. But don't worry"—Keefe draped an arm across Sophie's shoulders—"I'll take care of her for you."

Sophie wasn't sure who groaned louder, her or Dex.

Sandor grabbed Keefe's shoulders, lifting him off the ground. "If I find even one scratch on her—"

"Whoa, easy there, Gigantor," Keefe said, kicking the air, trying to squirm free. "I'm not going to let anything happen to her. But let's not forget that this is Sophie we're talking about. Odds are, we're going to need an Elwin visit."

Even Dex had to laugh at that one.

Sophie glared at all of them.

It wasn't her fault she'd set a record number of visits to the Healing Center at school, plus a ton of additional house calls from Elwin. She didn't choose to have a deadly allergy, or genetically enhanced abilities she couldn't always control. And she definitely didn't ask to have a group of rebels trying to kill her—which was probably why she should listen to Sandor and not leave his sight.

"We'll be fine," she promised, tucking her blond hair behind her ears and trying to sound more confident than she felt. "I can teleport us directly inside the Sanctuary, and security's been tripled since Silveny moved in."

"And you will come *straight* home afterward," Sandor added, waiting for Keefe to nod before setting him down. "I want you back here in an hour."

"Aw, come on," Keefe whined as he adjusted his dark blue cape. "We haven't seen Silveny in two weeks."

Sophie smiled.

She never would've guessed that Keefe could get so attached to a sparkly, winged horse. But he seemed to miss Silveny as much as she did. Maybe more, since he didn't get stuck with a head full of exuberant alicorn transmissions every time he saw her.

Silveny was the only creature that Sophie's unique telepathy couldn't block, probably because the Black Swan had modeled Sophie's genetics off an alicorn's DNA when they "created" her—a fact she was less than thrilled about. Her friends had assured her they didn't think it was weird, but she still felt like "the horse girl."

"You know how panicky Silveny can be," she reminded Sandor, trying to stay focused on the bigger problem. "It's going to take a few hours to calm her down."

Sandor grumbled under his breath. "Fine. You have until sunset—but if you're late, I'm holding you responsible, Mr. Sencen. And trust me when I say you do not want that to happen."

"Fear the wrath of Gigantor—got it." Keefe dragged Sophie back to the edge. "Let's do this!"

"I guess I'll see you at school on Monday," Dex mumbled, staring at the ground as he dug out his home crystal. "I reset the mechanism to make the lock open with your DNA, so you probably won't need me anymore."

"I'll always need you, Dex," Sophie told him, blushing as she quickly added, "you're my best friend."

"And dude, I'm telling you," Keefe jumped in. "When you're finally ready to go public with your ability—which you seriously need to get cracking on, by the way—we *have* to team up. We could break into Dame Alina's office and fill it with dinosaur poop. Or sparkly alicorn poop! Or we could—"

"And this is who you're entrusting your safety to?" Sandor interrupted, looking like he wanted to strangle Keefe again.

"I can take care of myself," Sophie reminded him, tapping her forehead. "Inflictor, remember?"

She might have mixed feelings about her rare ability to inflict pain on people, but it did come in handy if the rebels attacked.

"So we ready?" Keefe asked, swooping his arm to mime them diving off the edge.

Sophie's mouth went dry.

"You got this, Foster. Stop doubting yourself."

She nodded, trying not to look down as she asked, "Do you remember how teleporting works?"

"Well, last time we were kinda falling to our death and stuff, so it's a little blurry. But I'm pretty sure I just cling to you and scream like a banshee while you tear a crack into the universe, right?"

"Something like that. We go on three."

Sandor repeated his objections as they both bent their knees.

"One," Sophie counted, squeezing Keefe's hand so hard her knuckles cracked.

"Two."

She gave herself just slightly longer than a second before she closed her eyes and whispered the final command.

"Three."

The word was still on her lips as they both launched off the cliff.

Keefe whooped and hollered and flailed, but Sophie stayed quiet, trying to tune out everything except the warmth building in her mind and the adrenaline rushing through her veins.

Down down down they fell, until Sophie could feel the salty mist spraying her cheeks. But just when she was about to scream, something clicked inside her mind, and she channeled the burning mental energy out into the sky.

Thunder clapped as a crack formed in the air beneath them, and they dropped straight into the darkness.

Time and space didn't exist in the void. There was no up or down. No right or left. Just the pull of the force and the warmth of Keefe's hand. But Sophie knew that all she had to do was think about where she wanted to go and they'd be free.

The Sanctuary, she thought, picturing the lush meadows and sprawling forests she'd seen in pictures. Her photographic memory could recall every vivid detail, right down to the tiny drops of mist that coated every petal and leaf, sparkling like glitter in the sun.

"You with me, Foster?" Keefe called, when no exit appeared.

"I think so."

She squeezed her eyes tighter, picturing the hollowed out mountains that shielded the Sanctuary from the rest of the world, and the animals in every shape and color wandering through the pastures. She even tried imagining herself standing with Keefe in a meadow, watching Silveny soar above them with gleaming silver wings.

But when she opened her eyes, all she saw was black—thick and suffocating and inescapable.

Panic closed off her chest and Sophie gasped for breath, fighting to concentrate on the Sanctuary with the full power of her mind.

A migraine flared, so intense it felt like her brain was cracking. But the pain wasn't nearly as terrifying as the realization that came with it.

They were trapped in the void.

TWO

CALM DOWN, WE'LL FIGURE THIS out," Keefe promised as Sophie clutched her head and groaned from the migraine. "Are you doing anything different?"

She took a slow, deep breath and tried to think through her panic. "No—I can picture exactly where we need to go. But it's like my mind hits a wall when I try to take us there."

"Have you tried taking us somewhere else?" Keefe asked. "Maybe there's some sort of security around the Sanctuary to keep Teleporters away."

Sophie doubted that, since she was the only elf who could teleport. But it was worth a try.

She just couldn't think of anywhere else to go. Her mind

was racing a million directions, and they all ended in a blank.

"How about home?" Keefe asked. "Can you take us home?"

An image flashed in Sophie's mind, so sharp and clear it made her eyes water. Or maybe the tears were for the narrow crack that finally split through the darkness. She had just enough time to tighten her grip on Keefe's hand. Then the air filled with the boom of thunder as they blasted out of the void.

They hit the ground hard, tumbling across sloshy grass before landing in a heap. Sophie sat up first, untangling herself from Keefe's arms as she stared at the gray, overcast sky.

"Uh . . . this isn't Havenfield," Keefe said, squinting at the narrow street lined with plain, square houses.

"I know." Sophie rallied her concentration, imagining an invisible barrier wrapping around her head to shield herself from the voices pummeling her brain. She'd forgotten how loud human thoughts could be. "This is San Diego."

Keefe scrambled to his feet. "You teleported us to a Forbidden City? Okay. That. Is. Awesome! Don't get me wrong—I could do without the whole almost-getting-trapped-in-the-endless-black-nothingness thing. But this is epic! I mean, that's a human!"

He pointed across the street, to a mom in a bright blue tracksuit, jogging with her baby in a stroller.

"Yeah, and she can probably hear us," Sophie whispered.

Surely everyone must've noticed the teenagers in strange

clothes who fell out of the sky. But the few people outside weren't even glancing their way, too busy walking their dogs or checking their mail.

"I don't think they know we're here," Keefe said, pointing to a small black orb nestled in an overgrown daisy bush. There was another next to the trunk of the giant sycamore in the center of the yard. And three more along the path.

Obscurers.

Sophie had only seen the light-and-sound-bending gadgets once before, in the hands of her kidnappers when they ambushed her and Dex on a bridge in Paris.

One of them was the same blond elf who'd tried to snatch her months earlier, posing as a human jogger on the very street she was standing on.

She walked to the spot where she'd faced him, hoping it might help her remember something new. But all she could see was his face—and Alden had already entered his image in the Council's database, which was supposed to have a record of every elf ever born.

No match had been found.

He was a ghost. Only real when he jumped out of the shadows, like the rest of the rebels in their dark hooded cloaks with a creepy eye in a white circle sewn onto the sleeve.

"Maybe we should go," Sophie said, glancing over her shoulder, half expecting to spot the rebels jogging toward them.

"Are you kidding? I've been dying to see where the

Mysterious Miss Foster grew up." Keefe turned toward her weathered old house. "It's . . . small."

Compared to the crystal mansions of her new world, it was practically a hovel. But humans weren't given a birth fund, like elves were. They didn't get to start their lives with more money than they could ever possibly need.

"It smells weird too," Keefe decided. "What is that?"

"Smog, I think."

She'd forgotten how sour human air tasted. It made her not want to breathe. And the spots of oil staining the street and bits of litter in the gutters made her almost embarrassed to admit she used to live there.

And yet, it was the first place she'd thought of when Keefe had said "home."

A lump caught in her throat as she made her way to the front door. Of course it was locked—and the shutters on the windows were closed tight. But one had a crooked blind, and when Sophie peeked through, she could see that the house had been gutted, right down to the concrete slab and the insulation in the walls.

She shouldn't have been surprised. She knew her family had been relocated—and she'd already seen where the elves had stored all her old things in an unmarked building in Mysterium, one of the smaller Elvin cities.

But staring at the empty shell of her old life made it seem like all her memories had just been a dream. There was nothing left to prove any of it had been real.

Unless . . .

She rushed to the top step on the path, dropping to her knees where her dad's messy writing was still etched into the concrete.

W. D. F.

E. I. F.

S. E. F.

A. R. F.

She traced her fingers over her initials. "They didn't erase me."

Keefe squinted at the sloppy letters. "Does that say 'elf'?"

"No, that's an *I*. Emma Iris Foster. My dad was William David Foster, and my sister was Amy Rose Foster. I don't think my parents realized her initials spelled 'arf' until it was too late. Not that it matters anymore."

Now they were Connor, Kate, and Natalie Freeman.

Sophie wasn't supposed to know their new names. But the Black Swan had given them to her, and she'd been careful not to let anyone know she knew.

"So this is where Fitz found you?" Keefe asked. "I always wondered where he was disappearing to on his 'classified assignments'—and I would've found a way to follow him if I'd known he was off chasing girls."

"He wasn't *chasing* me," Sophie said, feeling her face heat up. "Well . . . he did have to chase me the first time we met. But he was freaking me out."

"Fitz *is* pretty terrifying."

"Hey, when you've been hiding a secret ability for seven years and a total stranger outs you in the middle of a museum, you run. No matter how cute he is."

She wanted to clamp her hands over her mouth as soon as the words left her lips, but that only would've made it worse.

All she could do was turn bright red and wait for Keefe to tease her.

He cleared his throat. "What about that other boy? The one who disappeared? Was that here?"

"I think so."

Part of her hated that Keefe knew her secrets—most of them, anyway. But she'd had to tell him when they were working together to save Alden, and Keefe would never let her forget it. Not that she could remember much about the mysterious disappearing boy.

She knew he had to be important because she had a blurry memory of him vanishing when she was five, *years* before Fitz found her and showed her she was an elf. And she could remember him wearing a blue bramble jersey, a game only elves played. It was also right around the time Mr. Forkle triggered her telepathy, so there had to be a connection.

But the Black Swan had torn the pages out of her journal and wiped the memory out of her mind, save for the few vague details she'd managed to recover.

"He stood right here," she said, moving closer to the syca-more and running her fingers along a branch.

He must've been taller than she'd realized. Not really a boy at all. More like a teenager. And there was something else—a detail so close she could feel it prickling her consciousness. But no matter how hard she concentrated, she couldn't reach it.

"Hey, no need to punish the innocent plant life," Keefe said as she kicked the tree. "I'm sure the Black Swan will tell you everything soon."

Sophie wished she could believe him. She'd thought the Black Swan would be working with her now, especially since she'd risked her life to let them heal her abilities. But two weeks had passed since she'd fled their hideout during the reb-els' attack, and she hadn't heard a peep. Not a note. Not a clue. Not even the slightest sign that they were still watching her.

She turned to the pale blue house next door, where Mr. Forkle used to sit every day, looking bloated and wrinkled in his ruckleberry-induced disguise. He spent twelve years sitting in the middle of his lawn, playing with his silly gnomes, so he could keep an eye on her. Now all that was left were a few weathered figures, peeking through the weeds with their tiny, ugly faces.

"What are those supposed to be?" Keefe asked as he fol-lowed her over to the planter.

"Garden gnomes."

"You've got to be kidding me."

"You should see what humans think elves look like. They give us bells on our shoes and pointy ears—though I guess they're right about the ears."

Sophie still wasn't thrilled that her ears would grow points as she aged. But at least she wouldn't have to worry about it for a few thousand years, thanks to the elves' indefinite lifespan.

Keefe laughed as he squatted to get a closer look at the tiny statues with pointy hats. "Okay, I have to take one of these home. My agriculture Mentor will pee his pants."

"Wait," Sophie said as Keefe reached for a gnome that was sitting on a rainbow-colored mushroom. "What if it's a clue?"

There was no rhyme or reason to the way the gnomes lined up, but something felt *familiar* about the arrangement. She let her eyes go out of focus, and as the shadows blended into a dark swirl, the memory slowly surfaced.

"Cygnus!"

"What's a Cygnus?" Keefe asked as she dropped to her knees and started to dig in the planter.

"A constellation. Each gnome is one of the stars. We call them Aquello, Fuschaire, Rosine, Grisenna, Sapphilene, Scarletina, Nievello, Gildere, and Peacerre—but humans call them Cygnus."

"Okay Miss I've-memorized-all-the-stars, no need to show off. And I still don't see why you're burrowing like a dwarf."

"Because Cygnus means 'swan,'" Sophie explained as she scooped out another handful of dirt. "And the constellation is made up of ten stars. But there are only nine gnomes. So I'm checking where the tenth star would be."

Slimy mud squished under her nails, but Sophie kept digging. After another minute her fingertips brushed something cold and smooth.

"It's . . . a bottle," Keefe said as she unearthed a tiny green vial and wiped the crystal clean on the grass.

"And a note," Sophie added, removing the stopper and tipping the bottle until a curl of paper slid free.

Keefe snatched the note before she could touch it. "Someone *not* covered in swamp sludge should read that."

He had a point.

She wiped her hands on the grass as Keefe frowned at the note. "What?" she asked.

"You're not going to like it."

"I usually don't." The Black Swan could be annoyingly vague with their clues. But she was happy to have them back in touch. Or, she was until Keefe showed her the message.

Wait for instructions and stick to the plan.

"They could've at least made it rhyme again," he said, stuffing the note back into the bottle. "And what plan?"

Sophie took the bottle and sniffed the nozzle, gagging at the familiar salty smell.

It was the same green bottle she'd drunk an entire ounce of

limbium from—and almost died in the process, thanks to her allergy—so she'd be able to heal minds again.

"Prentice is the plan," she told Keefe, rubbing the star-shaped scar on the back of her hand. Mr. Forkle had injected her with tweaked human medicine to stop the allergic reaction, and the needle wound had never gone away. "They're telling me to wait until they decide it's time to heal him."

"Yeah, well I still think they could've rhymed. *Wait for instructions and stick to the plan. Now get home safe as fast as you can!*"

Sophie was too disappointed to laugh.

She definitely wanted to heal Prentice. But she didn't want to *wait*.

Prentice had been a Keeper for the Black Swan, and thirteen years ago he'd let his mind get broken in a memory break to keep Sophie's existence secret from the rest of the elves. She hated knowing he was locked in a tiny cell in Exile, moaning and drooling and waiting for her to pull him out of the darkness.

Plus, every day that passed increased the chance that Alden would shatter again. His guilt over his role in Prentice's memory break had already broken his mind once—and even though Sophie had healed him, the only way to ensure his safety would be to bring Prentice back.

But the Councillors were still deciding if they were going to allow Prentice to be healed. And apparently the Black Swan were content to sit back and wait.

"Hey—how did they even know we'd come here?" Keefe asked as Sophie shoved the bottle into her pocket a little harder than she needed to. "I mean, they've pulled off some crazy things—but I doubt even they could guess you'd have trouble teleporting and accidentally bring us to your old house instead of your new one."

"No," Sophie agreed, hating that the only new note the Black Swan had given her probably wasn't new at all. "They must've just assumed I'd come here eventually."

Still, she had a more pressing problem to deal with than the Black Swan being stubborn—again.

Neither she nor Keefe were old enough to have their own pathfinders, so they'd have to get to a Leapmaster—a gadget made of leaping crystals—in order to leap to the Sanctuary.

"Do you have your home crystal with you?" she asked Keefe.

"Yeah. Why?"

"It's not safe to teleport until I figure out what went wrong. It's also not like there's a cliff to jump off. And if we go back to Havenfield, Sandor will never let us leave—especially now that we can only leap outside the Sanctuary gates and wait to be let in."

Keefe stared at his feet, looking about as unexcited by this idea as Sophie felt. His father definitely belonged on her list of People She Liked To Avoid.

"Silveny needs us," she said, reminding herself as much as him.

"I know. But . . ."

"What?" she asked when he didn't finish.

"I . . . don't bring friends home."

He fidgeted with the pin clasping his cape—the Sencen family crest. Two jeweled hands holding a candle with an emerald flame. His father had only given it to him a few weeks ago, even though most kids wore their family crest their whole lives.

"Okay," Sophie said slowly. "I guess we'll go back to Havenfield, then. If we run straight for the Leapmaster we might be able to get out of there before Sandor can stop us."

"No, we won't."

Probably not. Sandor's goblin supersenses would detect them the second they arrived.

"It's still worth a try." She dug out her home crystal—a pendant with a single facet—and held it up to the light.

Keefe glared at the beam refracting toward the ground. "This is stupid."

He pulled out his own home crystal and created another light path.

Sophie didn't have to be an Empath to feel the tension in his grip, or the way his fingers shook as they laced together with hers.

Her hands were shaking too.

But neither of them said anything as they stepped into the light. Then the warm, feathery rush pulled them both away.

THREE

WHOA," SOPHIE WHISPERED AS she stared at the mansion looming over her.

Actually, mansion wasn't the right word.

Skyscraper, maybe?

Though based on the squirmy feeling in her stomach, Ominous Tower of Doom might've been more appropriate.

"Yeah . . . my dad's a 'bigger is better' kind of guy," Keefe said as he led her through an iron archway with the word "Candleshade" laced into the design.

Sophie craned her neck, trying to guess how high the tower climbed. There had to be at least a hundred stories before the main building split into a series of narrow towers, each crowned with a curved golden roof that reminded Sophie of a flame. But there were no windows to count to tell her if she was right. The crystal walls were perfectly smooth, with no break except a single golden doorway, which was surprisingly small for such a massive place.

Keefe pressed his palm against the handle and the door swished open, gliding over the smooth black floor without so much as a hiss. The foyer they entered was empty except for a silver winding staircase that spiraled up and up and up some more, until Sophie lost sight of the twisting steps. The walls were just as smooth on the inside, but the crystal glowed with thousands of tiny blue flames tucked among the facets.

Balefire, Sophie realized.

Only a Pyrokinetic could spark a balefire flame, and pyrokinesis had been banned for millennia—ever since an accident that killed five people. But that wasn't why Sophie was struck by seeing it.

Balefire had been Fintan's trademark—until he moved on to Everblaze.

Before she could block it, Fintan's face filled her mind, and not the angry, rebellious Fintan she'd seen in Exile, or the reckless Fintan surrounded by neon yellow flames she'd seen when she probed his memories.

The pained, haunted Fintan after the memory break she'd helped perform, rocking back and forth in his cell, his screams echoing off the walls as she and Alden left him to his madness . . .

"You okay?" Keefe asked, grabbing her arm to snap her out of the flashback.

"Of course."

"You realize you can't lie to an Empath, right?"

"And yet you try it all the time," a deep voice boomed from above.

The sound of the stairway spinning to life muffled Keefe's groan, and a second later, Lord Cassius stepped off the stairs and into the foyer.

With their blond hair and ice blue eyes, the family resemblance between father and son was impossible to miss—though Keefe's artfully mussed hairstyle and untucked shirt stood in sharp contrast to Lord Cassius's immaculateness.

"Miss Foster," he said, flicking an invisible speck off his hunter green cape. "We run into each other again." He tilted his head, gazing at the blindingly high ceiling with obvious pride. "There's no other place quite like this, is there? But I'm guessing you didn't come here to marvel at the architecture—especially since you're supposed to be at the Sanctuary. So tell me, to what do I owe the honor?"

Sophie glanced at Keefe, wishing he would jump in with one of his easy lies—but he was too busy staring at the floor like it contained the deepest secrets of the universe.

"We just . . . took a slight detour," Sophie eventually said, avoiding Lord Cassius's eyes.

He had a way of studying her like he could see straight

through her—and maybe he could, because he cleared his throat and said, "Visiting a Forbidden City is more than a *slight* detour."

When her jaw dropped, he laughed—a sharp, hollow sound.

"The hot waves of guilt wafting off you completely give you away," he explained.

"You can feel that?" Keefe asked, sounding as stunned as Sophie felt.

Most Empaths could only read someone's emotions if they were touching them. But for some reason—probably another side effect of her freaky, manipulated genes—Keefe could read Sophie's from a distance. She'd hoped he was the only one who could, but apparently . . .

"You get your talent from me," Lord Cassius reminded Keefe. "Though I'll confess, female emotions are a bit harder to interpret. But that's where simple deduction comes in. I assumed you wouldn't miss your appointment at the Sanctuary without a *very* good reason. Pair that with your rather unique past, Miss Foster—and the reputations you both have for seeking out trouble—and it's the most logical conclusion."

It seemed like there were lots of other conclusions he could've come to.

Keefe must've agreed, because he stepped closer, touching his dad's wrist. "That's not how you knew."

Lord Cassius pulled his hand away and patted the back of his already perfect hair. "Well, I was trying to spare our guest from witnessing an uncomfortable conversation. But if you must know, I *have* noticed that my blue pathfinder is missing."

"And what? You think I took it?"

"Who else?"

Blue crystals were the only way to light leap to the Forbidden Cities, and they were restricted to specific members of the Nobility.

"It wasn't me this time," Keefe told him. "Check, if you don't believe me."

He held out his arm, daring his father to feel if he was lying.

Lord Cassius frowned. "How did you get to the Forbidden City, then?"

Keefe dropped his arm back to his side. "Doesn't matter."

"Actually, it does. I think you're forgetting that your trip today was *illegal*—and I don't mean that as a threat," he added quickly, glancing at Sophie. "I'm sure you had your reasons, and that *Sophie* was careful while you were there. But if I'm going to keep this secret for you, I need to understand what I'm protecting."

The smile he flashed came closer to reaching his eyes than any other smile Sophie had seen him give. But it wasn't enough to make her trust him.

"You don't have to keep it secret," she said. "I'll tell Alden the whole story the next time I see him."

The sound of the whirring staircase drowned out Lord Cassius's reply, and when it stopped a second later, Keefe's mother swept into the room in a sleek dress and cape the same pale peach as her skin. Her tall, jeweled heels clacked on the dark floor and her blond hair was swept into a twisted updo—like she should be walking a red carpet, not standing in the empty first floor of her home.

"Why didn't you tell me we had a visitor, Cassius?" she asked, clicking her tongue at her husband before turning to Sophie with a tight-looking smile. "I don't think we were properly introduced before. I'm Lady Gisela."

They hadn't been "properly introduced" because they'd met at Alden's sort-of-funeral, and Lady Gisela had been too busy sniping at her heartbroken son. But Sophie held her tongue, fumbling through an awkward curtsy as she said, "I'm Sophie."

"Yes, I know. Even if you weren't our world's most infamous new citizen, my son talks about you all the time."

"Not *all* the time," Keefe muttered, going back to staring at the floor.

Sophie copied him.

"So are you staying with us for dinner?" Lady Gisela asked, "Or wait—I thought you two were supposed to be somewhere, doing . . . something."

She tossed out the words like she couldn't bother to remember the specifics.

"We are." Keefe snatched Sophie's wrist and pulled her toward the stairs. "In fact, I'm sure they're waiting for us at the Sanctuary, so we should get going."

"Not like that, you won't," Lady Gisela said, blocking them. "Honestly, Keefe, what am I going to do with you?"

Sophie wished Keefe would snap back with one of his infamously snarky answers. Instead he froze, like he'd become a statue of The Most Miserable Boy on the Planet, as his mom smoothed his shirt and straightened his cape. He didn't even flinch when she licked her thumb and wiped an invisible smudge off his face. But he came back to life when she reached for his head.

"Not the hair!"

"You and your ridiculous hair." She reached for him again and he swatted her arm away. His hand barely touched her, but she still gasped and clutched her shoulder.

"I'm fine," she promised, glancing at Sophie.

But she was still rubbing her shoulder. And as she rearranged the peachy fabric of her cape, Sophie caught a glimpse of a red wound, near the top of her arm.

Lord Cassius stepped forward, blocking his wife from Sophie's view. "You two should go. The Sanctuary is waiting."

"Do you need to let them know we'll be leaping outside, instead of teleporting in?" Keefe asked him.

"Actually, I think they were expecting that."

"Why would they be—" Sophie started to ask, but Keefe dragged her onto the first stair.

"Ever been on a vortinator?" he asked.

"I don't think so." And she wished it didn't sound so much like a carnival ride from her nightmares.

29

"Better hold on tight, then." He grinned as she tightened her grip on his hand. "I meant to the railing."

"Oh."

Her face felt like it was on fire, and she'd barely grabbed the silver banister, when Keefe said, "Two Hundred!" Then everything turned into a spinning, sparkling blur of rushing air, and Sophie wanted to scream or throw up or pass out, but she didn't have time for anything because they'd already stopped.

"You with me, Foster?" Keefe asked as she leaned against the rail, wondering if her stomach was still on the ground floor.

"Do you really ride that thing every day?"

"You get used to it after a couple of turns. Come on." He offered her his hand, and Sophie was too dizzy not to take it.

It took ten deep breaths for her head to clear enough to realize they were in one of the golden-roofed towers. Dangling above them were more round crystals than Sophie had ever seen.

"The Leapmaster 10,000," Keefe explained.

Sophie couldn't even think of ten thousand places she'd want to go.

But there was one she was definitely ready to see.

"The Sanctuary," Keefe said, making the Leapmaster rotate. A single crystal dropped low enough to catch the sunlight from the window. "Okay, let's try this again."

FOUR

THE WARM, RACING LIGHT DROPPED them at the base of the Himalayas, and Keefe pulled his cape tighter around his shoulders.

"Couldn't they have picked a warmer mountain range to build this place?" he grumbled as they trudged up the snow-covered path to the Sanctuary.

"I'm pretty sure they needed as much room as possible," Sophie reminded him.

The Sanctuary housed all of the creatures that the elves had taken into protective custody—everything from dinosaurs to dodo birds, plus any animal that humans foolishly believed was "magical." They even kept endangered species, wanting to make sure they continued to thrive.

The elves believed every creature existed on the planet for a reason, and to allow even one to go extinct would cause irreparable damage to the delicate balance of their world.

An icy blast of wind cut through Sophie's tunic, making her wish she'd worn a cape. She always felt dumb wearing them—but braving the snow without a cloak was definitely dumber.

She also wished she'd taken Dex's offer a few months back, and let him teach her how to regulate her body temperature.

"Here," Keefe said, draping his cape over her shoulders.

"I'm f-f-fine. You d-d-don't h-h-have t-t-to—"

"That would be a lot more convincing without all the shivering," he interrupted. "Besides, it takes more than a little snow to get to me." He flashed a smug smirk, but she could see he was already shivering.

"You don't know how to regulate your body temperature either?" she asked, feeling her voice steady as Keefe fastened the warm cape under her chin.

"Eh, that only works when it's sorta cold, not freezing. But no, I've never learned. That's the kind of random skill you only learn in Exillium."

The name caused a whole different kind of shudder.

Exillium was a school the Council had threatened to send Sophie to if she couldn't hack it at Foxfire. She didn't know anything about it, except that people kept telling her she didn't want to go there.

"Why does Dex know how to regulate his temperature, then?" Sophie asked. The only school he'd ever attended was Foxfire.

Keefe laughed. "Are you really surprised his family would teach him something weird?"

"Good point."

Dex's parents were known for playing by their own rules and not following social conventions. His dad had even admitted that he designed their store, Slurps and Burps, to be intentionally bizarre and chaotic, just to make the stuffy nobles—as he liked to call them—squirm while they shopped for their elixirs.

Keefe shivered again, his whole body shaking, and Sophie tried to hand him back his cape.

"Nope. You deserve it, Foster," he insisted. "You have saved my life a few times, after all."

"Only once," Sophie corrected.

"Yeah, well you also saved the whole world from the Everblaze, so that counts too. Plus I'll face the wrath of Gigantor if I let you freeze to death, remember?"

"Well, thanks," she mumbled as he pulled the hood up over her head, warming her icy ears.

He held her gaze for a second too long before he backed away and shrugged. "Just don't lose the Sencen crest. My father will strangle me."

He clearly meant it as a joke—but it reminded Sophie of his mother's bruise.

And the way she'd tried to hide it.

And the way Lord Cassius had rushed them out of there after she saw it. . . .

"So," she said, not quite sure how to broach the subject as they went back to trudging through the snow. "Everything's okay at your house, right?"

"Um, if you leave out my father's constant lectures on how I'm 'not living up to my potential,' then yeah. Why?"

"No reason."

"Psh—there's always a reason with you, Foster. Spill it."

Sophie tugged out a snow-covered eyelash, wishing for a little extra courage as she flicked it away. "Just . . . your dad doesn't ever . . ."

Keefe stopped walking. "Ever what?"

Sophie sighed.

This was so much harder than it seemed on television.

"When your dad gets angry, does he ever . . . hurt anyone?"

The last words came out as a whisper.

Keefe laughed, but his smile quickly faded. "Wait, you're serious? Wow, uh, I know my dad has the whole stern and scary thing going for him, but still—that's crazy."

"So that's a no, then?" she asked, needing to hear him say it.

"Yeah, definitely a no. You really thought . . . ?"

"I don't know. Your mom had a red wound on her shoulder—"

"She did?"

"Yeah. And your dad looked like he didn't want me to see it."

Keefe frowned. "Well, I have no idea what that was about. But it's not what you're thinking. People don't do that around here. Remember, that whole guilt-shattering-our-sanity thing? That goes for violence, too."

The elves did seem to be incredibly peaceful. They didn't even have police.

And yet, Sophie could still remember the searing pain as her kidnapper burned her wrists, trying to force her to answer his questions. She could still see the dead look in Dex's eyes as the rebels blasted him with a paralyzing melder over and over. She could still hear the crunch of Silveny's wing breaking when the rebels dragged her out of the sky, right before they broke several of Keefe's ribs in a fight.

Either elves were capable of more than they realized, or the rebels were insane.

She didn't know which would be worse.

"Okay. Well. Sorry," she said quietly. "I just wanted to make sure."

"No need to apologize. It's nice to know the Mysterious Miss F. cares."

Neither of them seemed to know what to say after that, so they walked in uncomfortable silence as their flat shoes crunch crunch crunched through the snow.

"I don't understand how humans haven't found this place," Sophie said when they reached the towering silver gates set into the mountain. But then she spotted the round black Obscurers scattered among the various rocky outcroppings.

"Careful," Keefe warned, pointing at a bunch of silver fork-like gadgets that were stabbed into the ground next to some of the rocks. "Those are effluxers. Step too close, and they'll make you stink like you've been hanging around a pack of gulons. My dad set one off while the gnomes were installing them, and when he got home I could smell him all the way on the hundred-and-eighty-seventh floor. I guess the smell damages ogres' sinuses or something."

"Ogres?" Sophie asked, taking a giant step away from the stinky gadgets.

"Yep. One of the goblin patrols found some weird footprints a few nights ago, and thought they might be from ogres. They couldn't tell for sure, because the tracks had no scent, and by the time Alvar got here—"

"Fitz's brother?" Sophie interrupted.

"Yeah. He's been working with the ogres for a few years, so my dad figured he'd be able to tell if they were involved. But by the time he got there, it had snowed, and the tracks were gone. So the Council had the effluxers installed, just in case."

"Okay," Sophie said slowly. "But . . . I thought we had a treaty with the ogres."

"We do—but that doesn't mean we trust them. Look at what happened with humans."

Throughout the centuries, the elves had signed treaties with all of the "intelligent" creatures, trying to ensure peace. But humans decided *they* wanted to rule the world, and in order to prevent a war, the elves chose to disappear. They still watched from the shadows, finding subtle ways to share their wisdom when they could. But the humans continued their path of violence and destruction, and eventually the elves had to cut off contact completely.

And yet, the Black Swan broke every law—risking their sanity and their lives—specifically so they could hide Sophie among humans. She still didn't understand why.

"Why would the ogres care about the Sanctuary?" she asked, studying the massive gates.

"Uh, hello? Silveny's in there. Remember the whole Timeline to Extinction thing?"

She did. The elves had been searching for a female alicorn for decades, desperate to breed her with the only alicorn they'd ever found, a male already at the Sanctuary. If they couldn't start repopulating the species soon, alicorns would be the first creatures to go extinct.

But Sophie still didn't see why ogres would care about a couple of sparkly flying horses. Grady had told her once that ogres didn't value animals' lives the way elves did.

What else would've made the footprints, though?

"Do we need to knock or something?" she asked, ready to get to the other—much safer—side of the gates.

"I'm sure they're scanning our registry pendants right now, to make sure we have the right clearance."

Sophie's hand darted to her neck, her fingers closing around a triangular crystal hanging from her choker. The Council had added extra chains to hers, after the kidnappers cut her first pendant off. But she still liked to double-check that it was there.

"Finally," Keefe said as a loud clang echoed off the mountains.

The ground shook when the silver gates swung apart, and a blast of warmth prickled Sophie's skin as she followed Keefe into the sunny paradise.

She knew she was walking deep into a mountain range, but she had a hard time believing it as she stared at the lush meadows and forests of flowering trees that seemed to stretch on forever. The sky was a perfect cerulean blue—though it shifted with every step, flashing through the colors of the spectrum as if they were walking inside a rainbow—and the air had a crisp sweetness, like biting into an apple.

"How much of this is real?" she asked, rubbing her eyes, half expecting it to disappear.

"The sky is an illusion. And they hid the walls to make the space feel bigger. But everything else is real."

"How did they—"

"You're late," a tall, skinny elf interrupted as he stepped out of a clump of bushes. His chocolate brown tunic was covered in bright green patches, and his thick black hair hung in long tangles. "Do you have any idea how much trouble that's caused me?"

"Sorry, sir," Sophie mumbled, avoiding his piercing blue eyes.

He laughed—a bitter sound that felt sharp in her ears. "I am many things, Miss Foster, but I am definitely not a 'sir'. You may call me Jurek. I'm the equestrian caretaker for the Sanctuary. And I was right, wasn't I?"

Sophie glanced at Keefe, but he looked as confused as her. "Right?"

Jurek pulled a lumpy satchel out of one of the bushes and slung it over his shoulder, motioning for Sophie and Keefe to follow him. "You couldn't teleport here, could you?"

"Uh, no," she admitted. "How did you know?"

He smiled. "Tell me this: If you could teleport *into* the Sanctuary, why have the alicorns never teleported *out*?"

That . . . was a very good question.

She squinted at the rainbow sky, which wasn't really a sky at all. "Is it the mountains?"

"That'd be my guess. Keeps light leapers away—why not Teleporters? But then what do I know? I'm not the one with the fancy abilities and the strange eyes."

"Well, you clearly knew more than me," she said, ignoring the insult. She was getting used to being the only brown-eyed elf.

"So wait, she can't teleport through anything solid?" Keefe asked, frowning when Jurek and Sophie both nodded. "Dang—that's going to kill a bunch of my plans. But don't worry, Foster, there's still plenty of ways we can cause trouble."

He nudged Sophie, but she couldn't return his smile.

She'd liked knowing that if the Council didn't give permission to heal Prentice, she could teleport to Exile on her own. But the isolated prison was buried deep in the center of the earth, so if she couldn't teleport through anything solid, there was no way she could reach it on her own.

"Whoa, hang on a minute," Keefe said, stepping in front of Jurek to block his path. "You didn't think it might be a good idea to be like, 'Hey guys, that teleporting to the Sanctuary thing might not work out so well. You could get trapped in that creepy black voidy place'?"

"Actually, I told her father—who informed me that as a Talentless, it's my job to tend to the animals and prepare for visitors, not to pretend to know things about *special abilities*."

Sophie cringed.

Elves without special abilities were just as wealthy as other elves, and supposedly they were still equals. But they also didn't qualify for the elite levels at Foxfire, couldn't become members of the Nobility, and wore different clothes for their jobs in "working class" cities. And sometimes it seemed like people saw them as *lesser*.

But that mostly happened with jerks like Vika, Timkin, and Stina Heks, a family who loved to think they were better than *everyone*. Sophie hated to think that Grady was like that too.

"Grady really said that?" she asked quietly.

"Who's Grady?"

"My father." She was surprised at how easily the word rolled off her tongue. Grady and Edaline had only adopted Sophie about three months earlier—after a rocky process—and she still didn't quite feel comfortable calling them Mom and Dad.

Jurek pointed to the Sencen crest on her cape. "I thought Lord Cassius was your adoptive father."

40

"Oh! No, this is Keefe's." And she could *totally* see Keefe's dad saying that.

Jurek snorted. "I guess I should've known. They both have that same smug smirk."

"Yeah, but I have better hair," Keefe said, mussing it even more as Sophie gave him back his cape.

"Let's hope that's not the only way you're better." Jurek walked away without another word.

Keefe rolled his eyes like he didn't care. But Sophie noticed he hid the Sencen crest in the thick folds of his cape before he followed.

She trailed silently behind, staring at the shimmering flowers and trying to think of something to say.

After several awkward seconds, Keefe cleared his throat. "So, where's Glitter Butt?"

"He means Silveny," Sophie clarified. And she'd been wondering the same thing. The pastures around them only held grazing mammoths, feathery dinosaurs, and enormous wolf-bear things.

"All equestrians are in the violet pastures," Jurek explained as he veered off the path to cut straight over a line of hills.

The long blue grass was slick with dew and Sophie struggled not to slip as she ran behind him. By the time they crested the last hill she was sweaty and out of breath, but she didn't mind one bit when a familiar voice filled her mind.

Friend! Sophie! Keefe! Visit!

Yes, Sophie transmitted back, shielding her eyes as she tried to find her.

A pair of silver-and-black unicorns galloped in one of the purple-grassed fields, and a small river was lined with strange bluish-green horses that seemed almost slimy. But no sparkly alicorns in sight.

"She prefers the pastures down here," Jurek said before plopping to the grass and sliding down the hill.

Keefe launched after Jurek immediately, but Sophie stared at the slope, fairly certain the slide would end with an Elwin visit.

It was only when Keefe shouted, "Come on, Foster. Don't wimp out on me now!" that she dropped to the ground and pushed off after them.

Bits of grass and mud peppered her face—and she could tell her backside would be bruised for days—but she bumped and bobbed and somehow made it safely to the bottom.

Well . . . *almost* safely.

Stopping was harder than she'd thought, and she ended up crashing into Keefe, knocking him on top of her.

"Y'know, if you're trying to sweep me off my feet, there are less painful ways," he told her, laughing as she struggled to stand.

Sophie turned away to hide her burning cheeks. "Was the sliding really necessary?" she asked Jurek.

"No. But it was fun." Jurek tossed his wild hair, sending bits of grass flying.

42

Friend! Sophie! Keefe! Fly!

Sophie spun toward the sound, feeling tears prick her eyes as she spotted a glittering streak, flipping somersaults in the rainbow sky. Part of her had worried Silveny's wing wouldn't ever heal properly. But clearly she was good as new. And just as sparkly as ever.

"She's happy to see me, isn't she?" Keefe asked.

"Not as happy as she is to see *me*."

Though Sophie wished there was a bit less *Keefe! Keefe! Keefe!* filling her head. And she was less than thrilled when Silveny tucked her wings and dove, landing next to Keefe with an exuberant whinny.

"See? Glitter Butt loves me." Keefe reached to pat her sparkly rump, but Silveny scooted away, snapping at her tail.

"I told you she hates that nickname," Sophie said smugly.

She tried to call Silveny to her side, but Silveny was too busy chasing her tail to obey.

Keefe frowned. "Do you feel that, Foster?"

"Sort of." Sophie closed her eyes, trying to sort through the dizzying emotions swirling in her head. She'd forgotten how overwhelming Silveny's energy could be.

Calm, she transmitted. But Silveny kept on spinning, and the more she circled, the more Sophie picked up a darker emotion in the mix.

Why are you afraid? she asked, repeating the question until Silveny finally stopped to look at her.

A rush of fear clawed at Sophie's mind like an angry vermin-ion, and she stepped back, needing room to breathe. "What is she afraid of?"

"It's . . . probably easier to show you." Jurek opened the satchel he'd been carrying and pulled out a handful of twisted blue stalks, filling the air with a spicy, cinnamon scent.

Silveny's hunger clouded Sophie's mind, but the alicorn backed away from the treats.

"Why would she—"

An ear-splitting whinny cut Sophie off, and Silveny reared back as a blur of silver dropped out of the sky. Jurek barely managed to pull Keefe out of the way before a huge alicorn with blue-tipped wings landed right where he'd been standing.

"This is Greyfell," Jurek said, tossing the handful of treats to distract the new Alicorn while he swung a golden lasso around the massive horse's neck. Greyfell bucked and thrashed and wrestled against the restraint, but Jurek managed to hold tight. "He's our resident male. And up until a few days ago, he and Silveny were getting along just fine."

"So what changed?" Sophie asked as Silveny screeched and launched back into the sky.

"I have no idea." Jurek tried to stroke Greyfell's nose, but the alicorn glared at him with the coldest brown eyes Sophie had ever seen. "That's what you're here to figure out—and you'd bet-ter do it quick. Otherwise I'm afraid he's going to kill Silveny."

FIVE

IT'S OKAY, SOPHIE TRANSMITTED AS Silveny circled above them. *I won't let him hurt you.*

But as Greyfell thrashed again, nearly pulling Jurek over, she wondered if she could really keep that promise.

Everything about Greyfell was *fierce*. His wild eyes. The constant twitching in his bulky muscles. The gleam of his teeth as he tried—and thankfully failed—to snap through the thick rope holding him.

And yet, the cold waves rippling through Sophie's mind felt more like fear than rage.

"Careful," Keefe warned as Sophie took a step closer. "I'm getting some pretty serious I-will-bite-your-hand-off-if-you-touch-me vibes."

It's okay, Sophie transmitted. *I'm not going to hurt you.*

Greyfell stamped his hooves.

Silveny whinnied, transmitting, *Sophie! Danger! Fly!* But Sophie ordered her to stay back, wishing she could block Silveny's panicked shouts from her head.

She closed her eyes, letting everything else fade to a hum as she imagined her consciousness stretching toward Greyfell like a blanket of feathers. Most Telepaths couldn't open their minds to the thoughts of animals, but thanks to her enhanced abilities, Sophie's head filled with images of snowcapped mountains and towering trees and lakes so clear they looked like mirrors of the sky. Everything felt bright and open and free, and yet a hollow ache laced through every scene—the same mournful emptiness Sophie remembered feeling the first time she met Silveny.

You're not alone anymore, Sophie promised Greyfell. *Friend.*

She sent images along with the word: scenes of herself caring for Silveny, and flying with Silveny, and letting Silveny nuzzle her neck—anything to prove that Greyfell could trust her. She even showed him she could teleport, wanting him to know how deep their connection went.

A word filled her mind then—one that took Sophie a second to translate from the alicorn language Greyfell was using.

Kin.

Yes, Sophie transmitted, opening her eyes to study him. Greyfell's irises were flecked with gold—just like hers—and as he held her gaze, tiny bits of cold speckled her consciousness, like icy drops of rain inside her head.

The more she concentrated on them, the more they turned into a steady stream.

Then a downpour of nightmares.

Sharp-toothed beasts, and humans with gleaming weapons—chasing, hunting, out for blood. Screams and war cries echoed in her consciousness as the ache of scars still healing brought tears to her eyes.

She tried to pull her mind free, but Greyfell kept sending violent, bloody scenes filled with lumpy-faced monsters—ogres, she realized—beating and bludgeoning everything they touched until the whole world was red. She wanted to cry, scream, scratch the scenes out of her brain. But she could only stand there as the fear seemed to crystallize inside her, freezing her from the inside out.

"Whoa," Keefe said, dragging Sophie back. He held her tight as she shivered against his chest. "It's okay. I've got you."

"What happened?" she asked when her voice was working again.

"I have no idea. One minute you and Greyfell were becoming BFFs. Next minute you were shaking and Greyfell was thrashing so much Jurek had to sedate him."

"He did?" She tried to spin around and felt her knees collapse.

Keefe barely managed to catch her. "Hey—take it easy. He's fine, see?"

He turned so they were facing Greyfell's collapsed body, which didn't *look* fine. His wide eyes stared at nothing and his purple tongue drooped to the ground. But his chest was rising and falling with slow, heavy breaths.

"He'll wake up as soon as I remove this," Jurek said, pointing to a lei of tiny green-blue flowers around Greyfell's neck.

Sophie usually loved anything teal, but there was something ominous about the pointed petals, like nature was trying to warn everyone to stay away.

"Dreamlilies," Jurek explained. "The slightest touch of their pollen and you're out like a hibernating bugbear."

Sophie didn't know what a bugbear was, but she hoped they slept peacefully.

"So," Keefe said, making her realize she was still holding on to him. "You okay now?"

"Yeah. Sorry." She pulled away to stand on her own, hiding behind her hair so he couldn't see her blushing. "Greyfell's just had a *much* harder life than Silveny."

Her voice quivered as her mind replayed the horrors Greyfell had shown her. He must be centuries old, and had witnessed the murder of his own kind at the hands of all manner of vicious creature. Most of the time he'd barely escaped with his own life, while friends, family—even his mate—weren't as fortunate.

48

But one memory was far more terrifying than the others, partially because it was familiar, but mostly because it was *recent*.

"The rebels have been here," Sophie whispered.

"You're sure?" Keefe asked, the same time Jurek said, "That's impossible."

But Sophie knew what she'd seen. "Greyfell saw a black-cloaked figure do something to Silveny while she was sleeping. That's why he's afraid of her."

She called Silveny down, half hoping she was wrong as she led her a safe distance away from Greyfell's unconscious form. But when she traced her fingers through the shimmering silver strands of Silveny's tail, it didn't take long to find what she was looking for—right where Greyfell had shown her it would be.

"This is why Silveny keeps chasing her tail," Sophie said, holding out a quarter-size disk with five tiny crystals set into one side.

She'd never seen one so large or intricate, and she'd never seen one made of silver.

But she knew exactly what it was, even before Jurek tore his hands through his hair and said, "That looks like a tracker."

SIX

"THERE MUST BE SOME MISTAKE," JUREK said for the dozenth time as he combed through Silveny's mane, checking for other trackers. "No one could've gotten near either of the alicorns without my knowledge."

"The rebels always find a way," Sophie whispered.

They'd snatched her and Dex from a cave right outside her home, and tracked them down in the streets of Paris after the Black Swan helped them escape. They'd thwarted Sandor's goblin senses and snuck into Havenfield's pastures without being detected, leaving behind nothing but a single, unidentifiable footprint. And most impressive of all, they'd somehow followed her and Keefe across the ocean in the middle of the night, even though they were flying on the back of an alicorn, heading to a cave only the Black Swan knew existed.

"We need to tell the Council to move Silveny out of the Sanctuary," she decided.

"To where?" Jurek asked. "Where else could possibly be safer than this?"

"Uh, clearly there's a few holes in the security," Keefe said, stroking Silveny's nose to keep her calm. "How long has Greyfell been acting weird?"

"Not long. Maybe three days."

"You're sure it was three?" Keefe asked, glancing at Sophie like that was supposed to mean something.

Jurek nodded. "I remember him snapping at her when I was giving Silveny her bath, and I only bathe her once a week."

"What happened three days ago?" Sophie asked when Keefe turned slightly pale.

"That's when my dad had the effluxers installed."

Because the patrol had found those strange footprints.

"But Greyfell didn't see an ogre," Sophie reminded him. "He saw a figure in black."

"True," Keefe agreed. "Unless . . ."

Their eyes met again, and this time she did know what he was thinking.

Unless the rebels and the ogres were working together.

"Those footprints were *not* ogre tracks," Jurek interrupted as he dusted off his hands. "Ogres leave a trail of stink everywhere they step. But those prints smelled like ash."

"Ash?" The word tasted sour on Sophie's tongue.

The rebels had at least one Pyrokinetic in their ranks. Maybe he'd found a way to use fire to hide his scent.

But then why would the tracks look like ogre prints?

"Either way," Sophie said, holding out the tracker to remind them, "*Someone* put this in Silveny's tail. And I'd like to know why, wouldn't you?"

Keefe took the tracker from her and studied the glittering crystals. "Think they can hear us right now?"

Sophie backed a step away. "Can trackers do that?"

"No idea. But just in case . . ." He held the tracker up to his mouth like a microphone. "Yo, bad dudes. If you're listening, you should know that I've been practicing my aim with goblin throwing stars—a lot. If you touch one more hair on Silveny I will come at you with everything I have, and I promise, I won't miss again."

Sophie shuddered.

She'd watched Keefe clip one of the rebels across the shoulder with Sandor's bladed, disklike weapons, and she didn't want to be there when one hit the mark.

"Maybe this is all just . . . a misunderstanding," Jurek said after a second. "Maybe the disk is just a decoration or something. I've never seen a tracker with crystals on it, have you?"

"No," Sophie admitted. "But it still looks almost exactly like the trackers Sandor has sewn into my clothes." She could feel the faint outline of one in the lining of her sleeve. "They're gold, and they have slits where the crystals are. But the rebels probably went with sparkly silver so it would hide better in her tail."

"Right," Jurek mumbled, sounding as tired and defeated as he looked. "I just . . . I've worked around the clock trying to keep Silveny safe, and when I tell the Council that the rebels managed to get past me . . ."

"No one's going to blame you," Sophie promised.

"Won't they? The alicorns are *my* responsibility—and it's not a responsibility someone like me is normally given. When I started at the Sanctuary, I was basically a poop scooper. And now I have to tell the Council that the rebels slipped in under my nose and tagged their precious alicorn?"

"But the Council understands how sneaky the rebels are," Sophie reminded him.

Jurek laughed darkly. "The Council understands *nothing*. They sit in their crystal castles, basking in their own brilliance, while their Emissaries are out doing their dirty work. They have no concept of what it's like for the rest of us, and worse yet, they don't care. All they care about is keeping the status quo."

Sophie glanced at Keefe, not sure how to respond. She'd heard whispers and murmurs against the Councillors before—especially in the wake of her kidnapping. But she'd never had someone condemn the Council so openly. And she couldn't necessarily blame Jurek for what he was feeling. The longer she lived in the Lost Cities, the more she realized that things weren't as perfect as the elves wanted them to be.

"Let me talk to Alden," she said after a minute. "He *does* understand how ruthless the rebels are—and he's not afraid to stand up to the Council if he has to."

He'd come to her defense more times than she'd like to admit. And he didn't hesitate to bend, or even break, a few rules if he needed to. The fact that he'd spent years searching for her—when no one else was willing to believe she existed— was proof of his determination.

"Alden will know what to do," she assured Jurek. "And if he decides we should go to the Council, I know he'll make it clear to everyone that whatever happened wasn't your fault."

"I doubt *Alden Vacker* will give a second thought to someone like me. But . . ." Jurek moved to Greyfell's side, kneeling in the grass to stroke the still-unconscious alicorn's sleek silver mane. It was obvious how much Jurek cared about the precious creature, even before he whispered, "Do what you must."

"It's going to be okay." Sophie willed the words to be true as she took the tracker back from Keefe and stuffed it in her pocket. "We'll go to Everglen right now."

"This sounds like a great plan and all, but, uh, how are we supposed to get there?" Keefe asked. "You and I both only have home crystals, and I'd really rather not deal with my father right now."

"Why can't you teleport there?" Jurek asked.

"Well, I *thought* we established the whole, Foster-can't-teleport-through-solid-objects thing already. But maybe I missed something?"

"You did." Jurek motioned for them to follow him as he walked several paces away. "You're forgetting where we are."

It looked like they were standing in the middle of an empty meadow. But when Jurek pounded his palm in the air, it made a strange thumping sound, and when he curled his fingers and turned his wrist to the right, an arched doorway opened to the snowy world outside.

"Okay, that's awesome," Keefe said, staring at the icy mountains.

"You'd better hurry," Jurek warned them. "This exit is technically only for emergencies."

Silveny tried to follow, but Jurek held her back.

"It's going to be okay," Sophie promised, throwing her arms around Silveny's shimmering neck. "I'll visit again soon."

And I need you to be extra careful in the meantime, she added.

Careful! Silveny repeated. *Friend! Sophie! Keefe!*

"Come on, Foster," Keefe said, dragging Sophie out into the cold. "We gotta go. And let's try not to get trapped in the darkness this time, okay?"

Snowflakes and wind blasted their faces as they trudged across the icy ground, and Sophie was too freezing to hesitate when they reached the edge of the steep cliff. They jumped off the mountain together, screaming and flailing until the sky cracked open and they plummeted into the void.

Thunder crashed as the sky split, and Sophie and Keefe tumbled across a patch of sunlit grass, coming to a stop on the path leading up to Everglen.

Sophie had seen the crystal-and-gold mansion hundreds of times—even spent a few nights in one of the guest rooms. But she was still struck by the way the elegant building screamed *wealth* and *power* as it sparkled in the sunlight, like it was the kind of place only the best of the best were allowed to go.

The Elvin world didn't really have celebrities, but the Vackers were close—not that any of them seemed to notice their position.

Keefe groaned as he sat up, rubbing his left shoulder. "I think we need to work on your landings, Foster."

Sophie nodded, stretching her sore legs.

"Well, look who dropped out of the sky," Alden said behind them in his crisp, accented voice.

Sophie grinned as she turned to face him, but her lips fell when she noticed Alden wasn't alone—not that Sophie didn't like Councillor Kenric. In fact, the red-haired, wide-smiling Councillor was one of her favorites, and he was always one of the first to take her side. But there was something foreboding about Kenric's amber-encrusted circlet and jeweled cape—especially paired with Alden's equally regal attire.

Kenric clearly wasn't at Everglen for a friendly visit. And the Councillors only made house calls when something really important was going on.

"You two certainly know how to give someone a heart attack," Kenric said, laughing as he nudged Alden. "And I'm pretty sure you made this guy squeal."

Alden laughed. "I think you're right, my friend—though in my defense, no one's arrived directly inside Everglen since I had the gates installed a few decades ago."

An enormous glowing fence surrounded the entire estate of Everglen, and the metal bars somehow absorbed all the light, preventing anyone from being able to leap directly inside. It was a security measure Alden added when he became an Emissary for the Council, though he'd never explained exactly what—or who—he was trying to keep away.

"Sorry," Sophie mumbled. "I guess we should've hailed you before we came."

"Nonsense," Alden assured her. "You're welcome to drop in anytime. I just never realized you'd do it so literally. But I should've known you'd find a new way to amaze me."

"What about me—don't I amaze you too?" Keefe asked.

"Yes, I'm always amazed at how quickly you manage to find trouble," Alden teased. "And judging by the looks of you two, it seems you've had quite the adventure today. Did something happen at the Sanctuary?"

Sophie glanced at Keefe, trying to figure out how much to say. She hadn't planned on having to tell the Council herself.

"I think I'll let you guys talk privately," Kenric jumped in, almost like he knew what she was thinking. "But you'll let me know if there's anything I need to be aware of?" he asked Alden.

"Of course." Alden nodded a slight bow, and Kenric did the same as he pulled a pathfinder out of his cape's pocket and adjusted the round crystal at the end of the etched wand.

"I'll be back in touch as soon as the arrangements have been made," he said, glancing quickly at Sophie before he held his pathfinder up to the sun. "Oh, and give my congratulations to Biana!"

"What did he mean?" Sophie asked after Kenric glittered away.

She'd meant the mysterious "arrangements" Kenric had mentioned. But if Alden realized that, he pretended not to.

"I fear I must leave you in suspense," he said as he led them up the crystal steps and pulled open the towering silver doors to Everglen. "Biana will never forgive me if I spoil her surprise."

SEVEN

GIDDY SHRIEKS ECHOED OFF THE prismlike halls, followed by a huge fit of giggles. But when Alden led Sophie and Keefe to a wide sitting room filled with intricate statues and throne-size armchairs, they found Fitz standing alone.

"Where's Biana?" Sophie asked, hoping Keefe couldn't tell that her heart was doing the embarrassing fluttery thing it always did whenever she met Fitz's impossibly teal eyes.

"Right here!" Biana shouted.

The air shimmered in front of them, and Biana seemed to appear out of nowhere. She twirled, making her pale pink gown flare before she disappeared again, like a ghostly ballerina.

"I'm a Vanisher now—can you believe it?" she asked, though only her head blinked back into sight. She scowled at where her body should be. "I guess I'm still getting the hang of it."

"Of course you are," Della told her, appearing beside her daughter with a graceful swish. "It takes years to perfect the skill—though I must say, you're showing incredible control. Alvar took days before he could vanish completely, and he was a year older than you when he manifested."

Biana beamed at that, letting Della show her how to wiggle her shoulders to make the rest of her body reappear. Side by side with their pink gowns and long dark hair, Biana had never looked more like her strikingly beautiful mother—even before they both vanished again.

"Ugh, they've been at it all day," Fitz grumbled. "It's been hours of 'Look—I'm invisible. Now I'm not! Now I am!'"

Biana rolled her eyes as she reappeared. "Like you were any less annoying with your 'I can tell you what you're thinking right now! And now! And now!'"

Keefe snorted.

"Don't get so cocky, Mr. 'I keep laughing and crying at the same time!'" Fitz warned him.

"Hey—feeling people's emotions for the first time is *intense*," Keefe argued.

They all turned to Sophie like they were waiting for her to share her manifesting-a-special-ability story too. But she doubted they'd enjoy hearing about her waking up in the hospital at five years old, crying because the blaring thoughts were giving her a headache. Or waking up in a strange city after being kidnapped, and discovering she could suddenly understand other languages and inflict pain on people. Or even crashing toward the ocean, convinced she was about to die, until her instincts kicked in and she'd teleported them to safety—though Keefe had been there for that one.

"So I guess this means you'll start vanishing sessions, right?" Sophie asked, changing the subject as fast as she could.

"Yes," Alden agreed. "I guess I'll have to talk to Dame Alina about possible Mentors."

He sounded less than thrilled about it—though Fitz and Keefe found it hilarious.

Alden and Dame Alina had an *interesting* history—especially the part where Dame Alina showed up at Alden and Della's wedding and tried to convince him to marry her, instead.

"So I really don't have to take ability detecting anymore?" Biana asked, jumping up and down, and blinking like a strobe light in the process. "Stina's going to freak! She'll never admit it, but I know she's secretly hoping she'll be a Vanisher. Well, assuming she even *gets* an ability."

"Now, now, none of that," Della warned her. "You have every right to be proud of your ability—especially for manifesting at such a young age. But I won't have you judging others."

Della waited until Biana mumbled an apology.

Sophie became very interested in her shoes. She definitely

agreed about the judging-people thing, but . . . Stina won the prize for Most Awful Girl at Foxfire—ever. She acted like she was better than everyone, even though her own father didn't actually have a special ability. And Sophie had heard a bunch of rumors about how Stina's father was doing all kinds of shady things to work his way into the Nobility, despite the fact that he was Talentless—though she had no idea how much of that was true. All she knew was that the Hekses were horrible, and she wished they would move far, far away. Especially since they were still trying to convince the Council that *their family* should be the ones caring for Silveny.

"What?" Keefe asked as Sophie sucked in a breath.

She shook her head and forced a smile, pretending to listen to Biana talk about vanishing. But . . . if Stina's parents found out that the rebels had breached the security at the Sanctuary, they might be able to use that to convince the Council to turn Silveny over to their care. And if that happened, then—

"Did you hear anything I just said?" Biana asked, nudging Sophie's arm.

"Not really," she admitted.

Biana sighed. "Lame! I *said* we should all go play base quest! I finally have an ability—and it's an even better one than Sophie's!"

"I dunno about *that*," Keefe interrupted.

Sophie elbowed him before he could finish.

Thanks to a bunch of misunderstandings, her friendship

with Biana had been a bit rocky at times—but they were finally in a good place.

Besides, she didn't have time for games.

"I need to talk to you," she told Alden, stepping away from her friends.

Alden didn't look surprised by the news. "Why don't we go to my office? There's something I need to tell you as well—*privately*," he added when Keefe turned to join them.

Keefe didn't bother arguing. But he shot Sophie a look that seemed to say, *You will tell me everything later* as she followed Alden down the crystal hallway.

Fountains shot colored streams of water over their heads, and they passed room after room filled with fancy furniture and twinkling chandeliers before finally stopping at the all-too-familiar round office, where half the room was lined with a floor-to-ceiling aquarium, the other half made of windows overlooking a glassy lake.

Sophie sank into the same plush armchair she'd sat in when Alden had explained that she'd have to drug her human family and never see them again, and she tried to tell herself nothing could be worse news. But it was hard to believe it when she noticed the deep crease across Alden's usually smooth brow.

"I can see you're worried," he said after a second, "so I'll tell you my news first. Councillor Kenric came to see me today to let me know that the Council has finally come to a decision regarding mind healings."

The cautious tone to his voice made her heart feel heavy. "They're not going to let me heal Prentice, are they?"

"Actually, they still haven't reached a decision on that matter."

He cleared his throat and rose to stand by the curved window, staring at the slowly setting sun.

"Then what's wrong?" Sophie asked, gripping the arms of her chair to brace for the bad news.

"Hopefully nothing. But that's up to you." He turned back to face her, his expression impossible to read. "The decision may come as a surprise—it was certainly a surprise to me. And I should warn you that it was an *order*, not a request."

Sophie swallowed, hating how dry her mouth felt as her mind raced through a list of worst-case scenarios.

Still, she never could've guessed that Alden would tell her, "The Council has ordered you to perform a healing on Fintan."

EIGHT

WHY?"

It was a tiny word—much too small to hold the avalanche of emotions currently crashing through Sophie's head. But it was the only thing she could think to say.

"Why what?" Alden asked after a second.

"I don't know." Sophie stood, needing to move, to try and figure out why part of her wanted to cry and the rest of her wanted to punch something really, really hard.

"I guess I don't understand why the Council thinks Fintan deserves to be healed," she admitted. "I mean, you gave him a ton of chances to save himself, and he *chose* to have his mind broken instead."

She should probably feel horrible for saying that. But she'd seen Fintan's memories. She'd watched his hunger for power cause the death of five other Pyrokinetics. She'd seen him illegally training an unregistered Pyrokinetic to spark Everblaze—probably the same Pyrokinetic who'd kidnapped her and Dex and started the fires that killed hundreds of innocent humans. She'd felt his fury toward the Council and knew he would stop at nothing to take them down, even if it meant breaking her and Alden's sanity along with his—which he'd very nearly done.

Alden sighed. "I'm not convinced that anyone—even Fintan—deserves to spend an eternity trapped in the madness of a broken mind."

She reached for his hand, wondering how much he remembered about his own shattered days.

"I do understand why you're reluctant to heal Fintan, though," he added quietly. "And I hold many of the same reservations. But Fintan has information that could lead us to the rebels. He managed to stop us from taking it during the memory break, but thanks to you, we have a second chance to learn who he's protecting. And you know better than anyone how important that information is."

But the thought of entering Fintan's mind again . . .

"I'll be with you the whole time," Alden promised.

Sophie sank heavily into her chair. "It just seems so . . . unfair. Why does Fintan get to be healed when Prentice is stuck with a broken mind? The only crime Prentice committed was protecting me!"

Shadows settled into Alden's features, making him look twenty years older. "Believe me, no one is more aware of that than me."

"I'm sorry, I didn't mean—"

"I know you didn't—and you don't have to worry, I'm not feeling guilty. Well, not *too* guilty, anyway. I'm simply frustrated, like you. In fact, I made the same point to Kenric while he was here. But he explained to me that *that's* the problem. Fintan's easy. With or without his mind healed, he's guilty, and had he given us the information we needed in the first place, we still would've exiled him for his crimes. But Prentice is an entirely different situation. He's not necessarily guilty, but he's not exactly innocent either. The Black Swan are still classified as rebels. Yes, some of the things they've done are good things. But they've done them illegally. And that makes Prentice still technically a criminal. Essentially, Prentice is a lovely shade of gray. And the Council only knows what to do with black and white."

"So they'll leave his mind broken forever?"

"Nobody said *forever*, Sophie. But for now, when there is no obvious solution, the Council has decided to give themselves time to think through all the possible options, until the best course of action becomes clearer. I don't think you understand how ill equipped our world is for these kinds of issues. The Council is facing dilemmas that have never been seen in all the thousands of years of our history. They've accepted that now is a time for change. But they want to make sure it's the *right* change, and they need more information before they move forward—information that Fintan hopefully has. Will you help get it for them?"

"I thought I didn't have a choice."

"It was an order, yes. But that doesn't mean I'm not going to make sure you're okay with this. You're a very talented girl, and as a result you've had tremendous responsibilities heaped on your shoulders. But you're also thirteen. If this is too much, I *will* go back to the Council and make them reconsider. I already warned Kenric—and he agreed."

Sophie doubted Alden and Kenric would be able to change their minds. The Councillors seemed to be getting increasingly divided in decisions concerning her.

And it didn't matter. Much as she dreaded having to see Fintan again, he really was her best chance at stopping her kidnappers.

"I'll do the healing," she said, wishing her stomach didn't feel so squirmy as she said it.

Alden smiled sadly. "You never cease to amaze me, Sophie. And I promise, there *will* be a day when your life goes back to normal."

Sophie wasn't sure she even knew what a "normal life" meant for an elf. But she hoped she'd get to find out someday.

"So when am I supposed to heal him?" she asked.

"Kenric said the Council is still making the arrangements. Given what happened last time, they want to be sure they've considered every variable, so that there will be no issues."

"Issues" was putting it mildly.

She'd never forget the searing pain when Fintan burned her wrist to break their concentration, or finding Alden unconscious on the floor, his head streaked with red.

"It *will* be safe this time," Alden promised—and Sophie tried to believe him. But her legs were pretty shaky as she stood to leave.

"Wait, wasn't there something you wanted to talk to me about?" Alden asked.

"Oh, right." She couldn't believe she'd forgotten about Silveny.

Sophie showed him the silver tracker, explaining where she'd found it, and how Greyfell had known it was there. Alden's jaw clenched tighter with every word.

"Well," he said after an endless stretch of silence, "I'm sure there's no reason to worry."

Alden had said those words to her dozens of times since she'd met him. But she'd never believed them less.

"Don't you think we should move Silveny somewhere secret?" she asked. "Not that Jurek's not doing a great job. He's trying really hard. But the rebels still found a way in. Just like they found a way into Havenfield that time we found the footprint."

It might even be the same Pyrokinetic who snuck into both places. Unless . . .

"Do you think those tracks the goblins found outside the Sanctuary were made by ogres?"

"How did you know about that?" Alden asked.

"Keefe told me. And I saw the effluxers."

Alden nodded and turned to pace, crossing the room three times before he said, "The thing you have to keep in mind when it comes to goblins, Sophie, is that they tend to assume the ogres are behind *everything*. In fact, both species are always accusing the other of violating the treaties we've worked so hard to put in place. So yes, the goblins on patrol discovered some strange tracks—tracks that definitely shouldn't have been there, which was why we investigated them so thoroughly. But Alvar found no proof that the tracks were connected to the ogres in any way. And neither did Lady Cadence."

"Lady Cadence, my linguistics mentor?" Sophie interrupted.

"Yes. She was living with the ogres before she was brought back to mentor you, remember?"

Yes, and she seemed to deeply resent Sophie for it.

"Why *did* the Council choose her to mentor me?" Sophie couldn't resist asking.

"Because she's the most talented linguist in our world, and giving you the best training possible is far more important than her research into ogre technology. And it's good we have her back, because she was able to make us those effluxers, which we added outside the Sanctuary just to be safe. And speaking of safe"—he held out his hand—"I'll need to keep that tracker, so I can show it to the Council."

Sophie handed it over, happy to be rid of it. The last thing she wanted was to have the rebels know her every move—which made her wonder . . .

"Why would the rebels even bother tracking Silveny? I mean, they already know she's in the Sanctuary. Why risk getting caught, just to be able to monitor her every move?"

"*That* is what I intend to find out."

He flashed his most confident smile, and Sophie did her best to accept it. But she still vowed to do everything she could on her own.

"You're going home?" Alden asked as she held her home crystal up to the light.

"Yeah. If I'm not back by sunset, Sandor's going to murder Keefe."

Alden glanced out the window, where the last splashes of pink were fading into the purple twilight sky. "I guess I should warn Keefe to flee for his life."

Sandor was waiting outside Havenfield when Sophie arrived, and his glare told her he was very aware she'd missed her curfew. But all he said as he sheathed his long black sword and motioned for her to follow him inside was, "I'm glad you're safe."

Sophie turned in the opposite direction.

She knew the Black Swan wanted her to sit back and wait— but the rebels had just changed the game.

"Where do you think you're going?" Sandor asked, keeping pace with her as she made her way through the pastures.

Her palms turned sweaty as she pressed her thumb against the sensor on the padlock to the Cliffside gates, and the green flash seemed especially bright as it clicked open—or maybe that was because the path beyond the gate looked so much darker than normal.

"I demand to know what's going on," Sandor said as he blocked her from heading down the stairs.

She tried to push past him, but it was like slamming into a rough-skinned mountain. "I just . . . need to leave a note."

"A note," Sandor repeated.

"Yeah." She reached into her pocket, tracing her fingers around the tiny green bottle she'd unearthed earlier.

The Black Swan had sent her dozens of messages over the last few months.

It was time to send one of her own.

NINE

THE PLAN HAD SEEMED SO BRILLIANT, until Sophie reached the cold, sandy shore.

She'd never been to the cave at night, and now she understood why. The roar of the surf sounded like a snarl, and the shadowy rocks looked like faces and limbs. Even the moonlight—and the blue glowing sphere Sandor had pulled from one of his pockets—couldn't convince her eyes that she wasn't stumbling into the lair of giant beasts.

Sandor led the way, keeping his sword at the ready as he sniffed the air and tasted the wind. But as the icy waves crashed onto the shore, Sophie realized they had bigger problems than invisible enemies.

The cave she'd dreaded returning to—the place she and Dex

had been drugged and dragged away from—sat half-drowned by the high evening tide.

"Looks like we'll have to try again in the morning," Sandor said, turning to head back.

"No, I *have* to get in touch with the Black Swan as soon as possible. It's about Silveny," she added, before Sandor could ask.

If he knew it was actually about the rebels, he'd drag her straight to her room—and probably barricade her inside.

Sandor breathed a squeaky sigh. "You're positive you can reach them this way?"

"They left me a note here once before. And I'm pretty sure they're still watching me."

She hoped they were, anyway—which felt strange. Who knew she'd miss her Black Swan stalkers?

"Fine." Sandor let the word stretch out like a groan as he held out his hand. "Give me the note. I'll place it in there for you. A few piddly waves won't stop me."

Sophie doubted a rampaging T. rex could stop him. But as she reached into her pocket, she discovered another detail she hadn't really thought all the way through.

"Do you, uh . . . happen to have a pen?"

The look Sandor gave her could've withered flowers, but he dug a wide pencil out of his ankle pocket and handed it to her. "Tell me you brought paper."

"Of course." It wasn't necessarily paper she'd wanted to use, but it would do the job.

She slipped the Black Swan's note from the green vial and flipped it over to the back.

"I assume you'll be explaining where you found that once we're done here—and why it reeks of humans?" Sandor asked.

Sophie kept her eyes focused on the paper as she nodded. Not only was she *not* looking forward to telling Sandor about teleporting to the Forbidden Cities, but she was realizing that she'd forgotten to explain it to Alden, as well. She'd have to find a chance to tell him, before he heard about it from Lord Cassius.

"Better hurry," Sandor told her as a wave soaked them up to their ankles. "The tide is still rising."

"I'm trying," she said, hastily scribbling the only thing she could think of.

It wasn't particularly clever, and it definitely didn't rhyme. But she still made it clear that it was time for the Black Swan to come out of wherever they'd been hiding.

Things are happening, and I need your help.
When and where can we meet?

Sandor scowled when he read what she'd written. But all he said was, "Wait here," as he headed toward the cave. "And I expect you to sing the whole time I'm gone."

Sophie laughed. "Oh wait—you're serious?"

"Of course I'm serious. It's how I'll know you're not in trouble."

Sophie was about to argue that she could just scream if there were danger, but then she remembered the sweet-smelling cloth the kidnappers had pressed over her nose and mouth, knocking her out cold.

The only thing she could think to sing was a cheesy song her sister used to torment her with: a single verse repeated over and over, about how the song never actually ended. She was on the tenth repetition by the time Sandor was back at her side.

"That's going to be stuck in my head for the rest of my life," he grumbled.

"You're the one who told me to sing."

He didn't return her smile.

"You tucked the note somewhere they'll be able to see it, right?" she asked.

"The back of the cave has a small indent partway up the wall, well above the tide line but still low enough to see. If they're watching, there's no way they'll miss it."

The house was dark when Sophie and Sandor made it back to Havenfield, the only light a faint glow coming from the second floor. Sophie had a feeling she knew which room it was coming from, and as she made her way up the winding stairs, she braced for the worst.

Sixteen years ago, Grady and Edaline had lost their only daughter in a suspicious fire, and they'd left her room closed off ever since, only going in on their darkest, loneliest days. It felt like a shadow hung over that wing of the house, warning everyone to stay away.

But when Sophie entered the dusty bedroom, she found Edaline deep in discussion with two of the gnomes that lived in a grove of tree houses on the property. Edaline's simple turquoise gown was the exact same shade as her eyes—which weren't the least bit red or puffy—and her whole face lit up with a smile when she spotted Sophie.

"I was wondering when you'd be home," Edaline said, her smile fading as she got a closer look at Sophie's clothes. "Do I want to know why you're wet?"

"Nothing dangerous," Sophie promised, wishing her shoes didn't squish quite so loudly as she crossed the room to examine a row of trunks on the floor. "What's going on?"

"Oh, we were just trying to decide what to do with this room once it's all cleaned out. I was thinking maybe a conservatory, since Jolie always loved gardens. But Gerda's not sure if the lighting's really right."

A gnome in an earth-toned smock smiled at Sophie with bright green teeth. "It can be done if you truly desire it," she told Edaline in a dry, scratchy voice, "but we'll be limited in what we can grow."

Gnomes were expert gardeners, probably because they were almost plantlike themselves. They drew all their nourishment from the sun and needed very little sleep, which was why they'd chosen to live with the elves. They exchanged their unneeded produce for protection, and filled their long, waking hours by helping with any other tasks the elves needed.

"You're really getting rid of everything?" Sophie asked.

Edaline had mentioned this plan once before, but Sophie hadn't expected her to actually go through with it. Jolie's room had been a shrine, completely unchanged since her death, right down to the page markers in the dusty books and the pots of lip gloss on the dressing table.

"It's time," Edaline said quietly. She ran her hand over the lacy bedspread, then backed a few steps away.

"We should have it all packed up tonight," the other gnome—wearing what looked like overalls woven out of grass—told her. "Where do you want us to put the trunks when we're done?"

"In my office. If you can find room."

Sophie doubted they would. She'd been in Edaline's office once, and it was the Place Where Stuff Goes to Die. But she was glad Edaline wasn't planning to actually get rid of Jolie's things.

Still, as Sophie watched Gerda grab the first trunk and head to Jolie's closet, she couldn't stop herself from saying, "Wait—maybe I should do it!"

Prentice had shown Sophie a strange, almost visionlike memory when she'd tried to read his shattered mind, and ever since, she'd wondered if Jolie had somehow been connected to the Black Swan. She hadn't mentioned it to Grady or Edaline, wanting to wait until she understood Jolie's involvement. And her best chance of finding out the truth was to search Jolie's things.

"Are you sure?" Edaline asked. "This is a huge project. The only reason the gnomes can take it out in a night is because they'll have dozens of them."

"I know. I just . . . thought it would give me a chance to get to know Jolie a little better."

Edaline smiled, but sadness seemed to leak out of the corners. "You want to know Jolie?"

"Is that okay?" Sophie asked.

"Of course it's okay. In fact"—she dabbed her eyes—"I think it's wonderful. And I know Jolie would've wanted to know you, too. You remind me so much of her."

Sophie never knew what to do with that compliment. She had no doubt that Grady and Edaline loved her. She just hoped they were really seeing her for who she was, not for who they wanted her to be.

"Okay," Edaline said, clearing the thickness from her throat and turning to the gnomes. "I guess I won't be needing your help tonight after all. Thank you so much for offering."

They both nodded and shuffled away.

"And *you* should get out of those soggy clothes," she told Sophie, nudging her toward the door. "I'll send your dinner up when it's ready."

Sophie's bedroom took up the entire third floor, and was

bigger than every room in her old San Diego house—combined. Star-shaped crystals dangled from the ceiling, and they glowed to life when Sophie snapped her fingers, illuminating a crushed trail in the fragile flowers woven into her carpet.

"Someone was here," Sophie whispered, freezing in the doorway.

But her worry quickly melted into a giggle when she spotted the neon orange poof in the cage on her desk. "Dex dyed Iggy again!"

Sandor nodded. "He asked if he could stop by your room before he went home. Said he'd made the poor creature suffer with pink ringlets long enough."

Actually, Sophie's pet imp had quite enjoyed chewing on the hot pink curls Dex had given him a few weeks before. But he seemed to be having just as much fun chomping on his bright orange dreads.

"I don't think Dex is ever going to let you go back to your normal gray," Sophie warned the tiny creature as she let him out of his cage.

Iggy flitted to her shoulder with his black batlike wings and squeaked, making her gag from the toxic Iggy breath.

"So," Sandor said as a tray of food appeared out of nowhere on Sophie's bed—courtesy of Edaline's conjuring. "Ready to tell me where you really went today? And before you consider leaving out any details, need I remind you that your trackers will tell me the whole story when I check them."

"Is that the only thing the trackers do?" she asked, still trying to figure out why the rebels would bother tracking Silveny. "You can't use them to like . . . stun me or something, right?"

Sandor snorted—though it sounded more like a laugh. "Believe me, Miss Foster. If I were capable of incapacitating you, I would do it every time you and Keefe got one of your crazy schemes. Trackers simply gather information, and help me find you should I need to. Why do you ask?"

"And that's for all trackers?" she pressed, avoiding his question. "The silver ones aren't different?"

"What do you mean 'silver ones'? Did you find a silver tracker?"

"Not on me. I found one on Silveny."

Sandor reached for his sword as Sophie explained about Greyfell and the rebels and the unidentified footprints outside the Sanctuary. Each new detail made him grip the hilt tighter, until his skin was stretched so thin, she was sure it would tear.

"What?" she asked, taking a deep breath to brace for the bad news she could tell was coming. "Are the silver trackers more dangerous?"

"Trackers can't be made from silver," Sandor whispered, "because of the way the metal tarnishes. The tracker you found could only have been made from stalkenteene—a metal that isn't sold and isn't shared. The only creatures who use it are those who mine it, and it can only be mined in the deepest caves of an underground mountain in the heart of Ravagog, the ogres' largest and most powerful city."

81

TEN

BUT ALDEN DIDN'T THINK THE OGRES were involved—and neither did Alvar or Lady Cadence," Sophie argued, replaying her earlier conversation in her mind. "And why didn't he say anything about stalkenteene when I showed him the tracker?"

Sandor started a second sweep of her room, checking every shadow, like he expected an ogre to jump out any second. "I doubt Alden would've known. The ogres work hard to keep their technology secret, especially from elves. It's something my court has had *many* arguments with your Council about— though this tracker changes things. I need to ensure nothing prevents Alden from showing it to the Councillors."

"What—you think he's going to hide it?"

"No. I think the ogres might try to steal it. This tracker could finally prove they've been violating their treaty and carrying on a silent war."

A silent war.

The words felt cold, making Sophie shiver as she dug out her Imparter—a silver square that worked like a videophone—to call Alden and warn him. But when she said his name, the screen declared him "out of range." Same thing happened when she tried to reach Grady.

The only areas "out of range" were dark, dangerous places.

"I'm calling for reinforcements," Sandor said, taking out a black triangular gadget he'd never used before. "They'll make sure Alden is safe. Meanwhile, *you* are going to shower and go to bed."

Sophie knew better than to argue, so she ran to her bathroom and rushed through her shower. She raced back with soggy, dripping hair, and found Edaline sitting on the edge of her giant canopy bed.

"Where's Sandor?" Sophie asked, glancing around her room to make sure she wasn't missing him—not that it was easy to miss a seven-foot-tall goblin.

"In the hall, talking to Alden."

"Alden called? He's safe?"

"Yes, perfectly safe. And Grady is as well. He's off on a completely unrelated assignment."

Edaline's hands were twisting the fabric on her skirt back and forth.

Back and forth.

"Sandor told me about the tracker," she said after a second, "and your surprise trip to your old home."

"Oh." Sophie tugged on her pajamas, which were sticking to her still-damp skin. "Am I in trouble?"

"Not *trouble*. But I wish—"

Sandor stalked back into the room, stomping so hard he sent petals from her carpet flying with every step.

"Everything okay?" Edaline asked.

"Everything's fine, apparently. I have *no reason to worry*." Sandor kicked the carpet, scattering more petals. "What's it going to take for your Council to see what's really going on? An army of ogres marching across your capital?"

Sophie shuddered, hoping she'd never see a mob of lumpy-faced ogres parading through the glittering streets of Eternalia.

"What exactly did Alden say?" Edaline asked quietly.

"That all we know for the moment is that whoever planted the tracker got their hands on ogre technology—not that ogres are involved. And that he'll be conducting a full investigation into the matter."

Clearly Sandor was not in the mood to wait for an investigation, and Sophie couldn't blame him. She knew better than anyone how hard it was to be patient. But . . . Alden did have a point. The rebels could've stolen the tracker from the ogres without their knowledge.

Sandor sighed, rubbing the sides of his head like he had a migraine. "Forgive my outburst. I shall return to my post."

"If you'd like to take the night off—" Edaline started to offer.

"Thank you, Ms. Ruewen. But I fear Sophie needs my protection now more than ever."

He stalked out the door without another word.

Sophie leaned back on her bed, staring at the star-shaped crystals dangling above her.

"You okay?" Edaline asked, scooting closer.

"Yeah, just . . . worried about Silveny."

"I know." Edaline swept a soggy strand of hair off Sophie's forehead. "But I'm sure the Council's already adding extra security to keep her safe."

And hopefully it would actually work this time—though Sophie doubted it.

The rebels always find a way.

"You look tired, Sophie. Have you slept at all since Silveny moved to the Sanctuary?"

"Not much," Sophie admitted.

Silveny used to fill her mind at night with sweet, alicornish dreams. It was the only thing that ever chased away her nightmares.

"Want to try slumberberry tea? Even a small cup—"

"No sedatives," Sophie interrupted. She'd lost enough

hours in a drugged daze during her kidnapping.

"Well, if you change your mind, just call for me." Edaline kissed her goodnight and handed her Ella—the bright blue, Hawaiian-shirt-wearing stuffed elephant Sophie hadn't been able to sleep without since she was a kid. But she hesitated before turning out the lights. "I . . . wish you would've come to me about all of this tracker business, Sophie. Please don't feel like you have to wait for Alden or Grady."

"I don't feel like that," Sophie told her.

Though she did. A little.

Edaline had always been *the fragile one*, barely holding herself together as she battled through her grief. Sophie never wanted to be the one to make her lose her grip.

"I'm stronger now," Edaline whispered. "Next time, I hope you'll trust me."

Next time.

The words hung in the air as Edaline left her alone for the night.

As long as the rebels were free, there would always be a *next time.*

That night Sophie dreamed she was cornered by ogres. They licked their gray, pointy teeth, promising she would never be safe, as their clawed, nubby fingers reached for her throat. She woke up screaming and strangling Ella as Sandor burst into her room, sword at the ready.

"I'm fine," she told him, flopping back in her bed. She stared at the ceiling for a few minutes before she threw back the covers and headed for the door.

"Where are you going?" Sandor asked, following her down the stairs.

"I can't stay there tossing and turning all night," she whispered, hoping she hadn't woken Edaline.

The doorway to Grady and Edaline's bedroom was open a crack, and when Sophie peeked through, she could see Edaline curled up among her blankets.

Grady's side was still empty.

She knew if Edaline wasn't worried about him, she shouldn't be either. But she couldn't shake the churny feeling in her stomach as she padded down the hall and slipped into Jolie's old bedroom.

A soft snap of her fingers made the delicate crystal chandeliers glow, and Sophie carried a trunk to Jolie's dressing table and set to work packing up the drawers. She found more makeup than any girl could wear in two lifetimes, a dozen hairbrushes in every shape and size, and a huge collection of Slurps and Burps bottles with names like Raven Lovelylocks and Liquid Amber Eyes. But nothing gave her the slightest hint about Jolie's connection to the Black Swan.

The closet was just as unhelpful. Stacks of shoes. Handbags in all shapes and sizes. Row upon row of frilly gowns. Biana would've been in absolute girl-heaven. But clothes weren't really Sophie's thing. Her "style" was all about drawing as little attention to herself as possible.

"What about those?" Sandor asked, pointing to two small silver chests on the top shelf.

Sophie had searched them a few weeks before, when she'd first seen Jolie in Prentice's memories. But she'd been rushing at the time, so it was probably worth a second look.

The first chest was filled with old toys and dolls and dried flowers and all kinds of other things that probably had sentimental stories behind them, but were still really just a bunch of junk. The other chest was filled with letters.

Jolie's fiancé, Brant, had sent her hundreds of love letters while she was living in the elite towers in her final years at Foxfire, declaring over and over how much he cared for her and missed her and would be useless without her. Reading them felt like eavesdropping on a private conversation—an especially mushy conversation at that. But Sophie skimmed each one, just in case there was something important in them.

"What are you doing up?" Grady asked from the doorway, making her jump so hard she dropped all the letters.

"Sorry," he said, squatting to help her pick them up. "Didn't mean to scare you."

His eyes were rimmed with shadows and his blond hair was caked with sand. But the smile he gave her was 100 percent Grady.

"I'm so glad you're home," she whispered, hugging him tight.

"Yeah, me too. The dwarven caverns are *not* my favorite place to visit." He shook his head, showering them both with sand. "So what's keeping *you* up? More nightmares?"

"Kind of."

She told him about the tracker and the footprints, and Sandor's worries about the ogres, hating how tense Grady looked by the end of it.

All he said was, "Sounds like you've had a strange day. And I can see why you couldn't sleep. But what are you doing in here?" He scanned one of the letters. "Are these from Brant?"

"Love letters," Sophie agreed.

Grady read aloud. "'You're the spark, the kindling, the flame that never dies. The beauty and the wonder of the ever-burning skies.' That is some seriously sappy stuff."

He smiled, and Sophie tried to join him, but she couldn't stop thinking about Brant's scarred, ruined face. He'd been caught in the fire with Jolie—and even though he'd escaped with his life, his grief and guilt at not being able to save her had destroyed him more than the flames.

Grady cleared his throat as he handed the letters back to her. "So what made you want to get up in the middle of the night and read a bunch of gooey love letters? Did a *boy* inspire this?"

"No!" Sophie said, probably too quickly. "I just . . . wanted to get to know Jolie—and Brant," she added, pointing to the letters.

Grady's brows crunched together, and he opened his mouth to say something. Then shook his head.

"What?"

"Nothing. It's late. We can talk more in the morning."

"Uh, you know I'm imagining a billion terrible things now, right?"

He sighed, tracing his hands down his face before he said, "Fine. I know how vivid your imagination can be. But this is your choice—and Edaline and I will support you one hundred percent, regardless of what you decide."

"Okay," Sophie said slowly. "So . . . ?"

Grady bit his lip and turned to stare at the framed pictures on Jolie's desk. "I'd like to file a petition with the Council, requesting permission for you to heal Brant."

ELEVEN

SOPHIE KNEW WHAT GRADY WAS HOPing she'd say, what she *should* say, what she *wanted* to say.

But she couldn't make her mouth form the words.

"I think it's high time we both get some sleep," Grady said after an endless stretch of silence. "We can continue this conversation in the morning—or whenever you're ready, no matter how long that might be."

Sophie managed a nod.

Neither of them said anything as they made their way up the stairs to her bedroom. But as Grady tucked her in, he whispered, "I'll always love you no matter what—and Edaline will too. You know that, right?"

"I love you too," she whispered back.

She knew he meant every word. But her palms were still sweaty, and her heart was still racing, and when Grady left her alone, she buried her head under her pillow, feeling like everything was spinning too fast.

Healing Brant had originally been her idea—and if she could save him from the shattered mess he'd become, it would be a truly incredible thing.

But there was one word in that statement that was far more terrifying than the others. One that echoed in her mind, long after the sun rose and the darkness faded, ushering in a new day.

If.

"Looks like you had another rough night," Edaline said as Sophie stumbled into the kitchen for breakfast.

Sophie sank into her usual chair at the table and reached for one of the sugar-covered fluffcreams heaped on a platter, hoping it would erase the bitterness on her tongue. But her stomach lurched at the thought of food—even though the food was a delicious cloud of honey and cinnamon and butter.

She set it on the table, tearing at the flaky edge.

"What if I can't do it?" she whispered.

"Then that's fine," Grady promised as Edaline reached for Sophie's hand. "If you don't think you can handle it, we totally understand."

"No, it's not that." Sophie stared out the window, watching the feathered, colorful dinosaurs graze in the pastures. "I mean, what if I *can't* do it? Mind healing only works if some of the person's consciousness is left to save. And Mr. Forkle told me the Black Swan had to train all their Keepers to preserve their consciousness a special way—a way Brant wouldn't know. So what if the Council grants permission and I go there and get everyone's hopes up, and . . . I *can't* save him?"

"Then at least we'll know we tried everything we could," Grady told her.

"We would never blame you or be disappointed in you—if that's what you're worried about," Edaline added.

Sophie was a little afraid of that—not that she'd admit it.

But . . . what if the grief made Edaline go back to crying herself to sleep in Jolie's room?

Or worse: What if Grady's guilt and anger finally broke him?

"Hey," Edaline said, tucking Sophie's hair behind her ear. "Sometimes I think you're the oldest thirteen-year-old I've ever met. You shouldn't have a worry crease between your brows." She traced her finger along a line in Sophie's forehead, her soft touch making Sophie relax. "You should be thinking about what dress to wear or how you're doing in your Foxfire sessions or which boy you like best."

"Edaline's right," Grady said, scooting his chair closer to them. "Though I'm not sure how I feel about that last one. Especially if it involves that Sencen boy."

Edaline elbowed him.

"Sorry," Grady mumbled, not sounding sorry at all.

Sophie focused on the table, wishing she could crawl under it.

"So it's settled, then," Edaline said after a second. "We'll drop all of this for now and come back to it when you're older?"

Sophie smushed more of her fluffcream, tempted to take the easy way out and agree. But it wasn't fair to make Brant keep suffering—not if there was a chance she could help him.

She just wished there were a way to know if it were possible before everyone was counting on her.

Or maybe there was. . . .

"Do you think you could take me to see Brant?" Sophie asked.

"Why?" Grady was probably remembering Sophie's last encounter with Brant, which had been erratic at best and terrifying at worst.

But when Sophie had probed Prentice's mind—even though her abilities weren't working right and she wasn't able to heal him—she could tell that there was a glimmer of his consciousness left.

If she could probe Brant's thoughts, she might be able to find the same thing. Or she'd know once and for all that his mind was too far gone.

Either way, it was better than waiting on *if*.

"It's the only way to know for sure," she said, turning to Grady.

He glanced at Edaline, who nodded slowly.

"Okay, then." Grady stood so quickly he shook the table. "Finish your breakfast and get dressed. We'll go see him today."

TWELVE

BRANT'S STARK, WINDOWLESS HOUSE was just as bleak as Sophie remembered. Everything was gray—the dull stone walls, the jagged, dusty ground. Even the sky seemed to be in a perpetual state of gloom.

"There's something off about this place," Sandor said, pulling Sophie closer to his side. He'd insisted on coming, and after what happened last time, Grady had agreed—but he'd warned Sandor that he'd have to wait outside, doubting Brant could handle the sight of a goblin.

Sandor sniffed the frigid wind. "I can't detect a single sign of life."

"We burned everything before we built this place," Grady

explained, leading Sophie up the crooked path. "The only thing that lives here is Brant. The rest is just dust and ash."

"Well, I don't like it," Sandor muttered.

Sophie didn't either. But Brant was afraid of fire and heat and any kind of kindling. She could understand his reason for the phobias, but she couldn't imagine living somewhere so cold and empty.

Grady paused at the narrow steps that led to the metal front door. "You need to wait here, Sandor—and stay out of sight."

Sandor reached into one of his pockets and handed Grady a bladed throwing star. "Do not be afraid to use this."

"I can handle Brant. I've been taking care of him for sixteen years."

Sixteen years.

Sophie had never thought about what a burden taking care of Brant must be. His parents had been too mentally fragile from their grief to handle visiting their broken son, so Grady and Edaline had been the ones to find him somewhere to live and check on him from time to time—all while coping with their own loss.

"Take it for extra security," Sandor insisted. "You've said yourself that this elf is unpredictable."

Grady sighed as he shoved the blade into his cape pocket. "You're sure you're up for this?" he asked Sophie.

She nodded, not trusting her voice, as they started up the stairs.

They both hesitated at the top, taking several deep breaths.

Then Grady pulled the dangling chain, making a low chime echo through the silence. The tone was still ringing when the metal door flew open, slamming into the stone walls.

Grady clutched his chest. "I think you just gave me a heart attack, Brant. You've never met us at the door!"

"Well, you've never stopped by between anniversaries," Brant replied, his voice as hoarse and wheezy as Sophie remembered. "So I guess it's a day of firsts."

Don't stare at his scars, Sophie reminded herself, focusing on Brant's strange yellow-orange, bathrobelike shirt. But her eyes still darted to the bumps and dents and red splotches that ruined one side of his chin and cheek. Bitter souvenirs even Elwin couldn't erase.

"No Edaline?" Brant asked, stepping aside to let them pass.

"We're expecting a pair of apatosaurs to arrive this afternoon, and someone had to be there to assist." Grady explained. "Is that okay?"

Brant said nothing as he slammed the door and led them into his sparse sitting room. He motioned for them to take their pick of the four metal stools bound to the floor on large springs, but Sophie waited for Brant to choose his first. Then she sat in the one farthest away.

"No custard bursts either, I see," Brant said, shaking his head with a sigh. "So far this surprise isn't a very good one."

"No, I suppose it's not," Grady admitted. "But perhaps this might help."

He reached into his cape and pulled out a silver pouch tied with bright red string.

Brant leaned forward. "Is that . . . ?"

"Yep. A whole bag of Indigoobers, just for you."

Grady held it out to him, and Brant eyed it for a second, like Sophie's old cat used to do when she first showed him a new toy. He pounced just as quickly, snatching it away and tearing into his treasure.

It took him several seconds to untangle the string, shredding it to bits as he sank into his chair, pulled out a fist-size blue cluster, and shoved it into his mouth. Blue drool trickled down his lips and he struggled to chew the oversize mouthful, but that didn't stop him from saying, "I guess this is almost as good—but next time I want custard bursts."

"Edaline will bake a double batch," Grady promised.

"And I want more of these, too."

Brant shoved another in his mouth, covering his bottom lip with blue slime. Sophie had no idea what Indigoobers were, but she was pretty sure she never wanted to try them.

"So, are you going to tell me why you're here?" Brant asked, spraying spittle with each word. "Or do I have to guess? Actually, that might be fun." His sharp blue eyes bored into Sophie's like laser beams. "It has to do with *her*, doesn't it? You never made surprise visits before she came along. So what would *she* want?"

He rubbed his chin, smearing blue drool into his scars.

Sophie had to look away.

She studied the room, looking for any clues to how Brant spent his long, lonely days. There were no books or paper. No gadgets or tools. Nothing but bare walls and empty space, like a really clean prison.

"You can't have it!" Brant screamed, sending Sophie scrambling to her feet.

Grady rushed in front of her, but Brant was backing slowly away.

"You can't have it," he repeated, sinking to the floor in the corner. "It's mine. *Mine.*"

He said the word over and over, making Sophie realize what he meant. The last time she'd been there, Brant had tackled her and stolen her Ruewen crest pin.

"I gave the pin to you," she reminded him. "I don't want it back."

"Mine," Brant agreed, rocking back and forth. "Mine mine mine."

"Yes, Brant, it's yours. So can we calm down and get back to why we're really here?" Grady asked him.

Brant's eyes slowly cleared. "Sorry," he mumbled, crawling back to his chair. "Carry on."

Grady wrapped his arm around Sophie, keeping her at his side as he said, "Okay. You know how you get headaches sometimes? Sophie might be able to find the cause of them."

They'd decided not to tell Brant what they were really doing, not wanting to get his hopes up until they knew if the healing was a possibility.

Brant shoved another Indigoober into his mouth. "Oh, really?"

Sophie nodded. "It's a trick I learned a little while ago, and I think it might work on you."

"And what would I have to do?" he asked as he licked the blue slime off his lips.

"Just hold still for a second while Sophie sends a little warmth into your mind," Grady told him.

Brant shook his head, whipping it from side to side so hard it looked like it would detach from his neck. "Nothing warm! Nothing nothing nothing—"

"It's not really *warm*," Sophie jumped in. "More like a tingle. Like if you've ever had your leg fall asleep."

She had no idea if that was true. But that was how she imagined it would feel, and it seemed like a good enough explanation. It was enough to make Brant stop shaking.

"Okay," he said, a hint of a smile curling one side of his lips. "Let's see what you can do."

Grady squeezed Sophie's shoulder as she closed her eyes, reaching out with her consciousness for the feel of Brant's mind.

All she could find was heat.

A fire inside her head.

Sweat beaded on her skin as she stretched her mind further,

but no matter how hard she strained, she couldn't break through the wall of flames to make contact.

"I need to place my hands on your temples," she told Brant. "It won't hurt. It'll just help me focus the energy."

She moved slowly as she reached for his temples, like she was reaching to pet a wild dog that could bite her hand any second. But Brant held still, not even flinching when her fingers came to rest on his fever-hot skin.

The rush of heat was stronger this time, but Sophie was able to shove her way through, collapsing into a suffocating darkness with sharp edges that scratched at her mental barriers. She ignored the pain and rallied her concentration, pushing deeper into the mire.

A vivid scene rampaged into her mind.

Jolie, clinging to Brant as a firestorm explodes around them. The force tosses Brant backward, but Jolie is surrounded, the wild flames strangling tighter and tighter until her face is lost in the smoke and her screams fade to nothing.

"Stop!" Brant screamed, grabbing Sophie's wrist.

Pain launched up her arm as she tried to pull free, but she couldn't get away until Grady grabbed Brant and tossed him backward, slamming him into the wall.

Brant crumpled to the floor, pressing his hands over his ears and mumbling, "Stop stop stop stop stop stop stop stop stop."

"Are you okay?" Grady asked Sophie.

Before she could answer, Sandor charged into the room,

waving his sword and demanding to know what was going on. Brant covered his face and screamed.

"You're making it worse!" Grady shouted, shoving Sandor back toward the door. "I have everything under control."

"That's not what it looks like." Sandor's eyes focused on Sophie's wrist. She covered the wound with her hand, but he still insisted, "I'm taking Miss Foster with me."

"No," Sophie told him, relieved at the steadiness of her voice.

All of her instincts were telling her to run—flee—get far, far away.

But she couldn't ignore what she'd seen in Brant's mind.

His memory of Jolie's death had been sickening and horrifying. But it had also been *clear*—not scrambled up or shattered, like the broken memories she'd seen.

There had to be something left of Brant's consciousness.

"I can help you," she told Brant, waving Sandor back as she took a cautious step closer. "I can *heal* you."

"Heal me?" he asked, as Grady gasped.

The shadows seemed to crawl deeper into Brant's scars as he uncovered his face and asked, "What do you mean *heal* me?"

"Heal your mind," Sophie said quietly. "Make you better."

"Better," Brant repeated. "How will healing me make me *better*?"

"You'll be able to think clearly again," Grady jumped in. "Go back to normal—"

"Normal?" Brant screamed. "There is no *normal*!"

He whipped his bag of Indigoobers at Grady, and one of the clusters splattered Grady's cheek.

"Brant, please," Grady said as the goo slid down his face. "If you would just listen."

"No—you listen. Nothing will *ever* be normal because *nothing will ever bring her back!*"

Grady closed his eyes, and his voice was impossibly sad as he said. "I know you miss her. I do too."

"No, you don't. If you did you would've broken like me. *Then* you'd know that there's nothing without her. Nothing . . ." Brant's voice cracked and he buried his face in his hands. "Get out."

"Brant, please—"

"I SAID GET OUT!"

The words were so sharp, Sophie could practically feel them prick her skin.

But they weren't as scary as what Brant whispered while Sandor dragged her and Grady out the door.

"I never want to be healed. Never never never never."

Sophie didn't feel Grady take her hand, or the warm light whisk her away.

She didn't feel the pain in her wrist—though she was sure that would hit her when she got home.

All she felt were the claws of fear and doubt raging inside her, twisting and tearing and shredding her resolve.

Because if Brant didn't want to be healed, Prentice might not want to be either.

THIRTEEN

BUT PRENTICE IS THE PLAN, SOPHIE told herself for what felt like the hundredth time, as she pulled her memory log from its hiding place in the bottom drawer of her desk.

Alden had given her the teal book with the silver moonlark on the cover after she'd accidentally bottled quintessence—the highly dangerous fifth element, which could only be collected from one of the five unmapped stars—and he'd revealed the truth about her past. She'd been created as part of Project Moonlark, the Black Swan's secret genetic experiment, and after she'd been born they'd hidden classified secrets in her brain. The memories only resurfaced with the right trigger, so she'd been recording her dreams in her memory log, along with any clues that might lead her to her kidnappers, and any memories she'd recovered in the minds she'd probed.

She flipped to Prentice's pages, her clammy fingers sticking to the paper as she studied the twisted, nightmare scenes she'd recorded. Searching his mind had been one of the most terrifying things Sophie had ever experienced, and she couldn't imagine Prentice would want to live that way forever.

But he doesn't know what he'll be waking up to, she reminded herself.

A *lot* had changed since Prentice's mind had been broken.

Years had passed—more than a decade. His son, Wylie, had grown up without him. And his wife . . .

Sophie didn't know all the details—only that something had gone wrong while Cyrah was light leaping and she'd ended up fading away.

And Prentice had no idea. He would wake up expecting to find his wife and son waiting for him. Instead he'd learn his wife was dead and his son had been raised and adopted by an old family friend.

Would he be able to handle all of that tragedy?

Or would the grief and guilt and anger simply shatter him all over again?

Sophie sighed, stuffing the memory log away.

Mind healing was turning out to be *way* more complicated than she'd thought. And of course the Black Swan hadn't given her any guidance except, "Wait for instructions and stick to the plan."

Unless . . .

She ran to her door, threw it open and—

—slammed into a muscley goblin chest.

"Ow," she complained, pinching the bridge of her smashed nose. "You don't have to barricade me in."

"Actually, I do. I figured it was only a matter of time before you tried to sneak away."

"I'm not sneaking away. I was going down to check the caves to see if the Black Swan replied to my note."

"So you weren't going to pay a secret visit to Elwin on the way back?"

"Why would I . . ."

Sandor reached for her wrist, pointing to the ugly reddish bruise she'd forgotten about.

"It's not a big deal," she said, trying to pull her arm away.

"If you don't mind, I think *I* should be the one to decide that."

She rolled her eyes as Sandor sniffed the injury. "If you lick me I'm going to kick you."

"That would be like a kitten kicking a bear." His smile faded as he took another whiff. "This is more than a bruise."

"I think he twisted the skin as he squeezed—or maybe it happened when I tried to pull away." Her little sister used to do that to her all the time. It always stung like a burn.

Sandor frowned. "Well, it *does* seem like a surface wound, so it will probably clear up with a salve. But if it's still there tomorrow I will insist we stop by the Healing Center on your lunch break. Agreed?"

Sophie nodded, hoping one of the billions of ointments Edaline kept around the house in case of "Sophie Emergencies" would work. She was already holding the record for Most Physician Visits that year—and Foxfire had only been in session for a few weeks.

"Can I go now?" she asked, pulling her wrist free.

Sandor shook his head. "I'll check the cave. You stay here and treat that wound before it starts to fester."

"How do I know you won't hide their reply if you don't like it?"

"Because secrets hinder my ability to protect you—whether *I'm* keeping them, or you are. We need to work *together*. I know you're not used to trusting people, Sophie. But I'm on your side. I wish you would believe that."

Sophie touched the edge of her bruise. Her skin really was stinging. And she didn't exactly love going to that creepy cave. "Fiiiiiiiiiiiiiiiiiiiiiiiiiiiiiiine."

"Good. I'll be back in a few minutes," Sandor said, already on his way to the door. "And I hope when I come back I'll find you sleeping peacefully."

"It's the middle of the afternoon," she reminded him.

"Sounds like a perfect time for a nap. Trust me—you need one."

108

He left before she could argue, and Sophie checked her reflection in her floor-length mirror, surprised at how shadowed her eyes were.

"Ugh, what'd you do—get into a fist fight with your pillow?" Vertina asked as her tiny face appeared in the upper corner of the glass.

Sophie knew spectral mirrors were just a clever bit of Elvin programming. But she was always surprised by how lifelike Vertina seemed—and how much she wished she could reach through the glass and strangle her. If Vertina hadn't been such close friends with Jolie, Sophie would've left the obnoxious talking mirror to gather dust for all eternity.

"You should really think about using glimmer dust," Vertina told her, tossing her long black hair. "It worked wonders on Jolie—and she had the worst dark circles I've ever seen."

"Was Jolie having a hard time sleeping?"

"Toward the end, yeah. But that was when . . ."

"When what?" Sophie asked.

"Have you thought about trying gold eye shadow? It would really bring out the flecks in those freaky eyes of yours."

"When *what*?" Sophie pressed.

She'd been trying to get information out of Vertina for weeks, but so far all she'd gotten was snippy makeover advice.

Vertina chewed her lip. "I . . . can't tell you. Jolie said I couldn't tell anyone, even if she was gone. *Especially* if she was gone."

"Wait—are you saying she knew she might die?"

Vertina squeaked and tossed her hair to hide behind it. "I can't say any more. Not unless . . ."

"Unless what?" Sophie asked.

"If you don't know, I can't help you."

"What does that even mean?" Sophie was shouting now, but she didn't care if anyone heard her. Not that it made a difference.

"I'm sorry," Vertina told her, and it almost seemed like she meant it. "I can't say anything else. I've probably already said too much."

She blinked away with a faint click.

Sophie stared at the empty glass, not sure what surprised her more, that Vertina could turn herself off, or that Vertina really was hiding an important secret.

There had to be some sort of password—or maybe something she was supposed to show Vertina—in order to get her to share. Sophie tried to figure out what it would be as she searched the huge ebony armoire in her bathroom for a salve to treat her wrist. Edaline had bought Blister Blast and Scratches 'n Splits and Abrasion Persuasion. But Sophie grabbed the Bruise Cruse, hoping it wasn't made with any sort of animal pee as she smeared the yellowish sludge over her wound.

The cream felt prickly as it sank in, like she was rubbing her skin with a burr. And the longer it set, the hotter the zings grew until Sophie finally gave in and scrubbed her arm with soap and cold water.

"How's the wound?" Sandor asked, making her jump so hard she splashed herself.

"Sorry," he said, handing her one of the feather-soft towels. "I thought you heard me come in."

"Actually you walk pretty quiet, despite your giant goblin feet."

"I don't have giant goblin feet."

She moved her foot next to his, which looked like a lizard next to a dinosaur.

"Okay, maybe I do," Sandor conceded. "Let me see your wrist."

Sophie reluctantly held out her hand, revealing the angry welt. "I must've used the wrong ointment—but I'll try a different one in a few minutes. I just want to let my skin calm down."

"If it's not better in the morning—"

"I know, I know. So what'd you find in the cave?"

Sandor reached into his pocket, removing a clear glass vial with a note curled inside. The sign of the swan—a black curve like a swan's neck—had been pressed into a wax seal on the stopper.

"I waited for you to open it," he said as she grabbed the vial and pried at the seal.

Her pulse pounded in her ears as she removed the crystal stopper. She'd gotten dozens of notes from the Black Swan before, but this one felt bigger.

This time, they were responding to *her*.

But her excitement quickly faded as she read their carefully written message:

Your request is denied, for your own protection.

FOURTEEN

DUDE, WHAT IS UP WITH THEM NOT rhyming?" Keefe asked, holding up the note like he expected to find a secret message scratched into the paper.

Sophie had done the same thing—and searched the empty bottle for clues, and checked the cave to make sure Sandor hadn't missed anything. But of course the only thing the Black Swan had given her was the incredibly unhelpful message. Which meant her best option in the What Do I Do Now? category involved getting to Foxfire early the next day and ambushing Keefe on his way to morning orientation—though she was already regretting the decision.

Especially when Keefe tossed the note back to her and said,

"Okay, I figured out our reply. Write this down, Gigantor: *You may not want to meet, but we definitely do. Name a time and a place or we'll pelt you with sparkly poo.*"

Sophie was too angry to laugh.

After all the times she'd risked her life to help the Black Swan. All the times she'd blindly followed their vague instructions. When it was finally her turn to go to them for help—to protect *Silveny*, no less—they'd cast her aside with a single, poorly written sentence.

"Hey, don't go," Keefe said, grabbing her wrist to stop her.

Sophie flinched.

The other bruise ointment she'd tried had bleached most of the wound's reddish color, but her skin still felt raw and tingly, and throbbed every time she bumped it.

"I'm fine," she said under her breath, hoping Keefe would drop it and that Sandor hadn't noticed. She wasn't in the mood for another Elwin visit.

Keefe narrowed his eyes. But all he said was, "I know the Black Swan are being super jerky. But that means you need to get tougher. Make your next note a demand. Remember, you're Sophie Foster—Mysterious Girl Extraordinaire!"

He pumped his fist, making most of the prodigies around them turn to stare.

"I mean it," he added a bit quieter. "The Black Swan needs you *way* more than you need them. You're the one holding all the cards."

Even if that were true, she had no idea how to play the game. Her one move had been leaving them a note, and they'd tossed it back in her face.

"How is refusing to meet with me for my *protection*?" she asked as they walked along the winding path toward the main Foxfire building. "I mean, if they want to keep me safe, shouldn't they find out what I know?"

"Maybe they already know what you know," Keefe suggested. "Or maybe they don't trust themselves."

"What do you mean?"

"Well, the rebels *did* find their hideout somehow. And we had to fly across the ocean on an alicorn, so I'm pretty sure no one followed us."

She stopped walking. "Are you saying you think the Black Swan has a leak?"

"Maybe. Or maybe they're worried they do, and that's why they think it's safer not to meet with you right now."

"That . . . actually makes sense."

"Of course it does. I'm a genius. That's why you keep me around. Well, that and my stunning good looks."

He rumpled his hair and gave her his most confident smirk, but Sophie was too distracted to reply.

What if the Black Swan *did* have a leak?

Ten thousand questions swamped into her head, but the crowd had grown too thick for Sophie to say anything further. They'd reached the six-towered, six-colored, U-shaped main building, and everyone was funneling into the five-story glass pyramid in the center of the courtyard. Orientation was held every morning on the ground floor, and as they made their way inside, Sophie expected Keefe to join his fellow Level Fives in their fiery red uniforms. But he followed her over to the cluster of amber brown Level Threes, instead.

"Are you guys leaping to school together now?" Dex asked as they joined him.

"Ha—Foster wishes," Keefe jumped in, before Sophie could say anything. "I was just walking with her because, well, Gigantor misses me."

He wrapped an arm around Sandor, and Sandor shoved him away. "I'll be waiting over there," he said, glaring at Keefe before he stalked to his usual spot in the corner.

"What were you guys really doing?" Dex asked as soon as Sandor was gone. "And don't tell me 'nothing.' I'm not an idiot."

"But we *were* doing nothing. I just had to ask Keefe something. About . . . Silveny."

It was sort of the truth, but Dex clearly didn't buy it.

"Oh—Iggy looks awesome," she added, changing the subject to something safer.

"Really?" Dex's cheeks dimpled with his smile. "Thanks. I had a super hard time deciding between the orange dreads or green spikes."

"Dude, can I have the green-spiky elixir?" Keefe asked. "I've been trying to figure out what to do to Dame Alina next."

Sophie shook her head at him. "You're hopeless, you know that?"

"Not as long as I have you. Fix me, Foster. You're my only hope."

Sophie knew he was teasing, but her cheeks still felt hot—and when she glanced at Dex, she could tell he'd noticed.

"So," she said, trying to fill the awkward silence, "what have you been—"

"Boo!" Biana shouted, appearing out of thin air between them. She giggled as they all jumped back. "You guys should see your faces. Being a Vanisher is going to be *awesome!*"

She vanished again as Fitz made his way over to their group—another fiery red uniform among the golden brown. "Can you believe she's still at it? There's no way I was this annoying when I manifested."

"Wanna bet?" Dex mumbled.

Sophie elbowed him.

"No, Dex is right," Keefe said, smirking at Fitz. "Not only did I have him *constantly* begging to read my mind, but I had to keep hearing, 'I'm the youngest Telepath to ever manifest!'"

His impersonation of Fitz's precise accent was pretty dead-on.

"If only we'd known Foster had you beat by, like, eight years, we could've shut you up much sooner," Keefe added, earning himself a huge grin from Dex. "And wait—isn't Biana younger than you were?"

"Only by a few weeks," Fitz corrected. "Plus, telepathy is a rarer ability."

"Yeah, well, vanishing's cooler," Biana told him, disappearing again.

"Whoa," Jensi whispered, his eyes as round as his head as he and Marella joined them. "Biana manifested?"

His mouth fell open as Biana reappeared.

"That is the coolest thing ever! Did you manifest this weekend—and did it hurt? My brother said it hurt—he said he felt kind of achy all day before he manifested—and then his foot sank into the floor and he realized he was a Phaser and was like, 'oh, that's why!'—was it like that for you?"

Once Jensi started his rapid-fire questions, there was no stopping him, though Sophie was surprised at how quiet Marella was being. Usually Marella was the biggest gossip in the group, dominating their conversations with a surprisingly loud voice for someone so tiny.

"You okay?" Sophie asked, noticing Marella's uniform looked more wrinkled than usual. Her blond hair also wasn't twisted into any braids.

"Oh, um, yeah. I'm just tired. I overslept and—"

An intricate peal of chimes cut her off, and Dame Alina's projection appeared across the far wall of the pyramid.

"Good morning, prodigies!" she said, fluffing her caramel-colored hair and flashing a gleaming smile. "Welcome to a new week at Foxfire!"

Sophie only half listened as Dame Alina rattled off a lecture about Foxfire being a noble school and how they all needed to act like they were aware of the privilege they'd been given by attending. But she was forced to pay attention when Dame Alina declared that she had a special announcement to make.

"As some of you may already know, we've had our first prodigies manifest abilities this year. So would everyone please join me in congratulating our new Vanisher, Biana Vacker, and our new Technopath, Dex Dizznee!"

Spotlights flashed on both Dex and Biana and the room erupted into cheers.

As soon as the lights dimmed, Dex spun to face Keefe. "Did you tell Dame Alina about me?"

Keefe laughed. "Dude, I *never* talk to Dame Alina if I don't have to."

"Well maybe you had to," Dex pressed. "To get out of detention or something."

"Nope. I have detention for the rest of the month—you can check."

"Then was it you?" Dex asked, turning to Sophie.

"Do you really think I would do that?" She could hear the hurt in her voice, but she couldn't believe Dex would ask.

Dex's eyes dropped to his feet. "I don't know. Who else would it be?"

"I have no idea," Sophie admitted. "But I also don't think this is a bad thing. I mean, look around you."

"Exactly," Keefe jumped in, pointing to the crowd of whispering prodigies. "Everyone's talking about how cool you are!"

"No, they're saying Biana's cool. For me they're probably saying, 'Of course Dex got a lame ability.'"

"Nobody thinks it's lame," Sophie promised.

"How would you know? Are you reading their minds?"

"I could." Though she wasn't allowed to. According to the rules of telepathy, she wasn't supposed to read anyone's mind unless they gave her permission first.

Dex turned back to Keefe. "And you're sure you didn't tell *anyone*?"

"Uh, no offense, but if I'm going to brag about someone, I'll brag about me. Or Foster. But usually me."

Dex didn't look convinced. But he didn't say anything else as he turned and walked away.

Sophie waited until he'd disappeared into the crowd before she asked Keefe, "It wasn't you, right?"

He clutched his heart, pretending to be wounded.

"I wonder who it was, then. No one besides us . . ." Sophie's voice trailed off as she thought of someone else who knew.

Someone who was always watching.

Someone who might have a *leak*.

But . . . why would the Black Swan—or their leak—tell anyone about Dex's secret ability?

"Hey," Keefe said, waving his hand in front her eyes. "Don't let Dex get to you. He'll be over this by the end of the day."

She doubted that—Dex could hold a major grudge. But she nodded as she turned to follow the other prodigies out of the pyramid.

Keefe stayed beside her as Sandor led them through the main building. The crystal walls of each wing matched the color of the corresponding grade level's uniform, and when they reached the amber brown Level Three wing, Sophie turned to head toward her locker.

"Wait," Keefe said, jumping in front of her. "You should ditch with me. I mean, do you really want to suffer through elvin history?"

"Miss Foster will be going to her session," Sandor told him before Sophie could reply.

"Aw, come on. You can ditch with us too!"

Sandor cracked his knuckles ominously.

"You know you don't want to listen to two hours on the Troll Emancipation Act," Keefe told him.

"It's on the Elvin-Ogre Treaty, actually," Sophie corrected. "Which will probably be useful, considering everything happening."

Keefe's brows shot up, and she realized she hadn't told him about the tracker being made by ogres yet. But she didn't have time to get into it right then.

"Fine," Keefe said as she opened her locker and grabbed her history book. "Go be the model prodigy. But I'm coming over after school and you'll tell me whatever you're hiding. And then we'll come up with our epic *We are the cool, powerful ones, not you!* reply to the Black Swan and whip those dudes into shape. Deal?"

Sophie nodded so he'd be quiet, but she definitely wasn't agreeing.

She couldn't send the Black Swan any notes—and she realized with a start that she couldn't trust their notes anymore either.

Until she knew who their leak was, she was officially on her own.

FIFTEEN

DEX DIDN'T SHOW UP IN THE cafeteria during lunch, and Keefe was stuck in detention. The rest of the group sat with Sophie at their usual table in the corner, but Jensi was still peppering Biana with questions, and Marella was still sulking about whatever it was that was bothering her—and she *did not* want to talk about it when Sophie tried to ask.

Which left Sophie with nothing to do except pick at the weird green fruit she'd grabbed from the lunch line, and stare at the note the Black Swan had given her.

"This is when I miss transmitting to you," Fitz said, making her jump as he scooted into the seat across from her. "Then I could ask you what's wrong and you might actually tell me."

For a brief time, they'd been able to have telepathic conversations. But Fitz was only able to transmit past her blocking because of a crack in the barriers around her otherwise impenetrable mind. Now that her abilities had been healed, they had to talk out loud again.

"I could help, you know," Fitz said quietly.

"Not with this." This was a whole other realm of complicated.

How was she supposed to figure out if the Black Swan had a leak when she didn't even know who they were? The only member she'd met was Mr. Forkle, and she had no idea who he *really* was under the disguise. Plus, she was pretty sure it couldn't be him. Why would he rescue her when she'd been kidnapped?

Unless that was part of his cover . . .

"Come on, let me at least try," Fitz pressed. "You let Keefe help."

"Not by choice."

"So what if I don't give you a choice?" he asked, and the glint in his eye made her cheeks burn.

She leaned back in her chair. "No way you could ever be that annoying."

"Try me."

"I—"

"Ugh, check out the loser table," a snooty voice interrupted behind her, followed by an ugly laugh.

Sophie's hands curled into fists as a tall, bony girl plopped into the empty seat next to her.

"You do not have permission to sit there," Sandor snapped, stepping out of his hiding place in the shadows.

"I can handle Stina, Sandor." Sophie turned to glare at the girl beside her. "What do you want?"

"Oh, I don't know." Stina turned to Fitz with a sly smile. "I'm not interrupting something, am I?"

"Yeah, actually you are," Fitz told her. "I was talking to my *friend*."

Sophie knew why he was emphasizing the word, but it still stung—almost as much as the stupid bruise on her wrist.

"Yeah, what's up with that, by the way?" Stina asked. "I mean, I understand why these two are hiding over here"—she pointed to Jensi and Marella, who were both glaring at her—"they're just as bad as this one"—she pointed to Sophie. "But you guys used to be so cool. And now?" She turned to her two stringy-haired minions standing behind her and shrugged, unimpressed.

"Do you think I care what you think?" Biana asked.

"You should," Stina snapped. "I mean, look at you. I bet you feel so special now, just because you manifested an ability."

"Uh, I manifested before *you*," Biana reminded her, vanishing again for added effect.

Stina's jaw tightened—but only for a second. "Whatever. Abilities don't matter as much as people say they do."

"Is that what your dad tells you?" Marella jumped in.

"So what if it is? Look at your family—both parents with special abilities and you're still at the loser table."

"The only loser here is you," Jensi grumbled.

"Keep telling yourself that." Stina turned back to Fitz and Biana. "Don't you realize what people say about the Vackers now? They're calling your family traitors."

"Traitors?" Fitz repeated. "How do you figure that?"

Stina tossed her frizzy curls. "Simple. You spend all your time helping out the enemy."

Fitz laughed, his scowl fading to a look of pity. "Sophie is not our enemy."

"Are you sure about that?" Stina focused on Sophie, the glint in her eye as cold as her smile. "So you haven't agreed to heal an incredibly dangerous criminal?"

"Are you sure you don't want me to get rid of her for you?" Sandor offered again.

"No, I'm fine," Sophie said, her voice echoing around the suddenly silent room. "And Prentice isn't a criminal."

"Tell that to the guards at Exile—but that's not who I meant. My dad told me you're going to heal *Fintan*. And uh, didn't he have something to do with all those fires a few months ago?"

"How do you know that?"

As far as Sophie knew, all of that information was classified.

"I'll take that as a yes," Stina said smugly.

"Uh, are you forgetting that Sophie's the one who helped stop those fires?" Fitz asked. "And I'm sure the Council ordered Fintan's healing."

"So? Everyone knows the Councillors don't know what

they're doing—not since she came along. They need to replace, like, sixty percent of them."

"That. Is. Enough!"

All heads turned toward Dame Alina, who was striding toward Sophie's table. Her ruby-encrusted gown swished with every step, and it was the only sound in the room. She cleared her throat when she reached their table. "Miss Heks. Slanderous statements against the Council have no place at this school!"

"I wasn't—"

"I know what I heard. And I will not allow anyone to disparage our leaders—or one of our most prominent noble families—under my watch. Is. That. Clear?"

Stina stood, her beanpole body almost as tall as Dame Alina's. But she didn't argue.

She didn't *agree*, either. She just motioned for her minions to follow her and stalked away.

"You've earned yourself a week's worth of detention," Dame Alina called after her. "And you can count on me notifying your parents."

Sophie doubted Vika and Timkin would care. She'd heard them say even worse.

"All right, show's over," Dame Alina said, clapping her hands and ordering everyone to get back to their lunches. "And Miss Foster," she added, loud enough for everyone to hear. "If anyone says anything like that again, I expect you to tell me. Same goes for all of you."

She waited until every prodigy nodded.

"Good. Now eat up—you need brain food for all the learning ahead of you."

Sophie usually dreaded the long walk across campus to the twisted gold and silver towers that housed the elite levels—and her afternoon session. But it was a relief to get away from all the stares and whispers that had followed the lunch incident. She wished Fitz and Biana could do the same—especially since it was her fault they'd been dragged into the drama.

Then again, they didn't have to endure two hours of linguistics with Lady Cadence.

The session was an elite subject, taught only to prodigies in their eighth and final year at Foxfire. But since Sophie had discovered that she was also a Polyglot—able to speak any and all languages on instinct—the Council had decided she needed to start her training early. They'd also given her access to the usually restricted Silver Tower, even though she was too short to lick the DNA access strip on the door and had to wait outside for Master Leto, the Beacon of the Silver Tower, to let her in.

"You kids always need me right when I'm sitting down to lunch," he complained as he stepped aside to let Sophie pass.

She'd barely taken two steps before he spun on his heel, his long silver cloak swishing as he slammed the door in Sandor's face.

"I love how he looks ready to strangle me when I do that,"

Master Leto said, laughing to himself as he led her to the other side of the low-ceilinged foyer.

Balefire sconces bathed the silver walls with their blue tint, and the lone statue of a silver unicorn—the Level Eight mascot—seemed to stare at them as Master Leto placed his silver Beacon badge against a small black sensor, releasing a hidden compartment full of cloaks. While Sophie was in the Silver Tower, she was expected to dress like one of the elite. So she grabbed the silver cape that had been shortened just for her and clasped it across her shoulders.

"I heard you had some excitement today," Master Leto said, checking his overly gelled hair before pressing his palm against the wall and opening the hidden doorway to the main tower. "I've been telling Dame Alina for months that she needs to run those levels with a heavier hand. Perhaps now she'll be willing to listen to me. You'll find no such issue here. The Silver Tower is under my control."

Sophie would have loved to believe him. But when they entered the amphitheater-size common area, filled with book-shelves and chandeliers and plush silver armchairs, she could see someone waiting for her in the mostly empty room—impossible to miss at the base of the silver spiral staircase.

Prentice's son, Wylie.

SIXTEEN

NEED I REMIND YOU OF THE PUNISH-
ment for tardiness, Mr. Endal?" Master Leto
asked, pointing to his badge for emphasis.

Wylie's skin wasn't as dark as his father's,
and his features were sharper. But their eyes were the same.
Same shape. Same piercing blue. And they looked just as sad
and lost as he told Sophie, "I need to talk to you."

"No, you *need* to head to your session—immediately,"
Master Leto informed him.

Wylie didn't budge.

"I know what you're going to ask," Sophie told him quietly.
"And I . . ."

She had no idea how to finish that sentence.

Wylie hadn't spoken to her since the day she'd found him at his mother's grave, when he'd told her his father had promised him that someone would heal him. The poor guy had spent the majority of his life clinging to that dim hope for his father— even when he didn't know Sophie existed. And now that the possibility was finally a reality, she could practically smell the desperation radiating off him, thick and sour, like the bile coating her tongue.

Master Leto nudged her. "Miss Foster, you should head to your session. Lady Cadence *will* punish you, even if you're only a few seconds late."

She was sure he was right, and she was so tempted to climb the winding, twisted stairs and avoid the awkward conversation. But Wylie deserved to know what she was thinking. Maybe he'd even agree.

"I know you miss your dad," Sophie said, forcing herself to meet Wylie's eyes. "But I'm starting to wonder if healing him is a good idea. Think about what it would be like for him, waking up to find out how much time he's lost. How many things he's missed. And your mom . . ."

Wylie looked away, his hands curled into fists. "So, what? You think it's better to just leave him in Exile?"

"What I think is that this whole thing is *way* more complicated than any of us realized, and . . . maybe we need to take some time to really consider the consequences before we decide."

"Meanwhile you'll heal *Fintan*?" Wylie spat the name like it was a bad word.

Master Leto stepped closer. "That information is supposed to be classified."

"Well, word gets around. Especially when everyone disagrees."

Everyone disagrees?

Sophie wanted to know more, but stopped herself from asking. It didn't matter.

"I'm healing Fintan on the Council's order—and only because we need to know what he's hiding. But your dad is different. He's lost so much. What if all the grief is too much for him to handle?"

"Don't!" Wylie shouted, his voice crashing off the sleek walls. "Do not pretend to care about him. This is *your* fault. If he hadn't been protecting you—"

"That's enough, Mr. Endal!" Master Leto snapped, straightening up to his full height. He actually made a pretty imposing figure, especially when he told Wylie, "I would not recommend trying my patience any further."

Wylie gritted his teeth, and for a second Sophie wondered if he was going to clock Master Leto in the face. But all he did was shove past him, stomping up the stairs so loudly, each footfall sounded like a drumbeat. Once he'd disappeared around a few curves, Sophie slowly started up the stairs behind him.

"Did you mean what you said back there?" Master Leto called behind her.

Sophie turned back to face him. "Did I mean what?"

"You really think Prentice wouldn't want to be healed?"

"I . . . don't know. But how would you feel waking up after all those years and finding out your wife was dead?"

"I don't have a wife." His voice had turned thick, his face twisted with emotion—though Sophie doubted even an Empath could translate it.

"I'm sorry," she said quietly.

"It's not . . . And I still . . . Not that it matters . . ."

She wasn't sure if he was talking to her anymore. His gaze had turned distant, like he'd fallen deep into a memory. And as she studied his face, she realized Master Leto was much older than he looked. His ears weren't pointed, but he had ancient eyes.

The bells chimed their intricate peal, drawing him out of his trance.

"You'd better go," he reminded her.

He didn't follow her as she headed up the twisting staircase. And when she glanced down a few floors later he was still standing there, staring into space, looking even more confused than she felt.

Lady Cadence gave her a week's worth of lunch detention for being late—which wouldn't have been such a horrible punishment, if she hadn't also informed Sophie that she'd be the Mentor monitoring detention—and that she had a fresh batch of curdleroots for the prodigies to peel and juice.

Sophie had reeked of the rancid, squishy tubers for days after the last time she'd worked with them. But at least Stina would have to suffer with her.

"Now that you're done wasting my time," Lady Cadence said, knotting her raven black hair behind her head with a silver pencil, "let's get on with today's lesson. You've proven your aptitude with languages, so it's time to test your mimicking."

Sophie sank into the room's only chair—which was so cold and hard she was sure Lady Cadence had chosen it specifically to make her miserable. "Mimicking?"

"Don't tell me you thought we'd just be studying languages?"

"Well . . . the session *is* called linguistics."

"Yes, and if they wanted to simply teach you a few sentences in dwarven and troll they could've given you any Mentor. But they gave you to me, which I can only assume is because we're both Polyglots—"

"Wait—I thought you were a Conjurer." Sophie had seen Lady Cadence snap her fingers and make things appear or disappear several times.

Lady Cadence let out a slow sigh, like the mere thought of how much Sophie had to learn made her exhausted. "Polyglots often have more than one ability. And properly speaking a language is so much more than memorizing words. You must master the accent and pronunciation—sometimes even the tone. It's what makes Polyglots so remarkable. And also what allows us to mimic. For instance"—she cleared her throat and took a shallow breath—"I'm sorry I'm late. It won't happen again."

Sophie felt her mouth gape as she realized Lady Cadence had done a flawless impersonation of her voice.

"That's crazy."

"There's nothing crazy about it," Lady Cadence told her, mimicking Dame Alina. She followed with an impression of Alden's crisp accent that was so spot-on, it sounded like she was lip-synching to a recording.

"And I can do that too?" Sophie asked.

"With practice. So let's find your starting level, shall we?" She snapped her fingers and a golden gadget that looked somewhat like a metronome appeared in her hands. She flicked a lever and the needle swung back and forth. "Repeat after me, and make sure you say it just like I do: Someday I will return to Ravagog and continue my research."

Sophie repeated the sentence, trying to clip the words and emphasize the *T*s the way Lady Cadence had. Instead, she sounded like a grumpy Mary Poppins.

Lady Cadence sighed as she clicked off the gadget. "Three million, four hundred thousand, seven hundred and fifty three. I've seen toddlers with higher ratings."

They tried the same sentence three more times, and each time Sophie's rating fell lower.

"Well," Lady Cadence said, shoving the gadget into a pocket in her simple blue gown. "I suppose *this* is why they felt you needed my assistance."

Sophie doubted the Council could've known how horrible she'd be at mimicking. But she had a better question. "What was it like, living with the ogres?"

Lady Cadence leaned back, pulling the pen from her hair and letting the long, straight strands cascade around her face. "It was . . . very different from what I expected. They're so much more advanced than I'd realized they would be—their cities full of so many unknown wonders. There were unpleasant things, of course. The smell alone." She shuddered. "And they can be the most despicably violent creatures. But . . . there's shocking intelligence under all that brutality. So much drive and determination. I will never understand them—and I will always want to bathe them—but I have also learned to respect them. More important, they learned to respect me, and even to trust me. They were teaching me things no elf has ever learned before. That's what I miss. Knowing that the work I was doing could ensure the lasting peace between our people, as opposed to wasting hours teaching skills to a little girl who's already too smart for her own good."

Sophie couldn't tell if that was a compliment or an insult. Either way, she let it go. "So, knowing the ogres as well as you do, do you think they would give the rebels one of their stalkenteene trackers? Or would the rebels have to steal it?"

"Wait," Lady Cadence said, sitting up straighter. "Did you find one of their devices?"

"Yeah. Yesterday I found one tangled in Silveny's tail."

Lady Cadence scooted back like Sophie had the plague, muttering something under her breath as she snapped her fingers and made a tiny silver vial appear in her palm.

"Hold out your hands," she ordered, removing the stopper and sprinkling the fine silver powder over Sophie's skin.

"Please not red," she whispered. "Anything but red."

Sophie counted the passing seconds as they both stared at her hands. After one hundred and twenty-nine she was pretty sure nothing was going to happen.

But at one hundred and thirty, her skin glowed bright red.

SEVENTEEN

HAT DOES RED MEAN?"
Sophie asked, not sure if she
should scream or flail or run to the
nearest bathroom and wash her
hands with an entire bar of soap.

"It means you need to get to the Healing Center. Does Elwin
keep piquatine on hand?"

"I don't even know what that is."

Lady Cadence sprinkled the silver powder on her own
hands and rubbed it in. "It's an acid, second in strength only
to alkahest, so it should be strong enough to remove aromark.
Honestly—have you learned *nothing* in alchemy?"

Alchemy had been Sophie's worst subject—by far—and

she'd barely managed a passing grade. But she did remember that alkahest was the universal solvent, able to dissolve anything.

Wood.

Metal.

Flesh.

"What's aromark?" she asked, more than a little afraid of the answer.

Lady Cadence held her nonglowing hands up to sniff them. "Something I'm very thankful not to have on me. It won't hurt you. Not by itself, at least," she added when she noticed the way Sophie had started to tremble. "But you must get rid of it—quickly. Did anyone else handle the device besides you?"

"Alden and Keefe. And Jurek at the Sanctuary. And maybe some of the Councillors. Plus it was tangled in Silveny's tail, so I'm sure it touched her."

Lady Cadence rubbed her temples. "They'll all have to get tested." She handed Sophie the vial of powder. "Have them sprinkle this on their skin. Anywhere that glows red has to be purged. And if you need more, let me know. I have plenty of reveldust with my supplies."

"Reveldust?" Sophie repeated, trying not to think about the word "purged."

"It's a special type of spore that reacts to various ogre enzymes. It doesn't get rid of them. But it'll let you know they're there."

Sophie studied her glowing hands. "How come Alden and Sandor didn't know about this stuff?"

"Because they never asked. And most of the reports I sent the Council seemed to vanish into some sort of void, never to be mentioned again. I sent them all kinds of information about what I discovered of the true nature of ogre technology. For instance." She reached into her pocket and pulled out a necklace with a round silver pendant. "This is a Markchain. King Dimitar, the ogres' supreme leader, gave it to me when he finally granted my residency in their capital—which was no easy feat, I can assure you. He told me I had to wear it at all times if I wanted to remain safe, and for years I thought it was a gadget, like the registry pendants we wear. But I was wrong."

She rubbed her finger along the edge of the sphere and held out her hand. After a few seconds, her fingertip glowed green.

"That's the essenseal reacting with the reveldust still on my hands," she explained.

Sophie shook her head, struggling to keep all the weird names straight. "What does that have to do with aromark?"

"Because they're both enzymes. *That's* the ogres' true brilliance. Their technology is actually quite simplistic. But their biochemistry! I had no idea until I knocked over a vat of reveldust while I was working, and walked through the cloud it created. My skin glowed bright green everywhere my pendant had touched me, and I realized that the Markchain is actually an ecosystem. A tiny, self-sustaining world of microorganisms."

She dangled the silver pendant in front of Sophie's face, pointing to the nearly microscopic black holes that covered the outside like tiny pinpricks. "Essenseal is an enzyme secreted by the colony of microorganisms living inside this sphere. As elves we can't see the enzyme, smell it, or taste it without reveldust. But the ogres can. And if they don't detect it on someone walking through their city, they know they're dealing with an intruder."

Sophie frowned at her glowing red fingers. "If the scent is so strong, why didn't Sandor notice it?"

"Goblins are the ogres' greatest enemies—aside from humans. Of course their defense mechanisms evade goblin detection. The fact that elves can't see or smell them is just a bonus."

Sophie had to agree with the ogres' logic—though once again she found herself wishing that Sandor's goblin super-senses were a lot more *super*.

"So then what does aromark on the tracker do?" she asked, bracing for the worst possible answer. Still, nothing could've prepared her.

Lady Cadence held her green finger next to Sophie's red ones. "Green would mean it's a tracker, Sophie. Red means it's a homing device. All of their weapons—and they do have them, though they're supposedly for 'defense only'—use aromark as their targeting system. As long as they lock onto the enzyme, they're guaranteed a direct hit."

"You're sure Lady Cadence said *piquatine*?" Elwin asked as he searched the shelves of tiny bottles that lined the largest wall in the Healing Center.

He cringed when Sophie nodded, removing his iridescent spectacles and resting them on his forehead, amidst his wild, dark hair. "Well then. I'm going to have to prep your skin."

Nothing about that sentence sounded good.

"Relax, Foster," Keefe said as he flopped back in the bed across from her. "I swear I'm feeling more stress vibes from you than from Gigantor over there."

He pointed to Elwin's office, where Sandor was pacing back and forth, using his triangular-shaped gadget to convey the newest information to the captain of his army. The thin wall that separated the office from the larger treatment area muffled most of the conversation. But Sophie could still hear the tremble in Sandor's squeaky voice.

"I look like I've been dipped in foxfire," Keefe said, wiggling his glowing red fingers. "Think Dame Alina would give me extra credit if I told her I did this for school spirit?"

"I think Dame Alina is more worried that we might have gotten aromark somewhere else," Sophie told him.

The entire Foxfire campus was currently being swept with Lady Cadence's supply of reveldust, even though Lady Cadence had assured Dame Alina that ogre enzymes only transferred when they were freshly released—like how ink only smeared when it was wet—and only stuck to living skin through direct contact with the aromark's source.

Sophie, meanwhile, was much more concerned about getting in touch with Alden, so he could arrange for Silveny to get treated. Once again, Alden was "out of range." Same with Jurek and Grady.

Keefe kicked the edge of Sophie's mattress, making Bullhorn—Elwin's pet banshee, who must've been sleeping under her bed—streak across the room with an angry hiss. "If you keep squeezing your Imparter that tight, you're going to crush it."

Sophie loosened her grip and took a deep, calming breath.

It didn't help.

"Why aren't they answering?" she asked, fighting the urge to fling the useless gadget across the room. "And how can you be so calm? There could be ogre weapons aimed at us right this second. Or at Silveny. Or Alden. Or the Councillors. And if they lock onto this"—she held out her glowing fingers—"they can't miss."

"Yeah, but if they did that, they'd be starting a war," Keefe reminded her.

"A war they'd lose, by the way," Elwin chimed in. "Don't be fooled by our peaceful methods, Sophie. If anyone is foolish enough to attack, we have ways to shut them down—quickly. And the ogres know that. We've made sure *all* the intelligent species know it. Why do you think they signed our treaties?"

He sounded so sure. And Sophie *almost* believed him.

But she doubted the rebels—or ogres, or whoever it was that put the homing device on Silveny—would've gone to so much trouble if they weren't willing to pull the trigger.

"I think it's high time we get rid of that nasty stuff, don't you?" Elwin asked, placing a flat silver bowl in each of their laps and warning them not to spill.

Sophie gagged when she caught a whiff of the clear liquid inside.

"Yeah, trust me, you *don't* want to know what that is," Elwin told her. "Just soak your hands in there until I tell you to stop. Oh, and plan on it feeling strange."

"Strange how?" Sophie asked as she dunked her hands in the bowl—but then she knew what he meant because the liquid seeping into her skin was equal parts fire and ice. It didn't *hurt*—but it didn't feel good either. Mostly it made her sweat and shiver and itch like crazy.

"Just hang in for ten more seconds," Elwin said, starting to count down.

Ten seconds had never felt so slow, and when he finally got to one, Sophie couldn't pull her hands out fast enough. Elwin took their silver bowls away and handed them each a green silky cloth.

"Whoa," Keefe whispered, dropping the towel into his lap. He clapped his hands a few times, then pressed them against his face. "It's like, I know my hands are touching me, but I can't *feel* them doing it."

Sophie was just as numb—though she didn't find it nearly as entertaining.

Doctors only numbed someone if they were prepping them for *pain*.

"What's that?" she asked as Elwin pulled two small red vials out of the satchel he always wore across his shoulders.

"Last step—and it won't hurt, I promise."

Sophie stared at the hopping jackalopes on Elwin's tunic and reminded herself that she trusted him as he positioned her arms so they were straight out over the floor.

"It'll be less messy this way," he explained, which wasn't nearly as reassuring as he wanted it to be. "And don't freak out when you see what this does. It'll be over in a second."

Sophie had to force herself to hold still as Elwin poured the thin red liquid onto her hands. She couldn't feel the shiny fluid as it coated her palms, but that didn't make it any less horrifying when the top layers of her skin shriveled up and melted, dripping onto the floor in a slimy puddle of peach goo. The smell of burning flesh filled the air, making everyone gag as Elwin wrapped their hands in wet purple cloths.

"That might be the creepiest thing I've ever done," Keefe said quietly, staring at his soggy purple dressings. "I mean, it was also *awesome*. But dude. You should warn a guy before you melt his skin off."

Sophie hated that Alden would have to endure the same process. And Jurek. And—

"Oh no," she mumbled, struggling to grab her Imparter with her purple mummy hands. "They *can't* do that to Silveny. She'll be traumatized for months."

"Hey, easy," Elwin said, gently pinning her shoulders. "You

need to finish your treatment or it won't heal right. And I'm sure they'll sedate Silveny. I actually thought about doing that for you, but I know how you feel about sedatives and—"

"I might've volunteered to be knocked out," Keefe interrupted.

"Even if it meant spending the night at school?" Elwin asked.

"Oh—a slumber party! *Definitely* count me in for that."

"Yeah, well, somehow I doubt your parents would've wanted that—which was the other reason I kept you awake."

"You must not know my parents very well. They're always happy to be rid of me." Keefe said it with a smile, but Sophie knew him too well to buy it.

Elwin must've noticed too, because he dropped the subject. "Huh," he said as he unwrapped Sophie's hands. "I thought for sure this would've been gone."

He traced his finger along the star-shaped scar from the Black Swan's healing.

"It must sink too deep," she said as Elwin snapped his fingers to form an orange sphere of light around the scar.

He squinted through his iridescent spectacles, turning her hand from side to side. "But that doesn't make sense."

"That's Foster's trademark," Keefe reminded him.

"Yes, I suppose it is." Elwin flashed a green orb instead, frowning when he noticed her wrist. "Why didn't you tell me you had a burn?"

"It's not a burn, it's a bruise," Sophie corrected. "I just used the wrong ointments to treat it and made it worse—and before you give me a lecture, I didn't come to see you because it wasn't a big deal. My skin just got a little twisted while someone was squeezing my wrist."

"Whoa, wait a second—who was squeezing you?" Keefe asked. "Give me their name and I'll punish them, Sencen style."

"Nobody needs punishing," Sophie insisted. "If anything, it was my fault. I know how unstable Brant is. I should've been more careful."

"You definitely do need to learn to be more careful," Elwin agreed as he searched through his satchel. "But I also think it would be wise to stay away from him—and either way, *you must always come to see me when you have an injury!*"

"Okay, okay, no need to shout." Sophie rubbed her ringing ears.

Elwin gave her a stern glare as he took her hand and rubbed a purple salve on her wound. Instantly the cooling tingles eased the ache, and the redness vanished.

"What ointment is that?" Sophie asked, wanting to remember the name.

"It's called Get Your Butt To The Healing Center Next Time."

"Or, y'know, just don't *have* a next time," Keefe jumped in. "Though we all know that probably won't happen." He pointed to the picture of Sophie in her humiliating Opening Ceremonies mastodon costume, hanging over her bed. "Elwin should add a tally board so we can keep track of how many times you visit."

"I should add one for you, too, Keefe," Elwin told him. "You're starting to become quite the regular around here."

"Guess that's the downside of hanging with the Queen of Mystery over there—but don't worry, it's worth it."

Sophie forced a smile, knowing he was only teasing. But he was right. Since Keefe had been helping her, he'd had his skin melted off, gotten several broken ribs, and almost died. And Dex had been just as unlucky. Being her friend was dangerous.

But she'd worry about that later. First, she needed to warn someone about the ogre enzyme, and with Alden, Jurek, and Grady still not responding to her hails, she could only think of one other person who might be able to help. She'd promised herself—and Grady—that she'd only turn to him in the most extreme emergency, since his duties as a Councillor would always come first, and she knew from past experience that sometimes she had to bend a few rules.

But having Silveny under threat of attack *had* to fall into that category.

She grabbed her Imparter, wishing her hands weren't shaking as she held the sleek silver square up to her lips and whispered, "Show me Councillor Terik."

EIGHTEEN

THIS IS JUST A NORMAL DAY FOR YOU, isn't it?" Keefe asked as they shivered outside the Sanctuary gates, waiting for Councillor Terik to meet them. "Go to school, find out you're covered in a dangerous substance, melt off a few layers of skin, and then hail your besty the Councillor, tell him you're ditching study hall to save the world, and he says, 'Cool, I'll come with you!'"

"We're not saving the world, we're saving Silveny," Sophie corrected as she locked her knees to stop them from shaking. The half cape of her Foxfire uniform was keeping her shoulders warmer this time, but the skirt-plus-leggings combo was a *lot* draftier.

At least she wasn't shirtless like Sandor—though he didn't seem affected by the cold. Or maybe he was too busy checking for ogre tracks.

Keefe wrapped his cape higher around his neck, pinning it under his chin to cover every possible inch of skin. "It pretty much counts as saving the world, since, y'know, if anything happened to Silveny, we'd be back to worrying about the Timeline to Extinction."

Sophie sucked in a breath. "Do you think that's what this is about?"

"What do you mean?"

Sophie stepped closer, afraid to speak her theory too loudly. "Everyone knows how important Silveny is to the Council. So maybe they're trying to use that to their advantage. Like . . . as long as they have weapons locked onto her, they can force the Council to give them pretty much anything they want."

Keefe whistled. "I hate to say it, but that actually makes sense. Maybe that's why Councillor Terik flipped when you told him. It sounded like he peed himself."

"Did it?" a deep voice asked as Councillor Terik glittered onto the path in front of them. The emeralds in his circlet gleamed almost as brightly as the smile he shot Keefe before turning to Sophie. "I suppose I *was* a bit startled by the news—and I'm glad you felt comfortable coming to me."

Councillor Terik had programmed Sophie's Imparter so it could bypass the security restrictions and reach him anytime.

But he always seemed surprised when she used it. And he always answered her call.

He turned to Sandor, who had moved to their side, weapons drawn.

"Are there any threats in the area?" Councillor Terik asked him.

"None that I can tell, but I might not be the best person to ask. Apparently my senses aren't as valuable as I'd once thought."

"Trust me, Sandor, your senses are still incredibly valuable to me. But we probably should head inside the Sanctuary." He motioned for everyone to step forward as he explained, "I had Lord Cassius arrange our clearance, so, in theory . . ."

He took another step forward, and the gates clicked open.

"I love when things go according to plan. That so rarely seems to happen these days. After you?" he asked, stepping aside to let Sandor take the lead.

Sandor stalked ahead, his sword raised as Sophie, Keefe, and Councillor Terik followed. The warm, sunny paradise felt colder this time, but maybe that was because Sophie kept trying to guess how much force an ogre missile would need to collapse the mountain walls above them.

They'd only gone a few paces before Jurek stepped through a clump of bushes. His wild hair was pulled back into a simple braid, and he dropped to a bow in front of Councillor Terik. "I've sedated the alicorns as you instructed. They're waiting for you in their pastures."

He glanced at Sophie as he turned to lead the way, his face a mask of fear and betrayal. Guilt reminded her of her promise to protect him from the Council—but what choice did she have? This was bigger than all of them.

Sophie had tried to prepare herself to see Silveny unconscious. But her eyes still welled with tears when she did—and not sad tears.

Angry tears.

This was the second time she'd seen Silveny drugged because of the rebels. She had to make sure it was the last.

"She feels calm," Keefe promised, tracing his fingers along Silveny's neck. "And it doesn't feel like she was stressed while he sedated her, either. It's more like she just dozed off without realizing it."

"Yes, I *do* know how to sedate an ali—" Jurek started, cutting himself off when he glanced at Councillor Terik. Then he switched to another deep bow, and quietly said, "I was told there was a powder I should use to test the alicorns."

"I have it." Sophie dug through her pockets and pulled out the vial of reveldust.

She showed Jurek how to sprinkle a thin layer over Greyfell's limp body, then went to treat Silveny, ignoring Keefe when he called dibs on the top half. For all the times he'd called her Glitter Butt, he got to deal with the tail.

Plus, she wasn't sure she could handle seeing the aromark glow.

She'd barely begun dusting Silveny's mane when Keefe whispered, "Whoa," and Councillor Terik said, "So it's true."

At least the rest of Silveny's body turned out to be clear. Still, the halo of red from the skin around Silveny's tail was the brightest she'd ever seen.

"Greyfell's safe," Jurek announced as he rejoined them. "I checked twice to be sure. I guess they only want the girl."

"Of course. They know she's the most valuable," Sophie grumbled as she handed Jurek a vial of piquatine. "This stuff will remove it—but it's a creepy process."

"Elwin explained all the gory details," Jurek agreed.

Sophie backed away as he moved toward Silveny, heading for a part of the path that curved enough to block Silveny from her view.

"I can't watch," she whispered as Keefe joined her.

"Neither can I."

"I think that makes three of us," Councillor Terik agreed, coming to stand beside them. "I've witnessed many difficult things in my day, but . . . that magnificent creature . . ."

"Do you think she's going to be okay?" Sophie asked.

"Of course she will. Everything worked out for us, right?" Keefe held up his hands, wiggling his fingers.

Yes, but they weren't alicorns. Silveny's skin had a totally different composition.

Then again, Sophie and Silveny did share parts of their DNA . . .

"Ugh, you're worrying enough to make us both sick," Keefe told her, clutching his stomach.

"You can feel what she's feeling?" Councillor Terik asked, his brows shooting up when Keefe nodded. "Clearly you have your father's gift. You remind me of him, actually. Although . . ." He stroked his chin, his cobalt blue eyes boring into Keefe's. "There's much of your mother in you as well. It'll be interesting to see who you take after."

"Hopefully neither," Keefe mumbled.

Councillor Terik smiled. "We all wish to separate ourselves from our families when we're teenagers. But as you grow up, you'll learn to appreciate them."

"I doubt that."

Several awkward seconds passed. Then Councillor Terik asked Keefe, "So what *do* you want to be, then?"

Keefe shrugged. "Any openings in the Nobility for a professional troublemaker?"

That earned him a laugh, and Councillor Terik placed a hand on Keefe's shoulder. "Don't sell yourself short, Keefe. I see great potential in you."

"Yeah, adults love to tell me that."

"Yes, but I say it with a bit more authority. Need I remind you of my ability?"

Councillor Terik was a Descryer—the only one in the entire Elvin world. Which meant he was able to sense and interpret the potential of anyone he touched.

Keefe glanced at Councillor Terik's hand on his shoulder. "Did you just take a reading of me?"

"Couldn't resist," he admitted. "I don't often perform them, since I've found that knowing your potential tends to hinder your ability to live up to it. But I must admit, you fascinate me."

"Of course I do."

Keefe's grin was extra smug. But for all his bravado, Sophie could tell that Councillor Terik's words had affected him deeply.

"Well, you don't fascinate me as much as she does," Councillor Terik admitted, pointing to Sophie. "Hers was the only reading I couldn't translate. Everything I felt was too . . . divided."

"Divided how?" Sophie and Keefe asked at the same time.

"Ah, but if I told you that, it might unduly influence you. Best to let you choose for yourself."

"Wow, you're kind of evil, aren't you?" Keefe asked.

Councillor Terik laughed. "Once upon a time, I wasn't all that different from you." He winked as he turned to call to Jurek. "How's it going over there?"

"I think I'm done. Though I'd like to test the area with reveldust just to be safe."

Sophie brought him the vial of powder, though she nearly dropped it when she got a closer look at Silveny.

"Wow," Keefe said, coming up beside her. "Guess I can't call her Glitter Butt until her fur grows back. How do you think she'd feel about Bald Booty?"

Sophie looked away from the pinkish, furless hind. "I think she'd hate it as much as I do."

"Can one of you put the reveldust on the area?" Jurek asked. "My hands still have traces of the piquatine on them."

"I'll do it," Keefe offered before Sophie could find the courage to do the same.

She tried to thank him as he sprinkled the silver powder over Silveny's bare skin, rubbing it in with circular strokes. But every time she opened her mouth, her voice wanted to dissolve into a sob.

The only thing that snapped her out of it was when she noticed Keefe's hands.

"What?" Keefe asked as she gasped. "Is Silveny . . ."

His voice trailed off as he realized what she'd seen.

He'd gotten the reveldust on his skin when he'd rubbed it onto Silveny. And his fingertips were glowing vivid red.

NINETEEN

I DON'T GET IT," KEEFE SAID FOR WHAT HAD to be the tenth time. "I mean, seriously, where did the aromark come from?"

Everyone had retested themselves, and Keefe was the only one who showed any traces. Even Silveny was completely clear.

"Maybe Elwin missed some when he treated you?" Sophie suggested.

"*How?* He melted off my skin!"

Sophie wished she knew what to tell him. The stalkenteene device wasn't even with them anymore, so Elwin must've made a mistake.

"Guess this means I'm going back to the Healing Center," Keefe grumbled, kicking a pebble in the grass.

"Want me to go with you?" Sophie offered.

"Nah—then I have to act all brave and stuff. Freaking out sounds way more fun." He tried to smile, but she could tell he was forcing it.

"I'm sorry," she said quietly.

"Eh, it isn't your fault—unless you snuck aromark into my pockets."

"You caught me."

"I knew you couldn't be as innocent as you seemed."

"No one is ever as innocent as they seem," Councillor Terik interrupted. "It's one of the primary things I've learned as a Descryer. Everyone has potential for both good *and* bad."

"Foster's badness potential was off the charts, wasn't it?"

Councillor Terik laughed. "Not as much as yours. Now let's get you to Elwin, shall we?" He led them a few steps away, knocking on the air until he found the invisible exit to the snowy mountains outside. He used his pathfinder to create a beam of light. "This path will take you straight to Foxfire. Please have Elwin send me an update when he's done."

"Two Elwin visits in one day," Keefe mumbled. "Pretty sure that beats your record, Foster."

"I think it does," Sophie agreed sadly.

He squared his shoulders. "Well, all I can say is, Elwin better remove it *all* this time. If these fingers start glowing again, I'm going to re-create the Great Gulon Incident in his office."

"I thought you didn't have anything to do with that," Sophie reminded him. She still had no idea what the Great Gulon Incident even was. But apparently it had been one of Keefe's greatest triumphs. And he loved to deny being involved.

He flashed a slightly wicked smile as he stepped into the path. But Sophie could see the tension in his posture as the light carried him away.

"What about you, Miss Foster?" Councillor Terik asked, closing the door to block the freezing mountain wind. "Where would you like me to take you?"

"Back to Havenfield," Sandor answered for her. "Where I will be implementing additional safety protocols immediately."

"But what about Silveny?" Sophie asked, turning to Councillor Terik. "Whoever put that homing device on her knows she's here. What's to stop them from blowing up the whole Sanctuary?"

Councillor Terik smiled. "Well, I'm guessing it would be the same things that stopped them from doing that in the first place. After all, they went to quite a lot of trouble to put that device in her tail instead."

Maybe . . .

"But still, don't you think it would be safer to hide her somewhere no one knows about?" she asked.

"I'm not sure such a place exists," Councillor Terik said gently. "And even if it does, have you considered whether *that* could've been their plan all along? To trick us into moving Silveny? After all, she's far more vulnerable in transit than she is within these walls, which—by the way—have been reinforced in ways you can't even imagine. I guarantee, no weapon exists that could make even the slightest breach."

"How can you be so sure?" Sandor interrupted. "You didn't know about the aromark, and it exists. So how do you know that no one's developed a weapon without your knowledge?"

Councillor Terik's jaw set, and Sophie braced for him to yell. But when he spoke, his voice sounded more sad than angry. "Our world is definitely experiencing some growing pains. But giving in to doubt or mistrust only helps the rebels' cause, wouldn't you agree?"

Sandor studied him for a second before bowing his head. "Yes, sir."

Councillor Terik sighed. "Try not to worry too much, Miss Foster. We need your mind focused and sharp for the healing on Friday."

"Wait—*this* Friday?" Sophie repeated. "As in four days from now?"

"I suppose it is a bit sudden. But in light of all the contention surrounding the healing, we felt it was better to be done sooner, rather than later."

"How do people even know about it?" Sophie had to ask. "I thought it was classified."

"It is. Or it was supposed to be. But that was before . . ."

"Before what?" she asked when he didn't finish.

"Nothing you should trouble yourself with."

"Do you know how frustrating it is to constantly have people telling me not to worry?" she asked.

She wasn't sure if she was allowed to be so honest with a Councillor. But she was too annoyed to care.

Fortunately, Councillor Terik nodded kindly. "I do know, Sophie. And I don't blame your frustration. But I need you to concentrate all of your energy on preparing for this healing. Fintan's mind is ancient—and *strong*. There's no way to know if the shattered pieces of his consciousness will find a way to resist you while you're working."

Sophie's blood turned to ice at the thought.

He placed a hand on her shoulder, guiding her to the mountain door. But Sophie had to ask one last question before she could let the light carry her away.

"You're sure healing Fintan is the right thing to do?" she whispered, holding her breath as she waited for him to give her the yes she needed.

Instead he told her, "I hope so."

Laughter echoed through the halls when Sophie and Sandor returned to Havenfield, and Sophie followed the sound to Jolie's bedroom, where she found Edaline sitting on the edge of the bed. All the lace curtains had been pulled back, flooding the room with sunlight, and dresses were piled all over the floor.

Before Sophie could ask what was going on, Biana appeared in a silky teal gown.

"Well, look who finally showed up," she said, raising an eyebrow in Sophie's general direction. "I was starting to think you weren't coming back."

"So was I," Edaline agreed—though she didn't seem worried about it. She actually looked calmer than Sophie had ever seen as she helped Biana with her sash. "Did you forget you were having a friend over?"

"Um . . ."

Sophie didn't remember inviting her. And Biana had never once come over by herself.

"So where were you?" Biana jumped in, avoiding Sophie's eyes. "And where's Keefe? I thought I heard him say he'd be here after school."

"Keefe was planning to come over," Sophie said slowly, wondering if that was the real reason for Biana's visit. "But some stuff came up and he had to go see Elwin—"

"*What?*" Biana interrupted at the same time Edaline asked, "Is he okay?"

"Yeah, he's fine. He just had to get another treatment." Sophie glanced at her fingers, needing to make sure they hadn't started glowing again.

Edaline frowned. "And by *another* treatment, you mean . . ."

"That it's been kind of a crazy day," Sophie finished. "But I'm fine, I promise."

162

She could tell Edaline was less than satisfied with that answer, but she wasn't going to get into the complicated explanation with Biana there.

"So what are you guys doing in here?" Sophie asked, changing the subject—quickly. "It looks like the closet threw up."

Biana laughed. "Edaline said I could go through Jolie's clothes to see if there's anything I want to keep, and I swear she has the most amazing gowns ever. I mean look!"

She twirled, making the fabric of her dress shift from teal, to silver, and then back to teal.

"Jolie had that dress custom made for our annual solstice gala," Edaline explained. "Every other thread is made of lumenite. She wanted something that would shine like the moon when she danced. It was probably the most talked about thing at the party—even more than how many times Councillor Kenric asked Councillor Oralie to dance."

Sophie smiled, imagining Kenric following Oralie around like a lost puppy. She'd long suspected he had a crush on the blond-ringletted Councillor. And she'd known Grady and Edaline were famous for their incredible parties—or, they were before their grief turned them into social recluses. But for some reason she'd never pictured Jolie at any of them.

Now she could imagine her, flitting around the room like a princess at a ball. And something about the scene made her chest feel tight.

It twisted even tighter when Edaline told Biana, "You know,

I think this dress looks even better on you than it did on Jolie. It matches your eyes perfectly."

Biana's blush turned to a glow. "And you really don't mind if I take it?"

"Of course not. It'll just get packed away in a dusty trunk, otherwise. Might as well put it to use."

Biana squealed and twirled again. "I can't believe you didn't want any of these, Sophie."

"Oh, that's true—I probably should've checked. Do you mind?" Edaline asked.

"Of course not," Sophie promised, surprised at how thick her voice sounded. "You know I'm not into fancy dresses. Plus, Della bought me a billion of them when I moved here."

"Well, if you see anything in that pile you want"—Biana pointed to a monster stack of frills—"You can totally have it back."

"Nah. They'll look way better on you."

And they would. Sophie got attention because she was new and unique, and some people thought she was mysterious. But she would never be as beautiful as Biana.

"Well, I'll leave you girls to talk," Edaline said, taking one last look at Biana as she headed for the door.

When she'd closed it behind her, Sophie took Edaline's spot on the bed, not entirely sure what to say.

"So," Biana mumbled, fiddling with her dress. "I know you're probably wondering why I'm here."

164

"Kind of," Sophie admitted.

"I just . . . I'm tired of always being left out. I know it's partially my fault, because I've been a jerk to you a few times. But I'll never do that again. And I have a special ability now. And I really want to help with whatever you and Keefe are working on."

Sophie rubbed the star-shaped scar on her hand. "You don't know what you're asking."

"Yes, I do. I was there after you and Dex escaped from the kidnappers. I saw how messed up you both were. And I was at the planting for you guys too, when everyone thought you were dead."

Sophie squirmed, never sure what to feel when people told her they'd been to her funeral. The rebels had thrown her registry pendant into the ocean and made everyone believe she and Dex had drowned. So the Council gave them special trees in the Wanderling Woods—the elves' version of a cemetery— and held a big ceremony when the seeds were planted.

The trees were still there, growing side by side.

"You can't take down a whole band of rebels on your own," Biana added quietly. "And who else are you going to turn to? The Black Swan?"

"No," Sophie whispered. "I can't trust them."

Admitting it out loud felt so much scarier.

"So trust *me*," Biana said as she sat next to Sophie on the bed.

Sophie knew she should walk away and not drag in any more of her friends.

But she also needed more help.

So when Biana whispered, "Please," Sophie reluctantly told her, "Okay."

TWENTY

JUST . . . LET ME TELL DEX," SOPHIE TOLD
Biana, already imaging how much he would *flip* when he
found out she'd agreed to include a Vacker.

He'd warmed up to the family a little over the last few
months. But she had a feeling he would never actually like
them. Especially Fitz.

Biana shrugged. "Sure, if you want. But why was he mad at
you and Keefe earlier?"

"Oh, he thinks we told Dame Alina about him manifesting."

"Was that a secret?"

"Yeah. He wanted to keep taking ability detecting to see if
it would trigger another ability. He thinks being a Technopath
isn't cool enough to impress people."

"Or maybe he just wants to impress a *certain* person," Biana said with a sly smile.

Sophie had a feeling she knew what Biana was implying, but it was one of those weird, awkward things she didn't know how to handle. So all she said was, "Dex is my best friend."

Biana nodded. "Anyway, if you and Keefe didn't tell Dame Alina about his ability, who did?"

"I can answer that," Sandor said, making them both jump as he peeked his giant head through the doorway.

Biana clutched her chest. "Does he always eavesdrop like that?"

"Pretty much," Sophie grumbled. "Anyway, how do you know who told her?" she asked Sandor.

"Because it was me. I hailed the Council after I heard what you found at the Sanctuary. If we're dealing with ogres, we're going to need all the Technopaths we can get."

"But we don't even *know* that we're dealing with ogres," Sophie argued.

"So we must err on the side of caution."

"Whoa, wait. What about ogres?" Biana asked.

"I'll tell you later," Sophie promised. "And *you*," she told Sandor, "need to apologize to Dex."

"I know. I meant to warn him first. I did not realize the Council would move so fast. But I will explain it all to him tomorrow. First chance I get."

He left them then, closing the door as silently as he'd

opened it. But Sophie was sure he was still listening on the other side.

Biana didn't seem to care, immediately attacking Sophie with ten billion questions about ogres. Sophie did her best to explain about the aromark, and the homing device, and even the possible leak in the Black Swan. But there were a whole lot of *maybes* and *mights* and *I don't knows* in her answers.

Still, the question that stumped her the most was: "So what are we supposed to do now?"

"I have no idea. Usually I have a note or a clue to go on. But even if the Black Swan give me one, it's not like I can trust them enough to follow it."

"True," Biana agreed, standing up to pace.

She blinked in and out of sight as she moved, which was twice as trippy in her teal-and-lumenite dress.

"Okay!" she said after the third time she'd passed by. "It sounds like we need to figure out what's up with the Black Swan. How much do you actually know about them?"

"Pretty much nothing. I know what one of them looks like—but only when he's eaten a bunch of ruckleberries. And I guess I also know he starts sentences with 'you kids' a lot, since that's how I figured out that he was the one who rescued me. And . . . I know they have a few dwarves that help them. And that they used to have a hideout in a cave in the middle of the ocean. And . . ."

Her voice trailed off as she remembered one more thing

she knew about the Black Swan—assuming she'd understood what Prentice had shown her.

"Jolie."

"Okay . . . What about Jolie?" Biana asked when Sophie didn't say anything.

Sophie glanced over her shoulder to make sure the door was still closed. She couldn't believe she was about to tell Biana this—but she had to trust *someone*. And telling Biana felt easier than telling Keefe.

Still, her voice cracked as she said, "There's a chance Jolie might've been involved with the Black Swan."

Biana's eyes stretched about as wide as they could go. "Do you think that had something to do with what happened to her?"

"I know Grady will. That's why I haven't told him or Edaline about it."

For years Grady had believed the Black Swan set the fire that killed Jolie, because it happened right after they tried—and failed—to recruit him. Sophie had asked Mr. Forkle about it, and he promised they had nothing to do with it. But if Grady knew Jolie was connected to them—especially since they might have a traitor among them . . .

"So it sounds like we need to figure out how Jolie was involved," Biana said after a second. "And I'm guessing you've already searched all her things?"

"I'm actually still working on it. This place used to be kinda off-limits."

170

"Really?" Biana looked down at her teal dress. "Wow, Grady and Edaline have really come a long way, haven't they?"

They had.

And Sophie wasn't going to let *anything* set them back.

They set to work, packing up trunk after trunk of gowns and shoes and handbags and makeup and hats and jewelry. Every drawer they opened was crammed with more girly stuff. But they found nothing marked with the sign of the swan. Nothing that looked even remotely suspicious. And after a few hours of searching, they were running out of places to check.

"You know what I haven't found?" Biana asked as she added another gown to her Things To Take Home pile. "Foxfire stuff. Wasn't Jolie in the elite levels when she died?"

"Yeah. She was almost done with Level Eight."

"That's what I thought. So then where are all her uniforms and textbooks and notes and whatever else they need for those crazy sessions?"

"I . . . don't know." Sophie couldn't believe she hadn't noticed it.

She asked Edaline about it after Biana left, but Edaline seemed just as surprised as her. She even searched the room herself, like she was convinced Sophie and Biana missed something.

"I'm sorry," Edaline said, staring into Jolie's now-empty closet. "I wish I could snap my fingers and conjure everything up—but I have absolutely no idea what we've done with it. The whole first year after we lost her is just a hazy blur in my head."

"It's okay," Sophie said, wrapping an arm around Edaline's shoulders. "I'm sure they're somewhere. I can't see you and Grady throwing them away."

"No, we definitely didn't do that. I mean, look at all this stuff we kept." She pointed to the row of overstuffed trunks. "I can't believe there's more that's missing."

"Jolie must've been a big shopper."

"She was. And I'm sorry, by the way. I shouldn't have offered those clothes to Biana without asking you first."

"It's fine," Sophie promised. But some of the tightness had returned to her chest.

Edaline reached up to tuck Sophie's hair behind her ears.

"You *always* come first, Sophie. I hope you know that. And I'm really glad to see you hanging out with Biana. You know I love Dex—and Keefe is always very charming. But it's good to have girl friends too. They can be a lot less . . . complicated."

"Hey, Sophie, can I talk to you?" Dex asked, catching her on her way into the girls' locker room.

"Sure," Sophie said through a yawn.

She'd stayed up late, waiting for Grady to come home, but when she'd finally gone to bed he still wasn't back. Edaline had assured her that overnight assignments were normal for an Emissary, but she'd still had nightmares about Grady being hunted by ogres.

"I'm sorry I yelled at you yesterday," Dex mumbled, snapping her back to the present. "I shouldn't have blamed you. I know you would never tell."

"About that," Sandor interrupted. "I meant to tell you earlier. I was the one who informed the Council about your ability, Dex."

"I know," Dex told him, sounding surprisingly unirritated. "I went to Dame Alina's office during study hall yesterday and she told me how the Council called her to make sure I started training right away. Can you believe that? The *Council* cared enough about my ability to call the principal of Foxfire. They even insisted that I study with Lady Iskra!"

"Wow, that's awesome!" Sophie told him.

Dex laughed. "You have no idea who that is, do you?"

"Not a clue," she admitted.

"Yeah, neither did I. But I guess she, like, *invented all the things*. Imparters, nexuses—even Spyballs—were all her ideas. There's pretty much no other Technopath as talented as her— and the Council wants *me* to work with her. They told Dame Alina that with Lady Iskra's guidance, I'll invent things that will change our world!"

He was practically jumping up and down at that point, and his smile was so big his dimples looked like they were making his cheeks cave in.

"So hey," Sophie started, deciding to take advantage of his good mood. "Biana stopped by after school yesterday."

"Did she? That's weird. Oh—did I tell you my dad *freaked* when he found out I'd been hiding my ability from him?"

"Uh . . . no," Sophie said, surprised the Biana bombshell hadn't gotten a bigger reaction. "But I'm not surprised."

"Yeah. I thought he was going to ground me or something. But then he realized I'm basically guaranteed a spot in the elite levels, and we spent the rest of the night coming up with awesome ways to tell all the jerks who've judged us over the years."

Dex's father didn't have a special ability, and his marriage to Dex's mom had been classified as a bad match by the elvin matchmaking office. So more than a few people treated Dex and his triplet brothers and sister like they were all destined to be Talentless themselves.

"Anyway," Dex said, before Sophie could get too distracted by the craziness of the elvin social system, "I just wanted to apologize for being a brat. And I brought you something to make up for it. I've been working on it for a while, actually, but I finally finished it last night."

He reached into his pocket and handed her something small and silver.

"It's . . . a ring," Sophie said, staring at the plain silver band with a flat beige stone set into the middle.

"Yeah. I figured you already have a nexus on each wrist. And you have a ton of necklaces, between your registry pendant and your home crystal and the allergy elixirs Elwin makes you wear. So I thought I'd make something different."

A few of the girls around her giggled.

"Well . . . um . . . thanks," Sophie mumbled. "It's pretty."

"Nah. The stone is crooked and the band isn't as round as I wanted it to be. But the switch under the stone works perfectly." He leaned closer and whispered, "And if you press it, it triggers an alert right here." He held out his right hand, which had a matching silver band.

More girls giggled. And there were several whispers about *matching rings*.

Dex seemed oblivious as he explained, "It's a panic switch, in case you're ever in trouble."

"As long as she stays by my side, she won't be in any trouble," Sandor reminded him.

Sophie jumped. She never thought she'd forget that she had a seven-foot-tall goblin shadow. But apparently all it took was a ring.

"It's still good to have a backup plan, right?" Dex argued. "And this way, if something *does* happen, you won't have to use up all your mental energy trying to call Fitz telepathically. You can just call me."

Sophie hoped she'd never have to call either of them. But she could tell she'd hurt Dex's feelings if she didn't take his gift. So she shoved the ring onto her right pointer finger, hoping no one would notice her new accessory as she left to get ready for PE.

Of course they did, though. She might as well have had a

glowing beacon on her hand. And the crazy rumors took off like wildfire. By the time lunch break came around, Sophie was grateful she could escape to detention.

Keefe had saved her a seat in detention hall, and even though she sat on her hands, she was fully prepared for some serious ring-related teasing. But all he said was, "We'd better not be peeling curdleroots. I'm not touching *anything* else from the ogres."

Sophie glanced at his hands, hating how red they looked. "Was the treatment worse the second time?"

"Dunno. I made Elwin knock me out. Woke up at home in bed with no idea how I got there. My mom even brought me tea and asked me a ton of questions, like she was actually worried about me."

A tiny smile crept across his lips, which made Sophie incredibly sad. Before she could figure out what to say, Lady Cadence strode into the room.

Her elegant gown and cape had been replaced with a plain brown tunic and pants, and her hair was pulled back into a severe ponytail.

"This can't be good," Keefe muttered, earning himself a glare as Lady Cadence snapped her fingers and made a mountain of silver forklike gadgets appear in the center of the floor.

"I hope you're ready to get your hands dirty," she said, picking up one of the gadgets and grimacing as she sniffed it, "because you'll be spending the next hour crawling through bushes and climbing trees. Every single one of these efflux-ers needs to be hidden around the campus, according to my instructions."

"Ugh, can't we make the gnomes do it?" Stina grumbled.

Lady Cadence stalked to Stina's desk, slamming the effluxer down with a *clang*! "I'm sure the gnomes would be more than willing, Miss Heks. But they are busy with another task. Plus, that would rob you of your much-needed punishment. So for the suggestion alone, consider yourself the lucky recipient of an extra day of detention. Anyone else looking for an easy way to get out of today's assignment?"

She glanced around the silent room, her eyes lingering the longest on Sophie and Keefe. But neither of them said any-thing.

Not because they were afraid of more detention.

They both knew what Lady Cadence was really having them do.

They were protecting Foxfire from ogres.

TWENTY-ONE

DO YOU THINK THERE'S SOMETHING they're not telling us?" Sophie asked Keefe as she crawled under a shrubbery that had been trimmed to look like a mastodon. She stabbed the effluxer into the muddy soil between the toes of the back foot, right where it was marked on the map Lady Cadence had given her.

"All I know is my dad's been working crazy overtime at the Sanctuary, adding all kinds of new security. He won't tell me much, but I heard him say they're putting a force field around the mountain range. So there's no way anyone's getting near Silveny now. And as for these"—Keefe stabbed an effluxer into the ground under a saber-toothed tiger-shaped bush—"mostly I can't wait for a ditching prodigy to stumble across one. In fact . . ." He ran to the flowerbed lining the path and stabbed one among the flowers. "Man I hope Dame Alina walks by first."

"You really hate her that much?" Sophie asked, shuffling out of the bushes as Sandor removed Keefe's misplaced effluxer.

Keefe stabbed another in its place. "She's not as nice as she looks. Trust me, there was a *good* reason Alden ran screaming away from her."

"Well, I still thought it was cool the way she defended the Council and the Vackers at lunch yesterday," Sophie argued, removing the new effluxer Keefe had hidden.

Keefe replaced it immediately. "I could do this all day."

"So can I," she told him.

Keefe laughed. "You seriously need to cause more trouble, Foster. I mean, it's been months since you almost blew up the school."

"Miss Foster causes enough trouble without even trying," Sandor told him, holding out a giant hand, waiting for Keefe to give him the rest of his effluxers.

Keefe slapped him a low five instead. Then he snatched the rest of Sophie's effluxers and raced away, stabbing them in random places all over the grassy field. Sophie chased after him, trying to retrieve as many as she could. But he started putting them high in the trees—just out of her reach.

Lady Cadence's voice finally froze them in their tracks. "And here I thought that you two—of all people—would've understood the seriousness of this task!"

"We do," Sophie told her, glaring at Keefe.

"Obviously not! Give those to me." She held out her hands and Sophie passed over the effluxers she'd gathered. Keefe held on to his—though he only had two left.

"Honestly," Lady Cadence huffed. "You're lucky you didn't set one off. I knew I shouldn't have trusted this assignment to *children*."

"Then why did you?" Sandor asked. "A task this important—"

"It was not considered *important*," she interrupted. "In fact, when I presented the suggestion to the Council, they told me, 'If you must.'" She sighed, rearranging the effluxers into a neat stack. "I probably *am* being overly paranoid."

"When it comes to the ogres, I can assure you, you're not," Sandor promised.

"Typical thinking for a goblin," she told him. "All you see is an enemy."

"Because that's what ogres *are*," Sandor snapped back. "And clearly you agree if you've decided to install these gadgets."

"I don't know *what* to think, honestly," she said as she retrieved one of Keefe's effluxers from the tree he'd hidden it in. "I reached out to a few of my old friends in Ravagog—yes, *friends*," she added when Sandor rolled his eyes. "Many of the ogres were very good to me while I lived there. So I wanted to warn them that one of their homing devices turned up at the

180

Sanctuary. They should have the chance to prove they weren't involved."

"But they were?" Sandor finished for her, his squeaky voice more of a snarl.

"I never spoke to them. All my communication channels have been cut off—even with my friends. There could be any number of reasons—the most logical being they've forgotten me since I moved away. Ogres are fickle creatures. Out of sight, out of mind."

"But . . . ?" Sophie pressed.

Lady Cadence said nothing. But the stack of effluxers in her hand said it all.

Force field, Sophie reminded herself. *Silveny was now protected with a force field.*

She kind of wished Foxfire had one too. And her house. And . . .

"Anyway," Lady Cadence said, snatching Keefe's last two effluxers before he could stop her, "I'm giving you both an extra week of detention. And you should keep in mind, Miss Foster, that midterms aren't very far away. If you want to continue at this school, you should consider focusing more on your studies and less on *boys.*"

She stomped away before Sophie could reply.

"Okay, I've changed my mind," Keefe said, removing an effluxer he'd tucked under his cape. "Let's plant this somewhere *she'll* trigger it."

"Um, let's not give her an excuse to fail me, okay?" Sophie asked, rubbing her temples to ease the headache she could feel forming.

"Psh, you're a Polyglot. You could ace a linguistics midterm in your sleep."

"Not if there's mimicking on it."

"But mimicking's easy," he said, sounding remarkably like Lady Cadence.

"Wait—are you a Polyglot?"

"No, but my mom is, and I've picked up a few tricks here and there. Comes in pretty handy." He cleared his throat and straightened his posture. "Attention prodigies—study hall has been canceled. Please proceed to the Leapmaster."

It was a perfect impersonation of Dame Alina, and Sophie couldn't help smiling. "It's amazing you haven't been expelled."

"Did you just call me 'amazing'?"

Sophie was saved from a reply by the Foxfire chimes, announcing the end of lunch.

"Seriously though, if you need help, I can give you a few pointers," Keefe offered as they headed back into the main building.

"I might have to take you up on that."

They both headed for the red Level Five wing, where Keefe had his afternoon empathy session, and Sophie had telepathy. It was her favorite session by far—and not just because she was so good at it.

"Wow," Keefe said, fanning the air between them, "I always forget you have your special ability session with Fitz."

Sophie tried to keep her expression even. But she was pretty sure she was blushing.

Empaths were *so* annoying.

The Council had assigned Fitz to her telepathy session back when he could transmit past her blocking. She'd worried they'd move him once her abilities were fixed, but their Mentor, Sir Tiergan, felt they would still learn things from each other. So now they spent two hours, twice a week, working closely together. It was equal parts exciting and terrifying.

Keefe laughed and shook his head. "Tell Fitz he should join us in detention sometime."

"Has he ever even *had* detention?" Sophie asked.

"Only when he listens to me—which he really should do more often. You all should."

"I'll keep that in mind."

"I hope you do."

They reached the fork in the hallway where they would head down opposite paths.

"Hey, Foster," Keefe called as she started to turn away from him. "Nice ring."

He winked and walked away without another word.

Fitz was already waiting in the round red telepathy room, sitting in one of the three silver chairs covered in strange buttons and knobs that Sophie had yet to ever press or use. She ordered her palms not to sweat as she sank into the chair across from him—but that only made them sweat more. Especially when he asked, "Is that the ring everyone is talking about?"

She twisted the smooth silver band on her finger, wondering how mad Dex would be if she forgot to wear it the next day. "You heard about it, huh?"

"I think half the school heard about it. But I guess it's good they're talking about something other than my family."

Her eyes fell to her lap. "I'm so sorry you have to deal with that."

"Psh—you think I care?"

"How could you not?"

Fitz had always been the golden boy from the golden family. Being told he's at the "loser table" was a pretty long way to fall.

"I think you're forgetting that I've never been normal, Sophie. Remember, I used to miss school all the time to go on my dad's secret missions to find you. There were all kinds of crazy rumors about where I went. My favorite was that I had a horrible farting disease, and had to stay home to *unleash the stink*. I'm pretty sure that one was Keefe's doing."

"Sounds like him."

"Doesn't it? But that was also why we became friends. He was the weird kid who'd just skipped a grade, and I was the guy who kept disappearing. No one wanted to hang out with us."

"I . . . can't even picture that."

"That's because we're so awesome now."

"But you are!"

Or they were before she messed everything up.

Fitz grinned and leaned closer. "By the way, Biana told me you agreed to let her help. You know I want in on that too, right?"

"But there's nothing to be in on," she whispered back. "We don't even have a plan."

"So I'll help you come up with one."

Sophie pulled at the ends of her cape. "Did she tell you what I told her yesterday?"

"Nope. She said they weren't her secrets to share. So I'm hoping you trust me enough to tell me."

His eyes looked so intense, Sophie was tempted to tell him everything.

But as she opened her mouth to spill, Tiergan asked, "Am I interrupting something?"

He stood in the doorway, smoothing his pale blond hair, which always looked extra bright against his deep olive skin. He glanced at Sophie as he added, "If so, I can come back."

"No, it's fine, sir," Fitz promised, immediately straightening up in his chair. "Sorry. We were just waiting for you."

Sophie smiled. Fitz always seemed intimidated around Tiergan—probably because Tiergan used to hate the Vackers. He was the one who adopted and raised Prentice's son, Wylie, and for years he'd blamed Alden for his involvement in what

185

happened. But a lot had changed once Tiergan saw how deeply the guilt had affected Alden.

He smiled at Fitz. "First—*please* stop calling me 'sir.'" Tiergan despised noble titles almost as much as he hated the fancy capes and clothes. "And second, I was teasing. And I'm sorry I'm late. I was waiting for the Council to send me their instructions."

"Instructions?" Sophie asked.

"For the healing. They're still arranging some of the specifics, but they have confirmed that I'll be coming to collect you sometime on Friday evening and—"

"I'm going with you," Sandor interrupted from his shadowy spot in the corner.

Tiergan sighed. "I suspect you should prepare yourself for the possibility that I'll have to take Sophie alone. From what I understand, attendance will be severely restricted, in light of all the controversy surrounding the healing."

"All the more reason I should be there," Sandor insisted.

"I agree. But that is out of my hands. My only responsibilities are to escort Sophie there safely and prepare her beforehand."

"Prepare me how?" Sophie asked.

"That's what we'll be working on today. I've been developing a series of procedures and protocols for you to follow that should ensure you're able to maintain control. But first, you have a decision to make."

"I do?"

"Yes. And it's an incredibly important one. The Council has decided that you must choose a guide to assist you."

Her insides turned squirmy at the word. She'd been Alden's guide during Fintan's memory break, and it hadn't exactly gone well.

"But this is a healing, not a memory break," she reminded Tiergan. "I'm the only one who can enter a broken mind safely."

"That is definitely true," Tiergan agreed. "And whoever serves as your guide will need to keep their mind guarded until the healing is complete. But after that, you'll have to find what Fintan's been hiding, and his memories are going to be a murky, muddled mess. You'll need someone to help you keep control of the chaos."

"I'll do it," Fitz offered immediately.

"No—Fintan is way too dangerous," Sophie told him. She didn't want that crazy elf near anyone else she cared about.

"Actually, Fitz *is* on the list of potential candidates," Tiergan told her. "But I've asked the Council to let you pick who you'd like best. Under such stressful, complicated conditions, I want you to be completely comfortable with who you're working with. And yes, you *must* choose someone," he added, heading off her next question.

"Who else is on the list?" Fitz asked.

"Alden volunteered, of course."

Sophie shook her head so hard it hurt. "He's still too fragile."

"I agree," Tiergan told her. "Which leaves just three possibilities: Fitz. Quinlin Sonden. And myself."

That . . . wasn't a very long list.

"I don't know Quinlin well enough," Sophie said slowly. He'd been the one to perform the actual memory break on Prentice—and also discovered Sophie's existence. But she'd only met him once, in his office in Atlantis, after the Councillors had ordered her to have her memories probed. The whole process had been very unnerving.

"So that leaves Fitz and myself," Tiergan said quietly. "And before you decide, I'd like to say one thing. Of course I'd be more than happy to guide you, Sophie. But honestly? I think the wisest choice would be Fitz."

"You do?" Sandor and Fitz asked at the same time.

"Why?" Sophie asked.

Tiergan smiled. "I know Fitz isn't as experienced as I am. And I know he's your friend and you want to protect him. But you and Fitz have a very strong—very *special*—connection. I've seen you transmit to him anywhere, and with more ease than when we've tried with other prodigies. And let's not forget that you were able to reach him halfway across the world—while your mind was drugged and dazed, no less."

"I'm pretty sure panic and desperation helped with that," Sophie argued.

"I have no doubt it did. But it also says quite a lot that you chose to reach out to *him*. You trusted him with your life. And *that's* the kind of bond you should have with your guide."

Fitz leaned closer, making her suck in a breath with the intensity to his stare. "Please let me help you, Sophie."

He looked so much like his father in that moment, and Sophie couldn't help remembering Alden collapsed on the floor, his face streaked with red . . .

"Last time was so awful," she whispered.

"I know. But I'm not carrying around a huge load of guilt like my dad was. I promise, I can handle this. Have I ever let you down?"

He had, actually, a few weeks back when he'd blamed her for what happened to Alden.

But he was also the boy who'd shown up on her class field trip and shown her where she really belonged. The one who'd let her cry on his shoulder when she had to leave her family, and who'd gone out searching for her in the middle of nowhere, just because he'd heard her voice in his head.

"Okay," she said quietly, hoping she wouldn't regret the decision. "So what do we do next?"

TWENTY-TWO

TIERGAN SPENT THE REST OF THEIR session explaining his new "Guide Safety Procedures." The two primary rules were, "make eye contact every few minutes" and "don't do anything without warning." He also insisted that they "communicate in code," so that if Fintan's mind became conscious at any point, he wouldn't know what they were doing.

Their homework was to create their code words, and have them memorized by their telepathy session on Thursday. It took them all of study hall to create their list—though that was mostly because their friends kept interrupting. Dex kept grumbling about Telepaths. Biana kept begging to use her ability to sneak into the healing. And Keefe kept interrupting with unhelpful suggestions like, "snickerdoodle" and "hippity hop" and "Keefe is the awesome Lord of Everything." Only Jensi and Marella left them alone, though Sophie could tell they felt left out. But she wasn't dragging any more of her friends into all her drama.

The commands they finally picked were:

> "Alden": *No reason to worry*
> "Mallowmelt": *I found something good*
> "Dame Alina": *I'm in trouble*
> "Verminion": *Get out as fast as you can*
> "Everblaze": *I'm going to use a brain push*

Fitz hadn't understood why Sophie wanted a code word about brain pushes. But she'd used the rare method of channeling during Fintan's memory break, and it happened right before everything went wrong. Part of her kept wondering if the two elements were connected.

Hopefully she wouldn't need to take such an extreme measure this time, but in case she did, she wanted Fitz to be warned and ready.

She was going to protect him every way she could.

Sophie had figured her friends would want to come over after school, but Biana and Dex both got a ton of homework from their ability sessions, and Tiergan gave Fitz concentration exercises to practice. Even Keefe was stuck doing some sort of Empath practice with his dad. And with Grady still not home, and Edaline outside giving the verminion a bath, Sophie ended up roaming her empty house, trying to figure out where they would've put Jolie's old school things.

There weren't a lot of places to check. The downstairs was mostly one big open space, with no closets or cupboards or even any drawers. And half of the second floor was Grady and Edaline's room—which Sophie honestly wasn't sure if she was allowed to go into. So unless there was an attic she didn't know about, the only places left were Grady and Edaline's offices, and Sophie had a feeling Edaline's was the better bet. It *was* the Place Where Stuff Goes to Die, after all.

Sandor had to help her push open the door, because a huge bin of unopened letters was blocking most of it. And the office inside was far worse than Sophie remembered. She'd never seen so many trunks and boxes in one place, all stacked into chaotic piles and draped with more junk, turning the room into a dusty maze.

"One trunk at a time," Sophie whispered, opening the one closest to her.

A cloud of dust made her choke as she sifted through the tangle of silky lavender fabric inside. Sophie thought they were dresses, but when she pulled one out she realized they were tablecloths, edged with pearls and frilly lace. The trunk next to that held the same, and the one after that appeared to be the matching napkins. When the last trunk in the stack had diamond napkin rings, Sophie decided to move to a different spot.

Hours passed with more of the same, and Sophie was fairly certain the labyrinth was stretching around her, trapping her with the endless supply of dusty party decorations for the rest of her days. Her nose itched and her back ached but she forced herself to keep going, working through two more chests of crystal goblets before she opened a small black trunk stuffed with books and scrolls.

The Foxfire seal on a notebook made her heart triple in speed.

But when she looked closer she realized they were from Jolie's early levels. Pages of boring lecture notes from elvin history and multispeciesial studies—many with doodles in the margins of a boy who looked like the photos she'd seen of Brant. There were stacks of sketchbooks, too, filled with gorgeous renderings of landscapes, and creatures, and other prodigies at school. Sophie had never realized Jolie was so talented—and she'd never realized she was a Conjurer. But she found *The Elemental Guide to Conjuring and Translocation* with worn pages covered in hundreds of notes written in Jolie's loopy writing.

It was eye-opening and fascinating. But not particularly useful. And Sophie was about to move on to another chest when she noticed a crunched red scroll at the bottom, tied with gleaming gold ribbon and bearing a strange seal: two hands with fingers intertwined, their wrists bound with golden threads.

It took several tries to untie the extra tight knot in the ribbon, but when Sophie finally unrolled the scroll she found five curled pages, all stamped at the top with the same seal. Underneath in a fancy, frilly script it said:

By Official Arrangement of the Matchmakers:

Matches for Jolie Ruewen

Every scroll had a date at the top—each one exactly a month older than the last—and a title that implied the matches had been ranked. The first page said: *Top Tier*, the one after it: *Second Contenders*, followed by: *Third Considerations*, then: *Fourth Runners-Up*, and lastly: *Final Alternatives*. And underneath each heading was a list of one hundred names—five hundred different matches to choose from overall.

Sophie scanned the names, surprised that number thirty-seven on Jolie's *Top Tier* matches was someone named Ollie Heks, who must be Stina's uncle or cousin or something. Also on that page were two different Vackers—Benesh Vacker at number twenty-four, and Harlin Vacker at number seventy-seven—though neither were names Sophie recognized. In fact, none of the names seemed familiar, and it took her a minute to realize what that meant.

She rechecked each scroll, making sure her photographic memory hadn't failed her—but it was exactly like she'd remembered.

Five hundred names on the scrolls.

Five hundred approved matches for Jolie.

And Brant's name wasn't one of them.

TWENTY-THREE

WHAT ARE YOU DOING?" Edaline asked from the doorway, making Sophie fumble and drop the scrolls. "Sorry, didn't mean to sneak up on you."

"It's okay," Sophie told her, hoping she wasn't in trouble for being in Edaline's office. "I just thought this might be a good place to look for Jolie's school things."

"Oh, I bet you're right! This is where I usually stuff anything I don't know what to do with." Edaline clapped her hands, making an enormous crystal chandelier light the room—and reveal about a hundred more trunks that had been hidden in the shadows. "I've really let things get out of control in here, haven't I?

Hazard of being a Conjurer, I guess. It's too easy to snap my fingers and make anything I don't want to think about disappear."

She opened a nearby trunk and pulled out a garland of dangling diamonds and sparking amethysts and iridescent flowers that looked like they were woven from fairy wings.

"Decorations for the wedding," she explained quietly. "I'd been making everything myself to ensure it would be perfect. But now . . ."

She crushed a fragile flower in her hand, showering the ground with sparkly crumbs.

Sophie was still struggling to figure out how to respond, when Edaline cleared her throat and asked, "So have you found anything from Jolie?"

"One trunk so far, but it's all older stuff. It did have this, though." Sophie showed her the matchmaker's scrolls. "How come I couldn't find Brant's name?"

Edaline looked away, taking several deep breaths before she whispered, "Because Brant and Jolie were a bad match."

Sophie frowned. "So . . . what, if you don't marry someone on your list, it's a bad match?"

"Of course. How did you think it worked?"

"I don't know. I guess I figured you got a list that said, like, *Do Not Marry These People*. And if you chose to marry them anyway, it was a bad match."

"I suppose that would make it easier. But the only "good matches" are the ones the matchmakers arrange. That's why you can request up to five lists—though most of us find our match on the first. Grady was my number three, and I was his number seven."

Sophie couldn't help wondering who'd been their number ones as Edaline moved to her side and took the scrolls. Edaline traced her fingers along the names, shaking her head sadly. "Some of these options seem like such a wrong fit. And Jolie went back every month for a new list, hoping each time it would somehow have Brant's name. But we all knew he wouldn't be on there. Brant never manifested a special ability."

"Wait. People without special abilities can't get married?"

"No, they can. But they're only matched with other Talentless."

"That seems . . . really unfair."

"Brant and Jolie thought so too. The whole point of the matchmaking system is to ensure the strongest genetic potential for our offspring. And I know that probably seems strange, given your upbringing. But you have to consider that there are a lot fewer of us than humans, and we live a very long time—without physically aging. Left to our own devices, it would be far too easy to end up forming an attachment to a distant relative."

"Ew."

"Exactly. Varying the gene pool is essential. The matchmakers also ensure that different talents and skin colors and body types are all mixing. And of course they also work hard to consider our own personal tastes and preferences. They receive centuries of training before they're appointed to their positions. You'll see how extensive the questionnaire is when you're old enough to register. And until then, it's best to try to keep an open mind."

Sophie definitely *didn't* miss the part about her needing to register for matchmaking—but that was a prickly piece of weird her mind wasn't ready to wrap around. So all she asked was, "What do you mean by an 'open mind'?"

"Just . . . try not to form too strong of an attachment to anyone until you receive your lists." She was looking at Sophie's ring as she said it.

Sophie hid her hand behind her back.

Edaline pretended not to notice as she crouched beside the trunk of wedding stuff and started sifting through.

"Jolie was in love with Brant pretty much the moment they met," she said, lifting out a huge knot of fancy garland and trying to untangle it. "She was six, and we were in a pet store in Atlantis, and they both wanted the same gremlin. Brant offered to let her have it, but Jolie suggested they share, and that was all it took. Instant best friends—completely inseparable. For years Grady and I watched them, hoping it would work out. Brant's family was also in the Nobility, and we had no genetic connections—surely they would end up matched. But then Jolie manifested as a Conjurer, and Brant stayed in ability detecting. Poor boy tried so hard to manifest. His parents even hired extra tutors, and he'd work with them for hours, trying to trigger something—anything. But it never worked. And when it was time to register for the match, we all knew what would happen."

Edaline crunched more flowers on the garlands.

"But they were still getting married," Sophie reminded her.

"They were. And Grady and I struggled with it at first—not because we didn't adore Brant," she added quickly, going back to sorting through the trunk. "I'd just seen what my sister went through when she married Kesler. All the whispers and the stares and the friends who started avoiding them. Bad matches don't happen very often, so when they do, they draw lots of attention. And for years after, Juline was afraid to have children, worried something would turn out wrong with them. That's why Dex is your age, and the triplets are even younger. Fortunately, they're perfect and healthy—and I'm so happy to hear that Dex manifested an ability! That will make everything so much easier."

Something about Edaline's smile made Sophie very aware again of the ring on her finger.

"Ah, here it is," Edaline said quietly, lifting out a fragile headpiece—swirls of gold and silver set with amethysts and pearls and diamonds—and holding it up to the light. "Grady and I gave this to Jolie the day we finally consented to the wedding. We'd watched her yell at the matchmakers enough to know there would be no changing her mind. She loved Brant so much. But we still had one condition. We asked her to take the elite levels, even though Brant couldn't be with her."

That explained why Brant had written Jolie so many love letters while she'd been at the elite towers. And probably why he'd talked about feeling unworthy of her.

"She was so mad at us," Edaline whispered. "Accused us of trying to separate them so they'd fall out of love. But I told her that this was what my parents had asked of Kesler and Juline, to prove to others—but mostly to themselves—that they belonged together. If they couldn't survive two years of separation, how could they survive a lifetime of scorn? So she took us up on the challenge. Said she'd prove to everyone that she wasn't making a mistake. And she definitely did."

Edaline turned away, trying to hide the tears that had slipped down her cheeks. Sophie kneeled beside her, wrapping Edaline in a hug.

Edaline held on tight—so tight it was a little hard to breathe. Then she released her hold, clearing her throat several times before she dropped her arms and said, "I'm sorry. We're not here to dredge up sad memories." She stuffed the circlet back in the trunk, slamming it shut with a sort of finality. "We have more important things to find! Where do you want me to start looking?"

Sophie pointed to a row of trunks, and they both set to work. But even with Sandor's help, they'd still barely made it through a third of the room by dinnertime. Edaline conjured up two

201

plates of soggy purple leaves—which tasted uncannily like fried chicken—and they kept working while they ate.

They were just reaching the halfway point when Grady poked his head through the doorway. "Whoa—I can see the cloud of dust you guys are making all the way downstairs."

"You're home!" Sophie said, standing to give him a hug.

She froze when she got a better look at him. Thorny twigs were tangled in his hair, and his cape was caked with dried mud. But the four thin scratches on his left cheek were the most troubling, especially since one was still bleeding.

"What happened?" Edaline asked, sending several streamers crashing to the floor as she stood to inspect his injury.

"Nothing," Grady promised.

"That doesn't look like 'nothing.'" Edaline touched the skin around the wound, making Grady wince.

"I'm fine, I promise. I've just been in the dwarven capital, trying to help them solve a mystery."

"What kind of mystery?" Sophie asked, taking a step back as she realized his cape was caked with something other than mud—and whatever it was did *not* smell good.

"I don't know if mystery's the right word," Grady said, blotting his cheek on his dirty sleeve. "It's more like a *situation*."

"What's the situation?" Sophie pressed when he didn't continue.

Grady stared at the red stain on his cape. "A large group of dwarves seems to have disappeared."

TWENTY-FOUR

ISAPPEARING DWARVES?" SOPHIE asked, feeling foolish just saying it.

She was tempted to ask if they were journeying with a hobbit to reclaim the Lonely Mountain. But the blood on Grady's cheek kind of killed all her jokes.

"How do dwarves disappear?" she asked.

"That's what I'm trying to figure out—though I can't say I'm making much progress. Evidently they've gone missing one by one over the last year, and the dwarves didn't think to mention it to us until they realized that thirty have vanished."

"Thirty?" Edaline whispered.

"Is that a bad number?" Sophie asked.

"Not the number specifically. But last time we took a census, there were only three hundred and twenty-nine dwarves in the whole world. They're solitary creatures, very scattered. So for thirty to go missing is . . . well, we'd definitely like to know what's going on. Which is why I've been stuck crawling around their cramped tunnels for days, getting scraped and scratched and finding *nothing*. It's like they vanished into the ground and never came back out for air."

"What about the Black Swan?" Sophie asked. "They have dwarves secretly working with them. Maybe they have thirty?"

"I thought of that already. But I asked King Enki about them and he said the dwarves working with the Black Swan are all accounted for and checking in regularly."

"So wait, does that mean they could take us to the Black Swan?" Sophie asked.

"More than likely—but don't get your hopes up. The king wouldn't tell me who they are, and we can't force him. The guidelines of our treaty state only that the dwarves must work peacefully with the elves. And the Black Swan *are* elves, so the dwarves are well within their rights of privacy."

"What does that mean, then?" Edaline asked before Sophie could. "Someone is *stealing* dwarves?"

"They might be running away. Or perhaps they're all on a very extended vacation. Or . . . they could be getting abducted. We don't know. And before you assume the worst," he added, turning to Sophie, "keep in mind that mysteries like this happen way more often than we all realize. I'd forgotten just how much the Council deals with on a daily basis. This world is filled with complicated creatures and complicated problems. There's always someone, somewhere, having some sort of crisis. This is just business as usual."

"Not if you consider what's been going on with the ogres," Sandor interrupted. "Sophie uncovered some rather disturbing evidence yesterday, and I fear it might be related to your mystery."

"She did?" Edaline asked—her expression a mix of hurt and disappointment as she turned to Sophie. "Why haven't I heard about this?"

"Well, for one thing," Sophie said, glaring at Sandor, "we don't know for sure that ogres are involved. No one knows what any of it means."

"You still could've told me," Edaline said gently.

"I know." Sophie stared at the dust motes swirling in the air while she explained about the aromark and the homing device and Lady Cadence's effluxers at Foxfire. She even told them about the leak in the Black Swan. The only thing she kept secret were her theories about Jolie.

Grady's sigh sounded more like a groan as he ran his hands down his face, smearing the blood from his cut. "I don't think I have the energy to deal with any of this right now."

Sophie didn't either, honestly.

Ogres and goblins and missing dwarves?

Her life had officially turned into a fairy tale gone wrong.

"Hey," Grady said, strangling her with a hug. "Everything always looks worse after a long day. Let's all get some sleep and regroup tomorrow, okay?"

Sophie nodded, trying not to think about angry ogres and missing dwarves as she stumbled up to her messy bedroom. But as Iggy flitted to her pillow and curled up in a tangle of orange fluff, she couldn't help feeling just as small as him.

Her world—and its problems—was so much bigger than she'd ever imagined. And she couldn't shake the horrible feeling that this time no one could solve them.

"Hey," Sophie said as she caught up with Marella in the Level Three atrium.

The locker-lined quad was humongous, decorated with glittering crystal trees and a giant mastodon statue in the center. But it felt strangely small when Marella didn't smile back at her.

"You okay?" Sophie asked. "I couldn't find you at orientation."

Marella said nothing as she licked the sensor to open her locker, waiting until she'd grabbed all her books before she mumbled, "I'm surprised you noticed I was gone."

"Why wouldn't I?"

"No reason."

Marella tossed the tiny braids she'd woven into her hair as she turned to face Sophie. She looked more like her old self again—except for the scowl on her lips.

"Is this about Biana?" Sophie asked.

"Why would I care about her?"

"I don't know. You've been a little different since she manifested."

"Oh, so you think I'm jealous?"

"I never said that." Sophie kept her voice low, wishing they could have this conversation somewhere without so many staring prodigies.

Marella slammed her locker much harder than she needed to. "Good. And I don't care that she's suddenly in on all your secret stuff, either—in case that's what you're thinking."

"I wasn't," Sophie promised.

"Good," Marella repeated. "Because I wouldn't get sucked into your drama even if you wanted me too. It's way too dangerous."

She stalked away before Sophie could respond—not that she knew what to say.

Stina applauded.

"You know, I never thought I'd say this, but I'm starting to like that Redek girl," she told her minions as she followed Sophie over to her locker. "At least she's smart enough not to let you drag her down with you."

"No one's getting dragged anywhere," Sophie muttered.

"No—the Vacker losers are going voluntarily. And don't even get me started on Dizznee." She pointed to Sophie's ring and mimed gagging. "So tell me, who's going to be the next casualty? I mean, Dex already had one planting. And from what I hear, Keefe came pretty close to needing one himself. So who gets it this time? My money's on Fitz. The healing's on Friday, right? Anyone else think we might not see him after that?"

No one raised their hands. But Sophie could tell some of them wanted to.

Most of them, actually.

"Is there a problem, Miss Foster?" Dame Alina asked, striding toward them with a dramatic sweep of her cape. "It looked like Miss Heks was bothering you."

Sophie had never seen Dame Alina in the atrium, and she glanced over her shoulder, wondering if there was some sort of surveillance camera she was missing. And the snotty smirk on Stina's lips made it so tempting to get her in trouble. But that would only cause more drama, especially since everything Stina had said was technically true.

Being friends with Sophie *was* dangerous—and Sophie was just as worried about Fitz as everyone else seemed to be.

"We were just talking," she mumbled toward her feet.

Dame Alina sighed, clearly not convinced. But when Sophie didn't say anything else, she clapped her hands and ordered everyone to their sessions.

"Come on, girls," Stina told her minions. She grinned at Sophie as she tossed her giant hair. "Let's go find Redek and see if she wants to sit with us at lunch today."

"Actually, you still have detention," Dame Alina called after her. "And I think it might be best if you spend it with me today."

"What?" Stina asked, whipping back around.

Dame Alina smiled. "I'll be waiting for you in my office."

"But I didn't do anything wrong!"

"I never said you did."

Stina's eyes narrowed to slits, but she kept her mouth shut as she turned and stomped away.

Sophie leaned against her locker, letting the cold of the metal sink into her flushed skin. "You didn't have to do that," she told Dame Alina. "I'm fine."

"I'm sure you are. But I still think it's high time Miss Heks and I have a nice little chat. And you'd better get going, Miss Foster. You still have quite a long walk to your session, and . . ."

The bells chimed, right on schedule.

Sophie groaned, throwing her satchel over her shoulder as she raced down the hall. Her morning session was in the Silver Tower, and she'd picked the *worst* Mentor to be tardy for.

She was soaked with sweat by the time she pounded on the gleaming door, shouting for Master Leto to let her in.

"Are you okay?" he asked as she rushed past him.

She scrambled to put on her silver cape, feeling her eyes burn when she accidentally stabbed her finger with the pin. She squeezed them tight, ordering herself not to cry. But she felt a tear leak down her cheek.

"Here," Master Leto said, taking her hand and cleaning the blood off her finger with a silky handkerchief.

She waited for him to let go, but he leaned closer, squinting at Dex's ring before tracing his finger over her star-shaped scar.

"Looks like you've had an interesting few weeks."

He didn't say it like a question, but Sophie nodded anyway.

"Well, I know it does not change any of the things you're facing. But I hope you know that you're not alone."

Right. She had friends she could put in danger. Just what she always wanted.

"I mean it, Miss Foster. I'm sure you're hearing the same whispers that I am. But that does not speak for everyone. And the rest will understand with time."

"I hope so," she said, trying to hand back his handkerchief.

"Keep it. And let me solve one other problem as well." He placed a plain blue square of glass in her palm. "Show this to Councillor Bronte and you'll be off the hook for your tardiness. It should also make him go easy on you today—and if he doesn't, call for me."

The glass was cool to the touch, but it turned warm as she tucked it safely into her pocket. She meant to ask him what it was, but "Why are you helping me?" slipped out instead.

Master Leto smiled. "It's part of my job, Sophie—to give light when it's needed, and brighten up a bad day. Why else do you think they call me the Beacon?"

She'd honestly had no idea—and always thought it was a

stupid title. But maybe it fit better than she thought. Even if she still hated calling him "Master."

"Well, thank you," she mumbled.

He opened the door to the empty common room and she made her way to the stairs, wishing her session wasn't on the very top floor.

"There's a faster way," Master Leto told her as she climbed the first step. "But you're going to have to hold on tight."

He stomped his foot, making a rumbly thump, and Sophie barely managed to grab the gleaming banister before the silver stairway spun to life, whirling, faster than Keefe's vortinator. She spun sideways and slantways and upside down through all the twists and turns of the stairway, and by the time she reached the top she was fairly certain she'd never be able to eat again. Assuming she survived the next two hours.

She needed several deep breaths to stop her head from spinning spinning spinning. But her nausea came crashing back as she stumbled into the small dim room.

Councillor Bronte sat waiting for her in the room's only chair—a fancy silver throne that matched his fancy cape and crown.

He definitely looked ready to inflict some serious pain.

TWENTY-FIVE

YOU'RE LATE," BRONTE INFORMED her, and his gleeful smile made it clear he'd used the extra time to imagine all kinds of miserable punishments.

Before he could deliver any of them, a familiar red-haired figure stepped out of the shadows. "I'm sure she has a good excuse," Councillor Kenric told him. "And I'm sorry if I startled you, Sophie. Councillor Bronte apparently does not believe in providing his prodigies with light."

"Inflicting feeds on *darkness*," Bronte snapped back. "The fact that I have to explain that shows you have no place in this session."

"My *place*," Kenric corrected, "is to ensure Sophie's safety—

since you have proven that you will not always act with her best interests at heart."

That was putting it mildly. When Bronte wanted to prove that Sophie's abilities were broken, he'd basically used the session to torture her.

Still, she'd thought things between her and Bronte were getting better. He'd seemed genuinely interested in working with her after he'd discovered she could inflict positive emotions as well as negative—something he'd thought was impossible before then. But if Kenric felt he needed to chaperone . . .

"Regardless of what my weak-hearted assistant may claim," Bronte said, jolting her back to attention, "this tower has strict rules about tardiness—as I'm sure you're well aware."

"I am," Sophie agreed, pulling out the blue square Master Leto had given her. "That's why I was told to show you this."

Bronte's jaw fell so fast, she was surprised it didn't hit the floor.

"What could you have possibly done to deserve an amnesty?" he asked, lunging from his chair and snatching it from her hand. "When I attended here, these were reserved for extreme emergencies."

"Well, maybe things have changed since the dark ages," Sophie mumbled, earning a snicker from Kenric.

"The elves *never* had a dark ages," Bronte snapped. "And I graduated long before the time period you're referring to."

"Really?" She knew Bronte was one of the Ancients—and

he did have the pointiest ears she'd ever seen. But with his cropped brown hair and wrinkle-free skin it was so hard to imagine him being thousands of years old.

"Yes," he said, shoving the amnesty into the pocket of his jewel-encrusted cape before he pointed to his throne. "Now take a seat. We have wasted enough time."

"But . . . that's your chair."

"Thank you for that waste of words. Now sit."

Sophie glanced at Kenric and he nodded, so she reluctantly made her way to the chair, half expecting to spot a bucket of boiling acid dangling above it. The sharp edge cut into her legs, and the cold, rigid back pressed into her shoulders like ice. It felt like Bronte had custom ordered The Most Uncomfortable Chair Ever Invented—and the designer had exceeded his expectations.

"As you know, my fellow Councillors have ordered you to conduct a healing in two days," Bronte said to her, glancing sidelong at Kenric. "And they have asked me to ensure you're prepared. Now personally, I don't believe a twelve-year-old will *ever* be ready to handle such a task—"

"I'm thirteen," Sophie corrected.

"Oh, that's *much* better, then. Everyone knows teenagers are so full of *wisdom* and *experience*."

"Hey, you guys are the ones ordering me to do this," she reminded him.

"Actually, you can thank the other Councillors for that. I was—once again—outvoted."

214

Kenric cleared his throat.

"Oh, quit rattling your windpipe," Bronte snapped. "Now, as I was saying, I don't believe a *thirteen*-year-old will *ever* be ready to handle such a task. But I am open to being proven wrong." He crossed his arms and turned to face her. "Well, go ahead then."

Sophie shifted in the miserable chair. "Uh . . . go ahead with what?"

Bronte rolled his eyes. "Did you or did you not tell me that positive inflicting is an essential part of the healing process?"

"Right."

"Well then, show me how it's done."

"You . . . want me to inflict on you."

"*Positively*, yes. Is that a problem?"

Oh, it was a problem. She'd only inflicted positive emotions once, during Alden's healing, and she'd been so fueled by her desperation to bring him back that she'd acted almost entirely on instinct.

The only thing she was desperate to do now was pelt Bronte with sparkly alicorn poop.

"I believe the first step is to identify the emotion you want to unleash," Kenric offered quietly. "At least, that's what I remember studying. And with regular inflicting the primary choices are sorrow, envy, guilt, fear, and rage. So for positive inflicting they would be . . ."

"Happiness?" Sophie guessed. "And peace. And love. And, um . . ."

She tried to think of more, but they all seemed like versions of the emotions she'd already listed.

Were there really more negative emotions than positive ones?

"That's enough to start," Bronte told her. "So which is your objective?"

The thought of trying to make Bronte feel *love* made Sophie want to vomit. And she was feeling anything but peaceful at the moment. Which left her with: happy.

She squeezed her eyes tight and tried to remember happy things, hoping her instincts would kick in after that. Her childhood memories were mixed with too much sadness, now that she'd left her family, so she focused on her new life, remembering her friends, and Grady and Edaline, and Silveny. But even those memories were swirled with so much doubt and worry and uncertainty.

"I'm waiting, Miss Foster," Bronte interrupted.

"Oh please, it's only been a few seconds," Kenric told him. "You're doing great, Sophie."

The glimmer of praise helped her relax, and she shifted her mind to smaller memories: *the day she rescued Iggy, her first flight with Silveny, every time she stared into a pair of beautiful teal eyes* . . .

Warm energy swelled in her mind, and she fueled it with more memories until her brain felt ready to burst with the excess energy. Blue light rimmed her vision as she focused on Bronte and channeled the force out of her mind.

Bronte gasped as the emotion hit him, his sharp features softening as it sank in. A hint of a smile flitted across his lips, but it vanished just as quickly.

"That hardly counts as inflicting," he told her—though his voice sounded lighter than normal. "Is that really the best you can do?"

She gripped the armrests of the throne, focusing on the one memory that felt the purest: *the day Fitz had first shown her she was an elf.* It was before she'd known about the Black Swan or the kidnappers, before she'd realized she'd have to leave her family. He'd swept her away from her world of headaches and blaring thoughts and the inescapable sense that she was too strange, too different—and shown her where she truly belonged. And for that one brief moment everything felt right, like a missing piece of her life had finally clicked into place.

She drew on the feeling, wrapping her mind around the spark and letting it grow into an inferno in her mind. Then she met Bronte's cold, piercing eyes, wondering if he could see flames in hers as she shoved every ounce of energy toward him, slamming his mind with the hottest mass of happy she could muster.

Bronte gasped as the force hit him, but it quickly turned into a laugh.

No—a giggle.

She'd made Bronte *giggle*!

He covered his mouth like he was just as shocked as her, but more laughter slipped through his fingers, until his face turned red and his whole body was shaking.

"That's amazing!" Kenric told her as Bronte dropped to his knees, laughing so hard he started to cry.

But as Sophie watched the tears stream down his cheeks she realized they weren't tears of joy like they should be. His lips may have been smiling, but his eyes were pure terror.

She grabbed his shoulders, trying to shake him out of the frenzy. But Bronte kept right on laughing, turning more and more hysterical.

"Stay calm," Kenric told her, taking Sophie's hands and waiting for her to look at him. "Whatever's happening, you have the power within you to fix it."

"How can you be so sure?"

"Because I've seen the wonders you work, Sophie. You just have to believe."

She swallowed so hard it hurt as she reached for Bronte's temples. His pointy ears were much bendier than she'd thought, and when she pressed her fingers along each side of his face, his skin felt cold and clammy.

"You can do this," Kenric repeated.

Sophie hoped he was right, taking three deep breaths before she shoved her consciousness into Bronte's mind.

His memories felt like sludge. Thick and cold, like a snowdrift—and when she tried to sort through them, something kept shoving her back, sending her deeper and deeper into the mire.

Bronte? she transmitted, calling his name over and over.

He didn't respond. And when she tried sending happy thoughts—like she'd done when she healed Alden—the glimmers of warmth bounced off the sludge and stung her.

Stop it, Bronte! her mind yelled. *Or you can get out of this yourself.*

The harsh words sank into the darkness, which grew calmer and warmer as it absorbed the emotion behind them.

Is that the trick? she asked. Did Bronte need *more* anger?

It seemed like a backward approach, but she was out of ideas. So she thought about Stina, and Marella, and the whispers that followed her everywhere. Of the rebels and the ogres and anyone who dared to try to hurt Silveny. Of the nightmares and the worries and the massive burden the Black Swan had dumped on her—before they completely abandoned her.

Every bitter thought poured out of her like a river, and as they surged through Bronte's consciousness they melted the sludge, lifting her up and out until she was finally free.

Bronte sat up, gasping for breath and cradling his head.

Several seconds passed before he turned his tear-stained face to them and said, "We will never speak of this again."

TWENTY-SIX

NEXT TIME YOU ALMOST KILL A Councillor, can I be there?" Keefe asked as he tossed a handful of gold powder on the path leading to the main auditorium. Lady Cadence had given them something called musk-tang and told them to coat every walkway on the campus. It wouldn't have been such a terrible detention punishment if it hadn't smelled like rotting bananas. Keefe told her the whole Sanctuary had been dusted with it.

Another protection against ogres.

"I didn't almost kill him," Sophie whispered, glancing over her shoulder to make sure none of the other prodigies were around. "I don't know what happened—and neither did Bronte or Kenric. One second he was insulting me, next second he was collapsed on the floor."

"Clearly it's not a good idea to get you angry. Uh-oh, should I be afraid?" Keefe asked as she glared at him. "You going to knock me out or something, are you?"

"If only."

She wanted to kick herself for telling Keefe what happened.

But she'd had to tell *someone*. The more she'd replayed the session, the more she felt a nagging itch in the back of her mind, telling her something was off.

"Besides, it wasn't the anger that took him down. That was actually how I got him out of it. Which seems weird, doesn't it? I mean, he was basically allergic to happiness."

"Um, you have *met* Bronte, right?"

"I know. But I've been in some messed-up minds, and I've never felt anything like that sludgy darkness I felt today."

"Maybe that's what an Inflictor's mind feels like. I mean, no offense, but what you guys do *is* kinda creepy."

Sophie couldn't argue. If she had her way, she'd probably get rid of the dangerous ability. But talents couldn't be switched off once they'd been triggered. And creepy ability or no, she still didn't think that explained what had happened. Especially when she factored in the way Bronte's mind had blocked her from his memories. Almost like he had something to hide . . .

"You're cute when you worry, did you know that?" Keefe asked her.

Sophie flung a handful of musk-tang at his feet, surrounding him in a cloud of stinky golden dust.

He laughed as he coughed. "Oh, it is *so* on."

He pelted her with a giant handful, and Sophie struck back, nailing him in the shoulder before she took off running.

Keefe chased after her, hurling handful after handful as Sophie tried to swerve and duck. She was so busy launching counterattacks that she forgot to pay attention to where she was going. Which was how she ended up crashing into Lady Cadence, seconds before Keefe accidentally musk-tanged the furious Mentor's face.

"Don't let her get to you, Foster," Keefe said as they made their way to their afternoon sessions. "Lady Cadence can send as many disciplinary reports to Dame Alina as she wants. It still won't change the fact that watching her choke on that mouthful of musk-tang was one of the greatest moments of my life."

It *had* been pretty priceless.

And the disciplinary report wasn't what was bothering Sophie—though she wasn't exactly *thrilled* about that. Lady Cadence had gone on and on and on about how, given the controversy surrounding Fintan's healing, Sophie should be working harder than ever to prove herself a well-behaved citizen in her world. But what Sophie wanted to know was, *How did everyone know so many classified things?*

The information had to be leaking from someone in the

Nobility—and a lot of the things people had heard about were things only the Councillors would know. . . .

"What if Bronte's the one leaking secret information from the Council?" she whispered. "That would explain why he didn't want me to look through his memories."

"But why would he do that? He's just causing more problems for himself."

"Maybe not. He also told me today that he didn't vote in favor of Fintan's healing. So maybe he's trying to stop it by getting the public all riled up against it."

"I guess. But it still feels like a stretch. Bronte's the longest standing member of the Council—by a *lot*. I can't see him doing anything to undermine it."

Sophie sighed. "I wish there were some way to find out for sure. Oh! What if we—"

"If you're thinking of breaking into his office," Keefe interrupted, "you should know that the crystal castles are *impossible* to sneak into. Trust me, I tried several times when I was a kid."

"I wasn't going to suggest breaking and entering. But you're an Empath, right? And Empaths can detect lies."

"Only sort of. Lies aren't an emotion. All I can pick up on are the feelings that go with it—like the guilt and the stress and the worry. But if someone's a good enough liar they know how to hide that. I've pulled it off with my dad *many* times."

"Well, still, couldn't you test Bronte and see how he reacts?"

"Maybe. But it's not like I have weekly Councillor hang-out

time—and even if I did, as soon as I asked about the leak he'd know what I was doing."

He was right. Bronte was far too grumpy and suspicious not to catch on.

But he was also hiding something—she could *feel* it.

There had to be a way to figure out what it was.

Sophie came home to find her bedroom covered in boxes, each wrapped in opalescent paper and tied with a sparkling pink bow.

"I know you're not that into clothes and dresses," Edaline said, popping out of Sophie's closet carrying more boxes—and nearly giving Sophie a heart attack. "But I realized that we've never gone shopping together, and I've never really bought you anything, so . . . ta-da!"

She tried to set her boxes down, but there was no more empty space. "Hm. I might have gotten a little carried away."

"A little" was putting it mildly. Sophie doubted the stores in Atlantis had anything left to sell. And she was pretty sure this was leftover guilt from Edaline giving Biana Jolie's clothes. But it was nice of Edaline to think of her.

"Well, aren't you going to open them?" Edaline asked, grabbing a wide rectangular package from the top of the nearest pile. "Start with this one, it's my favorite."

Her enthusiasm was infectious, and Sophie couldn't help smiling as she untied the glittering ribbon. Pink sparkles stuck to her fingers as she pulled open the box to find . . .

A sea of wispy lavender chiffon, covered in diamonds and pearls.

"Isn't it gorgeous?" Edaline asked. "Most of the things I got are a bit simpler than this, since I know that's more your style. But I wanted you to have at least one special dress, and this one just reminded me so much of you. Hold it up—let's see if I guessed the right size."

Edaline showered the floor with glitter as she pulled out the dress and held it against Sophie's shoulders.

Sophie repressed a sigh when she realized it had a *train*.

As if she didn't have a hard enough time walking without tripping.

Edaline gasped. "The color, with your hair. It's—you look so much . . ."

She didn't finish the sentence, but Sophie knew how it ended.

You look so much like Jolie.

"Lady Ruewen?" one of the gnomes called from downstairs, saving Sophie from having to figure out a reply. "The new verminion tunneled out of its pen again."

"I am dreaming of the day those obnoxious creatures are ready for the Sanctuary," Edaline told Sophie, wiping pink glitter off her hands. "I'll be back as soon as I can. In the meantime, why don't you try that on and see how it fits?"

"Sure," Sophie said, not finding the idea nearly as exciting as Edaline seemed to. But there was something she wanted to see.

The lightweight fabric felt cool against her skin, and it swished and swirled with every step as she made her way to the floor-length mirror.

"Wow," Vertina said as she appeared in the corner. "You look so . . . pretty."

"You don't have to sound so surprised," Sophie grumbled.

"Oh please, you wear dull colors and never do anything with your hair—and don't get me started on your desperate need for lip gloss and—"

Sophie stepped out of range, making the tiny face disappear.

She counted to ten, then stepped back in front of the mirror.

"Just because I'm a gadget doesn't give you the right to flick me on and off at will," Vertina huffed. "Jolie never would've treated me that way. You may look like her, but—"

"So you really think I look like her?" Sophie interrupted, squinting at her reflection. That's what she kept trying to figure out—*what did Edaline see?*

Was there really a similarity? Or was it Edaline's wishful thinking.

"Well, it's not like you're twins or anything," Vertina told her. "Jolie's hair was shinier than yours—and she had the most gorgeous turquoise eyes, unlike *your* weird ones. But you do remind me of her. If I didn't know better I'd think you two were related."

The word was like a spark, igniting the firestorm of panic that had already been brewing in Sophie's stomach.

If Jolie had been working with the Black Swan, could she have been a part of Project Moonlark?

And if so . . . could she be Sophie's mother?

TWENTY-SEVEN

*I*T CAN'T BE, SOPHIE TOLD HERSELF, repeating it over and over and over.

Jolie died sixteen years ago.

And Sophie was only thirteen.

The numbers didn't lie.

But the numbers also didn't account for the fact that the Black Swan had built her in their lab, twisting and tweaking her genes for who knew how long before her embryo had been implanted in a human being. Sophie didn't know much about that process, but she knew embryos could be frozen. Which meant her mother could've been anyone, anywhere, any time.

"Please, Vertina," she begged. "You have to tell me what Jolie was hiding about the Black Swan."

"I can't. Not unless . . ."

"Unless what?" Sophie shouted, looking around for something heavy she could threaten the obnoxious mirror with. "Why can't you just tell me?"

"Because Jolie said it wasn't safe!" Vertina shouted back. "She said that someone was not who she thought they were, and even if I knew the person asking, I couldn't tell them unless they knew the password."

"But she couldn't have meant me—I wasn't even born yet!"

"You still don't know the password," Vertina reminded her.

She clicked away before Sophie could argue, and Sophie sank to the floor, the lavender gown crumpling around her.

She stared at her reflection in the mirror.

She knew she should be focusing on what Vertina had just told her, since it sounded like Jolie might've known about the Black Swan's leak—and maybe even who it was. But she was too distracted by a much stranger question.

If Jolie was her mother, and Grady and Edaline were her grandparents, did that mean she and Dex were . . . cousins?

"Are you avoiding me?" Dex asked, cornering Sophie the next morning in PE.

"Why would you think that?"

"Uh, maybe because every time I tried to find you at orientation you were somehow on the other side of the room—and now you've partnered with pretty much everyone except me."

She'd been hoping he wouldn't notice that. . . .

She forced herself to look at him—and then instantly regretted it. Suddenly she was noticing the curve of his chin and the lines of his cheekbones, realizing she could sorta see a resemblance to hers.

She didn't understand why that bothered her so much. But it did.

"Are you still mad at me?" Dex asked quietly.

"Of course not."

"Then what's wrong? Is it Marella? Because I heard about what she said to you yesterday, and if she thinks—"

"It's not Marella," Sophie interrupted, though Marella had gone out of her way to avoid her again. Even Jensi wasn't hanging around, though when she'd made eye contact with him, he'd still smiled. "I'm just not feeling good, okay?"

"What's this?" a deep voice asked behind her, and she spun around to face Sir Harding, her broad-shouldered PE mentor. "You do look pale," he decided after studying her face. "Perhaps you should go to the Healing Center."

An Elwin visit was *way* better than more Dex interrogation. So Sophie told him, "Maybe you're right."

She gave Dex a hasty wave and retreated from the gymnasium.

Sandor rushed after her, grabbing her arm to slow her down. "Why didn't you tell me you weren't feeling well?"

"Because it's not a big deal."

"Everything is a big deal."

"This isn't. I just needed a break. I'll hang out in the atrium until lunch."

"You most certainly will not. If you said you're going to the Healing Center, then to the Healing Center you'll go. I've been wanting Elwin to check that wound on your wrist again anyway."

She could tell there would be no changing his mind, so she switched direction, muttering under her breath about stubborn goblins.

"Let me guess," Elwin said as she walked into the Healing Center. "You overestimated the strength of your levitating abilities and crashed into the ceiling."

"Very funny. Actually, I . . ." Her voice trailed off when she realized Elwin wasn't alone.

Master Leto bowed. "Hello, Miss Foster. I would say this is a surprise, but from what I hear, you stop by quite often. In fact, we were just talking about you."

"I was telling him how the piquatine worked when I treated you," Elwin explained, pointing to the egg-shaped vial in Master Leto's hands.

Sophie scrambled back. "Did you find more aromark?"

"Preparatory measure only," Master Leto promised. "Lady Cadence feels it would be prudent for us to keep a supply in the tower, along with reveldust, and two other enzymes Elwin is attempting to track down."

"And I'm not having much luck," Elwin warned him. "I thought yeti pee was tough to come by—but it'd be easier to fill a whole lake with it than to get my hands on anything from the ogres. All the trade lines have closed."

Master Leto frowned, but he didn't ask about any of the things Sophie was dying to know.

Before she could jump in on her own, Elwin asked her, "So what brings you by today?"

"An overprotective bodyguard," she grumbled.

"She would like you to check the burn on her wrist," Sandor clarified.

Elwin nodded, slipping on his crazy spectacles and flashing a green orb of light around her wrist. "I thought you said it wasn't a burn."

"It wasn't," Sophie agreed. "It was just a bruise that I treated with the wrong medicine."

"Ah, yes. And I believe I already gave you my, 'Always Come See Me First' lecture last time. So I'll spare you this time—but I hope you've learned your lesson."

"I have."

Elwin turned her hand from side to side, switching the light from red, to blue, to purple before he told her, "Well, the good news is, the wound healed perfectly. Not even the slightest trace that anything used to be there."

"And the bad news?" Sophie had to ask.

"You have some of the most exhausted-looking cells I've

ever seen. And don't even get me started on those dark circles under your eyes." He flashed an orange orb around her head. "When was the last time you actually slept?"

"It's . . . been a while," she admitted.

"I haven't heard her sleep through the night since Silveny moved to the Sanctuary," Sandor added.

Elwin whistled. "You can't keep that up, Sophie. I know you don't like sedatives—"

"Then don't try to talk me into taking them," she interrupted.

"But you *need* sleep."

"Wait," Master Leto interrupted. "Forgive my intrusion, but I have to ask. What does sleep have to do with Silveny being at the Sanctuary?"

It really wasn't any of his business. But he had given her that amnesty thing, so she told him, "Silveny used to keep my nightmares away. We can communicate telepathically, and she would send her memories into my mind while I slept."

"So why don't you still have her do that?"

"Uh . . . because she's on the other side of the world now."

Was he actually serious with that question?

Clearly he was, because Master Leto laughed. "And here I thought you were the girl with all the impossibly strong powers. Did you or did you not transmit to someone more than half a world away—and with your mind drugged, no less?"

"I did," she admitted. "But I'm pretty sure that was mostly

adrenaline. Plus, the Sanctuary is a different situation. I couldn't even teleport there when I tried."

His brows shot up. "Really?"

"Yeah. I can't teleport through anything solid."

"Fascinating," he mumbled, mostly to himself. Several long seconds passed before he added, "Well, last I checked, teleporting and telepathy were two completely different things. And I promise you, Sophie, the only barrier stopping you from reaching your alicorn friend is the imaginary wall you put there yourself. Tear it down and discover an entirely new realm of possibilities."

"How can you be so sure?" Sophie had to ask.

He smiled and tapped the side of his head. "I know rather more about the mind than you might expect."

He left before she could ask what that meant, and she didn't see how he could be right. But if there was even the slightest chance she could connect with Silveny, it was worth trying. The healing was tomorrow, and the Councillors—and Fitz—were counting on her to get through it safely.

She was going to need all the help she could get.

TWENTY-EIGHT

TELL ME THIS," TIERGAN SAID AS HE stood from his chair and started to pace the small telepathy room. "What will be your greatest asset during the healing—during any telepathic endeavor, actually?"

"My impenetrable mind?" Sophie guessed.

"That is a strength, Sophie, but not an asset," Tiergan corrected. "And you've already seen how our strengths can fail us. An asset, on the other hand, is a tool, ready to be utilized the second we should call upon it—and there's one asset in particular that you both must rely upon to the fullest extent of your abilities. Any other guesses what it might be?"

Sophie glanced at Fitz, but he seemed just as clueless as her.

"It's *trust*," Tiergan told them. "Trust is what gives us confidence to step outside the safety of our own headspace and enter the darkness of another. What fuels us, guides us, pushes us to keep going, even when all hope feels lost. And for the two of you, *trust* is what will bond you together, so that your minds can face the coming challenge as one. So tell me, Fitz," he said, turning to face him, "do you trust Sophie?"

"Of course."

"Are you certain—and I mean *absolutely* certain?" Tiergan pressed. "If memory serves me, the two of you have had a somewhat tumultuous relationship recently."

Fitz lowered his head. "I know I was a total jerk for a few weeks. But I *do* trust you," he told Sophie. "I hope you trust me."

"Of course I do!" Sophie said—probably too quickly.

Tiergan studied them for a second, rubbing his chin. "Nope. I'm not convinced. I see friendship and familiarity. But what you need is *absolute* confidence in each other. Which is why I've prepared a special exercise." He folded his hands as he waited for them to look at him. "The better we understand someone, the more we can trust them, wouldn't you agree?"

Sophie and Fitz both nodded.

"I'm so glad you feel that way, because the success of the assignment will depend entirely upon how willing you are to open up and truly put faith in each other."

236

Something about his tone felt almost ominous, and when Sophie swallowed she realized her mouth had gone dry.

"Sophie," Tiergan said, forcing her to pay attention, "since Fitz can no longer transmit to you, I'm going to need you to open your mind to his for this exercise—and for now I want you both to keep your thoughts focused on something unimportant. Like socks, or napkins, or uvulas."

"Uvulas?" Fitz and Sophie both asked at the same time.

Tiergan smiled. "And now you won't be able to think of anything else."

He was right—Sophie's mind was filled with images of the hangy ball that dangled from the back of her throat, and when she opened her thoughts to Fitz's, he was picturing the same thing.

She couldn't decide if she wanted to laugh or gag.

"Okay, I'm in," she said.

Like old times, huh? Fitz thought.

Pretty much, Sophie transmitted—deciding not to mention that his thoughts were way easier to listen to than the blaring transmissions he used to send.

"So now what?" Fitz asked Tiergan.

"Now comes the fun part—though you may consider it rather challenging. I want you both to privately tell each other three things about yourself that no one else knows—"

"Three?" Sophie interrupted.

"Would you like more?" Tiergan asked.

237

"No—three is good!" Fitz jumped in.

He sounded just as nervous as Sophie, which actually made her feel better.

"They can't be things you've shared with anyone else," Tiergan added, sealing their misery, "and they need to be important secrets. Not 'I didn't eat breakfast this morning' or 'I always fall asleep during elvin history.' You need to push yourself beyond your comfort zone and really trust each other. Understand?"

They both nodded, and Sophie wished she hadn't shared quite so many secrets with Biana as Tiergan sank into his chair. He turned one of the silver knobs on his armrest, dimming the lights, and the darkness made everything feel more intimate—which was probably the point. But it made Sophie's palms so clammy they stuck to her cape.

"Pretend I'm not here," Tiergan told them. "And try to forget about Sandor as well. This exercise will work best if you concentrate only on each other. And keep in mind that the more you share, the better you'll be able to work together."

An endless stretch of silence followed, before Sophie transmitted, *So . . . how do you want to do this?*

I guess we could take turns, Fitz thought back.

They both shifted in their chairs, neither seeming to want to go first.

We could play rock, paper, scissors, Sophie suggested, *and the loser has to start.*

I have no idea what that is.

Wow, really? Sophie explained the rules, and, even though Fitz didn't seem to understand how paper could ever beat rock, they decided to play.

Naturally, Fitz chose paper.

And naturally, Sophie won with scissors.

Fitz slumped in his chair. *Argh—this is so awkward. I mean, it's not that I don't trust you. It's just . . . the only things I can come up with are going to make you think I'm such a dork.*

That's not possible. You're pretty much the coolest guy I know.

Cooler than Keefe?

Well . . . maybe it's a tie.

A slow smile curled his lips. *I guess I can live with that. And I should probably stop stalling, huh?*

Nah—take your time. In fact, feel free to stall for the rest of the session. Then I don't have to take a turn either.

Think we could get away with that?

Somehow I doubt it.

Okay—let's do this. He squared his shoulders as he told her, *I . . . can't sleep without this bright red stuffed dragon Elwin gave me.*

A giggle slipped out of Sophie's lips before she could stop it.

See? I knew you'd think I was a dork!

Uh, you already know I'm a huge fan of sleeping with stuffed animals. I just never realized you were.

Yeah. It's a recent thing. Elwin brought it to me after everything that happened with my dad, and at first I wanted to tear its head off or something—I was pretty angry back then.

A wave of bitter memories flooded his mind and Sophie did her best to block them. She didn't want to relive those moments any more than Fitz did.

Anyway, he thought, turning his head away and blinking a few times, *I'd shoved the stupid dragon under my bed and forgotten about it for a few days. But then I had a really bad nightmare and I couldn't stop shaking. And I remembered that day when I had to take you away from your family, how you were sobbing on the floor and nothing seemed to help until you told me to go get Ella. As soon as I gave her to you, you were suddenly okay. I mean, I could see you were still struggling. But you were better, too. So I grabbed the stupid fluffy dragon and held on tight, and for some reason I can't sleep without it now—even though things are back to normal. Well . . . mostly normal.*

His mind filled with the same fears Sophie felt when she thought about Alden—only about a thousand times worse.

Your dad's going to be okay, she promised.

I know. But she could see there were still doubts in his mind.

Does the dragon have a name? she asked, trying to lighten the mood.

I was hoping you wouldn't ask. He didn't look at her as he added, *Elwin named it . . . Mr. Snuggles.*

Sophie covered her mouth to block her laugh, but it slipped out her nose in a snort.

Fitz snorted too, and they both burst into a fit of giggles.

"I take it things are going well?" Tiergan asked, opening one eye to study them. "Keep it up, you'll see the value in this exercise by the end."

Next time I'm at your house I want to meet Mr. Snuggles, Sophie transmitted to Fitz.

I figured you were going to say that. And fine—but only if Biana's not around. She'd tell Keefe and then it'd be over.

I can't believe they haven't found Mr. Snuggles already.

I have him very *well hidden. And I think that's more than enough humiliation for me right now. Your turn.*

Sophie's stomach dropped with a thud.

She reached up to tug out an eyelash, trying to think of something that wasn't too embarrassing.

Okay, she transmitted after at least another minute had passed. *But this is a* big *secret. You seriously can't tell anyone, okay?*

Of course, Fitz promised. *Just like I'm counting on you to keep Mr. Snuggles to yourself.*

Sophie smiled. But two more eyelashes were flicked to the floor before she quietly transmitted, *The Black Swan gave me a Spyball.*

Wow. I'm super jealous. I've been begging my dad for one for years. You have it hidden, right?

Yeah. Though she wondered if Sandor knew about it.

Good, Fitz told her. *Because you're right, you could get yourself*

241

another tribunal. All Spyballs have to be registered and monitored to make sure they're not being abused.

I know. I thought about turning it in. But . . . it's the only way I can see my old family. Make sure the rebels aren't doing anything to them to try to get to me.

Do you think they'd do that?

I have no idea. They seem to be willing to do anything.

An image of Silveny's unconscious body filled her mind, and she had to remind herself that there were extra security measures at the Sanctuary now.

And you don't think the Council will protect them? Fitz asked.

Sophie shifted, choosing her answer carefully. *I think the Council underestimates the danger we're in.*

I do too, Fitz admitted. *In fact, sometimes . . .*

Sometimes what? Sophie asked when he didn't finish. *It can be your second secret, if that helps.*

Fitz twisted his fingers, cracking each knuckle before he told her, *Sometimes I wish my dad would resign as an Emissary. I know, it's crazy, right?*

Why is it crazy?

Because it's, like, the most important position anyone can have—besides Councillor.

And one of the most dangerous, Sophie reminded him.

Fitz's head snapped up, and she worried she'd transmitted the wrong thing. But he smiled. *Sometimes I forget how nice it is to talk to you.*

Sophie's face burned, and it was the best kind of warm. Like the steam from a thick cup of hot chocolate wafting against her cheeks.

I mean it, Fitz thought. *I think you might be the only person who really understands how messy our world is getting. Everyone else—even my dad—wants to pretend everything is about to go back to normal.*

But you don't think it will?

I think things are going to get way worse before they get better. Look how many close calls we've already had.

His mind replayed the different plantings he'd been to.

His dad's.

Dex's.

Hers.

It was bizarre to watch her own funeral from someone else's eyes, and Sophie wasn't sure if she wanted to cry or run away or reach out and take Fitz's hand. Especially when he told her, *I stood there and watched your tree sprout out of the ground. Then you came back, but you were so faded it looked like you were going to disappear. And even though I wasn't there for this*—he traced his finger over the star-shaped scar on her hand—*Keefe painted a pretty painful picture of how almost dead you looked. So I want you to know that I'm not going to sit at home anymore, worrying about what might be happening to you, or Keefe, or Biana, or my dad. I'm going to be right there with you guys, helping any way I can.*

Maybe it was the absolute conviction of his words.

Or the warm touch of his hand.

Whatever it was, Sophie softly transmitted, *Okay.*

Fitz let out a breath and leaned back in his chair. *Wow, you agreed to that way easier than I thought you would.*

I know, Sophie told him. *And I'm still tempted to take it back.*

Uh-uh, no takesies backsies—especially after I told you about Mr. Snuggles. But I'll make you a deal. You agree to let me help, and we'll count it as one of your secrets. So that would mean we'd each only have one left.

Getting out of a secret sounded like a pretty good trade—especially since she had a feeling she wouldn't be able to stop Fitz from helping her anyway.

Deal, she told him, smiling as he nodded.

But her smile faded when he told her, *I think you should have to go first this time.*

The only other thing she could think to share was something she didn't even want to admit to herself. But she didn't have anything else.

Okay, here goes, she transmitted, shoving out the words before she could change her mind. *I . . . don't want to know who my biological parents are.*

Wow—you're not even a tiny bit curious?

About the people who gave me up to be some crazy experiment—knowing the kind of danger it would put me in?

Do you think they knew?

How could they not?

244

How could they? Remember, Sophie, before you came along, kidnappings didn't happen.

Maybe. But don't forget, the Black Swan hid me. They wouldn't have done that if they weren't worried about my safety.

Yeah, I guess that's true. Fitz sighed, his fingers absently tracing the Vacker crest on his Foxfire cape—a pair of yellow, diamond-encrusted wings. *But I think I'd still have to know who my parents are. I mean, what if I ran into them and I had no idea?*

Sophie looked away.

You think you know who they are, don't you? Fitz guessed.

I have a few theories—which I'm hoping are wrong.

She let the silence that followed make it clear she wasn't going to share them.

Okay, so I guess that leaves me with one last secret, Fitz thought, letting her off the hook.

And you'd better make it a good one, Sophie added, trying to smile.

Well, I don't know if this counts as good, but back when my dad used to send me places to look for you, I always took a souvenir from everywhere I went. It was just little things no one would notice—and half the time I didn't even know what they were. But I wanted something to remember every Forbidden City and prove I'd been there.

Sophie could see from his memories that he'd taken a crunched soda can from the gutters of New York, a discarded gold coin from the steps outside Buckingham Palace, and a "Lost Dog" flyer from a park in San Francisco, plus all kinds of odds and ends from cities she didn't recognize. She couldn't believe how many places he'd searched for her.

What'd you take the day you met me? she asked.

Nothing. I was so shocked that I'd actually found you that I forgot. Especially since I botched it and scared you away, and then I had to take you to our world to prove I wasn't crazy—which I totally got busted for that night, by the way.

Did you?

Oh yeah. Longest lecture my dad's ever given me. But I knew you wouldn't tell anyone—and you didn't, did you?

Of course not.

See, I knew I could trust you. His brow puckered. *Huh. I guess I've always trusted you—even from the first day.*

I've always trusted you, too, Sophie told him. *Well, once I knew you weren't a serial killer or something.*

They both laughed, and Sophie felt her heartbeat change.

But it wasn't the usual silly flutter.

This time it beat slower, like her heart was settling into the easy comfort of knowing she was with someone who knew her better than anyone else.

Fitz was the first elf she'd met, and the only one who knew what she really gained—and *lost*—the day he found her.

"Whoa," Fitz said, jumping to his feet.

"Is something wrong?" Sophie asked.

"I don't know. Just don't do anything for a second. I need to see something."

His eyes turned all intense, like he was trying to bore inside her brain. It reminded her of Lord Cassius, though maybe a little less creepy.

Fitz laughed. "Keefe's dad does have the creepiest stare, doesn't he?"

"He—" Sophie froze. "I didn't say anything about Keefe's dad."

"I know." Fitz's voice was hushed, but the words still felt like a bomb going off inside Sophie's head. She sucked in a breath, trying not to panic as she thought, *Can you . . . hear me?*

She was careful not to transmit the question, or let her expression give the thought away.

And still, Fitz nodded.

He could read her mind.

TWENTY-NINE

HOW—WHEN—WHY—" SOPHIE STARTED,
not sure which question she wanted to ask
first.

Or maybe she knew.

Can you still hear me?

"Yep!" Fitz said, bouncing on the balls his feet. "Though,
wow, your thoughts are *racing*. I can't make sense of any of
them."

Sophie covered her ears, like it could somehow shield her
mind—which was when she realized she knew a better way to
shield.

"No—don't—" Fitz tried to tell her, but he was too late.
"Ugh, you just blocked me."

"Good." She focused on the invisible wall she'd built around her mind, imagining it as thick and solid as possible.

"I thought you trusted me."

"I *do*. I just . . ."

How could she explain that it was terrifying to have him poking around her brain—especially when he had no problem letting her do the same thing to him?

"I imagine it's rather jarring, given Sophie's upbringing," Tiergan said quietly, reminding them they weren't alone. "We must remember that Sophie didn't grow up in a world of Telepaths, and even now that she's with us, she's gotten rather used to her mind being impenetrable. Can you blame her for panicking?"

"I guess not," Fitz mumbled. But he still looked annoyed.

Tiergan turned to Sophie. "I'll confess, I'd hoped you'd handle the connection a bit differently."

"Wait—you knew Fitz would be able to read my mind? Why didn't you warn me?"

"Because it was only a theory. You'd told me this Mr. Forkle— whoever he is—can slip past your mental blocking. And if the barrier around your consciousness is free of imperfection— which it has to be, otherwise the madness of a broken mind could seep in—there would be no way he could sneak through. So I began to wonder if it's *your* mind that pulls him in, because your mind trusts him."

"But I don't trust Mr. Forkle." Especially not now that she knew the Black Swan had a leak.

"Consciously, that may be true—and with good reason. His preference for subterfuge and disguise hardly instills confidence. But *subconsciously*, I suspect your minds share a mutual trust based on years of close training. Don't you believe that it was Mr. Forkle who planted the Black Swan's secrets carefully within your memories?"

"Yes," Sophie admitted. "But . . ."

She didn't know what she wanted to say. Her mind was still too overloaded with the realization that *Fitz got into her head.*

"So you're saying all Sophie has to do is trust me enough to let me in, and then I can read her mind?" Fitz asked.

"In the simplest of terms, yes," Tiergan told him. "But trust is rarely so simple. That's why I came up with today's exercise. I'd hoped that if you were forced to share things you'd never shared with anyone else, it would trigger an even deeper connection between you two. Obviously it worked. But I'm not sure how easily it can be replicated—especially now that Sophie knows to have her guard up."

Sophie felt her cheeks flush. "Sorry. I guess I shouldn't have freaked out the way I did."

"There's no need to apologize, Sophie," Tiergan assured her. "But I meant what I said about trust being your greatest asset. Letting Fitz into your mind will only make you both stronger during this healing. So I hope you're willing to try the exercise again—and to not shove Fitz away if he does manage to bypass your blocking."

Sophie glanced at Fitz as she nodded, wondering if he was thinking the same thing she was.

He must have been, because he asked Tiergan, "Does that mean we have to share three more secrets?"

Tiergan smiled as he sank back into his chair. "No, I think this time it should be five."

"So what's going on with you and Wonderboy?" Dex asked as soon as Sandor had left them alone. He'd stopped by after school to make sure Sophie was feeling okay. But she wasn't really in the mood for company.

"I saw the way he ignored you in study hall," he pressed as he plopped down beside her. "Something has to be up."

Sophie stared at the elvin history book she was pretending to read.

What was up was that she'd been so busy trying to keep her mind clear of anything embarrassing that she'd barely listened to the secrets Fitz had shared with her. Even now, the only thing she could remember was that he'd put Fart a la Carte in Biana's breakfast before her Level One Opening Ceremonies, and gave her a raging case of stinky gas.

And the secrets she'd shared had been fairly lame. So basically, the entire exercise had been a total failure, and Fitz hadn't talked to her since.

Dex nudged Sophie's elbow, making it clear he wasn't going to let it go. So she closed her book—a little harder than she meant to—and told him, "Fitz was just upset because I freaked out when he got past my blocking and—"

"Wait," Dex interrupted. "He got past your blocking?"

"Yeah. Tiergan had us do this exercise where we had to share all these secrets, and something about the process made my mind pull Fitz past my defenses. Which is cool—but I wasn't expecting it. So I totally freaked out and blocked Fitz again. And then we couldn't re-create it, so now he thinks I don't trust him."

"*Do* you trust him?" Dex asked.

"Of course. It was just super weird having someone in my head. But I have to get over it. Tiergan gave me this long lecture on how crucial it is that I let Fitz in, and I know he's right."

"Why?" Dex asked. "I mean, you're the one with all the superspecial telepathy. What do you need Fitz for?"

"For backup. Plus, my telepathy is strongest when I'm working with him—and his is strongest with me. It's like we have a connection or something."

"A *connection*," Dex repeated.

He shook his head as he walked over to her wall of windows, keeping his eyes focused on the glass. "He's not that special, you know. I could make a gadget that does everything he does. In fact, I could make one that does it better."

"I'm . . . pretty sure you can't," Sophie said gently.

"Why? You don't think I'm talented enough?"

"Of course not. It's just, if someone could invent a telepathy gadget, don't you think they would've done it already?"

"Maybe no one's ever tried."

Sophie actually didn't see why they would. If anyone needed a Telepath for something, they could just *ask a Telepath*.

Luckily she stopped herself from saying that. Dex's ears had turned the same color her elixirs used to turn in alchemy, right before they exploded.

"Listen, Dex. I didn't mean your ability isn't awesome—"

"Not awesome enough, apparently."

"That's not what I meant. There are just some things only a Telepath can do."

"Yeah, well, we'll see about *that*."

"What do you mean?"

He didn't answer as he pulled out his home crystal.

"Are you leaving?"

"Yup." But he didn't sound angry. He even flashed a confident smile as he told her, "I'm going to build you a gadget that does everything Wonderboy can do—and then you'll see which one of us you should trust."

"Oh—I thought Dex was here," Edaline said from the doorway. She held a crystal tray with three extra-thick slices of mallow-melt balanced on it.

Standing behind her was Biana.

"He just left," Sophie told them as they made their way into her bedroom.

Clearly Edaline thought that was strange, but all she said

was, "Well, I guess you'll just have to share his piece, then," and set the tray on the bed.

She left them alone with their snack, and they each grabbed their plates of mallowmelt, letting the gooey sweetness—and the sound of chewing—fill the awkward silence.

"Sorry to drop by out of the blue again," Biana eventually told her. "You left so fast after study hall that I didn't get a chance to ask if you were busy."

"Yeah. Sorry. I kinda just wanted to get out of there."

"I know. So did my brother. You guys must've had quite an interesting telepathy session."

Sophie could feel her blush burn her ears. "So how mad is he?"

"Oh, he wasn't mad. When he's mad, he yells—though I guess you already know that." She stared at her plate, squishing what was left of her cake with her fork. "Today he just seemed . . . disappointed."

"Disappointed," Sophie repeated.

Somehow that felt so much worse than mad.

"Can you tell him I'm sorry?" she asked, but Biana was already shaking her head.

"Uh-uh. I'm *so* not getting in the middle."

"Yeah, that's probably better," Sophie agreed.

Not that there was anything for Biana to be in the middle of—unless she knew something Sophie didn't, which Sophie couldn't exactly ask her.

254

"So what's the deal with Dex?" Biana asked, switching from one awkward subject to another.

Sophie told her about Dex's new invention plan, figuring Biana would think he was as crazy as she did.

Instead she told Sophie, "Aw, just try to go easy on him. He's fighting such an impossible battle." And something about the way she said it made Sophie wonder if she was even referring to the invention.

She cleared her throat. "Anyway, how come you came over? Nothing's changed since the last time you were here."

Well, nothing she was ready to talk about. Her newest Jolie revelations had been carefully tucked away into the *I'm not ready to deal with this* section of her mind.

"I figured, since you hadn't told me anything," Biana told her. "But . . . I did a little searching on my own. I snuck into my dad's office and vanished, so I was there while he did his nightly update with the Council."

Sophie leaned closer, not sure if she should feel excited or guilty about what Biana had done.

"Most of it was boring stuff. Complaints he was getting about tomorrow's healing. Something about Grady not making any progress on the dwarves. But there was one thing I knew I had to tell you. A goblin patrol found some new tracks outside the Sanctuary. They were far away from the gates, and whoever made them was only there briefly. But one of the footprints definitely belonged to an ogre."

THIRTY

SOPHIE HAD WANTED TO HAIL ALDEN,
but Biana wouldn't let her.

They couldn't risk that he'd figure out how
they'd heard about the footprints, and if he did,
they'd never be able to use that trick again. Plus, Biana would
probably be grounded for the rest of eternity.

But Sophie *had* to make sure Silveny was okay.

She lay back on her bed, staring at the crystal stars that
dangled from her ceiling and hoping Master Leto was right
about her abilities. She had no idea how she'd been able to
transmit to Fitz from so far away—she'd operated mostly on
instinct, mixed with a healthy dash of desperation.

But she was feeling pretty desperate right then, so she

hoped that would be enough to create a connection.

Silveny? she called, fueling the transmission with every ounce of fear she could muster. *Can you hear me? I need you to know you're okay. Please, please reply.*

No answer.

She closed her eyes, letting her worries feed off one another until her head buzzed with static-like energy. It hummed and thrummed and hissed and swished until she couldn't bear the noise any longer. Then she shoved it out of her mind, along with another desperate transmission to Silveny. And as she lay there, gasping for breath, her mind filled with the most wonderful sound ever.

Friend?

Yes! Sophie transmitted back, afraid to move or breathe or do anything to sever the connection.

Friend! Sophie! Visit! Treats!

No, I'm not visiting right now—and I can't send you any treats. But I'm so glad you're safe.

Safe! Silveny agreed. She filled Sophie's mind with scenes of her galloping through the violet pastures, and streaking through the rainbow sky with Greyfell at her side.

Sophie couldn't decide what made her happier—knowing Silveny was safe, or seeing her getting along with Greyfell. Either way, she sank into the feeling, letting her mind drift with Silveny's cool, breezy memories.

And for the first time in weeks, she finally slept.

• • •

"Can we talk?" Sophie asked, stopping Fitz on their way to the main Foxfire building.

Fitz glanced at all the prodigies lingering around them. "We should probably talk in my head."

Sophie nodded, opening her mind to his thoughts before she transmitted, *I just wanted to say I'm sorry. I shouldn't have panicked like that.*

No, I'm sorry, too. I still get freaked out sometimes when I let someone into my head—and I'm used to it.

It's definitely weird, Sophie agreed. *But . . . I'm glad you can do it. And I'm going to do my best not to block you the next time it happens.*

Fitz grinned.

So you trust me? she asked softly.

Of course. Do you still trust me?

Probably more than anyone.

So will you at least tell me what you and Biana have been working on, then?

If you really want to know—but it's not as awesome as you think it is.

Fitz insisted he didn't care, so she told him about the leak in the Black Swan and the homing device and the ogre footprints outside the Sanctuary. His brows rose higher with each new detail. But before she got to the part about Jolie, Stina shoved her way between them.

258

"Aw, look at the traitors having their secret conversation," she said, tossing her hair into Sophie's face. "All set to heal a worthless criminal tonight?"

"None of your business," Sophie told her.

"Actually, it's *everyone's* business. And don't think we won't be watching to see what mess you make this time."

She tossed her hair again as she stalked away, and Sophie glanced at the crowd of prodigies still watching them—most of them looking less than supportive.

You sure you want to deal with stuff like this? she transmitted to Fitz.

Oh, I'm definitely in. And nothing's going to go wrong, okay?

There wasn't a hint of doubt in his mind, and Sophie wished she could feel the same. But all she could hear was Fintan's mocking laughter from the last time she'd had to see him.

She could worry about ogres and Black Swan leaks later. Right now she needed to focus on getting them through the healing.

Practice during study hall? she asked Fitz.

He nodded. *See you there. And try not to stress too much until then.*

They both smiled sadly, knowing it was an impossible request.

Fortunately, Lady Veda—Sophie's elementalism Mentor—had her working on something far less dangerous than her usual tornado-bottling fare. She'd placed an etched crystal basin filled with water in the center of the table and showed Sophie how to bottle the ripples that formed when she tapped the water with her fingers. Sophie didn't see the point of collecting such an insignificant amount of force, but when the bells chimed the end of session, Lady Veda held out one of the bottles.

"Never underestimate the power of a small change," she told her, pressing it into Sophie's hand.

She was obviously referring to the healing, but whether she was in favor or against, Sophie couldn't decide. And the rest of her fellow prodigies seemed just as unsure. Stares and whispers trailed Sophie like a shadow, and when she let herself pay attention, she couldn't find a consensus. Some thought she was brave. Others clearly agreed with Stina.

But the majority were simply afraid.

It was so strange having everyone know so much about her assignment. Even her agriculture Mentor—a stocky gnome who insisted on being called Barth the Reaper—had heard about the scandal. And when Sophie walked into study hall, the whole room went quiet.

"All right—nothing to see," Keefe told them, rushing Sophie to a table in the dimmest corner. Fitz was already there, slouching in his chair.

"That Stina girl's been telling people that you're going to do some sort of freaky Inflictor thing on Fitz to prepare, and everyone's waiting to see," Keefe explained. "I'm guessing that's a total lie—but I gotta say, that *would* be awesome."

"Yeah, well it's not happening." Sophie sat, hiding her face behind her hair as she transmitted, *You still want to practice?* to Fitz.

He nodded, and she opened her thoughts to his mind, cringing when she saw his mental turmoil.

Has your day been as weird as mine? he asked. *People are taping notes to my locker saying, "Keep the criminals where they belong" and "Whose side are you on?"*

It's not too late to change your—

"Will you stop worrying?" Keefe asked, waving Sophie's stress vibes away from his face. "Trust me—my boy can handle himself."

"Or you could let me help," Dex said, marching up behind them.

He pulled a slightly-less-than-round silver circlet out of his satchel and set it proudly on the table.

"What is that?" Fitz asked.

"Something I whipped up last night after Sophie and I talked."

He picked up the circlet and slipped it over Sophie's head. It slid down to her ears, covering her eyes and matting her hair against her face.

"Huh, your head must be smaller than mine," Dex said as he spun the circlet so the clear trillion-cut crystals on each side rested over her temples, and tilted it so it wouldn't cover her eyes. "I can tighten it when I get home. The healing's not till this evening, right?"

261

"Right," Sophie told him. "But I'm not wearing this—whatever it is."

She reached up to remove it, but Dex blocked her.

"It'll help enhance all your telepathic abilities!"

"Seriously?" Fitz asked as Keefe snatched the circlet off Sophie's head and said, "Cool—will it tell me what Foster's thinking?"

"No, I only made it enhance existing abilities—so far," Dex told him, taking his creation back.

"What do you mean, 'so far'?" Dame Alina asked, stalking up to their table. She checked her reflection in one of the windows as she asked, "You really think a gadget can affect someone's ability?"

"Why not?" Dex asked.

"I can think of several reasons—but the fact that it's never been done in all our years of history seems to be the strongest argument," Dame Alina replied.

"Maybe no one's cared enough to try," Dex argued.

"Or maybe you're just trying to fix your Talentless dad," someone called, triggering a wave of snickers.

"That's enough of that!" Dame Alina shouted, reeling around to face the rest of her prodigies. "I will not warn you again."

She turned back to Dex. "Mr. Dizznee—put that contraption away and take a seat. And the rest of you'd best spend the rest of this session perfecting the art of silence, or you will give me an opportunity to put some of my newest—and, I daresay, most *ingenious*—punishments into effect. Understood?"

Shuffling paper was the only reply.

"Good," she said, waiting until the circlet was safely out of sight before returning to her desk.

"So you're not going to use my invention?" Dex whispered while pretending to write in his notebook.

Sophie shook her head.

Dex was incredibly talented with gadgets. But she wasn't about to bring an untested piece of technology into an already dangerous situation.

Dex sighed, but didn't say anything, using the rest of study hall to sketch a diagram of the circlet, covered in lines and numbers and all kinds of crazy things Sophie couldn't translate.

Sophie—on the other hand—spent the rest of the time transmitting anything she could remember about Fintan's memory break to Fitz, trying to prepare him for what they would be facing. She'd figured Fitz would want to keep working after school, but when the bells chimed the end of the day he told her he had to go home.

"My dad thinks a big part of his problem last time was how exhausted he was that day," he explained as they made their way to the Leapmaster. "He made me promise I'd take a nap before tonight. I hope that's okay."

"Of course," Sophie said, realizing this had to be just as stressful for Alden as it was for her. Maybe worse, since he probably had even scarier memories of the last Break than she did. "There's not much to practice anyway."

"Then maybe you should rest too," Fitz suggested.

But they both knew that was so not going to happen.

Sophie decided to stay busy and search more of Edaline's office instead.

She had Sandor dig her a trail through the trunks and boxes so she could get to the chests in the back, hoping Edaline would've shoved Jolie's school things as far away as she could. But when she opened the first trunk . . .

. . . books.

Thick, heavy-bound journals filled with Edaline's intricate writing. A quick flip through the pages told Sophie there were probably some interesting stories in there—the words "monitoring the mermaid migration" particularly caught her attention. But she'd have to come back to them later. At the moment, she was a girl on a mission.

The next trunk was filled with what had to be bramble jerseys, and Sophie couldn't resist stopping to count how many different games they represented. Keefe had told her that the elves only had a bramble championship once every three years, and that was when they printed the jerseys. So if all the jerseys belonged to Grady, he was way older than she'd realized—by at least a couple of hundred years.

She couldn't quite wrap her head around that.

The trunks got increasingly boring from then on, some filled with curtains, others with shoes, and there was a particularly stinky one that was currently empty but must've once held some sort of cheese.

Sophie had gotten so used to finding useless things that she'd already closed the next chest before she realized what she'd just seen.

She pulled the lid open again, feeling her heart pick up speed.

Inside were neat rows of textbooks and carefully folded silver uniforms and capes.

All of Jolie's missing Foxfire things.

THIRTY-ONE

DON'T GET YOUR HOPES UP, SOPHIE tried to tell herself as she unpacked the trunk. But that didn't stop her brain from thinking, *THIS HAS TO BE IT!!!*

She scanned every page in each textbook, emptied every pocket and purse, disassembled every picture frame to see if any notes or clues had been tucked into the back. She even read an entire journal of sappy love poems Jolie had written about Brant.

And she found . . . a lot of old, dusty junk that couldn't tell her anything.

"But it *has* to be here," Sophie said, like saying it out loud would somehow make it true. She was running out of places to look.

"Careful," Sandor warned as she tried to pry the mirror out of one of the compacts she'd found in Jolie's purse. "You're going to break that and cut yourself."

"But what if there's a note or something behind it?" Jolie also had a regular compact filled with a shimmering peach powder and a mirror. So why would she need a second compact with nothing inside except two more mirrors?

No one besides Dame Alina was *that* vain.

She tried to dig her fingernails along the sides of the glass, but the mirrors seemed to be welded in. And no matter how many times she pressed on the tiny pearls mounted along the outside, it never triggered a secret latch.

"Sometimes a mirror is just a mirror," Sandor told her.

"Maybe." But something bothered her about the compact.

It took endless minutes of staring at her reflections before she realized what it was.

"I think this side is a human mirror," Sophie said, scooting into better light and checking her Ruewen crest in the reflection.

The letters read backward.

Elvin mirrors didn't invert things the way human mirrors did, which was probably why Sophie's eyes were drawn to the right side. The human mirror looked more like *her*—or the *her* she'd grown up with, at least.

"Why would Jolie have a human mirror?" Sandor asked, taking the compact from Sophie to examine it. He tried to pry the

267

mirror off, but didn't have any better success. "There's no way to remove these without breaking them."

Sophie agreed. Which meant there couldn't be anything hidden behind them. In fact, nothing about the compact seemed related to the Black Swan. There were no runes etched into the silver. The pearls mounted on the outside were definitely not shaped into the sign of the swan. The compact wasn't even black. The enamel on the outside was a pale sky blue.

Sophie sat up straighter.

The Black Swan didn't always use the sign of the swan to identify themselves. Sometimes they'd used a phrase from an old dwarven song.

"Follow the pretty bird across the sky."

"What bird?" Sandor asked—but Sophie was way ahead of him.

She'd thought the pearls on the outside looked like a lopsided *X*. But when she turned the mirror a different way, she recognized the constellation.

"It's Cygnus again," she whispered, tracing her finger over the familiar pattern.

So the mirror *had* come from the Black Swan.

But what was she supposed to do with it?

A mirror was really only useful for one thing. And she didn't understand how reflecting something was going to help.

"Hey, kiddo," Grady said from the doorway, making Sophie almost drop the compact.

She shoved it quickly into her pocket, hoping Grady didn't notice as she told him, "I didn't realize you were home."

"Just got in. I wanted to see you before you left. Plus, the Council wants you to wear these for the healing." He handed Sophie a golden satchel—which was surprisingly heavy. "Fireproof clothes," he explained. "The cloth is woven from flareadon fur and bennu feathers. Both creatures are naturally resistant to fire."

Sophie was tempted to point out that Gildie—the flareadon who'd helped her bottle a sample of the Everblaze—had come back badly singed by the unstoppable flames. But she decided she'd rather not think about it.

It couldn't be a good sign that the Council was preparing for fire.

"It's just a precaution," Grady told her as she made her way upstairs to change. And they really weren't *that* different from her normal clothes. Just far less comfortable.

The tunic and pants were so fitted, she looked like a cheesy superhero. And the enormous cape and knee-high boots didn't help. The whole outfit probably weighed more than she did, and the fabric definitely didn't breathe. She was sweaty and gross within five minutes.

"How's it going?" Grady asked as she sprayed on a thick layer of Stink Shrink, hoping it worked like deodorant. "Tiergan should be here any minute to pick you up."

"You mean 'us,' don't you?" Sandor asked. "Pick *us* up?"

269

"Unfortunately no," Grady said quietly. "Even the Councillors won't have their bodyguards. They're trying to keep the amount of body heat to a minimum."

Sophie shivered under her stuffy clothes.

Last time, Fintan had pulled warmth from Alden's skin and used it to burn them both.

"So their plan," Sandor said bitterly, "is to gather all of their important people in one place and then not give them any goblin protection? Why not coat the whole place with aromark, while they're at it?"

"I thought the same thing, at first," Grady told him. "And I didn't understand why they were moving Fintan out of Exile. But then they told me the healing would be in Oblivimyre."

"What's Oblivimyre?" Sophie asked when Sandor sucked in a breath.

Her insides tangled into more knots than a friendship bracelet when they both whispered, "A place best forgotten."

Cold silence settled over the room, until Sandor raised his head and sniffed the air. "It seems Tiergan has arrived. Excuse me, I have some instructions to give him."

He marched down the stairs, and Sophie hoped Tiergan was prepared for an epic goblin safety lecture.

"You seem calm," Grady said, studying Sophie like he wasn't sure if he believed it.

"So do you," she pointed out.

"Do I?" He held out his hands, showing her they were shaking. "I know Alden and Tiergan will do everything in their power to keep you safe. And Kenric also promised to personally keep an eye on you. But Fintan . . ."

His face creased with lines and shadows. "Do *not* underestimate him, Sophie. The level of evil he's protecting is far worse than you realize. I won't say anything else, because I don't want you to feel any more pressure."

"Uh-uh. You have to tell me," she interrupted.

Grady sighed, his face aging another twenty years as he mumbled, "I suspect Fintan knows who killed Jolie."

Everything in Sophie froze. "What?"

"It's just a theory, of course. But I know her fire wasn't an accident, and it makes sense that it would've been set by a Pyrokinetic."

"And Fintan trained an unregistered Pyrokinetic," she finished for him.

Grady nodded.

"Whoa," she whispered, trying to fit the new idea with the dozens of other tiny bits she'd already pieced together. "Do you think one of my kidnappers was the person who killed Jolie?"

"I think it's very possible," Grady admitted. "And honestly, that would be better. I'm hoping there aren't too many unregistered Pyrokinetics running wild in the shadows."

"Yeah," Sophie mumbled, not sure how to process the revelation.

271

"Hey," Grady said, pulling her close for a hug. "This doesn't change anything, okay?"

Of course it did.

It changed everything.

Now she wasn't just hunting her kidnappers. She was on the verge of solving Jolie's murder.

"I mean it, Sophie. Your number one priority is getting you and Fitz out of there safely. Do *not* take any unnecessary risks trying to find Jolie's killer. Understood?"

"Understood," Sophie repeated.

But she also had a chance to find her kidnapper *and* Jolie's murderer.

Nothing was going to stop her from finally getting to the truth.

THIRTY-TWO

SOPHIE STARED AT THE GLITTERING tower built from brick-size amethysts. "That . . . isn't what I was expecting,"

She'd been to the jeweled city of Eternalia several times over the last year—though never to this section, far from the tree-lined river, where the lone tower stood surrounded by a silver fence. But the shimmering purple walls and the diamond-shaped windows made it look like it should house a princess with ridiculously long hair—not an insane, pyromaniac elf.

And it definitely didn't match the name Oblivimyre.

"Do not let the beauty deceive you," Tiergan warned, his long, heavy cloak—identical to Sophie's—swishing noisily along the crystal path. "This tower is from a different time. Back before the ancient treaties were signed. When we needed to make an example."

He whispered the last word, like it was too horrible to say louder.

"I thought elves hated violence."

"Yes, but violence isn't the only way to instill fear."

She decided to take him at his word, following him silently to the locked silver gate. Thin strands of tinsel were draped over the fence like webs, and when they drew closer Sophie could see tiny prickles and barbs hidden among the sparkles.

A thunderous clang shattered the silence, and the gates whipped open, revealing a dark courtyard filled with leafless trees. A chill seemed to hang in the air as they entered, and after a few steps even Tiergan started to shiver. Sophie pulled her cape tighter as the gates latched behind them with a groan.

"Where is everyone?" Sophie asked, searching the shadows for signs of life.

"Waiting for us inside."

He offered her his hand and Sophie gratefully took it, happy to feel some tiny hint of warmth.

"At least there's no angry mob protesting the healing," she said, trying to stay positive.

"Yes, it appears at least *some* secrets can be kept."

"So do you think that means the leaked information isn't

coming from the Council?" she asked, remembering her theories about Bronte.

"I hope so. Though . . . I'd almost prefer that to the alternative."

"What's the alternative?"

He glanced around like he was afraid someone might be listening. "I shouldn't be distracting you with unnecessary worries."

"Yes, you should."

She locked her knees when he tried to pull her forward, earning herself a sigh as he leaned closer and whispered, "All right, fine. I can think of a race of creatures that are far better at eavesdropping—can't you?"

It took Sophie a minute to piece out what he meant. "The missing dwarves?"

"What do you mean, 'missing'?"

Now it was Sophie's turn to glance over her shoulder. "I guess thirty dwarves have disappeared. Grady's been looking for them, but so far he hasn't found any clue to where they might be."

"You're certain?"

Sophie nodded—not liking the way his grip was tightening on her hand. "But the dwarves are on our side, right?"

"As a whole, yes. But as you well know, that does not mean there can't be deviants among the group."

And dwarves might be small and squinty and rather

molelike, but Sophie had seen them crack the earth with a single well-placed step.

"So what do we do?" she whispered, half expecting thirty dwarves to burst out of the ground and attack.

"Nothing right now—except to shove this far, *far* from your mind and rally your full concentration. Let us not forget that we're here for something much more crucial."

"Right," Sophie agreed, squaring her shoulders as she followed Tiergan through a narrow silver door into the tower.

Once inside, Sophie could see fissures marring each brick—glistening purple veins that made the jewels look ready to shatter. Two glowing chains hung from the ceiling to the floor, providing the only light. Otherwise the room was round and bare and cold.

Beyond cold.

Their breath practically crystallized in the air, and Sophie pulled her hood over her head, grateful the fabric was so thick.

"I th-th-thought you said the o-o-others were here," she said between chattering teeth, searching for a door or a flight of stairs.

"They're above us," Tiergan explained as he grabbed the nearest chain and pulled it toward her. "This will take us to them."

The words would've sounded much better if there weren't a sharp hook dangling from the end that was bigger than Sophie's head. She tried to hold still as Tiergan looped the chain twice around her ankles. But when he latched the hook through a link in the chain, she fidgeted enough to lose her balance.

"Easy," Tiergan said, catching her before she could collapse. "This won't hurt, I promise. The chain will absorb all the force."

Actually, Sophie was much more concerned about the low—and very solid—jeweled ceiling. She'd jumped into whirlpools and launched out of the ocean in a giant bubble and sunk into the middle of the earth through a choking patch of quicksand. Still, she couldn't help worrying this would be the one thing that was simply too impossible to survive.

"Pull the chain three times," Tiergan told her, stepping out of the way.

Part of her was tempted to stand there forever.

But the brave part of her—or perhaps the part that was troublingly insane—wrapped her fingers around the chain and tugged.

The world flipped and her stomach launched into her throat as she passed through something that felt like frozen mashed potatoes. She hadn't even had a chance to scream before she was dangling like a piñata in the center of a bright room with purple walls and a purple floor and lots of staring faces in identical fireproof clothes.

"The girl of the hour arrives," Alden said, grabbing Sophie's shoulders to stop her from swaying. "You okay?"

"Yeah, I'm fine—though next time I'd prefer a tower with stairs."

He smiled. "One somersault will have you back on your feet. Just make sure you flip forward, not backward."

Gymnastics of any kind had never been Sophie's strong suit. So she was grateful she could blame her red cheeks on the head rush as she twisted and squirmed and eventually flipped in a lopsided-tumble to freedom.

Seconds later Tiergan launched through the floor in a shower of amethyst glitter. Sophie watched him somersault effortlessly to his feet, wondering how the ground could feel so solid. But she wasn't about to ask. Not in front of the entire Council. And Fitz. And Alden. And—

"Where's Fintan?" Sophie asked, trying not to sound too relieved that she didn't have to face him yet.

Councillor Emery pointed to the ceiling, which once again looked incredibly solid. The dark-skinned Councillor generally radiated calm and confidence. But his deep voice hid the slightest hint of a tremble as he told her, "He is being kept in absolute-zero conditions until you are prepared to face him."

"The cold won't kill him?" Fitz asked, taking the question right out of Sophie's mouth.

Bronte snorted. "That would be pointless, wouldn't it?"

"What Bronte means"—Councillor Kenric jumped in—"is that Pyrokinetics generate a much higher amount of body heat. And Councillor Terik has been checking on Fintan regularly to make sure he's still conscious—or as conscious as he's capable of being, given his current mental state."

Several of the other Councillors fidgeted at his words. Sophie didn't understand their discomfort, until she remembered that Fintan had been a member of the Council before pyrokinesis became a forbidden ability.

"Perhaps we should get started," Councillor Terik suggested. "We'll all feel much better once this is over, right?"

"Yes," Councillor Emery agreed, turning to Sophie and Fitz. "Only Alden, Tiergan, and Councillors Kenric, Terik, and Oralie will go up with you. The rest will stay here with me—and I'll transmit updates to them from Kenric."

"I still don't understand why Terik is going instead of me," Bronte grumbled. "Need I remind you that this process involves *inflicting*?"

"And need I remind *you* that you have shown your weakness?" Kenric asked him, glancing at Sophie in a way that made her wonder if he was referring to what happened during their session. "Besides, Sophie needs to feel safe and comfortable—two sentiments you certainly don't let her experience when you're around."

"I've done nothing to—" Bronte started, but Councillor Emery held up his hand.

"There will be no further debate on this matter." He waited until Bronte stepped back before he added, "As I was saying, the seven of you will go up to the top floor and begin the healing immediately. Sophie, you and Fitz will stand on either side of Fintan, and Oralie will stand behind you to keep track of your emotions. Alden, Kenric, and Tiergan will monitor the situation telepathically. And Terik will be descrying Fintan, searching his potential for warning signs. We feel this arrangement will be the strongest way to ensure your safety. But if you have any concerns, now is the time to address them."

Sophie had *many* concerns—but nothing was going to fix that. So she went with the only other thought on her mind. "Councillor Kenric's a Telepath?"

"Did I never mention?" Kenric asked with a grin. "That's why I was part of your original committee of three. They wanted an Empath to get a reading on who you were as a person, a Telepath to judge your capabilities, and Councillor Grumpypants because, well, he insisted."

The mood was too tense for anyone to actually laugh. But Sophie did notice a plethora of smiles.

Bronte threw up his hands. "Don't we have a healing to perform?"

"Yes, I suppose Bronte's right," Councillor Emery murmured. "Sophie, do you need a minute to prepare yourself?"

"I do!" Fitz jumped in before she could answer. His face flamed as all eyes turned to him. "It'll be quick, I promise."

Sophie opened her mind to his and found his thoughts on auto-repeat of the code words they'd created:

Alden means there's no reason to worry. Mallowmelt means

she found something. Dame Alina means trouble. The verminion means run away. Everblaze means brain push.

Was there something you needed to talk about? she asked.

I don't know. I'm just starting to get why you're always saying this stuff is so scary. I mean—look at this place. I remember reading about it in Elvin History. The whole tower is a trap, designed to make people go insane.

It's pretty creepy, Sophie agreed.

When he went back to repeating the code words again, she added, *Fitz, if you don't want to do this, I'm sure Tiergan can step in.*

No, I'm fine. I'm sorry. I just . . . I'm scared I'm going to mess something up.

It's going to be okay, Sophie promised, ordering herself to believe it. *Remember, I have a perfect track record with healings.*

Fitz glanced at his father, who looked strong and healthy and very much healed. *Yeah, you're right. Let's do this.*

"I think we're ready," Sophie said, half hoping no one would hear her.

But Alden, Tiergan, Kenric, Oralie, and Terik moved to her side, and the Councillors who were staying behind pulled glowing chains out of the ceiling and started wrapping them around everyone's ankles.

"From this moment on, I want you both to be in *constant* communication with each other," Tiergan told Sophie and Fitz. "Hold nothing back. Check in regularly. And above all else, *trust.*"

281

"We will," Fitz promised, taking Sophie's hand.

They tangled their fingers together, and Sophie took one deep breath for courage. Then the chains dragged them up— too fast and too sharply and way too painfully—into a room so cold, it felt like her blood was freezing.

Everyone toppled out of their chains, collapsing to the icy ground with a chorus of groans. Sophie pulled her hood over her head as she turned to face a hunched figure in the center of the floor.

If she hadn't known who he was, she wouldn't have recognized him.

Pale, papery skin covered his withered, shadowed face, which was crusted with grime and ice. Frozen tears clung to his hair and eyelashes, and his lips were cracked and blue. The only sounds filling the room were his ragged, raspy gasps for air, each one more a death rattle than a breath.

Sophie had spent days questioning the rightness of this healing. But in that moment she *needed* to help him.

You with me? she transmitted as Fitz backed away from Fintan's crumpled figure.

Yeah. Sorry, he thought, forcing himself to move to her side. *What do you need?*

Just stay close—and don't try to open your mind to his until I tell you it's safe.

Oralie took her place between them and placed a soft, fragile hand on each of their shoulders.

"If I feel too much stress or fear I will pull you away," Oralie explained, her voice too sweet and warm for such a cold, miserable place.

But Sophie doubted she would need it.

Her mind was ready.

Her instincts were ready.

All that was left to do was press her fingers against Fintan's swollen temples, and push her mind into his consciousness.

THIRTY-THREE

THE THICK, PIERCING DARKNESS FELT shockingly warm as it stabbed and scraped and smashed. Sophie held her breath, wondering if any madness would break through—but her mental defenses held strong, deflecting each attack like an invisible shield.

Now if only she had any idea what to do.

She'd been planning to search for a trail of warmth and follow it to the nook in Fintan's mind. But there was warmth *everywhere*. A stifling, suffocating fog that slowed her thoughts and blurred all the pathways.

Fintan, she transmitted over and over, but the echoes shredded as they bounced around his jagged mind.

She shoved her way through a cloud of shattered memories, searching each one for a clue to steer her through the chaos. She could see glints of color and shadow, slivers and slices of faces and places—but nothing she could recognize.

Nothing except fire.

Sparks of red and orange and blue and white—each more blinding than the last—swarmed around her, burning hotter, brighter, wilder with each second, until they erupted into neon yellow flames.

Everblaze.

Somewhere in the back of her consciousness Sophie knew she should run away. But the Everblaze traced a glinting path through the endless darkness. She had to follow the trail.

The flames led her deeper, into a pit of pure black heat. The space was empty of memories but thick with the breath of so many emotions, Sophie didn't know which one to feel:

Fear.

Pride.

Regret.

Envy.

Triumph.

Sadness.

Hopelessness.

And rage.

So much rage.

It burned hotter than the other emotions—hotter than the Everblaze.

Boiling and bubbling and consuming everything.

Every thought.

Every memory.

Every glint of light and hope and reason.

Leaving her empty.

Except for the rage.

The rage was her power. Her force. Her fire to unleash on the world, to stop the—

Sharp jostling pulled her out of the frenzy, and Sophie realized Oralie and Fitz were shaking her shoulders.

Sorry, she transmitted, concentrating on Fitz's thoughts.

His worry was so thick she could feel it tangling around her.

We've been trying to wake you up for a really long time, he told her.

Really? I don't know what happened. I followed the warmth like I always do. But I ended up in a very dark place.

Is it something I could help with?

Not yet. His mind is still too broken.

And you're sure you can handle it? It's not worth risking your sanity, Sophie.

Actually, it was.

This was her chance to find the rebels—and Jolie's killer.

She wasn't giving up that easily.

I know what to expect this time. And I'll let you know if I need you, she promised.

No—you'll let me know when he's healed and it's safe for me to join you, whether you think you need me or not, he corrected.

Fine, she told him, feeling her lips smile.

She gave herself three slow, deep breaths to steady her nerves. Then she channeled her mental energy back into Fintan's mind.

The heat felt stronger this time, like standing in the middle of a fire. But Sophie rallied her concentration and pushed through the fog of splinters, deep into the center of his consciousness. She could go anywhere from there, and every path looked the same. But she had a plan this time. A trick she'd forgotten about earlier.

Inflicting.

She doubted Fintan would respond to love or joy or peace. But she could feed him pride and triumph, and hope it drew him back. So she inflicted the victory of every A she'd earned in school, and the confidence from every compliment she'd ever been paid.

The positive energy hummed through the darkness, a deep rumble that seemed to build with each infliction, parting the sea of shredded memories and creating a new path.

Sophie followed it slowly, watching for signs of another trap. But the way was clear. And when she reached the end of the trail, she found the nook she'd been searching for.

She transmitted Fintan's name again, begging him to find her—and when there was still no reply she went back to inflicting.

She shared more triumphs, more celebrations, and the sweet relief of forgiveness. But nothing seemed to reach him—until she realized she'd been overlooking his greatest passion. The triumph that had defined him and ruined him in the same instant.

Everblaze.

She drew on the wonder and power she'd felt when she faced down a fire line of the neon yellow flames, letting the energy swell into a force before she shoved it into Fintan's mind.

Something started to stir, and she used the momentum, drawing on her memories of the heat and the smoke.

Each emotion she inflicted made the fog around her shift, until it swirled into a storm that showered her with splintered memories.

But still, no sign of Fintan.

Unsure what to do, she drew on the only other emotion she could think of—the strongest reaction she'd felt when she faced the unstoppable flames.

Fear.

She relived every panicked second of that day, letting the terror swell inside her mind until she thought she might burst from the pressure. Then she called for Fintan one last time and blasted him with the energy, gasping when it melted the darkness and set fire to the rain of memories.

Somewhere among the flames, Fintan's deep voice whispered through the smoke.

I knew you'd come back for me, Sophie. And now everyone will pay.

THIRTY-FOUR

WHAT'S WRONG?" SOMEONE shouted as Sophie jerked backward, shivering and flailing in someone's icy grip. It took her a second to realize it was Fitz.

"He was waiting for me," she whispered, glancing behind her, expecting Fintan to spring up and attack.

He was still unconscious on the floor.

"I don't understand." She tried to pull away from Fitz, but her legs weren't ready. "I—He . . ."

"You're safe," Fitz promised. "He's not even awake."

"But he should be. I brought him back and it was like he'd been waiting for me. He told me everyone was going to pay."

"Are you sure it wasn't a memory?" Tiergan asked, moving to Fintan's side.

He lifted one of Fintan's arms and dropped it, letting it fall to the floor with an icy crunch.

"He hasn't moved this whole time," Kenric added. "I was watching him closely, and nothing changed until you started screaming."

"And I felt only the slightest shift in his mood," Oralie added quietly.

"Hmm." Tiergan closed his eyes and reached for Fintan's temples, and . . .

. . . ripped his hands away as fast as he could.

"I *can* see his memories piecing themselves back together," he told them, shaking his head—hard. "But his mind is *very* overwhelming."

"How so?" Alden asked, reaching for Fintan's temples.

Tiergan grabbed his hands to stop him. "I wouldn't recommend it. Especially given your past experiences."

Alden looked torn for a second. Then slowly dropped his hands to his sides. "Well, his mind was devastatingly shattered in the break. Perhaps it's taking him longer to recover?"

"Then why was he able to threaten me?" Sophie asked.

Tiergan lifted Fintan's eyelids before he answered. "I'm not sure if it really was *him*. You said he seemed very prepared for the memory break before you performed it, right?"

Alden and Sophie both nodded.

"Well, then perhaps he built in certain defense mechanisms, and you inadvertently triggered one."

"Then . . . it's safe to search his memories?" Sophie asked, cursing herself for falling for a cheap trick.

"I'm not sure *safe* is the right word," Alden said, running his hands through his hair. "Perhaps we should give it a bit more time?"

"But what if that was his plan?" Sophie argued. "What if he left that message to frighten me away so he'd have time to destroy important memories?"

"I don't know if the mind truly works that way," Kenric said, taking Alden's place at Fintan's side. "But let's see . . ."

He pressed his fingers against Fintan's forehead, gritting his teeth and sucking in sharp breaths until he finally stumbled back.

"Wow," he whispered, wiping his sweaty brow with his sleeve. "His mind is a *maze*. I can't . . ."

He groaned and rubbed his temples.

Oralie rushed to his side, tracing one soft finger across the crease puckering his brow.

"Thanks," he whispered, sighing as he pressed his face into her palm. "You always make everything better."

Oralie smiled, gently cradling his head, before they both seemed to realize they weren't alone.

"Sorry," Kenric mumbled, clearing his throat. He straightened up as he told them, "I've never entered a mind so twisted before. I don't know how you lasted so long in there, Sophie."

"It wasn't fun," she admitted, though she hadn't noticed that the mind was a maze. Had it shifted since she'd been in there?

"I have to go back," she decided, moving toward Fintan.

"Not without me," Fitz insisted. "He's healed now, right?"

"I don't know what he is," Tiergan admitted. "You saw how he affected Kenric."

"Yes, but Kenric's a big softie," Councillor Terik teased. "Every time we take a vote, we can count on Kenric to vote for mercy."

"That's why I'm everyone's favorite. Well, *second* favorite. Empaths always win."

Oralie blushed.

"I'm sure I can handle it," Fitz insisted.

"And I applaud your bravery, son," Alden told him, "I also understand your urgency, Sophie. But haste is never a wise course."

"Neither is wasting time and overthinking things," Sophie argued.

"If it helps, I'm not picking up any potential for danger," Councillor Terik offered.

"Actually, I find that rather more upsetting," Alden told him.

"So do I," Tiergan agreed.

"Me too," Kenric added.

"Are you doubting my abilities?" Councillor Terik's tone was light—but there was a definite edge of annoyance.

Oralie made her way over to Fintan, tracing her fingertips across his forehead. "He's feeling everything and nothing all at once. Surely that could confuse your descrying."

"Perhaps," Councillor Terik reluctantly agreed.

"It doesn't matter," Sophie jumped in. "We all knew this was going to be dangerous. I still have to try."

"I think you mean *we*," Fitz corrected. "*We* have to try."

Sophie sighed. "Fitz—"

"Who thinks Sophie should go back into the crazy mind-maze without a guide?" Fitz interrupted, looking to see if anyone would raise their hand.

Alden looked the most tempted—though Councillor Terik was a surprisingly close second.

But no one did.

"If something happens—" Sophie tried.

"What if something happens to you?" Fitz argued. "I can't sit here uselessly anymore. You trust me, don't you?"

"I do, but . . ."

"You either trust me or you don't."

She really wished there were a Secret Answer Number Three that would keep Fitz safe.

But she knew he was right—and she probably *was* going to need him.

Get ready, she told him. *We're going in.*

Okay, this is way creepier than I thought it would be, Fitz admitted, trying to keep up as Sophie raced through the web of eerie flashing memories.

Kenric had definitely been right about Fintan's mind being a maze. Every turn they made only led to more paths of blaring, mismatched scenes—flickering like living projections—and Sophie quickly lost all track of which way was up or down or where they were supposed to be.

Is this how it was last time with my dad? Fitz asked as they backtracked from yet another dead end.

It was still overwhelming. But not so . . . calculated.

During Fintan's memory break, his mind had been a raging river, flooding too fast for her to make sense of most of what she saw. But the maze was slow and deliberate, as if Fintan—however conscious he was—was specifically choosing what he would and wouldn't let them see. He was stalling them, buying himself time, and Sophie didn't want to be there when he was finally ready to face them.

Do you think Everblaze would help? Fitz asked.

Why would I want to . . . her transmission stopped when she realized Fitz meant their code word.

I don't think it would. A brain push needed to have a reason or a direction.

But the thought did give her another idea. . . .

I'm going to try something I never made up a code word for, she transmitted.

Great—because that's not terrifying.

Sorry.

She'd totally overlooked her inflicting ability when they

made up their list, and she was starting to think emotion might be the key.

Every memory would be linked to both thoughts *and* feelings. So if she could inflict the right emotion into Fintan's mind, it might lead them to all the related memories attached to the same emotion.

She had no idea if that was actually possible. But it was the only plan she could think of.

She replayed the partial memory she recovered the last time, focusing on the way Fintan had looked as he watched his unknown, unregistered prodigy call down Everblaze from the sky. His lips were curled with a smile—but not a happy smile.

A *proud* smile.

You ready? she transmitted to Fitz.

I guess. Let's hope this turns out to be Alden.

She was thinking the same thing—though she felt many reasons to worry.

Still, she focused on the day she'd found out she'd passed all her Level Two midterms, after struggling so hard with some of the tests. A warm rush of pride blossomed inside her head, and she coddled it, nurtured it, fed it bits of other proud moments until she'd built up enough force to blast it out of her mind.

What on earth is that? Fitz asked as the warmth rushed past them, swirling through the maze of images and turning down a new path.

Sophie chased the warm trail, weaving and dipping and climbing and dropping until they reached a row of images that seemed almost connected.

A younger, kinder Fintan bowed and accepted his Councillor's crown.

A somewhat older, more serious Fintan stopped the firestorm of an erupting volcano and saved a large family of apatosaurs.

A mishmash of smiling people he'd helped—both human and elvin.

Glimpses of places he'd visited and struggles he'd braved.

He used to be a good person, Sophie thought quietly.

But this was all before pyrokinesis was banned, Fitz reminded her.

He was right. In fact, most of the scenes looked ancient—and many of them involved fire. But there was a distinct lack of glowing neon yellow.

Do you see any Everblaze? Sophie transmitted, wondering if her eyes were missing something.

Everblaze Everblaze? Or code word Everblaze? Fitz asked.

Everblaze Everblaze, Sophie clarified, wishing she'd picked a less confusing code word. *I don't see any in these memories, do you?*

No, he thought after a second. *Is that bad?*

It just doesn't make sense. The way Fintan had talked about Everblaze when she'd met him—it was like he'd been talking about his deepest love. His greatest creation.

But his creation had killed five of his friends and gotten his ability banned . . .

I think we're looking in the wrong place.

Maybe she'd gotten mushy after seeing all the good things Fintan had done. But she couldn't help wondering if the memory they needed was tucked away with Fintan's regrets.

Sophie tried to remember moments when she'd felt the right kind of shame. She'd tripped or fallen or humiliated herself thousands of different ways—and of course there were her numerous medical disasters. The Great Cape Destruction had also been pretty epic.

But none of those carried the kind of regret and remorse like the time she'd cheated on her alchemy midterm.

She drew on her shame and sadness—mixed with a dash of guilt and embarrassment—and let it stew and simmer until she felt like she was back in Dame Alina's office, facing the consequences of her actions. The feeling was equal parts hot and cold and Sophie let herself drown in it, until the force was strong enough to blast out of her mind.

She raced through the trail it blazed, spiraling down and down and down some more, until the light was gone and all that was left was her, and Fitz, and a wall of fragmented memories—many blazing with unstoppable flames.

You'll never find what you're looking for, Fintan's mind shouted. But Sophie knew he was too late.

Mallowmelt, she told Fitz, using the code word to stop him from retreating away.

She'd definitely found something good. In fact, she'd found the exact memory they needed.

Please, please, please, Sophie thought as she watched the familiar scene replay.

The memory started earlier this time, and she stared through Fintan's eyes as he stood behind an elf in long red robes and pointed up to the night sky—to one star that seemed to burn brighter than the others.

Turn around, Sophie begged as the elf murmured something to the stars.

She couldn't understand the words.

But she *knew* that voice.

The hollow, empty tone had been etched into her brain the day her kidnapper had dragged her out of her drugged haze and burned her wrists for not answering his questions.

This was it. The clue she'd been waiting for.

All she needed was for him to turn around and show his face.

Turn around. Turn around. Turn around.

The figure stretched his palm toward the sky, curling his fingers, still whispering something Sophie couldn't understand.

Turnaroundturnaroundturnaround.

Instead, the memory sputtered to a halt, like Fintan had just hit pause.

No you don't, Sophie transmitted, focusing harder, trying to push through whatever barrier Fintan had just made.

His mind fought back, and no matter how many times she lunged for the memory, Fintan kept shoving her away.

Everblaze, Sophie warned Fitz, concentrating on the humming energy in the back of her mind and blasting it at the guarded memory.

The brain push broke through, whirling the scene back to life—but it was blurry now. She could barely make out pale skin and dark hair—not enough to identify him. But hopefully another brain push would clear away the rest of the fog.

The memory sped up as Sophie tried to focus on the energy left in her head, and by the time she called *Everblaze* again, the scene had skipped to the moment the neon yellow flames erupted, burning wilder than the last time she'd watched the memory.

Not just a ball of flame.

An inferno.

And so we begin, Fintan told her as she pushed at the memory from every side, trying to catch a different view of her kidnapper's face through the smoke.

Everblaze, Fitz transmitted.

But Sophie had nothing left to give. Her mind was too drained, and she could barely think through the heat and the blinding flames that seemed to be consuming the memory from the outside in.

His identity dies with me, Fintan told her.

Everblaze! Everblaze! EVERBLAZE! Fitz screamed.

It was only when he added *VERMINION!!!* to the mix that she realized he might not be using the code.

She pulled her mind free, dragging Fitz in her wake, and opened her eyes to the nightmare he'd been trying to save her from. Bright yellow sparks rained from the ceiling, merging with the flames that were no longer just in her mind.

An unstoppable wall of Everblaze.

THIRTY-FIVE

*T*HE FLAMES ARE REAL.

It was Sophie's only thought as Fitz yanked her and Oralie away from the neon yellow inferno that had erupted before them.

The jeweled floor cracked beneath their feet and Sophie pulled her hood over her head, trying to shield her skin from the heat as much as possible. "Where's everyone else?" she managed to shout between coughs from the thick smoke.

Oralie pointed a trembling arm toward the raging Everblaze.

"No!" Fitz screamed. "No! No! NO!"

He ran toward the flames and Sophie barely managed to grab his arm in time.

"The clothes won't protect you," she warned him. "Everblaze

burns *everything*." Even without direct contact, they could only last a few more minutes in the firestorm.

"But my father—"

"Is finding his own way out."

She promised herself the words were true as she squinted at the fire, searching for any sign of life. All she could see was smoke and flame.

Oralie screamed and Sophie spun toward her, finding her thrashing in pain, her shoulder covered in a splotch of liquid amethyst.

"The jewels are melting!" Fitz shouted between coughs, pointing to the walls, which were starting to bubble like boiling sugar. "This whole place is going to collapse."

Another crack split the floor and Sophie grabbed his and Oralie's hands, dragging them toward what used to be one of the windows—but was now a hole, dripping with bubbling jewel.

Please let us fit, Sophie begged as she charged full speed, pulling Fitz and Oralie as close to her as possible.

She didn't have time to think or scream as they charged through the gap and plummeted toward the ground—which was now a flaming lake of molten jewel. Sophie closed her eyes, trusting her instincts, and . . .

. . . heard the thunderous clap as they crashed through a crack into the void.

"Where should we go?" Sophie asked—hacking and coughing as the smoke-free air hit her scorched lungs.

Fitz and Oralie were too busy doing the same, but she realized there was really only one place they'd want her to take them.

She pictured Oblivimyre in her mind, concentrating on the shadowy field she'd seen a safe distance away as a crack split the air in front of them and they launched back to the raging Everblaze.

They tumbled across the grass and Sophie was glad she'd picked an arrival point farther away. The flames had already spread to the bare trees along the glittering crystal path. Any minute now the fire would advance beyond the silver fence.

"Dad!" Fitz shouted, running toward what was left of the tower. Oralie raced after him, calling for Kenric and Tiergan and the rest of the Councillors.

But Sophie couldn't find her voice.

She couldn't find her brain.

Everything was shutting down, and she wanted to close her eyes and cover her ears and wish it all away.

"I found them!" Fitz shouted, and Sophie could suddenly move again.

She chased the sound, ducking flying sparks and jumping over sparkly purple puddles until she spotted a cluster of heavy-cloaked figures.

Alden raced to meet both of them and they crashed into his arms, nearly knocking everyone over as the sobs Sophie had been fighting burst free.

"Thank goodness," Alden said, his voice thick with tears of his own. "The flames tore me away from you, and when I tried to go back in I couldn't get through the blaze."

"How did you get away?" Fitz asked him.

"Light leaping—Tiergan's idea. He was the only one thinking clearly."

"So he's okay?" Sophie asked.

"Yes, Tiergan is safe, but you'll have to see him later. I'm so sorry to ask this of you, Sophie, but we need quintessence. As fast as you can get it."

They must be planning to make frissyn—the only substance that could extinguish the Everblaze—which needed a healthy dose of the rare fifth element. She was surprised they didn't have any already made.

"I'll need a stellarscope," Sophie reminded him, smearing away her tears.

Alden nodded, leading her and Fitz to where the others were already working. "Councillor Liora is a Conjurer."

"Where's everyone else?" Sophie asked, realizing there were far fewer people than there should've been. She was glad to see Tiergan and Councillor Terik among them—but what about Kenric and Councillor Emery and all the other Councillors?

"They're working to gather the rest of the ingredients for the frissyn," Alden explained as a Councillor with bronze-colored skin rushed over. She snapped her fingers—making Sophie realize she must be Councillor Liora—and a stellarscope appeared in her hands.

"We need two dozen," she told Sophie, snapping her fingers again to conjure up a satchel filled with twenty-four small empty bottles.

Alden tightened his grip on Sophie's shoulder. "You need to be *very* careful when you transport the bottles back. That's enough quintessence to take out a few hundred miles."

"Great," Sophie mumbled, grabbing the stellarscope. "Wait—what do you mean transport?"

He pulled his pathfinder out of his pocket and gave it to Fitz. "There's too much smoke here blocking the stars. I've set the path to Siren Rock. Hail me before you leap back."

"I know which facet will take us here," Fitz said, shouldering the bag of tiny bottles as he reached for Sophie's hand.

"Yes, I know," Alden said sadly. "But you'll need to make sure it's safe to return. The Everblaze has caught the wind and is heading toward the river. By the time you've bottled the quintessence, this whole city could be up in flames."

THIRTY-SIX

WARM SALTY WIND PRICKLED their noses as Sophie and Fitz reappeared on a long stretch of pristine beach. The waves glowed with swirls of pink and green, but it felt wrong to be somewhere safe and breathtaking while the world was burning.

"How did this happen?" Fitz asked quietly. "I didn't even feel Fintan move. How could he have called down Everblaze?"

Sophie didn't have an answer.

"We should get started," she said, tucking the stellarscope under her arm and reaching for the first glass bottle. She didn't realize she was shaking until the bottle slipped from her hands, landing with a soft thud in the silky white sand.

"Hey," Fitz said, catching the scope as she nearly dropped it, too. "You okay?"

"I'm fine."

But she could hear the tears rising in her throat, and now that she felt them, she couldn't hold them back.

Fitz pulled her close, letting her cry on his shoulder as he whispered, "Everything's going to be okay."

"Is it?" She wiped her runny nose on her smoky, singed sleeve. "Do you think everyone got out in time?"

"I don't think my dad would've kept that from us, do you?"

"I guess not."

But they both knew Alden was very good at hiding things.

"I'm sorry I wouldn't let you search for your dad," she whispered.

"You mean when I wanted to run into the fire like an idiot?" His chest heaved with a sigh. "Thank you for stopping me. And um . . . thanks for saving my life. I was way too panicked to figure out how to get out of there."

"Yeah, well you saved me first. I had no idea the Everblaze was burning. If you hadn't pulled me back, I doubt I would've gotten out of there in time."

"I guess this proves we make a good team."

A stretch of silence passed before he whispered, "Do you really think Eternalia is going to burn?"

"Not if I can help it."

She pulled away and grabbed the stellarscope, remembering

why they were there. A tiny spout protruded from the narrow end of the scope, and she attached a bottle and hefted the heavy gadget up to her eye.

"Which star do you need to find?" Fitz asked, lining up the other bottles on the sand.

"Elementine is one of the unmapped stars." She could only find it because of the Black Swan's carefully planted secrets.

She searched the sky for the six stars her Universe assignment had taught her to look for. The list had actually been prepared by the Black Swan as a clue, and when she connected the dots between the stars, the lines pointed to an empty space, where Elementine was hidden by the darkness.

"Wait," Fitz said, removing his cape. He tore off two long shreds from the end and handed them to her. "Elwin still talks about how bad the burns on your hands were."

Sophie could definitely remember the pain—though the yeti pee balm he'd used to treat the injuries had probably been the worst part of the experience.

She handed Fitz the stellarscope and tied the strips around her hands like bandages. The thick fabric should keep her skin protected, but it also made her grip super slippery.

"Here," Fitz said, tying up his own hands with more cape shreds and moving behind her. He cupped his mummy palms under hers, cradling the scope from underneath. "Is that better? Or is this weird?"

"It's not weird," she promised, surprised to realize she meant it.

It *had* felt weird when she'd stood in a nearly identical position with Dex a few months back. But it was different with Fitz.

"So which way are we looking?" Fitz asked, resting his arms on Sophie's shoulders.

Sophie squinted through the viewfinder, tracing the trails through the stars until she focused on a patch of darkness.

She could tell Fitz was skeptical as she adjusted the knobs—and then adjusted them again. And again. But when she flipped the switch, thick silvery starlight streaked from the sky—knocking them both backward as it crashed into the scope.

"Is it supposed to be freezing?" Fitz asked as he carefully removed the sealed bottle.

"That's how it was last time. Only the scope gets hot." White hot, actually. She adjusted her grip, relieved to feel only a hint of warmth seeping through her makeshift gloves as she screwed on the next empty bottle.

Fitz nestled the quintessence in the sand, making sure it couldn't tip over.

They worked through the majority of the bottles just as quickly. But the strain of the concentration gave Sophie a headache, and by the time they reached the final five, she could barely see straight.

"Can I help?" Fitz asked as she rubbed her blurry eyes. "If you tell me how to find Elementine, I should be able to do the rest."

"It's not really something I can tell. You have to know what to look for, otherwise you'll never find it."

"Okay, then can you *show* me? Transmit your memories of everything you look at when you're finding it—I'm sure I'll be able to figure it out from there."

Sophie wasn't convinced that would work, but her raging headache insisted she try it. She handed Fitz the stellarscope and they traded places—which felt way more awkward given their height difference.

"I think you're shorter than Biana," Fitz teased as she stood on her tiptoes so she could see the sky over his shoulders.

"She always wears heels."

"I guess that is sort of cheating," Fitz agreed. "You ready?"

"One second."

She opened her mind to his, then realized she'd forgotten to ask his permission beforehand.

Fitz shrugged as she apologized, his shoulder blade nearly clipping her nose. *I don't mind having you know what I'm thinking, Sophie. I trust you.*

Her cheeks turned warm. *I trust you, too.*

Then send me those images and let's finish this.

Right.

She tried to transmit the memories, but sending images took more energy than she'd expected. And with her mind already so tired, she couldn't seem to find enough force.

But she could feel a hint of brain push energy tucked deep in the back of her mind, and when she mixed it with what was left of her concentration, she was finally able to

310

shove the memories into Fitz's head.

"Wow, that was crazy. I think you sent me *all* of your memories of the stars."

"Did I?"

She checked his thoughts and sure enough, his mind was struggling to process a never-ending stream of star maps.

"Oh—sorry!"

"Are you kidding? I'll never have to study for the Universe again!"

It did take a couple of minutes for him to find the information he needed—precious time they couldn't spare. But once he found it, he bottled the quintessence on the first try.

"I can see why you have a headache," he told her as she changed out the bottle for him. "I feel like my brain started to stretch as I concentrated."

Still, he bottled the last four just as quickly, and a few minutes later they had all the quintessence wrapped in shredded cape and loaded carefully into the bag.

"I'll hail Alden," Sophie said as Fitz pulled out the pathfinder and spun the crystal.

Alden didn't answer.

She told herself he was just busy, and that everything was going to be okay.

But when they finally leaped to the outskirts of Eternalia, they found the glittering city burning wildly with Everblaze.

THIRTY-SEVEN

SOPHIE AND FITZ SPRINTED TOWARD the city, weaving around rivers of melted-jewel lava. Dozens of buildings had already oozed away—with more catching fire every second—and Sophie sent a silent plea into the night, hoping no one was inside.

"We have to find my dad!" Fitz yelled as Sophie stopped and pressed her hands to her head.

"I know. I'm trying to track him."

Her mind could trace the sound of someone's thoughts to their exact location. But she was having a hard time concentrating, between the heat and the crackling and the pound-pound-pounding of her heart. She wished she could take a deep breath to clear her throbbing head. But the smoke was too thick and bitter, so she closed her eyes and forced herself to tune out everything except the voice she needed to find.

For several seconds she couldn't hear anything. Then Tiergan's panicked, overwhelmed thoughts filled her mind.

"They're by the river!" she shouted, cradling the bottles of quintessence as she took off downstream with Fitz right behind her.

Everything burned—her chest, her legs, her eyes—but she pushed herself to move faster, wanting to cry with relief when she spotted what looked like a makeshift lab, complete with glowing beakers and test tubes and some sort of bubbling cauldron. Standing next to a white-robed figure was a blissfully familiar face.

"Tiergan!" Sophie shouted, doubling her speed.

He ran toward her once he spotted her, and even though she knew he wasn't a hugger—and she was carrying a large bag of very explosive bottles—she threw her arms around him, clinging to him in the eerie, flickering light.

"Where's my father?" Fitz asked between wheezing breaths.

"He's safe. He went with Lady Galvin to collect the only other ingredient we need for the frissyn. She's been giving us a long lecture on how we should've kept some in reserve after last time."

"She's right," Sophie said, surprised she actually agreed with her evil ex–alchemy instructor about anything.

"I know." Tiergan took the bag of quintessence from her

and led them back toward the lab. "I'll have Kesler start prepping this."

"Kesler's here?" Sophie asked, wondering if that meant Dex was as well.

"Every alchemist we could find is here. Plus a fleet of gnomes who volunteered to help us distribute the frissyn. The fire should be out quickly once we have what we need."

Sophie hoped he was right. And she felt better handing the quintessence over to Kesler and seeing him immediately add some to the cauldron. He also assured her that Dex was home safe.

Still, it was agonizing to stand there, watching the beautiful jeweled city melt in the flames, while Kesler stirred beakers and measured liquids and they waited waited waited.

Fitz had worn a groove into the ground from his pacing when Alden's familiar voice called, "Thank goodness you're both back!" and Sophie and Fitz ran to tackle him.

"I was so worried about you," Alden told them, hugging so tight Sophie couldn't breathe—but maybe that was a good thing.

"Ugh—why do you stink?" Fitz asked, leaning back as far as Alden would let him.

"Sasquatch saliva was the last ingredient we needed."

"But we got it," a sharp voice said behind him, making them realize Alden hadn't returned alone.

Lady Galvin—who looked less terrifying than usual with

green sasquatch fur sticking out of her bun—held up a large flask filled with cloudy yellow liquid. Even though it had a cork, Sophie could smell the rancid stench radiating from it.

"I'm assuming you collected the quintessence?" she asked Sophie, stalking over to Kesler and examining his cauldron. "It looks like you managed to do it without anything exploding, either. Well done. Now we can finally clean up this mess."

Everyone cheered when they finished brewing the first batch of frissyn—which turned out to be a shimmering silver powder. But Sophie didn't feel like celebrating as she watched a group of gnomes set to work dusting the first line of flames. All she could see was the destruction all around her. And she knew none of it would've happened if she hadn't healed Fintan.

She closed her eyes and let the truth nestle deep into her brain.

She needed to face it.

Accept it.

Own up to the reality.

Partially for her own sanity—but mostly because there would surely be backlash when the news hit the public.

"You two have had a very long night," Alden said, joining Sophie and Fitz on the hill where they'd been watching. "I think it's time we go home, don't you?"

"Do Grady and Edaline know about the Everblaze?" Sophie asked.

"Not yet. I didn't think it would be wise to involve them until the fires were contained. But now . . . there is much to explain."

Sophie met his eyes, realizing there was a deeper emotion hiding behind the stress and exhaustion and worry.

Grief.

"Everything's okay, right?" she asked quietly. "Nobody was . . . ?"

She couldn't say it.

Hated even having to think it.

"We'll talk in the morning," Alden told her, offering her a hand.

"No—you have to tell me what happened. I can't . . ." A lump lodged in her throat, threatening to choke her. "If someone was hurt, I need to know."

Alden's lips formed one word—but at the last second he changed it to, "I really think you should rest before we talk about this."

"Like I'll be able to sleep *now*."

"She's right, Dad," Fitz agreed.

Alden looked about a thousand years old as he sat down between them and buried his face in his hands. "I don't know how to tell you this."

The words seemed to swallow the air around them.

Alden had told Sophie she'd be facing a tribunal, and that she had to go to Exile, and that she had to leave her human family and have her whole life erased.

What could be worse than that?

And then she knew.

"Someone's dead," she said quietly, as her mind ran through a list of names and faces.

It was hard to remember who she'd seen safe and who she hadn't—but as she played the night back she realized someone was missing.

Fitz reached for her hand, squeezing so hard it probably would've hurt if Sophie hadn't already turned numb.

Still, she felt a million needles press into her heart when Alden swallowed back a sob and said, "Actually, it was two people. Both Fintan and Councillor Kenric never made it out of the tower."

THIRTY-EIGHT

N O," SOPHIE SAID, JERKING AWAY from Fitz. "Not Kenric."

There had to be a mistake.

She raced down the hill, promising herself that she would find a smiling Kenric standing with the cluster of figures in the distance.

Instead she found the rest of the Councillors gathered around a sobbing Oralie.

"No!" Sophie shouted, spinning around to head to Oblivimyre.

The ground felt slippery as she ran, but Sophie pushed forward, ordering her legs not to trip.

Everything would be better once she got there. She'd find

a secret compartment he'd hidden in, or a clue to where he'd leaped to, or . . .

She screeched to a halt when she realized the slick ground was purple.

A few feet away, a lone silver fencepost stuck out of the sea of melted jewel—all that remained of Oblivimyre.

"No," she cried again, dropping to her knees.

"I'm sorry," Alden said behind her, placing a gentle hand on her trembling shoulder. "I'm so, so sorry."

She didn't even know Kenric that well. But he'd always been kind—and was always the first to take her side. She couldn't imagine the Council without him.

"He can't really be gone," she whispered, feeling hot tears streak down her face.

Alden pulled her close, his body shaking harder than hers as he told her, "I'm afraid he is. Kenric charged Fintan when the room started raining Everblaze. He managed to shove you, Fitz, and Oralie away, but then Fintan's body exploded with flames. There was nothing we could do. I—"

His voice broke, and he needed several deep breaths before he could speak again.

"We're going to have to be brave, Sophie. I'm sorry to ask that of you, but Kenric's loss is going to be deeply, *deeply* felt by our citizens. People are going to need to see that everything is going to be okay."

"But it's not!" she yelled, backing away from him.

The loss was too huge this time.

They'd lost a *Councillor*.

A hole opened inside of her as she thought of how many people had told her not to do the healing.

"I should've listened," she whispered, barely able to breathe. "It's my fault."

"If it's anyone's fault, it's mine," Fitz said as he stepped out of the darkness. "If I'd noticed the flames earlier, or been a better guide—"

"This was not your fault, Fitz," Sophie promised.

"Nor was it yours," Alden said firmly. "No matter what you think. No matter what happens in the coming days. I want you both to know this, and hold to it, and believe it. This. Wasn't. Your. Fault. Remember that. And remember what happened to me when I tried to hold on to guilt and blame."

The reminder felt like a bucket of ice water, splashing them both awake.

But Sophie couldn't make herself believe him.

Like it or not, she *had* played a role in Kenric's death—and she would have to square with that someday.

But if she let the guilt break her, his sacrifice would be a waste, and she refused to let that happen either.

She'd hold herself together the same way Grady had when he lost Jolie.

She would focus on *rage*.

Her anger boiled inside her and she drank it in, letting it settle into her heart and burn the fear and sadness away.

She wouldn't rest until she found the Pyrokinetic Fintan was protecting. And once she did, she *would* make him pay.

THIRTY-NINE

TIERGAN BROUGHT SOPHIE HOME, and she took him up on his offer to break the news to Grady and Edaline without her.

When Alden's mind had broken, she'd insisted on being there, wanting to be brave and strong and support her family. But she couldn't handle another teary, heartbreaking scene.

She needed to hold on to her rage.

She left everyone downstairs—avoiding their worried glances—as she dropped her singed cape in a heap on the floor and followed Sandor up to her room. He said nothing as she closed him outside, probably too busy eavesdropping on what Tiergan was saying. But Sophie didn't want to hear. She locked herself in her bathroom and turned on the shower, letting the sound of falling water drown out the world.

Flakes of ash sprinkled the floor as she kicked her clothes to the corner, wishing she could tear them to tiny threads. She grabbed every bottle of shampoo she could find and stepped under the colored streams of cold water, glad to feel her body shiver.

She'd had enough heat to last a lifetime.

She washed her hair so many times she lost count, though when she finally turned off the water, she could still smell the smoke. She tied the dripping, soggy strands away from her face, threw on her pajamas, and stumbled to bed. But she could see the Everblaze behind her eyes.

The bright, neon yellow flashes were seared to her eyelids, and no matter how hard she blinked, they wouldn't fade away.

"How can I help?" Sandor asked, hovering in the doorway, silhouetted by a sliver of light.

Sophie rolled to her side, not wanting to look at him as she whispered, "I think I'd like to try slumberberry tea."

She'd expected some sort of triumphant "It's about time!" But all she heard were the heavy thuds of Sandor's feet as he rushed to grant her request.

She lay still, trying not to think about what she was doing, until the footsteps returned, bringing with them the scent of something sweet. But when she turned to grab the tea, the person offering it to her was Edaline.

"Sandor said you requested this," she said, holding out the fragile pink teacup.

Sophie took it slowly, trying not to let her shaky hands spill the steaming liquid. But she froze with the cup halfway to her lips.

The tea was purple, with a slight shimmer—like the bubbling flows of amethyst lava coating the ground outside Oblivimyre.

Edaline grabbed the cup as it started to slip from Sophie's hands, and she set it down on Sophie's nightstand.

"Slumberberry tea can be a wonderful thing," Edaline said, sounding surprisingly calm as she sat next to Sophie on the edge of the bed. "But I know how you feel about sedatives. That's why I also brought you these."

She pulled a black vial from her pocket and placed it in Sophie's lap. The bottle was small and narrow—no wider than Sophie's finger—and covered in tiny silver dots, with a strange silver lid that felt squishy when Sophie touched it.

"It's called somnalene," Edaline explained. "It's the nectar of the starglass flower, and it's not a drug. All you need is one drop in each eye to help you sleep. It used to work for me."

"How?" Sophie asked, unscrewing the bottle and filling the eyedropper with the shimmering silver liquid.

"It's hard to explain until you see."

Sophie scooted down, tipping her head back so Edaline could hold her eyelids open and squeeze one drop into each of her eyes. The cool silver liquid felt blindingly bright as it spread across her corneas. But as the tears settled, she sucked in a breath.

"It's beautiful, isn't it?" Edaline asked.

Beautiful wasn't a strong enough word.

A million flecks of light shimmered and flashed behind her eyes, like she had a tiny universe tucked inside her mind.

"They call the effect 'midnighting,'" Edaline explained. "It'll last about eight hours before it fades."

"It's amazing," Sophie breathed.

The lingering yellow glow of the Everblaze faded in the twinkling lights, and Sophie breathed a sigh of relief—even as her insides squirmed like snakes.

She didn't deserve to have her guilt fade—not until she made the rebels pay.

"Hey," Edaline said, wiping a tear off Sophie's cheek. "If you cry it all out, it can't help you sleep."

"Good," Sophie mumbled, rolling away.

Edaline placed a gentle hand on Sophie's shoulder. "You're missing the point of the somnalene. It reminds us just how small we really are, and how big the rest of the world is by comparison. One person is not the source of anything—it's millions of pieces all working together. And it shows us that there's always hope—always light. No matter how much darkness we might be facing."

Her hand had started to trace slow, careful circles down

Sophie's spine, just like Sophie's human mother used to do when she was a little kid.

"I never should have come here," Sophie whispered. "If I'd just stayed with the humans, none of this would have happened."

"Our world has been teetering on the edge of a blade for a very long time, Sophie. In fact . . . I think that's why you're here—why you grew up where you did. So you could see our world through different eyes. Help us find our way. Just like you did for Grady and me. You've made us whole again. Given us back our lives. Now it's our turn to help *you*."

She brushed another tear off Sophie's cheek.

"I want you to know that Grady and I are here for you, okay? I know you try to protect us. And I know you like to do things on your own. But we're all going to lean on each other this time. Please don't push us away."

Maybe it was because Edaline sounded so strong and sure.

Or maybe Sophie just couldn't face another long, lonely night.

Either way, she tightened her grip on Edaline's wrist and whispered, "Will you stay here tonight?"

"Of course." Edaline kissed Sophie's cheek and settled under the covers, stroking Sophie's back again.

Slowly, very very slowly, Sophie finally fell asleep.

And when she woke up and found Edaline still sleeping peacefully next to her, she knew she was ready to face the day.

FORTY

NEWS OF THE FIRE SPREAD FASTER than the Everblaze, and when Sophie came downstairs for breakfast, a scroll from the Council sat waiting on the kitchen table.

Sophie sank into her chair next to Grady and took one of the colorful pastries from the platter in the center. The gooey cake was covered in sugar and sprinkles—but it turned to sour in her mouth when she read the Council's message:

TOMORROW AT MIDDAY WE WILL HONOR THE LIFE AND LEGACY OF

COUNCILLOR KENRIC ELGAR FATHDON

BY PLANTING HIS SEED IN THE WANDERLING WOODS

"What do they mean by nominations?" Sophie asked, rolling up the scroll so she wouldn't have to look at it.

"Nominations for the next Councillor."

"They're replacing him already?"

"They have to, Sophie. The very foundation of our world has been shattered, and we must rebuild it immediately. That doesn't mean we won't grieve. But we must also keep working to protect our people. You can't tell me that's not what Kenric would've wanted."

She couldn't.

But she still hated it.

She stood, wandering to the wall of windows, watching the dinosaurs graze in the pastures beyond.

"How do the nominations work?" she asked, not sure she'd be able to survive a long campaign with speeches and debates.

Grady moved to stand beside her. "The public will be allowed to privately submit nominations for members of the Nobility who qualify for consideration. Then the Council will ultimately decide."

"And how long does that normally take?"

"It depends on how quickly the Councillors agree. But I suspect this time will move incredibly quickly. I only hope they'll elect a Councillor as compassionate and considerate as Kenric."

Sophie couldn't help hoping the new Councillor would also be on her side. She hated to admit it—hated herself for even thinking it. But Kenric had always been one of her strongest supporters. Losing even one vote could sway the rulings against her.

"Is there any chance you or Alden will be nominated?" she asked quietly.

"No—thankfully. The Councillors aren't allowed to be married. It's their responsibility to make decisions for the good of *all* people, and having a wife or children could threaten their impartiality."

"But . . . what if they fall in love?"

"Then they can choose to resign from the Council—which definitely has happened in the past. Or they can opt to ignore the feelings. The choice is entirely up to them."

Suddenly Kenric's longing looks at Oralie made much more sense. Which made Sophie's heart extra heavy.

Kenric sacrificed so much for the good of his world—and look how his world repaid him.

No—not his whole *world,* Sophie corrected.

A small band with their own agenda.

Villains.

She was tired of calling them "rebels."

They were kidnappers.

Killers.

And she was going to stop them.

"I've seen that look in your eye before, Sophie," Grady said, resting a hand on her shoulder, "and I can't say I blame you for it. I also doubt I can stop you. So I'm only going to ask you one thing: *Remember who you can trust, and keep them close.* Don't push them away."

Sophie nodded, and he pulled her into a hug.

"If I might add something," Sandor said behind them. "I would like to renew my request for you to stay by my side. I am already getting reports of highly increased unrest among the public, and I fear in the coming days you will need more protection than normal."

"Because everyone blames me," Sophie mumbled, trying to pull away from Grady.

Grady tightened his hold. "The people of our world fear the new and the different. But you are brave and strong and smart enough to not believe what they say. Trust your friends and your family, know that they love you and will support you no matter what."

"And keep your bodyguard close," Sandor added.

"Yes, and that." Grady sighed, trailing his hand through Sophie's hair. "I know you don't want to talk about yesterday, Sophie—and I respect that. But if you change your mind, I'm here."

Sophie squeezed him tighter, blinking back her tears.

She wasn't going to cry.

She was going to *fight*.

"By the way," Grady said, slowly letting her go. "Tiergan asked me to tell you to record *everything* you remember from yesterday—not just what you saw in Fintan's mind. The Council is trying to piece together what happened during the fire."

Sophie's eyes dropped to her feet. "I doubt I'm going to be much help. If Fitz hadn't warned me about the Everblaze, I probably wouldn't have realized what was happening until it was too late. I think that was Fintan's plan."

Grady's expression turned murderous. But he said nothing as Sophie turned and headed upstairs.

She pulled out her memory log and spent the rest of the day fighting to remember anything that might give her something to go on.

She projected the memory Fintan had once again managed to stop her from recovering and placed it side by side with her other projection from the first break with Alden.

She could see more of the mysterious pyrokinetic's robe—though there was nothing special about it, except perhaps the vivid red color. She could also see the shape of his face. The edges were blurred, but his chin was prominent and his dark hair looked neatly styled. So he was probably someone who cared about his appearance.

Probably, Sophie thought bitterly, shoving the memory log aside.

All she could do was guess and speculate about pointless details—hardly the revelation she needed.

She was about to close the log and tuck it away, when she noticed one final difference between the two projected scenes. She'd been concentrating so hard on her kidnapper, she'd forgotten to notice that she could see more of Fintan, too—especially in the early part of the memory, when he was pointing at the star he was teaching her kidnapper to call.

His cloak was black, with long, thick sleeves. And near the top of his shoulder was a white patch with an eye.

Keefe had seen the same patch on the rebels, so to see Fintan wearing it wasn't necessarily earth-shattering. But she could see a word this time—written in runes that she wouldn't have expected she'd be able to read.

The word triggered no memories in her mind, so the Black Swan must not be familiar with it.

But the nameless rebels had a name.

Neverseen.

FORTY-ONE

S OMETHING BAD HAPPENED AGAIN, didn't it?" Vertina asked as Sophie squinted at her reflection, trying to make sure she didn't miss any of the tiny silver hooks that fastened the bodice of her shimmering green gown.

She still felt strange wearing something so bright and cheerful at a funeral. But the elves' tradition was to wear green, to symbolize life.

Not that it made the funerals any less depressing.

Sophie sighed and pinned back part of her hair with an emerald comb. "Yes. One of the Councillors died."

Vertina closed her eyes, her tiny face looking pinched. "I'm sorry. Did you know him?"

"Not as well as I would've liked," Sophie admitted as she spread a little pink gloss over her lips. "Not as well as I should have."

"I'm so sorry," Vertina repeated. "What happened?"

"He was killed in a fire, by a group called the Neverseen."

Sophie had told Grady and Edaline the name she'd discovered—and hailed Alden and done the same. None of them had heard any trace of it ever mentioned.

So Sophie's heart picked up speed when Vertina shook her tiny head and whispered, "Not them again."

"What do you mean? Do you know who they are?"

Vertina's eyes stretched as wide as they could go, and she squeaked something about saying too much and clicked away.

"I'm going to have Dex reprogram you to tell me!" Sophie shouted, pounding on the glass.

Vertina clicked back. "He'd never have the chance. I have an auto erase feature—I can wipe my memory clean and reset if I have to."

"Why would you do that?"

"I don't *want* to. I want you to give me the password so I can trust you. Haven't you found it yet?"

No. All she'd found was a stupid human mirror. Unless . . .

"Is it 'follow the pretty bird across the sky'?"

Vertina shook her head sadly. "No. But a bird *is* connected to it."

Sophie knew Vertina probably meant the clue to be helpful.

But it wasn't exactly a revelation. The Black Swan used birds for *everything*.

"A bird is connected to what?" Grady asked from the doorway.

"Oh, um, just a game Vertina and I are playing," Sophie told him, throwing her green velvet cape over her shoulders and pinning it with her Ruewen crest.

She could tell Grady was less than impressed with her lie. But all he said was, "You look beautiful."

"Thanks."

She took another glance at her reflection, hating that she looked more like she was heading off to prom. But Grady was dressed just as formally: velvet pants, an intricately embroidered jerkin, and a gold-trimmed silk cape—though his clothes were a deep hunter green.

The hint of dark matched the shadows under his eyes as he offered Sophie his hand and told her, "Today is probably going to be pretty miserable."

"I know. I keep wishing it could be like last time, when I still had a little hope to hold on to."

"There's always hope, Sophie. Just because Kenric is gone doesn't mean that his work, and the things he stood for, will vanish. It's just going to take everyone a little time to heal."

Sophie cringed.

"Sorry. Bad choice of word." Grady sighed, mussing his hair. "You ready?"

She wasn't. But she took his hand and they made their way up the stairs, with Sandor close behind.

Edaline was waiting for them in the fourth floor cupola, standing under the glittering crystals of the Leapmaster. Her wispy, silky dress floated around her like a summer breeze, and Sophie was relieved to see how calm Edaline looked. No tears. No shadows. Just a sad smile as she strangled Sophie with a hug.

"Remember, we're here for you," she whispered into Sophie's ear.

"I'm fine," Sophie promised.

But she didn't feel fine as Grady called the Leapmaster to bring them the crystal for the Wanderling Woods. Especially when Sandor joined them under the crystals.

The Council would only allow a goblin into the Wanderling Woods if they were expecting some sort of danger.

Sophie had thought the crowd for Alden's planting had been huge—but it was nothing compared to the turnout for Kenric. A never-ending line of green-clad figures stretched down the silvery path, waiting silently for their turn to pass through the archway that proclaimed *Those who wander are not lost.*

And they weren't just elves. Gnomes, goblins, dwarves, and some sort of wet-looking, grayish-green creatures—trolls, maybe?—were all in the mix.

But no ogres.

336

Sophie wondered if any of the Neverseen were lurking among the crowd.

She wouldn't put it past them.

She reached for Grady's hand, expecting him to head to the back of the line. But Grady led them to a side entrance, hidden among a thick vine of white star-shaped flowers.

The goblin guarding the gate was so large he made Sandor look scrawny, and his voice was even squeakier as he told them, "There's a space reserved for you in the clearing. Just look for the silver ropes."

"Thank you," Grady said, pausing in the middle of the gateway. "Is there a path I'm not seeing?"

"The crowd keeps closing it off," the goblin told them. "And I suggest you move quickly."

Sandor saluted the guard and took the lead, ordering Sophie to stay right behind him as he pushed into the mass of bodies, creating a narrow wake for them to follow.

Despite the suffocating crowd, the Wanderling Woods maintained its eerie, unnatural silence, swallowing the sound of their footsteps as they wove through the carefully arranged trees. Each Wanderling's seed was wrapped with a hair from the person who'd been lost, making the tree reflect their appearance as it grew and absorbed their DNA. There were tall trees, thin trees, leaves in every color of the rainbow, trees with dark bark, or light bark, or flowers, or berries.

Plus three small saplings that never should've been planted.

They passed Alden's Wanderling first, and Sophie was stunned at how tall the dark-leafed tree had grown in such a short time. If it weren't for the vivid teal flowers peppered among the branches, she never would've guessed it was his.

Hers and Dex's trees looked taller too, though it was hard to tell from a distance. Their Wanderlings had been planted side by side, high on a hill, and Sophie was tempted to climb up and check on them. But Sandor moved like a bull who'd seen red, rushing past tree after tree after tree—each more ancient looking than the last—until they reached the clearing for the ceremony.

A silver stage had been set up in the center for the Councillors, and the crowd around it was packed so tightly, Sophie could barely breathe.

"That must be the area the guard meant," Grady said, pointing to a pale yellow tree where a small spot of shade had been blocked off with thick silver ropes.

Three goblins were guarding the area, and once they'd let Sandor pass, they positioned themselves to the left, right, and front of Sophie. Sandor stood behind, and his grip stayed locked around his sword, ready to unsheathe it any second.

Sophie was tempted to tell him he was being overly paranoid. But then she noticed the crowd's faces.

They weren't staring at her.

They were *glaring*.

Whispers followed—and this time they weren't calling her *the girl who was taken*.

They used the same two words over and over—the same words Sophie was fighting so hard not to think:

Her fault.

Sophie searched the faces, desperate to find a friend. But the closest she came was Marella—and when their eyes met, Marella looked away.

A muffled gasp finally silenced the crowd, and Sophie craned her neck to see that the remaining eleven members of the Council had arrived in the clearing. Four goblins guarded each Councillor, cramming the small silver stage with their muscular bodies. But it still looked empty without Kenric's bright, smiling face.

The Councillors all wore the same pale shade of green—but instead of the simple gowns and tunics they'd worn for Alden's planting, their clothes were covered in emeralds and peridots, and their circlets were crusted with diamonds. Their hair was perfectly styled and their clothes were perfectly pressed. But the finery didn't make them look any less weary and miserable. Especially Oralie.

Her eyes were nothing more than puffy red slits, and she leaned on her goblin bodyguards like they were the only things keeping her standing.

"We appreciate your support on this challenging day," Councillor Emery said, his voice hoarse as he stepped forward to address the crowd, "and I know many of you have questions about what will happen next. But now is not the time to focus on such matters. We will have a brief announcement after these proceedings. Before that, we must celebrate the life and loss of our dear friend—and inspiring Councillor—Kenric Fathdon.

Soft sniffles hissed through the air as Councillor Terik stepped off the stage and dug a small hole in the ground with a silver shovel. When the seed was completely buried, Councillor Liora poured a shimmering syrup from a green bottle on top, then cracked the glass against her palm, letting it shatter into a million shimmering specks that blanketed the freshly turned ground.

The sniffles turned to quiet sobs as a tiny sapling sprang from the earth and sprouted vivid red leaves. But Sophie battled back her tears, knowing if she let herself fall down the rabbit hole of grief, she might never find her way back.

"She doesn't even look sorry," someone near Sophie whispered.

"Of course she isn't. This was probably what she was created for all along."

"She should be exiled."

"Or banished."

"To the goblins!"

"Or the ogres!"

The crowd pressed closer and closer, until Sandor ordered the other goblins to evacuate. Before Sophie knew what was happening, the bodyguards lifted her over their heads and rushed her outside the woods to the normal forest that surrounded the Wanderlings.

"We should be safer here," Sandor told her, setting Sophie down in the shade of a tall pine tree. "I'll bring you back in after the receiving line has finished, so you can hear the Council's announcement."

"Can't I go through the line?" Sophie asked.

"The Councillors asked that you don't," Grady said quietly, as he and Edaline caught up with them. "The less interaction you have with the crowd, the better."

"Great—maybe they should just lock me away in Exile."

Edaline hugged her. "It's going to be okay. We just need to give the public some time to reset."

"Or to gather the torches and pitchforks and come after me," Sophie mumbled.

"They'd come after me, too—if it makes you feel any better," Fitz said behind her.

Sophie turned to find him leaning against a nearby tree. His smile was too sad to make her heart do anything except break.

"We'll let you two talk," Edaline said, taking Grady's hand and leading him back toward the woods. "Sandor will keep an eye on things while we pay our respects."

"Tell them I'm sorry," Sophie called after them.

Edaline turned back. "You have nothing to be sorry for, Sophie. But we *will* give them your condolences."

Sophie watched them go, not sure if she should be grateful for not having to face the heartbreaking scene, or mad that the angry crowds were keeping her away.

"My parents are in there too," Fitz said after a second, waving her over to join him in the shade. "I stayed with them as long as I could, but we were standing near the Hekses and they got everyone all riled up pretty quickly."

"What were they saying?"

"The usual. That my family needs to get away from you to save our reputation, that we're ruining the world, blah, blah." He tore a piece of dead bark from the tree and flung it away.

Sophie's stomach wrenched as she sat beside him. "If you want to stop hanging out with me—"

"I told you, I'm *in*. In fact, there's something I have to tell you—"

"*There* you are," Keefe interrupted, stomping over from the exit to the Wanderling Woods. "You could've told me about your little private party out here. I've been stuck watching my parents play *who can pretend to be the saddest?* in the middle of a mob that smelled like a goblin's armpit."

"I'd be careful what you say," Sandor warned, pointing to the three scowling goblins behind him.

Keefe shrugged, unfazed. "So . . . ," he said, his smile fading as he turned to Fitz and Sophie. "Rough weekend?"

"You could say that," Fitz mumbled, tearing off another piece of dead bark.

"And you," Keefe said, turning to Sophie, "didn't I tell you I wanted to be there the next time you—nope, actually, I can't joke about this." He shook his head—hard—and sat down facing them. "Are you guys okay?"

"Yeah, I guess," Fitz answered when Sophie didn't say anything. "I think I'm still . . . processing it."

"I think we all are." Keefe turned to stare at the Wanderlings. "And I'm guessing there's no chance this could all be a mistake again?"

Fitz shook his head, twisting the piece of bark in his hands until it crumbled. "My dad saw it happen."

Sophie shuddered, trying not to imagine it.

"So what's the plan now?" Keefe asked after a painful silence. "And don't pretend you don't have one, Foster."

"But I *don't* have one. That's the problem."

She'd found no other record of the Neverseen. Jolie's mirrored compact had been a bust. Vertina wasn't cooperating. The Black Swan was compromised. And everyone was so distracted by the fire that there'd been no more news about the missing dwarves or the ogre footprints.

All she had were questions and problems.

Fitz glanced over his shoulder and leaned closer. "I might have a plan."

"Hmm," Keefe jumped in before Sophie could say anything. "Team Keefe-Foster-Fitz doesn't have quite the same ring, but I'm still in. Oh—maybe we could be the Keefitzter!"

"Not unless it's the Keefianaitzter," Biana informed them as she appeared next to Keefe. "Or the Keefitzteriana."

343

"That doesn't really have the same ring," Keefe told her. "And have you been there the whole time?"

"Yep. I followed Fitz after he left, figuring I could sneak up on anyone if they tried to hassle him. And then Sophie came out, and I stayed hidden so I could make sure they couldn't leave me out of their plans."

Fitz rolled his eyes. "This vanishing thing is going to be a problem, isn't it?"

"Not if you include me."

"You guys shouldn't be doing this," Sophie said, wondering if Dex was about show up to complete the Let's Ruin Our Lives Club. "Don't you see? Everyone blames me for what happened, and they'll hold that against anyone who's friends with me."

"So?" Biana asked.

"So . . . don't you care that you're stuck outside the Wanderling Woods instead of standing in the receiving line with the normal people?"

"No," Keefe answered immediately, with Fitz and Biana only a fraction of a second later.

"You think I care about not getting to be around the people saying horrible things about my best friend and my brother?" Biana asked.

"I'm your best friend?" Sophie said—then realized she was focusing on the wrong thing. "Never mind, what I mean is, they're only saying that because of me. Because of this like . . . aura of doom that seems to ruin everything I touch."

"Aura of doom?" Keefe asked, a smirk curling his lips. "Sounds like my kind of party."

"Mine too," Fitz chimed in.

"And mine," Biana agreed. "Besides, you already agreed to this, remember?"

"And I'm the only one with a plan," Fitz reminded them.

"Hey—I've got plans," Keefe argued.

"Plans that don't involve tormenting Dame Alina," Fitz clarified.

"But those are always the best plans!"

Fitz and Biana laughed, and Sophie couldn't decide if she wanted to join them or scold them. Kenric was *dead*—and they were sitting outside his funeral, making jokes and . . .

Actually, that was probably exactly what Kenric would've wanted. If he were still there, he would've laughed right along with them.

"Fine," she told them, wondering what she was getting herself into. "So what's the plan?"

"Wait," Sandor shouted before Fitz could say anything.

"Aw, don't be like that, Gigantor. We'll play by your rules—mostly."

"No," Sandor insisted, waving Keefe silent and sniffing the air. "Do you smell that?" He turned to the other goblins, who were all unsheathing their swords.

"What is it?" Sophie whispered.

Sandor tightened his grip on his weapon. "Something unpleasant is coming."

Before he could say anything else, the ground rumbled, creating a wide sinkhole.

Sophie and her friends scrambled back as the goblins shouted orders at each other and surrounded the opening, holding their swords at the ready.

One . . . two . . . three seconds passed.

Then a stocky brown beast leaped out of the fissure, scattering rocks and dirt and grass as it landed with a heavy thud.

"Is that an ogre?" Sophie whispered, staring at the creature's lumpy face, trying to understand why none of the goblins were attacking.

"Yes," Sandor said, a snarl in his voice as he lowered his head with a reluctant bow. "This is their king."

FORTY-TWO

THE OGRE KING, SOPHIE THOUGHT slowly, fairly certain her brain was about to call it quits.

He wasn't dressed like a king—at least not by elvin standards. Or human standards, for that matter.

The only clothing he wore looked like riveted steel underwear, and his body was shaped like a hairless gorilla on a massive amount of steroids, with skin that reminded Sophie of weathered marble. He carried no weapons and arrived with no guards. And while he did have enormous glittering yellow stones set into the centers of his stretched-out earlobes, he had no crown, no scepter, no signet ring. His bald head was marked with some sort of black, squiggly patterns, but it didn't look kingly. It pretty much just screamed, *This dude is scary.*

Still, there was something regal about the way he fearlessly faced the goblins, all of whom were at least a foot taller than him. And his scratchy voice held authority as he turned to Sandor and said, "Settle down, goblin. I'm only here to pay my respects."

For a second Sophie thought Sandor was going to pounce. But his snarl faded to a glare as he stepped back and said, "Then allow us to clear you a path."

Sandor glanced at Sophie as he turned to leave, and his eyes seemed to be saying, *Follow us and I will clobber you!*

But there was no way Sophie was going to miss this.

"I'm pretty sure that was the freakiest thing I've ever seen," Fitz whispered as he, Keefe, and Biana caught up with her.

"Yeah, not gonna lie—I almost peed my pants. Did you see his nose?" Keefe curled his fingers in front of his face to mime the gigantic bulbous mass. "He could've taken us all out with one sneeze. And his *teeth*?"

He shuddered.

Fitz and Biana did too—and the king's gray pointed teeth *were* terrifying. But Sophie was much more bothered by his eyes.

The two cold silver orbs tucked among the lumps and bumps of his face had a glint to them. A hint of glee that didn't belong on the face of someone coming to a funeral.

The crowd toppled over themselves to get out of the king's

way, and Sophie and her friends rode the wake, ducking back into the masses when they had a clear view of the stage.

The Councillors stood hand in hand in a precise line, and their bodyguards had formed two lines surrounding them: one on the ground with their backs against the stage, the other behind them, their swords raised.

"King Dimitar," Councillor Emery said from the center of the line, while all eleven Councillors bowed as one. "How generous of you to come."

King Dimitar bobbed his head in the briefest bow possible—though he didn't have much of a neck, so that might have been the best he could do. His droopy chin seemed to connect directly to his muscle-bound shoulders, giving him a permanent hunch.

"I assumed all the kings would be here," he said, turning to study the sea of curious faces. "But perhaps I was too late to catch them?"

"No," Councillor Emery said carefully. "They were otherwise engaged."

"Of course they were," King Dimitar agreed. "And I'm sure you will have their full support for whomever you elect as your newest Councillor."

His cold smile said otherwise, and it stretched wider as he scraped one of his teeth with a black fingernail. "I stopped by your capital on my way here, by the way. The damage is *far* more extensive than I'd been led to believe."

349

That earned him a few gasps from the audience, but Councillor Emery held up his hand. He addressed the crowd, not the king, as he said, "We'd been waiting to share that announcement until we'd completed the memorial proceedings, but yes, King Dimitar speaks correctly. The Everblaze consumed much of Eternalia. *However*"—he paused, waiting for the murmurs to die down—"the gnomes and dwarves have surveyed the damage and believe they can rebuild before the equinox, which, as you all know, is less than four months away. And they've assured us that the new buildings will be even greater than the former."

Whispers followed—most of them sounding pleased. Though it was a far cry from the cheers Sophie suspected the Council had been hoping for.

"And when will you hold your election?" King Dimitar asked, triggering another silence.

"That is also an announcement we had planned to make momentarily," Emery told him. He closed his eyes, like he was listening to the thoughts of the other Councillors, before he said, "The period for nominations will begin tonight, and last for exactly one week, after which we will work to select our newest member as quickly as possible. And once the Councillor is elected," he added, turning to King Dimitar, "a gathering will be held in Lumenaria with yourself and all the other leaders, so that we all can prepare to move forward together."

"Looking forward to it," King Dimitar told him.

"One final announcement—since I've covered all the

others," Councillor Emery added. "Given recent events, we've decided to declare a period of grieving, effective immediately. All noble facilities—including Foxfire Academy—are closed until the new Councillor is elected."

Sophie glanced at her friends as the crowd hissed with more whispers.

No school for at least a week?

"I assume that includes your legendary Sanctuary?" King Dimitar asked, forcing Sophie to pay attention. She wanted to strangle something when he added, "I'd been hoping to pay a visit before I left. I've heard wonders about your newest transplant."

"The Council better not let him anywhere near Silveny," Keefe told her under his breath.

Sophie nodded, resisting the urge to cheer when Councillor Emery told the king, "We must respect the grieving period."

"Perhaps after the gathering in Lumenaria, then," King Dimitar pressed.

"Yes, perhaps," Councillor Emery agreed. "We appreciate your patience—and the time you shared with us today. Please bring our regards to the rest of your court."

"That's it?" Sophie asked—a little louder than she meant to—as all eleven Councillors bowed.

But seriously, what was the Council thinking?

They should be demanding to know why he was interested in Silveny—and if he knew anything about the homing device and the Neverseen and the footprints outside the Sanctuary.

And if he refused to tell them, they should arrest him, or have Alden probe his mind or . . . something—*anything*.

Instead, they stood silent as King Dimitar bobbed another halfhearted bow and told them, "Should you need any assistance from my people, all you must do is ask. We're always there for our neighbors—especially in their hour of need."

"Thank you," Councillor Emery said with a tight smile. "We ask only what we always do. Patience. Kindness. And the continued pursuit of peace."

King Dimitar snorted, his wide nostrils spraying something wet in the process. But he said nothing further as he turned to leave.

Sophie had to bite her tongue to stop herself from screaming *Wait!*

"We have to do something," she whispered to Fitz and Keefe.

"Like what?" Biana asked.

Sophie was pretty sure jumping in front of King Dimitar and demanding he answer her questions wouldn't be very effective—especially when she took another look at his rippled chest. He had muscles on top of muscles, and paired with his freakishly long arms, he could probably tear her in half.

But there was more than one way to find out what he was hiding.

"I have a plan," she told her friends, before she darted into the crowd, moving parallel to the king.

Keefe was the first to catch up with her. "Okay, I have no

idea what you're thinking, but the amount of panic radiating off you tells me it's probably not a good thing."

It wasn't.

This was arguably the most dangerous idea she'd ever had.

But what was the point of being an unstoppable Telepath if she couldn't use the ability to protect Silveny and maybe even catch Kenric's killers?

Somewhere deep in the back of her brain, a tiny voice reminded her of the laws of telepathy. But a *much* more desperate voice convinced her those rules only applied to elves.

Plus, she'd broken rules before, when the situation called for it—and if any situation called for it, it was this.

"Cover me," Sophie whispered.

Keefe grabbed her arm as she tried to duck behind him. "Cover you how? Don't you think you should at least tell me your crazy plan before you start doing it?"

"What crazy plan?" Fitz asked, pushing through the crowd to join them.

"Ask her—she's the one wigging out over here," Keefe told him.

"I'm not wigging out, I'm just trying to do something and I need you to cover me so no one knows I have my eyes closed."

"You better not be doing what I think you're doing," Fitz told her.

But he was too late.

Sophie had already opened her mind to the ogre king's.

FORTY-THREE

SOPHIE HAD NO IDEA WHAT AN OGRE'S mind was supposed to feel like. But she definitely wasn't expecting it to be so . . . soft.

And *blank*.

No color.

No sound.

Just a thick, endless sea of fuzzy white nothing. Like trying to shove her way through a giant ball of cotton.

She took a deep breath, rallying her mental energy as she tried to decide if a brain push would be too risky.

She knew from past experience that she could slip in and out of a mind completely undetected. But if she pressed too hard, she could accidentally give herself away.

Deciding to play it safe, she tried to imagine her mind sweeping away the cottony thickness in layers—like carefully pulling back sheer drapes, trying to find the window underneath. Each pass did seem to brighten the fog around her, revealing hints of shadows and shapes, and filling the silence with the trace of whispers. But nothing she could translate or recognize.

Maybe if she—

"Sophie, please *stop!*" Fitz begged, shaking her so hard it knocked her off balance.

She was about to ask him what he was doing when she noticed where Keefe was pointing.

King Dimitar stood in the middle of the path. And his eyes were locked on *her*.

"Oh, Councillors," the king called, his lips curling back to show every one of his pointed teeth. "Perhaps you can explain why this little girl has taken it upon herself to probe my mind without my permission. And don't even think about denying it," he told Sophie, as gasps echoed through the silent woods—along with a squeaky groan, which had to have come from Sandor. "I felt you the second you slipped in."

Sophie tried to choke down the lump in her throat, but it wouldn't budge. "I'm sorry. I . . . shouldn't have."

"No, you shouldn't," King Ditmar agreed. "And *sorry* doesn't change the fact that you just violated our treaty."

Their treaty? Sophie thought, the world spinning too fast around her.

"She didn't know!" Councillor Emery shouted over the flurry of raised voices. "Sophie is very new to our world and still learning the specifics of our laws. She's what you might call a *special case*."

The crowd fell silent as King Dimitar stroked his lumpy chin. "I see nothing *special* about her."

"Neither do I," someone nearby muttered, stirring other grumblings.

"Breathe, Foster," Keefe whispered, giving her palm a quick, reassuring squeeze.

She clung to his hand like it could keep her alive and forced herself to take a shaky breath.

"So tell me," King Dimitar said, turning back to the Council. "If she's new to your world, where has she been all this time?"

Councillor Emery closed his eyes, deliberating with the other Councillors.

Before they came to a decision, someone in the crowd shouted, "She was raised by humans!"

"Humans!" King Dimitar snarled. "I thought the elves had severed ties with those vermin."

"We have," Councillor Emery promised. "Like I said, Sophie is a *special case*."

"Well then, let's see how *special* she is." King Dimitar stalked toward Sophie, sending the crowd around her scurrying.

Sophie locked her knees, begging them not to give out as she faced the monstrous king. From the corner of her eye, she could see Sandor fighting his way toward her, but the fleeing masses kept knocking him back. Only Fitz and Keefe stayed by her side—though Sophie had a feeling Biana was hiding nearby.

The king leaned so close, Sophie could smell his breath—rotten meat and burned garlic—as he sniffed her hair and said, "I feel everything that goes on in my head. *Everything*. Do you?"

"Y-yes," she managed to stutter.

King Dimitar's eyes narrowed and Sophie braced for him to raise one of his massive arms and smash her.

Instead, Biana reappeared with a yelp as she, Fitz, and Keefe dropped to their knees, covering their ears and squeezing their heads.

"What's wrong?" Sophie shouted, trying to shake them out of whatever was happening. "What are you doing to them?"

"The better question," King Dimitar said as he relaxed his brow and halted whatever torture he'd been delivering, "is why didn't it work on you?"

"Like the Councillors already said, Sophie is *special*," Alden spat as he pushed his way to his children's side.

Grady and Edaline were right behind him, and they pulled Sophie close as Sandor moved in front of them and straightened to his full height, leaving the king in his shadow.

"Those children you just harmed were innocent," Sandor snarled.

"Guilty by association," King Dimitar argued. "And they'll be fine in a minute. Meanwhile, *this one* . . ."

He reached for Sophie, and Sandor shoved his hand away.

King Dimitar laughed, a wet, gurgley sound. "You have no place here, goblin."

"That girl is my charge."

"Is she now?" His eyes traced over Sophie, lingering on the scar on her hand. "Raised by humans, strange talents, *and* a bodyguard. I'd heard rumors that the elves had a new trick up their sleeves. I just never expected it to be in such an unimpressive package."

"Sophie is not a trick," Alden assured him. "She's a child. A child who made a very grave mistake—and she will be punished accordingly."

"Yes, she will," King Dimitar agreed, slamming his gigantic fist into Sandor's stomach.

Sandor dropped to his knees, coughing and wheezing as the King grabbed him by the shoulders and tossed him into a nearby Wanderling.

Sophie wasn't sure if the loud *crack* was the tree or Sandor's head, and when she tried to run to check on him, King Dimitar snatched her wrist.

"This child invaded *my* mind and challenged *my* authority!" he shouted, dragging her to his side. "That means *I* get to decide her punishment. And I've decided she's coming back to Ravagog with me, to serve a life sentence."

FORTY-FOUR

THAT'S NOT WHAT THE TREATY SAYS!"
Grady shouted, grabbing Sophie's free hand and starting a tug-of-war. "If you don't let go of my daughter right now, I will make you cut off your own arm."

"Your mind tricks don't work on us," King Dimitar sneered.

"Don't they?" Grady narrowed his eyes, and the King dropped Sophie's hand and punched himself in the nose—hard.

Dark maroon streamed down his face as the king screamed, *"This is an act of war!"*

He lunged for Grady's throat, but Grady narrowed his eyes again and King Dimitar froze like a statue, his vicious mouth barely moving enough to breathe.

"All right—enough!" Councillor Emery shouted, pushing his way through the panicking crowd, followed by the rest of the Council and their furious bodyguards.

When they reached Grady's side, Councillor Terik squeezed Grady's shoulder and told him, "You've made your point."

Grady hesitated a fraction of a second. Then stepped back, dragging Sophie safely behind him as King Dimitar collapsed in a heap, panting and clawing at the ground with rage.

"The treaty is *over*," he growled between gasping breaths.

"Is it?" Councillor Emery asked, waving his hands to silence the shouting elves all around. "I think you need to check again."

"We have the treaty right here," Councillor Liora said as she conjured a golden scroll.

"And as you can see," Councillor Emery said, taking the scroll from her and quickly scanning it, "it says, 'No elf shall use their ability on an ogre without their permission in times of peace.' But trying to drag someone's daughter away does not constitute a 'time of peace.' So Grady's act was *not* a violation— end of discussion."

King Dimitar spit, splattering the grass with dark blood. "What about the girl?"

"Yes, let's examine that, shall we?" Councillor Emery scrolled down and pointed to a block of text. "It says, 'Should a serious violation occur, a punishment must be agreed upon by both sides.'"

360

"The only punishment I'll agree to will be in *my* city under *my* control!" King Dimitar shouted.

"Then we are apparently at an impasse."

"No—we're at *war*!"

"Is that really what you want?" someone called, causing the crowd to part again as Lady Cadence stalked forward.

She dipped a slow, elaborate curtsy and held up her Markchain to show King Dimitar. "I remember when you gave this to me, I thought, *here* is a king who cares about the safety of his people. Such a king would not want them needlessly slaughtered in battles."

"Who says they would be?" King Dimitar argued. "Elves do not fight."

"We fight for them," Sandor growled, unsheathing his blade. The Councillor's bodyguards did the same.

King Dimitar feigned a yawn. "Goblins are no match for us."

Sandor stomped closer, pointing his sword at the ogre king's heart. "Tell that to the thousands you lost in the last war. Trust me, if my hands were no longer tied by the restrictions of peace, you would not still be standing."

"Neither would you," King Dimitar growled back.

"Neither would any of us," Lady Cadence said firmly. "Which is why we all agreed to the treaties in the first place. So our children would not have to grow up without fathers. Is that really something you would give up because of your wounded pride?"

"You speak too boldly," King Dimitar warned, his words switching to the ogre language.

"Perhaps I do," Lady Cadence replied in the same tongue. "But that is only because I know you as a king who understands reason. A king who came here today to offer his sympathy in our dark hour. A king who knows that war should never be sparked by the mistake of a child—a child who *will* be punished by her own for the shame she's brought on everyone today."

King Dimitar gritted his teeth so hard Sophie swore she could hear them cracking.

"You also told us if we needed your assistance, we just had to ask," Councillor Oralie said quietly, her ogre words slightly stilted but perfectly understandable. "This is our need."

The king spat at Sophie's feet, splashing the bottom of her gown with bloody spittle. But he told the Council, "Fine, punish her as you see fit. But know that I will be following up."

"We will send you a full report," Councillor Emery promised. "But we must wait until we are a complete body of twelve again."

"I'll give you two weeks," the King told them, turning to face Sophie. "Then I'll be back to check on things—and I'd better be satisfied with what I see. Otherwise you can consider your treaty over."

"Please say *something*," Sophie whispered, twisting one of her nexuses so many times it was starting to rub her wrist raw.

She'd already torn out every loose eyelash she could find—plus several that had been very much attached. And still, she sat on the pristine couch of Havenfield's main room, feeling the glass walls close in while Grady, Edaline, Tiergan, Alden, and Sandor all seemed to be competing in some sort of Who Can Glare At Sophie The Longest contest.

"I'm so sorry," she repeated for the ten millionth time. "I didn't think—"

"That's just it," Grady interrupted. "You didn't *think*. Do you have any idea what would've happened to you if he'd dragged you away before we could stop him?

She didn't.

But she was very aware that she'd almost started a *war*.

And that she'd forced Grady to use his ability, which had been the most terrifying part of the day—by far. She never wanted to see that side of Grady again.

"Is the Council going to exile me?" she whispered.

Tiergan shook his head. "The ogres do not support that prison—largely because some of their own are being held there. King Dimitar would never approve."

"So what *will* he approve?" Sophie asked, hearing the panic in her voice but unable to hide it.

What could be worse than Exile?

Alden sighed and sat down beside her. "There's no reason to worry *too* much, Sophie. What you did was very serious. But the Council is also well aware that King Dimitar's visit today was hardly the concerned check-in he claimed it to be. His sole purpose was to assess the unrest in our world and increase it. He wants us to crumble so he can swoop in and conquer the pieces, and he was looking for anything that might help him accomplish it. You were simply his convenient excuse."

"Incredibly convenient," Tiergan muttered. "You might as well have wrapped yourself in shiny paper and tied your hair with a bow."

Sophie hung her head. "I'm—"

"I know you're sorry," Alden interrupted. "I even know *why* you did it. I just hope you understand that this is one dilemma I will not be able to protect you from. Not only will King Dimitar insist that there be consequences, but our people need to see you punished as well. Most of the public sees you as a dangerous experiment run amok, and today's drama essentially confirmed it. The Council is going to have to devise a punishment that will satisfy King Dimitar *and* prove to everyone that you are being sufficiently controlled."

Sophie swallowed, and it felt like choking down an entire bucket of sharp ice. "Any idea what the punishment will be?"

"It could be any number of things. But if I had to guess, it'll be some sort of mandatory public service assignment that you'll be expected to do every day after school. That way our people will see you humbled, and know that you're being supervised more thoroughly. And since it's essentially equivalent to an ogre work camp sentence, King Dimitar should be satisfied."

Grady and Tiergan both nodded, like they'd been thinking the same thing, and Sophie felt her heart rate start to slow down to normal.

"What kind of public service?" Edaline asked, looking just as relieved as Sophie felt.

Alden glanced at Grady again before he answered. "I'd assume they'd send her to the Sanctuary, since Sophie's skills with Silveny would be most useful to us there—but before you go smiling too widely, Sophie," he added, and Sophie's face fell immediately, "know that it will be hard, filthy work, probably involving a large amount of animal feces—most of which will not be sparkly. And you will likely serve there for the rest of the school year. Perhaps longer."

"It's better than an ogre work camp," Sophie told him.

"It is, indeed."

"But let us hope it is still awful enough to deter you from doing anything like this ever again," Sandor added, gripping the handle of his weapon like he was wishing he could shred her with it.

"Believe me, I've learned my lesson," Sophie promised, staring at the stain where the King had spit on her, vowing to throw away the dress.

"I'm not sure you have, so you can count on us spending a lot of time reviewing the laws of telepathy," Tiergan warned her. "We clearly also need to discuss the differences between our minds, and the minds of the other intelligent creatures.

You're very lucky you were spared the pain of the *grusom-daj*. Fitz, Biana, and Keefe weren't so fortunate."

Sophie shut her eyes, wishing she could shut out the memory of her three friends collapsing in agony. "What's a *grusom-daj*?"

"An ogre mind trick," Alden said quietly. "They're not telepathic, but their minds can transmit a single high-pitched frequency that feels like a tuning fork is being rammed into our brain. You really couldn't hear it?"

"Not at all."

"Another gift from the Black Swan," Tiergan murmured, and Sophie couldn't tell if he thought that was good or bad. "Could you hear anything in his mind when you probed it?"

"No, it was totally silent—and weirdly soft. I felt like I was trying to push my way though a fluffy blanket."

"Wait—his mind felt *soft*?" Tiergan asked.

Sophie nodded. "Was it not supposed to?"

"'Supposed' is the wrong word," Alden said after an uncomfortably long pause. "It *is* different from what others have experienced—which is admittedly a very small number of elves. They described an ogre's mind as a bed of needles. The fact that it felt soft to you suggests you might have come closer to breaching their defenses—which shouldn't surprise us at this point, given all we've seen when it comes to your abilities. But it's still interesting."

"*Not* interesting enough that we ever want you to try it again," Tiergan clarified.

"Indeed," Alden agreed. "Trying to invade an ogre's mind is like a fly trying to dance on a spider's web. Nothing gets past their detection. Not even you."

Sophie shrank lower in her chair.

"I still think King Dimitar was *looking* for something to cause a scene over," Edaline said quietly.

"Of course he was," Sandor agreed. "That's why he came here today. I'm sure the ogres know we found their homing device, and the best defense is always a strong offense. Then Sophie handed it to him on a silver platter."

He slashed the air with his blade and Sophie shrank even further, wishing the plush cushions could swallow her whole.

Especially when Alden said, "This does tie the Council's hands. They can't accuse King Dimitar of not exercising enough control over his populace when one of our own just broke a fundamental rule—at a public ceremony, no less."

"So I made it worse," Sophie mumbled miserably.

"Sadly . . . yes," Alden admitted. He took her hand, waiting for her to look at him. "I know you want to catch these Neverseen—and believe me, I do too. But we're going to have to be patient. Our Council is incomplete. Our people are scared and divided. And now we have the ogres on high alert, ready for a fight. It is not the time for investigating leads and demanding answers about their involvement. It's the time to focus on restoring peace. And you must work extra hard to prove to our world—and the Council—that you are not the out-of-control problem they fear. Then we can seek the justice that you, and Dex, and Prentice, and Kenric and anyone else the rebels have hurt, deserve. Okay?"

Sophie nodded, even though she didn't really have a choice.

She'd messed up too huge this time. Nothing could change until it was fixed.

That didn't mean she was going to stop investigating, though. She'd just have to keep her focus on the Black Swan. Use the empty days to uncover their leak.

"I guess I'd better get going," Alden said, pulling Sophie close for a hug. "I'll see if there's anything I can do to help smooth over the Council before they decide on your punishment."

"I'll go with you," Tiergan told him, sounding anything but happy about it.

Grady promised he'd join them soon, once he'd dealt with a few other things—and the edge to his voice left no doubt that Sophie had more punishments to come.

Alden and Tiergan both gave her sympathetic smiles as they leaped away.

"Let me guess," Sophie said after another painful silence. "I'm grounded for the rest of eternity?"

"I'm considering it," Grady said, taking the place next to her on the couch now that Alden had vacated it. "But . . . I know your heart was in the right place—even if your brain had clearly gone on vacation for the afternoon."

The words were too true to be insulting.

"Plus, I have no doubt that with Bronte on the Council, whatever punishment they settle on will be as miserable as possible. So I won't add much to it. Only this: It's time to brush Verdi's teeth again, and I think that should be your job. And watch out—she spits."

Sophie cringed, but didn't argue.

Besides, after ogre spit, she doubted T. rex spit could be any worse.

"Also, since you don't have school right now, I'm going to make it your job to get my office clean and organized," Edaline added. "You're not done until every single thing is either cleared out or put away."

Sandor snorted. "You're both far too soft. If she were my child, she'd be locked in her room for the rest of her life, for her own protection."

"That would definitely be easier," Grady said, hugging Sophie so tightly she coughed. "But I'll settle for the rest of the night, and a promise to keep the war starting to a minimum from now on? What do you say?"

Sophie responded by tightening her hold.

Edaline joined the hug, and Sophie lost track of how long they sat there clinging to one another. But by the time she let go, the sun was already starting to set.

She spent the rest of the night in her room, examining Jolie's mirrored compact for clues, which turned out to be a more miserable punishment than anything Grady and Edaline could've given her.

No matter which way she squinted at it, twisted it, or tried to use it, the mirrors never did anything except reflect two slightly different versions of herself—both of which looked like a girl who was far better at getting herself into trouble than she was at getting out of it.

Which meant Fitz's plan—whatever it was—was officially her only option at the moment.

She hoped it was a good one.

FORTY-FIVE

I WASN'T SURE IF GRADY AND EDALINE would let me see you," Fitz said as he settled on the flowered carpet of Sophie's bedroom. "Aren't you grounded?"

"Surprisingly, no," Sophie told him, resisting the urge to check her reflection and see how disastrous she looked. "But Grady always finds more interesting ways to punish me."

"Is that why you smell like T. rex breath?" Fitz asked, laughing when she blushed.

She'd just finished brushing Verdi's teeth when Fitz showed up, and she could still feel a slimy blob of dinosaur drool crawling down her back like a cold, sticky slug. It really wasn't fair that Fitz got to look like a teen model in his tailored blue jerkin with gray pants and a gray satchel slung across his shoulders, while she got to look—and apparently *smell*—like The Thing A Dinosaur's Been Chewing On.

"I'm sorry I didn't listen to you yesterday," Sophie mumbled, crossing her arms, trying to hide the fang-size holes scattered along her tunic sleeves. "I know you tried to stop me."

"I probably should've tried harder. It just happened so fast. But I wasn't going to let him take you. I'd transmitted to Keefe that if the ground started to open up I was going to tackle the king and he should grab you and leap you somewhere safe."

Sophie smiled, trying to imagine that. "What did Keefe say?"

"That I was crazier than you, and that I couldn't even tackle my little sister without getting pinned. But I told him I was still going to try. And I really thought I was going to have to. At least half of the Councillors were nodding along as King Dimitar was talking. If Lady Cadence hadn't stepped in, I don't know what would've happened."

"Really?" Sophie whispered.

She knew she didn't have the full support of the Council, but . . . *half*?

"Yeah. It was pretty scary."

"Seriously."

She pulled at the edges of one of the holes in her sleeve, stretching it wider. "You must think I'm a total idiot."

"Nah. I *am* starting to wonder if you're trying to beat Keefe's record for biggest interspeciesial episode—and if you are, I'm pretty sure you've won. The Great Gulon Incident was epic, but it didn't almost spark a war." His voice hitched on the last word. "I do get why you did it, though," he added quietly. "And I'm guessing you didn't learn anything?"

"Only that I've made it even harder for the Council to investigate what's going on with the ogres. Your dad said we'd have to wait until my punishment is delivered and things *hopefully* go back to normal."

Fitz sighed. "Well, my dad said the punishment wouldn't be *that* severe."

"I hope he's right. But it's up to the Council, so . . ."

She didn't finish the sentence, but Fitz must've guessed what she was thinking, because he asked, "Who do you think the new Councillor will be?"

"I have no idea. Hopefully someone who likes me."

"Yeah. I was hoping for Sir Tiergan, but my dad said the 'no kids' rule applies to him, even though his son is adopted."

"Who does your dad think it will be?"

"Master Leto from the Silver Tower. I guess he's had the most nominations. Do you know him?"

"Only a little. He's kind of weird." But he'd been nice to her the last few times she'd seen him, so he might be an okay choice. "Who are the other nominees?"

"A bunch of ancient guys I've never met. Oh, and Lady Cadence. She's kind of a long shot, considering how many years she's been away. But after she smoothed things over yesterday, she got a lot of people nominating her."

She also seemed to despise Sophie, but, maybe she was getting over it. She *had* come to Sophie's defense.

Then again, she'd also talked quite a lot about Sophie being punished . . .

"Hey, it's going to be okay," Fitz promised. "And in the meantime, I brought something to cheer you up. You have no idea how hard it was sneaking this out past Biana. She wanted to come with me today, but . . ."

He opened his satchel and pulled out a fluffy red stuffed animal that reminded Sophie of a lizard, but with short fur and a bushy red-and-white tail.

"Mr. Snuggles!"

Fitz turned as red as his stuffed dragon.

Especially when she said, "You didn't tell me he was sparkly."

"Yeah. Um. Dragons have a sheen on their fur—plus Elwin picked him, not me."

"Sparkles also make everything better. Well, except alicorn poop."

"I don't know. I think sparkly poop is way better than regular poop."

"That's because you've never fallen into a pile of it."

"You're right about that." His smile faded. "You don't think he's stupid?"

"Mr. Snuggles? He's adorable. He might even be better than Ella."

374

They both turned to look at the bright blue elephant propped among the pillows on her bed.

"Well, maybe it's a tie," Sophie decided.

Fitz laughed and set Mr. Snuggles down next to him—with a quick pat to the head—before he reached into his bag again.

"So, um, there was another reason I didn't want Biana to come with me today too," he said, pulling out a silver memory log with a jeweled Vacker crest on the cover. "I've been working on Tiergan's assignment, recording everything I remember from the day of the fire. And it's been taking a while, since you sent me a *lot* of star maps when were bottling the quintessence."

She'd forgotten about that. "I bet you can skip them. I doubt the Council's going to need to see any of those. It's all information they can find anywhere."

"I wasn't sure, so I thought I'd try." He opened the memory log, flipping through page after page of black sky and carefully labeled stars. "And I thought it was weird how clear the memories are. They're so much more detailed than my usual projections."

He flipped to the beginning of the memory log, showing her a scene he'd recorded of a dark-haired girl. She looked like Biana, but the features of her face were slightly off. Her nose was too broad and her eyes were too far apart.

"I recorded this in my telepathy session last year to test the accuracy of my memories. I was supposed to project an image of someone in my family and see how close it comes to the reality. Obviously I messed a few things up."

"It's not perfect. But I still knew who it was."

"Exactly. And my Mentor said that's normal for those of us without photographic memories. Our minds hold onto an overall impression, not an exact re-creation. Except for these." He flipped to the star maps again. "In these, I remember every. Single. Star."

"Right. But I shared that memory with you, so I'm the one who remembered those details."

"But it would still be my memory of your memory—or it's supposed to be. And I would never be able to remember it so perfectly. Not unless it came from you."

"But it *did* come from me."

"Yeah, but what I'm saying is, I think you sent it to me differently. If you'd transmitted it, the memory would've flashed through my mind just long enough for me to make my own record of it, which wouldn't have been as detailed. Only if you'd *implanted* it would the memory stay perfectly intact."

"Implanted?"

The word made Sophie think of microchips and alien probes and needles poking through skin.

"It's where you stick the memory in someone's mind—like shoving a book on someone else's bookshelf, and leaving it there for them to reference later," Fitz explained, which at least sounded less creepy than what she'd been imagining. Or it was until he said, "I'm sure that's how the Black Swan put their secrets in your head. Otherwise you would've known the memories were there. You can implant something without the person ever really looking at it."

"Okay . . . ," Sophie said slowly, her brain struggling to keep up. "So is implanting bad?"

"Of course not. It's just a super-hard skill only a few people can really pull off—but I guess I shouldn't be surprised anymore. You can pretty much do anything."

He grinned at her, and Sophie wanted to take it as a compliment. But she wasn't sure she liked that she'd done it without even realizing.

"Did I implant anything else?" she asked.

"That's what I'm trying to figure out. I've been searching my mind for anything that seems sharper and more detailed than my other memories. And I found this."

He flipped over a few more pages and showed her an image of a formula so complex it might as well have been written in gibberish. Still, each number, line, and squiggle was exactly where it should be.

"That's how they make frissyn," Sophie said, remembering when she'd projected the classified formula in her memory log a few months back. "Why would I have sent you that?"

"Maybe it was on your mind, since that's what we were gathering the quintessence for."

"Yeah. Maybe." But the explanation sounded as empty as she felt. "Did you find anything else?"

Fitz flipped through more pages, settling on another star map.

Most of the stars weren't labeled. But there were five dark splotches with names:

Lucilliant

Phosforien

Marquiseire

Candesia

Elementine

"But . . . these are the unmapped stars . . . ," Sophie mumbled, holding the image closer to make sure she was seeing it correctly.

"That's what I thought. Weird that there's a *map* of the unmapped stars, isn't it?"

"I don't understand. I don't know these stars. I mean . . . I do now that I'm looking at them. But I didn't know that I knew them, you know? Not until I read them."

"Isn't that how it always is when a memory gets triggered for you?" Fitz asked.

"It is. But how could I implant a memory before I even remembered it?"

"I don't know. I figured you must've remembered it, since you knew how to find Elementine. Maybe this is where your brain pulled that information from without you realizing. So it would be like you knew it, but you didn't know you knew it, you know?"

Sophie wasn't entirely sure if that sentence even made sense.

But how could she argue with what was right in front of her eyes.

"Was this it? Was that the only other memory I implanted?"

"I'm still searching, so there could be more. But I definitely found one other."

He flipped through the pages again, stopping on a scene of a round window with black iron bars crisscrossed over it.

"Can you read that?" Fitz asked, pointing to a square sign hanging from a nearby lamppost, right under a red circle with a wide white line.

"It says 'except authorized,'" Sophie told him, surprised Fitz had to ask.

She studied the letters again, feeling her stomach tighten when she realized they actually said *"eccetto autorizzati."* Which did mean the same thing.

In *Italian*.

"This is in the Forbidden Cities!" Sophie practically shouted, grabbing the journal to get a better look.

"I figured it had to be," Fitz agreed. "But it's not from any of my memories, so you must've implanted it."

He was right—the memory was too sharp and clear.

"But I don't remember it either."

She also couldn't find any other memories to connect it to, or any reason why she would've been thinking about a window— in *Italy*—during the middle of a deadly fire.

And why would the Black Swan bother implanting the stupid window in her head in the first place?

Then she noticed the dark stain discoloring the yellow stones around the window.

She'd thought it was just wear and weathering. But the perfectly curved shape was unmistakable.

The sign of the swan.

FORTY-SIX

WHERE IS THIS?" SOPHIE ASKED, flipping the page like it would somehow show her more of the scene.

"I was hoping you would know," Fitz admitted. "Seeing the memory again doesn't trigger anything?"

Sophie closed her eyes, willing her brain to pull the pieces together.

"I'm not getting anything."

"Well, then I guess I don't have a plan after all. I figured we'd go there and see what we can learn about the Black Swan. But that's kind of hard to do if we don't know where it is."

"And who knows if it's even safe? Remember, last time

Keefe and I tracked down one of their hideouts, there was an ambush waiting for us." She slammed the memory log harder than she needed to. "It's all such a mess. I can't trust the Black Swan, and now the Council hates me and the ogres are out to get me and Eternalia is gone and Kenric . . ."

Just saying his name ripped the hole inside her a little wider.

"Here," Fitz said, handing her Mr. Snuggles.

He waved it under her nose until she took it, and she had to admit, hugging the super soft dragon did help.

"Sorry," she mumbled.

"No need to apologize. If anyone deserves to freak out, it's you. I seriously don't know how you deal with it all." He grabbed the memory log and flipped back to the Italian window, turning it round and round, like seeing it upside down would magically tell them which one of the dozens of cities in Italy they were supposed to go to.

"I still feel like this is the answer," he said quietly. "I mean, something had to trigger this, right? Your mind wouldn't have just pulled up some random memory, would it?"

"Who knows anymore?"

Her sulky tone made her realize how pouty she was being.

She took the memory log back and stared at the sign of the swan.

It was clever the way they'd hidden it—glaringly obvious now that she knew where to look, but perfectly camouflaged to everyone else.

She tried to think of any famous landmarks it could be a part of, but nothing seemed to fit. Sometimes she really missed the Internet. She doubted the answer was as easy as searching "round windows in Italy." But it had worked in Paris when she was with Dex.

"Why would they give me an image of one of their bases? And what would've triggered me to think of it?" she asked.

She'd hardly been thinking about windows or Italy—or even the Black Swan—when she was racing to collect enough quintessence to save Eternalia.

She was so terrified she could barely think straight.

"Maybe that's it," she said slowly, trying to let the idea settle before she fed it any hope. "Maybe it was fear—like a panic switch."

She sometimes wondered how the Black Swan could send her into such dangerous situations and not seem to care what happened to her. Maybe they'd stacked her memories in a way to make her remember how to find them if she ever really needed them.

"Why didn't it happen the other times you've been in danger, then?" Fitz asked. "It's not like you haven't almost died a few billion times."

"True."

Plus, she hadn't been *that* scared when she was with Fitz on the beach. She'd actually felt almost . . . safe. They were away from the fire, and she wasn't alone, and Fitz was helping her and—

"What if it was trust?" Sophie asked, sitting up straighter. "Sir Tiergan said it was our most powerful asset. And it helped me let you into my head once."

"That's true! *And,*"—he took the memory log and turned to a blank page—"that would be awesome, because then we should be able to re-create it!"

"Re-create what?"

"Whatever you did to dig up that memory. We do *exactly* what we did that night, and hope it helps your mind dig up the missing pieces." He stood, offering her a hand to pull her up. "How were we standing? You were behind me, right?"

"Yeah," Sophie said, blushing as she remembered how close they'd been.

Somehow she managed to make her legs drag her toward him, wishing for the fiftieth time that she'd had a chance to wash away the dino drool first.

"No—you were closer than that," he told her. "I remember feeling more heat—body heat," he corrected, like that somehow made it less embarrassing. "It was really cold, remember?"

Sophie had been trying not to relive even a second of that horrible night. But if she was going to make this work, she had to take her mind back.

She pictured the beach.

The vibrant, glowing waves.

The freezing ocean breeze.

Her arms were so weary from holding the heavy stellarscope that she'd leaned on Fitz, clinging to him like he was all she had left.

"Yeah, it was more like that," Fitz said, making her realize she'd started to lean on him again.

She wrapped her arms around him, resting her hands on his wrists as he pretended to hold a stellarscope.

"I think your hands were a little higher," he told her, "resting on top of mine."

She willed her palms not to sweat as she slid them into place.

"I think that's it," Fitz whispered.

"Yeah. Me too."

She could practically hear the crashing waves and see the twinkling stars. Their last safe moment, before everything went up in smoke.

"So . . . now what?" she asked.

"I think you have to open your mind to mine."

"Right." She took a deep breath and stretched out her consciousness, letting Fitz's thoughts fill her head.

It's so crazy how you do that, he thought. *I always try to block you—just to see if I can. But I swear you slip through faster every time.*

Sorry, Sophie transmitted.

Stop apologizing! You have an amazing talent, Sophie. I'd give anything to be like you.

And I'd give anything to be normal, like you.

And that *is why we trust each other.*

Was it?

Could it really be that simple?

Want to try implanting something, to see if you remember how? Fitz asked. *Make sure you pick something I wouldn't already have a memory of, so we can tell.*

Right.

But she knew she had to do better than that.

If this was about trust, she needed to tell him something she hadn't told anyone else.

You ready? she asked, trying to remember what she'd done that night. She knew she'd mixed brain push energy along with the transmission to make it stronger, so she focused on the warmth buzzing in the back of her mind, letting the tingling heat mix with her concentration before she pushed the memory into Fitz's head.

"Whoa," Fitz breathed. "I think that worked."

He scrambled for his memory log and flipped to a blank page, projecting the memory Sophie had just sent him in vivid, photographic detail.

"What is this?" Fitz asked, frowning at the scene.

A blond woman in a purple gown stood holding a black swan.

Sophie swallowed to find her voice. "It's a memory I saw in Prentice's mind—or maybe 'vision' is the better word. I'm not sure. All I know is . . . that's Jolie."

Fitz's eyes widened at the name, and he pointed to the swan she was holding. "Does this mean what I think it means?"

"That's what Biana and I have been trying to figure out. I haven't told Grady and Edaline. The only other person I've told is Tiergan, and it was back when he thought a broken mind could never be healed, so he said it was all just random madness."

"Are you sure it's not?"

She showed him the mirrored compact, letting him trace his fingers over the constellation on the cover. She even told him about Vertina and the missing password. But if she was *really* going to trust him, there was one more thing she had to share.

"You know what else this means, right?" she whispered, trying to work up the courage. "Or what it could mean, anyway."

Fitz shook his head, taking his eyes off the memory log to study her.

She squared her shoulders, taking a deep breath. "It could mean Jolie is my mother."

The words seemed to vanish as soon as they left her lips, and Sophie wondered if Fitz had even heard them.

Then he took her hand, squeezing it tight. "I get why that would be scary."

"Do you?" Sophie asked. "Sometimes I'm not even sure how to explain it."

"Yeah. I'm sure it would be super weird to find out your parents are actually your grandparents."

"That's part of it," Sophie whispered. "But also . . . I don't know."

"What?"

She picked up Mr. Snuggles again, squeezing tight as she told him, "It's hard enough knowing that I remind Grady and Edaline of her. If they knew I was her daughter . . ."

"You'd worry that's the only reason they want you," Fitz finished for her.

Sophie nodded, burying her face in Mr. Snuggles's soft fur.

"If it helps, I don't think that's the case. They seem like they really care about you."

"I know. But it would still change everything."

"It probably would," he admitted. "Wait—would that mean you're related to Dex, too?"

Sophie nodded, still not sure why that bothered her.

She'd hoped Fitz might be able to explain it, but all he said was, "Wow."

Then he totally cracked up. "Dex is going to freak if that's true," he said between laughs.

"If what's true?" a painfully familiar voice asked from the doorway.

Fitz fell silent and Sophie forced herself to turn toward the sound.

Just as she'd feared, she found a red-faced, fuming Dex.

FORTY-SEVEN

IF WHAT'S TRUE?" DEX REPEATED, "AND IF you tell me it's 'nothing,' I swear I'm going to slip an honesty elixir in your next bottle of lushberry juice."

"You don't even make those," Sophie argued, hoping it was true.

"I can figure out how," he promised.

Sophie glared at Sandor, wondering what the point was of having a goblin constantly eavesdropping outside her door if he couldn't give her a heads-up about surprise visitors. He shrugged innocently—but the glint in his eye told her he'd kept silent on purpose. Probably *his* punishment for the trouble she'd caused with King Dimitar.

"Seriously, what were you guys talking about?" Dex asked. "I'm not going to 'freak out.'"

"It was just a joke, okay?" Fitz told him, looking like he wished he could leap out of there.

"What kind of joke?" Dex pressed. "And what is *that*?"

Sophie shoved Mr. Snuggles behind her back. "Just something Fitz brought to cheer me up."

"How nice of him."

"It was, actually," Sophie said—a little sharper than she meant to.

She'd been trying not to let it bother her, but . . . she'd been through a fire, a funeral, and almost been kidnapped by an ogre king, and Dex hadn't even hailed her on her Imparter to make sure she was okay.

"I'm sorry I haven't come by sooner," Dex mumbled, like he knew what she'd been thinking. "I've been stuck working on an assignment from the Council."

"Really?" Fitz asked, the same time Sophie asked, "What assignment?"

"I'm not allowed to talk about it. But you don't have to worry, it's totally safe. I'm just testing some gadgets to see if I can improve them. Oh—and get this. I showed Councillor Terik my telepathy enhancer and he thought it had great potential."

"Seriously?" Fitz asked. "He actually thinks you can enhance someone's abilities?"

"No," Dex admitted. "But he thinks I might be able restrict

390

someone's ability instead. I haven't had time to tweak it yet because they needed me to finish the other weap—um, gadgets, first. But I think I know what I need to do to make that change."

"Why would the Council want to restrict someone's abilities?" Fitz asked, clearly disgusted by the idea.

Sophie was more bothered by Dex's little slip.

Were the Councillors making *weapons*?

"Uh, because some people shouldn't be allowed to have abilities," Dex argued.

"Allowed," Fitz repeated.

"Yeah. *Allowed.* Think about it. Restricting Fintan's ability would've saved Councillor Kenric's life. And his own life. And all of Eternalia."

"But . . . ," Sophie started, then realized she had nothing to say.

The Councillors had done everything they could to keep the healing safe. But they could only control the temperature, their clothes, how many people were in the room. They couldn't control *Fintan.*

"Okay, but . . . controlling *people* with gadgets?" Fitz asked. "That's creepy."

He turned to Sophie, like he was expecting her to agree. But she was too stuck on the idea that the whole fire could've been prevented with a simple silver circlet.

"They wouldn't be controlling everyone," Dex argued. "Just the people who need it."

"And who decides that?" Fitz asked.

"The Council, obviously. What?" Dex asked when Fitz cringed. "I thought your family was like, the Council's number one fan club."

"You clearly know nothing about my family. But I'm not saying I don't trust the Council. I'm saying I don't think it's right to mess with people's brains."

"Ha—this coming from a Telepath!"

"Telepaths have rules and restrictions to follow to make sure we don't abuse our abilities. Sounds like Technopaths need the same."

"Um, the *Council* is the one asking me to make that gadget, remember?"

"Yeah. That's what worries me. I think I'm going to go home and see if my dad knows about this. Want to meet up tomorrow to try again?" Fitz asked Sophie as he packed away his memory log.

She nodded, still struggling to process the information overload from the last few minutes.

Fitz gave one quick longing look to Mr. Snuggles as he pulled out his home crystal. Then he left him behind and stepped into the light.

"So what was the 'joke' I'm apparently going to freak out about?" Dex asked the second Fitz glittered away.

Sophie sighed and set Mr. Snuggles on her bed. "It was nothing, Dex. Really, honestly, nothing."

"You're seriously not going to tell me?"

"Not right now, okay? It's not important, and maybe you haven't noticed, but I'm having kind of a bad week."

Her voice caught on the last words.

"You're right," Dex said, moving closer. "I just . . . No—no excuses. I'm sorry."

"Thanks," Sophie mumbled, wiping her nose.

He reached for her hand, then stopped halfway there, leaving his fingers dangling. "I'm sorry I didn't check on you. I begged my dad to let me help with the Everblaze—mostly so I could make sure you were okay. But he said I wasn't experienced enough to handle quintessence. So I stayed up all night, watching my panic switch in case you called me. I even kept my shoes on so I wouldn't have anything to slow me down. But you never called."

"I'm not going to drag you into danger, Dex."

"But I *want* you to. That's why I made you that ring. And I'm sorry I let the Council's assignment keep me from checking on you. I should've made time—though I also wasn't at the planting, so I didn't know about King Dimitar until today. That's why I rushed over."

"Why weren't you at the planting?"

"Councillor Terik needed all the gadgets back by this morning, so he could pass them on to the next Technopath—and they needed a ton of work."

"You can stop calling them gadgets, Dex. I know they're weapons."

He hesitated before he said, "Not all of them. Besides, don't you think it's good that the Council is realizing they need to be prepared? My dad said that if they'd had a batch of frissyn on hand, most of Eternalia would still be standing."

"Yeah, I guess."

But if the elves needed *weapons* . . .

She sat on the edge of her bed and Dex sat beside her—not so subtly knocking Mr. Snuggles to the floor in the process.

"You sure you're okay?" he asked. "You look . . . pretty awful."

"Gee, thanks."

"No, I just mean . . . you can talk to me, you know. Maybe I can help?"

Sophie wished he could. But unless he knew how to find a random window in Italy . . .

"Wait," she said, rushing to her desk and digging through the drawers.

If she wanted to learn about anything human, she was going to need to access *human* information.

She pulled out her old iPod and switched it on, showing Dex how it said *Searching* on the screen. "I know this is probably going to sound weird, but do you think there's any way you could make this pick up human signals from where we are?"

He'd already made it solar powered a few months back. Maybe he could use his ability to amplify the antenna or something.

Dex traced his fingers along the screen. "What kind of signals?"

"Anything. Satellite. Wi-Fi. I just need to access the Internet.

Remember how I used it to find the bridge we needed when we were in Paris?"

"Yeah, and I still can't believe that clunky machine was able to help us. But"—he flipped the iPod over and squinted at the back—"I can sense a receiver in here, and it's super weak. I'm sure if I boost that it'll pick up whatever you want. It might take me a few days, though. Councillor Terik wanted that ability restrictor as soon as possible."

"A few days is fine," she told him—though she hoped it would be sooner.

And that there was a FamousRoundWindowsInItaly.com, complete with detailed directions.

But even if there wasn't, she was going to find that building.

After Dex left, Sophie spent the rest of the afternoon trying to make a dent in the other half of her punishment: cleaning and organizing Edaline's office.

She was up to her elbows in tiny silver butterflies when someone behind her snapped their fingers, making all the shimmering insects spring to life and fly around her.

"Whoa, too bad those aren't spiders or stinkbugs or something," Keefe said from the doorway. "I could cause some serious chaos."

"I'm sure you could," Sophie agreed, watching the butterflies flit and flutter. "It really would've been a beautiful wedding, wouldn't it?"

"Maybe," Keefe agreed. "But robotic spiders would've been cooler. They could've put them under everyone's chairs and triggered them during the vows."

"Wow—you should be a wedding planner."

"Nah. I'll save it for my own wedding. Make my bride feel even luckier." He winked.

"So what's up?" Sophie asked, before the conversation got any weirder.

"You don't know why I'm here?"

"Should I?"

"I don't know. Didn't you get one of these?"

He stumbled through the maze of boxes and handed her a tiny scroll.

The wax seal had been broken—split in half from when Keefe must've opened it.

But Sophie could still perfectly make out the sign of the swan.

FORTY-EIGHT

WHERE DID YOU GET THIS?" Sophie asked, not sure if she should feel excited or terrified. Mostly she felt confused.

Especially when Keefe told her. "I found it in my cape pocket this morning—*no* idea how it got there. You didn't get one?"

She checked her pockets to make sure, surprised at how disappointed she was when they were empty. She felt even worse when she read the Black Swan's message:

Careful plans have now been changed
So a meeting must be arranged.

In three days time, when the evening star ascends
Find us where the lost have no end.

"They want to meet with you," Sophie mumbled, reading the message again to be sure.

"I know—they're finally including me on the team! Hope they know this means their little rule book just went out the window—and the first change I'll be implementing is *clearer stinking directions*. Any idea 'where the lost have no end'?"

"Probably in the Wanderling Woods, by my tree. They've left me notes there before."

"And the evening star ascends . . . ?"

"Right after sunset," Sophie finished.

"Cool. Party with the Black Swan in three days. Bring your dancing shoes, Foster. And maybe try to look a *little* less miserable than you do right now, because it's a serious bummer. Come on, this is good news!"

"Is it?" she asked. "How do you know it's not a trap?"

"I don't," Keefe admitted. "But even if it is, remember: Last time we met with them you got your abilities fixed and that Forkle dude gave you some answers."

"And then we almost died," she reminded him.

"Details, details." He laughed when she didn't smile. "I'm kidding, Foster. I do realize it's a risk. But I think it's worth it—especially since they want us to meet in the Wanderling Woods. I mean, how bad could that be?"

"Well, for one thing, they only gave a note to you. Not me. Don't you find that suspicious?"

"That *is* weird," Keefe admitted. "When was the last time you checked the cave?"

"Not since we realized they had a leak."

"Then maybe there's a note there waiting for you. That would make sense, if you think about it. Sandor's got so many security things around here, the cave is probably the closest they can get."

"Maybe . . ."

"Gee, try to sound *less* excited. Actually, never mind. Get your shoes on—we're going to the cave. And get ready for an epic 'I told you so' when we find your note waiting."

Keefe kept true to his word, and his "I told you so" was so loud, it was still echoing around them as Sophie unrolled the tiny scroll. Her note showed the same instructions—but it also included an extra verse:

The days ahead will be dark and dour.
You must not fear yourself or your power.

"Not cool—I didn't get a present with mine," Keefe complained as he unhooked a familiar black magsidian swan charm from where it had been latched through the paper.

Magsidian was a rare mineral only the dwarves could mine, and it had the ability to affect certain forces, depending on how it had been cut. The last time they'd used the charm, it had steered the needle of Sophie's compass toward the Black Swan's hideout.

She had no idea what they'd need it for this time—but that was the least of her worries at the moment.

"Do you *really* think we should trust them?" she whispered, glancing over her shoulder like she expected a fleet of dwarves to pop out of the sand.

"You most definitely should not," Sandor interrupted, to neither of their surprise.

Sophie was honestly shocked he'd kept quiet as long as he had. Other than a few squeaky sighs, he hadn't even argued about them going down to the caves. But he was back in full-fledged Overprotective Bodyguard mode as he added, "They've already proven that they cannot ensure your protection. I will not let you blindly follow these instructions!"

"But they gave us three days to prepare," Keefe reminded him. "And they told us where we're going. I'm betting they knew you were going to freak out about this. So now you can do whatever obsessive safety stuff you want to do first."

Sandor couldn't argue with that logic. But he still mumbled, "I do not like it."

"I don't either," Sophie admitted. "I mean, why reach out to us now, after all these weeks of silence?"

"I don't know—you *did* just tick off the ogre king and almost start a war," Keefe said with a smirk. "Maybe they decided you shouldn't be left to your own devices."

Sandor released another squeaky sigh. "That almost makes sense."

"Of course it does!" Keefe told him.

Next thing Sophie knew, Sandor and Keefe were coming up with a plan. She tried to listen, but mostly she kept rereading the Black Swan's note, wondering if they knew something she didn't.

One line in particular stood out from the others:

The days ahead will be dark and dour.

Despite the Black Swan's prediction, nothing dark or dour happened during the next three days.

Sandor haunted Sophie's every move, even though all she did was organize more trunks of wedding decorations in Edaline's office—finding nothing useful, interesting, or related to the Black Swan in any of them—and hang out in her room.

Dex was too busy working on the ability restrictor to visit. But he hailed her every night, and didn't even freak out—too much—when she told him about the meeting with the Black Swan. He did, of course, ask if he could go. But Sophie told him the same thing she'd told Fitz and Biana: *She couldn't risk scaring the Black Swan away.*

Biana tried to convince Sophie that she could sneak along as a Vanisher, but since she couldn't stay invisible for longer than a few minutes, she had to admit she couldn't handle it. She stopped coming over as often, so she could practice vanishing with Della. Which worked out well because Fitz wanted to work with Sophie on triggering her memories.

He'd stop by every afternoon to test new trust exercises, but nothing seemed to work—even when he had her stand on a chair and fall backward into his arms. He did catch her, without even bruising her. But all it earned them was some serious teasing from Keefe, who'd showed up just in time to find Fitz cradling her.

Keefe spent the rest of the day begging for a turn and promising he'd only drop her once.

It was frustrating and discouraging—but somehow comforting at the same time. Like life had found a path back to normal, despite school being canceled and news of the Councillor nominations trickling in.

Most of the nominees Sophie had never heard of. But she was surprised to hear Dame Alina's name in the mix.

"Do you think she'll win?" Sophie asked Grady when she finally caught him at breakfast on the third morning.

With all noble assignments on hold during the mourning period, Grady had been working long hours in Eternalia, helping the gnomes organize their cleanup project. Apparently they were saving all the shards of jewels to build a monument to Kenric's legacy—which Sophie knew was an awesome idea. But she wasn't sure she could bear seeing it when it was finished.

"Alden seems to think Dame Alina has several supporters,"

Grady said, serving Sophie a huge slice of the purple porcaroot pie Edaline had conjured up before heading out to work in the pastures. "Why? Are you afraid of losing your principal?"

Actually, Dame Alina was Sophie's top pick. She'd been extra kind and supportive at Foxfire lately—and she always sided with Alden. Having her on the Council would guarantee another vote in Sophie's favor.

Sophie took a bite of her breakfast, relieved when it tasted like bacon mixed with more bacon and covered in melting cheese. Gnomes really did grow the best tasting vegetables.

"How long do you think it's going to take the Council to come to a decision," she asked between mouthfuls.

"Oh, I think they'll elect someone as soon as the nomination period has ended. Not only is King Dimitar waiting on your punishment"—he cleared his throat—"but our world needs to know we have our leaders settled again. People need to feel safe. And speaking of *safe* . . ."

He scooted closer, taking her hand. "Just because we haven't talked about this meeting with the Black Swan tonight doesn't mean I'm totally okay with it."

"So . . . you don't think I should go?" Sophie asked, still having doubts herself.

"Actually, I think we need to find out what the Black Swan wants. But I don't trust them—and I definitely don't trust the Neverseen—so I'm going to insist that Sandor go with you. And not just to the Wanderling Woods. *Anywhere* they take you. None of that *drugging you and taking you somewhere all alone* stuff like last time. "

"They might not allow that," Sophie warned him. "Last time they wouldn't let Keefe go with me."

"I can be *much* more persuasive than Mr. Sencen," Sandor said, patting his weapon-filled pockets. "And if they refuse, I shall drag the two of you home—immediately."

"But—"

"This is not up for debate," Grady interrupted. "You are not to go anywhere without your bodyguard—and that applies to everything for right now. If Sandor's not with, you don't go, understood? Not until things settle down."

"Fine," Sophie mumbled. She knew a losing fight when she saw it.

Plus, she had a feeling she knew what "things" Grady meant. She'd caught Fitz and Keefe whispering about an Exile Sophie Foster! campaign that apparently had a ton of supporters.

As she'd heard Keefe put it, the Lost Cities were not a "Foster friendly" place at the moment.

She pushed aside her plate, no longer feeling hungry.

Grady pushed it back—and added two pink folded pastries. "That's another thing. I know you're under a lot of stress. But you still need to eat. And sleep. And do things with your friends that don't involve conspiracies or rebels or testing your abilities. Childhood is a precious gift, Sophie. Don't let anything steal it away."

Sophie nibbled on one of the pastries—which tasted like crepes soaked in butter and sugar. "It's not really my choice, is it?"

"Yes, it is. I wish I could give you a world where everything was perfect and shining and safe. I used to think that's what we had, but . . ." He shook his head. "I've realized now that our world doesn't define us. We define our world. And I hope you'll fill yours with as much light and happiness as you can."

"You realize how silly that sounds, right?"

"I do. But after everything that's happened, I think we could all use a bit more silly in our lives."

The rest of the day passed in a blur, and all too soon the sun was setting and Sophie was bundled in a thick black cape and heading to the Leapmaster, hopeful she was doing the right thing.

Of course Grady and Edaline were waiting for her.

She braced for a long lecture—and an even longer list of rules and warnings.

All they did was hug her.

"Really? That's it?" Sophie asked as they called the crystal for the Wanderling Woods.

"Why?" Edaline asked.

"Because I'm going off to a dark, lonely forest to meet with a group of rebels, one of whom might be a traitor."

"We trust you," Edaline promised.

"And we trust Sandor," Grady added.

Sandor pounded his burly chest—which was now strapped with two rather terrifying daggers. Sheathed next to his sword was an obscurer and a melder—one of the rare Elvin weapons Sophie kept hoping she'd never have to see again.

"Nothing will get past me," he promised.

Sophie nodded. But she couldn't help remembering the way King Dimitar had tossed him aside like a piece of trash.

"If you don't want to do this, you don't have to," Grady told her quietly.

"Yes, I do."

She repeated the words in her mind until her legs felt strong enough to move. Then she took Sandor's hand—glad she had someone to hold on to—and let the light carry her to the Black Swan.

FORTY-NINE

ABOUT TIME YOU GOT HERE," Keefe said, smirking at Sophie from the archway to the Wanderling Woods. "And it looks like we have a chaperone. What kind of lame party is this?"

"One where you will both come home alive—and without any broken bones," Sandor said, sniffing the air and scanning the trees around them.

"But Sophie didn't have any broken bones last ti—wait! Does this mean Gigantor is starting to *care* about me? Should we hug it out?"

He held out his arms.

Sandor shoved past him. "Stay behind me—and keep in

mind that Miss Foster is, and always will be, my first priority."

"Mine too," Keefe said as he fell in step beside Sophie.

As soon as they crossed into the Woods, Sandor strayed off the regular path, cutting through the grassy knolls that looked far less tranquil covered in shadow. The Wanderlings had hidden their flowers and leaves, turning the trees into a forest of skeletons. And the silence felt different in the twilight. Sharper and colder—like the woods was holding its breath. Waiting to pounce.

"Relax, Foster," Keefe said, taking her hand—and then immediately dropping it. "Sheesh—keep up that kind of worrying and you're going to make us both hurl. Plus, that clenched jaw thing you're doing makes you look like an angry chipmunk."

Sophie pretended to ignore him—but she did force her jaw to relax.

"Did your parents give you a hard time about going tonight?" she asked, needing to break the eerie silence.

"A little," Keefe admitted. "My dad has apparently decided that my connection to you could ruin the Sencen name— which is awesome, by the way. Now I get to hang with you *and* tick my dad off. Win and win!"

He elbowed Sophie until she smiled.

"What about your mom?" Sophie asked.

"Eh, she said, and I quote, 'Can't you rescue the alicorn again? It's been nice actually having a son I can brag about.'"

408

He mimicked Lady Gisela's voice perfectly, which made the words that much more awful.

Sophie reached for his hand. "I'm sorry."

Keefe shrugged.

Several seconds passed before he added, "My dad did make sure I wore a cape to keep warm. So I guess that counts as worrying about me. Maybe?"

"Definitely," Sophie agreed, with as much enthusiasm as she could muster.

"Yeah. Though of course my mom told me I fastened it too loosely and insisted I repin it. *Twice.*"

Now it looked tight enough to choke him, and his Sencen crest was digging into his chin.

Sophie squeezed his hand harder.

They walked the rest of the way in silence, their breaths turning to huffs as the ground became steeper and steeper. Cold sweat dripped down Sophie's back as they crested the hill, but it was worth the climb when she spotted her Wanderling.

Dangling from one of the thin, fragile branches was a small twinkling bottle strung with a silver satin ribbon.

Sandor shoved Keefe and Sophie behind him as he sniffed the air, and then the fragile vial. Then he slowly untied the ribbon and offered it to Sophie. "It appears to be safe—but I would not advise opening it."

"I don't think we need to," she said, lifting the bottle to study it against the night sky.

The blue glow was filled with tiny flecks of darkness and shimmer, all of which swirled like glitter in a snow globe. And when she traced her finger along the cold, damp glass, the memory finally triggered.

"This is light from Lucilliant. It's one of the unmapped stars."

"Okay," Keefe said, leaning closer to the bottle. "That explains why it looks so freaky. Any idea what we do with it? Or is it just like . . . a fun souvenir we get to keep from tonight's daring journey?"

"Actually, I'm pretty sure the journey is just getting started." She pulled back her sleeve and removed her charm bracelet, holding up the black swan charm. "Magsidian can also serve as a leaping crystal, and I've seen it work differently with different kinds of light. I'm betting they want us to use the glow from Lucilliant to leap to the real meeting place."

Keefe grinned. "Cute *and* smart. No wonder Dex gave you a ring."

"That's—I . . ." Sophie hid behind her hair. "You ready?"

"I should go first," Sandor decided.

"You can't leap without one of us," Sophie reminded him. "And even if you could, you might not be able to come back here. We don't know how this is going to work."

"Then perhaps we shouldn't go," Sandor argued.

"Aw, come on—where's your sense of adventure?" Keefe asked.

"It is overshadowed by my sense of responsibility. My job is to bring you home safe."

"There you go, caring about me again," Keefe said with a grin. "But come on, you know we need to find out what the Black Swan is up to—that's why we came here."

Sandor looked like he wanted to pick them both up and drag them back to Havenfield. But he released his death grip on Sophie's hand, letting her press the charm against the glowing vial.

The tiny swan crusted with a thin layer of frost as a beam of sparkling, swirling blue light refracted at her feet.

"That. Is. Awesome!" Keefe said as he looped his arm through hers. "You ready, Gigantor?"

A squeaky snort was Sandor's only reply. But he curled one massive hand around Sophie's arm, keeping his other on the hilt of his blade as Keefe pulled them into the icy light.

The cold rush was a tempest.

Tearing and shredding and turning turning turning.

Sophie tried to scream or cry or call someone's name, but she couldn't think—couldn't function. She was empty. She was nothing. She was—

—slamming into the hot ground like a bug against a windshield, then tumbling tumbling tumbling until she collapsed in a heap.

"Okay," Keefe said, choking on the dry, dusty air. "I am definitely not a fan of that kind of leaping. Let's call a normal beam of light for the way home, shall we?"

"I don't think we can." Sophie pulled herself to her feet—coughing and hacking as she used the glow of Lucilliant to show him the stalagmite-covered ceiling. "We just leaped underground."

"So *that's* why it felt like getting stepped on by an ogre."

"Actually, the ogre stomping would've been preferable," Sandor told him.

"I guess you would know," Keefe agreed. "How hard was it not to go all *goblin rage* on King Dimitar when he punched you like that? I *know* you held back."

"It is not my place to attack the ogre king. Not *yet*. But that is a conversation for another day. Right now, I see two much more concerning issues." He stood and waved his arm around the cave—which was much smaller than Sophie realized. Barely larger than her closet. "There are no tunnels and no stairs in or out of this place."

"Yeah, and where's the Black Swan?" Keefe cupped his hands around his mouth and shouted, "Yo guys—what gives? Even my dad's a better host than this!"

A shower of dust, as his echo ricocheted off the ceiling, was the only reply.

"Wait," Sophie said, making her way over to a stalagmite that seemed slightly less dark than the others. She wasn't sure if it was just a trick of the light. But as she ran her hands over the jagged point, her fingers felt the cool smoothness of glass. "It's another bottle!"

She tied the bottle of Lucilliant around her neck before picking up the round, bulbous vial filled with a glow so pale, it barely counted as starlight. But she could feel the energy pulsing through the glass, and knew the glow came from Candesia.

"Another unmapped star," Sophie whispered, holding it out to show the others. "I wonder if that means we'll have three more leaps after this."

"Let's hope not," Sandor grumbled.

"For once Gigantor and I agree."

Sophie knew how they were feeling. But the only way out of the cramped pocket of earth was to keep going.

"On three," she decided, pressing the charm against the glass.

Another beam of light flashed from the swan's beak, dull and smoky and hardly inviting.

"One," she called as Keefe and Sandor wrapped their arms around her. "Two."

She hesitated half a second longer. Then she pulled them forward on, "Three!"

Light leaping had never felt so slow. Each second was a thousand years, and the gray emptiness seemed to drain their energy away. A blast of wind finally shoved them out of the gloom, and then they were crumpling onto a patch of soggy sand.

If Keefe hadn't said, "Okay, I don't mean to freak anyone out, but I'm pretty sure that's a kraken," Sophie might never have gotten up again.

Sandor dragged her to her feet, shoving her behind him as he raised his sword at the monstrous green beast. It looked like some strange combination of an octopus, an elephant, and a lion, and when it opened its six-fanged mouth and roared, Sophie couldn't believe she'd come all that way just to be eaten by a sea monster.

But when the kraken lunged for them, it smacked into some sort of invisible shield, flattening its trunklike, tentacled nose and knocking the slimy beast back. It tried three more times to break the unseen barrier, then zipped away with another roar, vanishing into the dark water.

"So . . . we're under the ocean," Sophie mumbled, knowing she was stating the obvious but needing to say it anyway. "I thought light couldn't pass through the water, and that's why we have to slide down a whirlpool to get to Atlantis."

"It's not supposed to pass through rock, either," Keefe reminded her. "The light from the unmapped stars must be different. Maybe that's why they're secret. And look. There's another one."

They all stared at the curved bottle nestled into the sand, glowing with the rosy light of Marquiseire.

"Okay, what do we think?" Keefe asked as Sophie used the charm to create a pink glittery beam. "Better or worse than the others?"

"Worse," Sandor decided, and Keefe had to agree.

But Sophie chose "better" as she pulled them into the shimmering light, since sparkles made everything better—didn't they?

But she was wrong.

So. Very. Wrong.

Each glinting speck turned coarse as they traveled—grating and scraping, like they were leaping through a glitterbomb. She was starting to worry the pain would never end when the warmth fizzled and the ground rushed up at them, leaving them in a shivering heap on a misty hilltop, right by . . .

. . . another bottle.

"Phosforien," Sophie mumbled as she tied it around her neck with the others.

The swirly opalescent light was a sensory overload of color and motion, and the leap was a nonstop rollercoaster of spinning and dipping and swerving.

Sophie was sure she would've hurled all over the neon colors if her stomach hadn't been broken and scattered into a million pieces. And when they finally collapsed onto hard, frosty ground, it took several seconds before her eyes could focus on the stretch of empty tundra.

A silvery bottle was buried in the hoarfrost.

"Last one," she said, her hands shaking as she carefully grabbed the bottle of quintessence. "And I have a feeling this is going to be the toughest one yet. Remember—this stuff can blow up cities."

"Wonderful," Sandor grumbled.

"Aren't you glad you insisted on coming along?" Sophie asked him.

"Yes, I am. I'm always happiest when I know I'm keeping you safe."

"Awwwwww, Gigantor's so cute!" Keefe interrupted. "Who knew under all those muscles was a ball of marshmallowy sweetness?"

Sandor growled at him—but Keefe just laughed.

"Squeak all you want. It only makes you more precious."

"Okay, this is it," Sophie said, reminding them why they were all there. "The Black Swan should be waiting for us at the end of this. We just need to survive one more leap."

"Uh, you had me all excited until you used the word 'survive,'" Keefe told her as Sophie held her breath and pressed the charm against the last vial, casting a blindingly bright silver beam at their feet.

Now that the moment was here, she wasn't sure she was ready to face the Black Swan—and whatever terrifying plans came with them. But she clung to Sandor and Keefe, and they held on to her just as tightly.

Slowly . . . bravely . . . they all stepped into the light.

FIFTY

THEY'RE . . . NOT HERE," SOPHIE SAID, rolling the words around on her tongue, like that would somehow change their meaning. "Why aren't they here?"

The quintessence had carried them to an island—a tiny spit of sand and palms where Sophie would've expected to find a marooned pirate searching for the X that marked the spot. But there was no treasure. Just beach and trees and empty ocean, looking extra eerie in the dim moonlight.

"Maybe we're early," Keefe said, plopping down in the soft sand as Sandor went to patrol the trees. "I bet they'll be here any minute."

He motioned for Sophie to join him, but she was too tense

to sit. She made her way to the shore, grabbing one of the smooth stones from the beach and hurling it into the water as hard as she could—followed by another and another. Each stone flew just a little shorter than the last.

"You should be skipping them," Keefe told her as he came up behind her.

He placed a wide, flat rock in her palm and showed her how to flick her wrist. They practiced the motion one, two, three times. On the fourth they let it fly, and the rock skipped and skipped and skipped some more before they lost sight of it in the dark waves.

"See how much more fun it is when you relax?" Keefe asked her.

"How am I supposed to relax, Keefe? Look at this place—it's a deserted island."

An extra creepy one. She couldn't put her finger on what it was, but there was something *off* about it. Like all the color had been bleached out. Even the moonlight was a faded gray.

Sophie turned to pace, dredging a rut in the sand. "Something's wrong. I don't think they're coming."

"But why would they go to all the trouble of giving us these?" Keefe asked, pointing to the five glowing bottles dangling from her neck.

"Who knows? Maybe they needed to get rid of them because they're illegal and they knew I would get in less trouble."

"Uh, they could just open the bottles and release the light

back into the sky. Plus, after the whole ogre king thing, you're on pretty thin ice, y'know? I bet if you sneeze too loud, Bronte will call a Tribunal."

Sophie straightened. "Maybe *that's* their plan."

"What is?"

"Having me get caught with these, so I'll be exiled. They want me to heal Prentice, right? And they know there's no way the Council is going to approve that now. So if they can't bring him to me, they'll force me to go to him."

Keefe stared at the glowing bottles like he was seeing them in a whole new light. But then he shook his head. "I still don't buy it. There are easier ways to get you exiled. Plus, why would they invite me? Remember, I didn't just tag along this time."

He was right—inviting him didn't make sense.

Unless . . .

"What if this whole thing was a distraction?" she asked. "A trick to get you, me, and Sandor away from something." She grabbed Keefe's arm. "What if they're trying to get to Silveny?"

"But Silveny's not with us anymore. She's at the Sanctuary."

"Still—we should get back. There's no reason to stay here."

She pulled out her home crystal, holding it up to the pale moonlight. But it wouldn't cast a beam. She tried several directions, and nothing changed.

"Okay, that's not cool," Keefe mumbled when his home crystal did the same. "It's like the light's too weak, somehow."

Or something was filtering it. If the Black Swan could create a pocket of air under the ocean, surely they could put some sort of shield around an island. And the palm trees didn't look tall enough for her to teleport from. . . .

"This is a trap," Sophie whispered, squinting through the darkness, trying to see what hid in the shadows. "They must've picked this place because they know we can't leave."

"We can try those," Keefe said, pointing to the glowing bottles dangling around her neck.

"Won't they just take us back to the places we've already been?" Sophie asked. "They were all pretty cramped places. I'd rather be out here."

"I guess."

Maybe it was the weird moonlight. But Keefe looked genuinely afraid.

"Sandor!" Sophie shouted, wanting some extra muscle—and weapons—close by.

Sandor must've been listening to their conversation, because he was already on his way, sword raised.

"I detect no trace of life," he told them, sniffing the air once more. "But we must find a way to get out of here."

"What if we, like, combined the different lights or something?" Keefe suggested. "That might take us somewhere different, right?"

"Would that work?" Sandor asked.

"I don't know," Sophie admitted. "But if it did, where would it even take us?"

Keefe shrugged. "It's gotta be safer than waiting around here."

No one could argue with that, so Sophie untied all the bottles and placed them in a small circle in the sand. Their colorful glows turned white where they converged, and when Keefe nodded, she carefully placed the magsidian charm in the brightest spot in the center.

A blinding flash shot out of the swan's beak, turning everything to a blur.

Sophie rubbed her eyes, trying to focus through the glare. But Keefe must've recovered first, because he grabbed her arm and whispered, "I think I see something."

"Where?" Sandor asked, and Keefe pointed toward the ocean.

The light had faded, leaving nothing but shadows and more shadows.

But when Keefe took the charm from Sophie and created another gleaming flash, she spotted what his sharp eyes had caught the first time.

Three figures in dark hooded cloaks, coming toward them across the waves.

FIFTY-ONE

THEY'RE WALKING ON WATER," Sophie whispered, staring at the white eyes sewn on the cloaked figures' sleeves. "How are they doing that?"

"Let's worry about it later, okay?" Keefe asked, grabbing the glowing bottles and pulling a goblin throwing star out of a pocket on his sleeve. "Right now there's three of them and three of us. I think we can take them."

"The only one 'taking them' will be *me*," Sandor growled, throwing Sophie and Keefe over each of his shoulders and running them into the palm trees. He dropped them behind a wall of fernlike bushes and took the bottles of starlight. "Stay here—I mean it, Sophie. Do not move unless absolutely necessary."

"But—"

"DO NOT ARGUE WITH ME!"

Sophie cowered.

"I'll cover us," Keefe promised as Sandor handed him one of his melders.

"Good. And I"—Sandor gripped his other melder—"am going to catch these villains once and for all."

He slashed his sword over their heads, covering them with fallen leaves before he charged back toward the waves.

The bushes blocked their view of the beach, but Sophie could hear deep voices mixed with the roar of the ocean.

It sounded like they were arguing.

"How did they find us?" she whispered, scooting closer to Keefe. "Do you think they're the ones that led us here?"

"If they were, why pick this spot for their ambush? That underground cave would've been a way easier place to catch us."

"True. But how could they have followed us through all those leaps? And why aren't the Black Swan here?"

"We are."

Furry hands blocked Sophie's scream as a dozen dwarves popped out of the ground. Two of them pinned Keefe to a tree, snatching his melder and cutting off his cry for help.

"What's happening over there?" Sandor called from the beach.

"Tell him to come to you," the dwarf holding Sophie whispered. "We're here to capture the rebels, and he's ruining our plan."

Plan? Sophie wondered as he held up his wrist, pointing to a cuff bearing the sign of the swan.

A dozen dwarves *did* have better odds of winning than a lone goblin did. Plus, if they were there to capture her, they could've just taken her.

"Fine," she mumbled into his palm, wishing she didn't have to taste his sandy fur.

The dwarf let her go, begging her to call Sandor quickly. "He's keeping the rebels off the sand. That's where we have our advantage."

Sophie *really* hoped she was doing the right thing as she took a breath and shouted, "Sandor, we need your help!"

"On my way," Sandor called, tearing into the bushes.

The dwarves dove back into the ground, and their feet had barely disappeared when Sandor burst through the ferns behind Keefe, sword raised. "What's going on? Are you okay?"

Sophie nodded, trying to figure out how to explain.

But Sandor was already sniffing the air. "Dwarves have been here."

He took off after them, despite Sophie's cries to stop, and the starlight around his neck cast a glow over the shadowy beach.

The cloaked figures had just set foot on the sand when they spotted Sandor—and the line of dwarves sending cracks rippling across the beach. They scrambled back into the water just in time to avoid sinking into the shore.

Sophie and Keefe caught up to Sandor as he drew his sword

at the dwarves. "They're with the Black Swan," she told him. "They were trying to get us to lure the Neverseen onto the beach."

"Yes, and it didn't work," the dwarves mumbled, shaking their furry heads.

The one who'd grabbed Sophie pointed to where the Neverseen were diving under the waves. "They came here through the water. I'm sure they're leaving the way they came."

Sandor reeled on him. "How do you know so much about them?"

"We know only what we observed."

"And why were you observing?" Sandor demanded.

"Part of the plan. Which you have now ruined."

Sandor lifted the dwarf by his furry shoulders. "Excuse me?"

The dwarf didn't so much as blink—though his friends raised their feet, ready to stomp the ground any second.

"Uh, careful there, Gigantor," Keefe warned. "I'm pretty sure they're about to drop you into a sinkhole."

"Only if he gives us a reason," the dwarves told him.

Sandor pulled his hostage closer. "I'm only going to ask this once. What. Was. Your. Plan?"

"Watch, and wait, and if the rebels show up—catch them. It would've worked, if you hadn't chased them off the sand."

"You *planned* for us to be ambushed?" Sandor snarled.

"We suspected that you would be."

"Why?" Sophie asked. "And why didn't you warn us?"

"It was not our decision," the dwarf told her, squirming out of Sandor's grip like a cat. "I am sure our commander had his reasons."

"And where is your *commander*?" Sandor asked.

"Monitoring the situation off site."

Sophie rolled her eyes. "Of course he is. Why bother showing up for the meeting that *he* called?"

"This was never a meeting, Miss Foster. It was a test."

"A test of what?" Keefe asked.

"Our security. And yours. And that is all I can tell you. Also, I must give you this." He dug around his fur, pulling out a smooth, slightly opaque stone with a single facet along one edge. "Hold the moonstone to the light and it will create a path back to your home."

Sophie reached to take it, but he insisted they give him the bottles of starlight—and the magsidian charm—first.

"Will you give your commander a message for us?" Keefe asked as Sandor grumpily made the trade.

The dwarves exchanged a glance, before their leader told Keefe, "Go ahead."

Keefe stalked closer, crossing his arms with a smirk. "Tell him we passed his little test, so now he can pass one of ours. He'll find instructions waiting in the cave in five days—and if he doesn't follow them *exactly*, well . . . let's just say there will be a mountain of sparkly poop with his name on it."

FIFTY-TWO

REMIND ME NEVER TO LIGHT LEAP again," Keefe mumbled as Elwin sprayed a misty elixir under his nose and told him to take a deep breath.

Fade Fuel.

Sophie had hoped she'd never need the all-too-familiar elixir again. But Grady took one look at them when they got home and shouted for Edaline to hail Elwin.

"At least there are no other injuries this time," Elwin said, flashing a yellow orb of light around Keefe and putting on his iridescent spectacles. "But you do have the most traumatized cells I've ever seen."

"I'm not surprised, given what little I know about the unmapped stars," Alden said as he paced the living room.

Sophie had hailed him the second they were home safe.

"Did you know it was possible to leap underground or under the ocean?" Grady asked him.

Alden shook his head. "I knew the light of the unmapped stars granted unusual abilities, but I never realized they defied our physical laws."

"At quite a cost," Elwin muttered, handing Sophie and Keefe two bloodred vials. "I need to completely rebuild your cells. Don't worry—it's painless. You'll feel a bit itchy tonight, but I have a poultice that should help."

Sophie downed the remedy, gagging as the cold liquid hit her throat.

Keefe barely managed to choke his down. "Okay, that's not the worst thing I've ever tasted—but it might be a close second."

"Oh, trust me, I have lots worse," Elwin assured him. "Keep hanging around her and I bet you'll get to try them. As for you"— he turned to Sandor—"I'm not sure any of my elixirs will work on your physiology. I can probably make some tweaks tonight—"

"I have a remedy of my own," Sandor promised, removing a flat black flask from one of his pockets.

He took a huge swig, making his chest heave and his eyes tear. But the fit passed after a few seconds, and he looked much less pale.

"What is that?" Elwin asked, taking the flask and sniffing it.

He gagged and handed it back. "Never mind—I don't want to know."

"You don't," Sandor agreed.

"So they're going to be okay?" Edaline asked, smiling when Elwin nodded.

Her eyes looked tight and tired—but her voice was calm and steady as she asked, "Then what are we going to do about the next meeting with the Black Swan?"

"Assuming they even show up," Sophie said through a sigh.

"Oh, they'll show," Keefe promised. "I threatened them with sparkly poop. Plus, we passed their test, so it's only fair."

"*Did* we pass?" Sophie asked. "The Neverseen still got away."

"I'm not sure that's what was being tested," Alden said quietly. "I can only speculate of course, but it seems logical that today's meeting was designed to discover the source of their leak. It's what I would've done—create a scenario with a limited number of variables."

"Like an island that can only be reached by very specific means," Grady jumped in.

"Exactly," Alden agreed. "Then send you there using a convoluted trail no one could possibly follow—"

"Like the light of five unmapped stars," Edaline suggested.

Alden nodded. "And then monitor the situation from both inside and out, to gather the most possible information. I suspect that's why this Mr. Forkle figure wasn't there. He was likely following up on certain leads."

"Meanwhile, we got to be the bait," Sandor said, squeezing his flask so hard, he left dents in it.

"Highly protected bait," Alden corrected. "They did have an entire fleet of dwarves there to protect you. And it was also meant to be a trap for the Neverseen, which would've been brilliant had it succeeded."

But Sandor had scared them away too quickly.

"I wish they would've *told* us what they were doing," Sophie said, kicking at the floor.

"Ah, but if they'd tipped you off, it would've tipped off their leak, as well," Alden reminded her. "Everything is infinitely more complicated when you cannot trust your own organization."

He shared a look with Grady that made Sophie wonder if he was referring to the Council, as well. Classified secrets were still continuing to leak.

But Sophie would have to worry about that another day.

For now, she was going to check on Silveny and try to get some sleep, despite the itch tickling her cells.

And then they had a meeting with the Black Swan to plan.

Keefe had agreed to come over the next day to brainstorm ideas, but he hailed Sophie in the morning to let her know he couldn't make it. His parents had been surprisingly worried after he told them about the attack—especially his mom. And even though he promised he was okay, they'd asked him to stay home so they'd know he was safe.

Keefe sounded horrified at the idea of a long family day. But Sophie was happy for him. Maybe his parents were finally realizing how awesome their son was.

She tried to brainstorm plans alone, but everything sounded too obvious. Fitz and Biana weren't much help either when they stopped by to check on her. Plotting and scheming really were Keefe's forte.

But Keefe was busy the next day too. His dad had set them up a whole day together at the Sanctuary—and while Sophie was a little jealous that he got to check on Silveny, she knew once the Council ordered her punishment, she'd probably see the hyper alicorn every day.

Instead she used the time to finish organizing Edaline's office, trying to keep her mind off the fact that the Councillors could be electing their newest member as early as the next day. The period for nominations closed at midday, and Grady explained that afterward they would sequester themselves in their castles and cast their votes using a network of mirrors. When all the mirrors aligned, a beam of light would refract off the castles, bright enough to be seen anywhere in the Lost Cities.

Everyone was expecting the consensus to happen immediately.

And yet when Sophie ran outside at noon the next day, she found nothing but blue sky and puffy white clouds. She stood there so long her neck started to ache, and still no flash appeared. When the sunset tinted everything pink and orange,

Edaline served dinner picnic style and Grady gave an update on what little information he'd learned.

Master Leto was still the favorite—though an ancient elf Sophie had never heard of was a close second. Everyone was expecting the new Councillor to be male, since the Council usually had an even number of males and females. Still, there was no requirement that took females out of the running.

The night wore on, turning cold enough that Edaline conjured up fluffy blankets and warm petit fours called mooncakes, which tasted like fudge dipped in marshmallow and then drizzled with chocolate cream. They stretched out in the grass and watched the stars while Grady told stories about his adventures tracking down lost animals in the human world. He was in the middle of a story about an uncatchable yeti—which Sophie was pretty sure had inspired the abominable snowman legends—when a bright flash turned the night to day.

"Is that it?" she asked, already on her feet. "That has to be it, right?"

"It definitely is," Grady agreed, glancing at Edaline.

"Okay, so . . . how do we know who it is?"

"A scroll should be delivered in the next few minutes."

He'd barely finished the sentence when a courier glittered into the pastures and handed Grady a scroll sealed with golden wax.

"We can't open it for another twenty-three minutes," Grady explained, tucking the scroll in his pocket for safekeeping.

The elves liked to time their messages so everyone could hear the news as one. But the twenty-three minutes felt like twenty-three centuries, and Sophie had to resist the urge to tackle Grady and take it.

When it was time to break the seal, Sophie ripped it out of his hands. Her palms were sweaty and her heart was racing, but her lips curled into a smile when she finally read the name.

Their newest Councillor would be Dame Alina.

FIFTY-THREE

THE CROWD THAT GATHERED IN FRONT of the Councillor's castles the next morning seemed to have mixed feelings about the election.

Dressed in their finest and bearing lavish gifts, they greeted their newest Councillor with a standing ovation as she appeared with the other eleven Councillors on the arched crystal stage that had been created for the occasion.

But when the applause died down, Sophie could hear the whispers and mutterings:

We needed someone stronger.

Someone with more experience.

Someone to take control.

Even those in favor were concerned about the upheaval this would cause at Foxfire.

But Dame Alina—no, *Councillor* Alina, Sophie corrected—smiled and waved like she had no idea they were discontent. Her pale green gown was understated compared to her usual fare, but her silver cape and peridot-encrusted circlet made her every bit as regal as the rest of the Council. And she held her head high, dipping the most elegant curtsy Sophie had ever seen as she stepped forward to address her people.

"Thank you," she called, her sharp voice slicing through the chilly morning air. "Thank you for such an incredible welcome. It is truly my honor to come before you today."

She fell silent, and Sophie wondered if that was all she was going to say.

But Councillor Alina turned and pointed to the ruins of Eternalia in the distance. "I cannot ignore that this position I've been given is the result of one of the greatest tragedies our world has ever seen. Nor would I want to. That's why I've chosen this color for my crown. I want my time ruling to stand in memorial to what we've lost, and as a testimony to what we will regain."

She turned back to the crowd, pausing to let her glassy eyes study the faces of the people standing before her.

"I hear your cries for justice and change. And I realize that trust is earned, not given. But I want you to know that I *am* ready to brave the long road ahead. I'm ready to make the hard choices. I'm ready to grow and learn and regain control. Past wounds will heal and past wrongs *will* be corrected. The life we used to know will return. We are all part of the most dramatic time we've ever faced in our long history. But it's an exciting time. An inspiring time. A time we will look back on centuries from now as a pivotal moment. A chance to prove the superiority of the Elvin Way. And I am honored to help us rise to the occasion."

The crowd erupted into another round of applause, this time sounding more sincere. And as Councillor Emery stepped forward and called for silence, Sophie noticed that none of the whispers returned.

His dark skin was silhouetted against the bright sky, giving him an aura of power and confidence as he cleared his throat and called, "Thank you for joining us this morning, and for all your patience during these long, tumultuous days. Like you, we are still mourning and healing. But we are also rebuilding—and we stand before you ready to rule. Many changes are already in the works, and we will share them over the course of the coming days. But to start, I have an announcement to make. As you know, Councillor Alina's appointment has opened up the position of Foxfire's principal—and in order to ensure that our prestigious academy in no way falls into disarray, our first order of business was to elect her replacement. Numerous names were discussed and considered, and we selected a candidate with both the strong leadership required, and the experience at Foxfire to transition quickly. So from this day forward, the principal at Foxfire will be Master Leto Kerlof, who shall henceforth be called

Magnate Leto Kerlof. Correspondingly, the Beacon of the Silver Tower will now be Lady Cadence Talle, who shall henceforth be called Master Cadence Talle. She will maintain her session with her sole prodigy in addition to her new responsibilities, and all transitions will be made in time for the return of regular sessions at Foxfire on Monday. Meanwhile all members of the Nobility will return to work today."

He paused to let that information settle, but not long enough for Sophie to decide how she felt about any of it.

She tried to applaud as the Councillors slowly glittered away. But something about the speeches had unsettled her, and it had nothing to do with all the shifts and changes.

She didn't figure it out until late that night as she lay in bed tossing and turning, unable to find her way to sleep.

Councillor Alina had met Sophie's eyes only once during her speech. And it was when she'd promised she was ready to make the hard choices.

"So when are the Councillors going to decide on my punishment?" Sophie asked, stopping Grady at the Leapmaster before he could leave for his latest assignment.

Now that the Council was back in session, they wanted him crawling through tunnels, searching for the missing dwarves again. Which meant she might not see him for days.

Grady adjusted his heavy cape, looking particularly uncomfortable as he told her. "I'm still waiting for word on that myself. King Dimitar's deadline is only a few days away, so I expect it will happen rather swiftly. But it depends on how quickly they agree."

"How will I know when they've decided?"

"No one has told me that, either. But I promise, Alden and I are both staying on top of it. We're as eager to have this settled as you are."

He pulled her close, kissing the top of her head as he whispered, "In the meantime, stay safe. I'll be home as soon as I can."

She watched him glitter away, then headed back to her room to hail Keefe. His dad was back on assignment too, which meant he was finally free to brainstorm meeting options for the Black Swan—and just in time, since the deadline they'd given the Black Swan was that day.

She'd expected Keefe's ideas to be complicated and crazy—and there were definitely a few like that in the mix. One even involved forcing the Black Swan to visit five of the places on Keefe's Stinkiest Spots in the World list before coming full circle back to the cave. But in the end, Keefe surprised her with what he pushed for:

We meet tomorrow at sunset.
Outside my old home.
You bring the answers.
We'll rearrange the gnomes.

"You don't think we should at least push for them to meet us at that window in Italy—that way we can find out where it is?" Sophie asked.

"Nah, we can find it ourselves. Plus, then we'd have to tell them we know about it. Why give away a secret if we don't need to? Trust me—San Diego's perfect. This Forkle dude has just as much history there as you do, which should throw him off his game. And it'll make it way easier to nag him about what happened the day he activated your telepathy, and about the Boy Who Disappeared, and anything else you've been stressing about, since it all happened right there."

"I guess you're right."

"What do you mean you 'guess'? Of course I'm right—I'm a genius, remember?"

"A genius who's dressed all fancy," Sophie pointed out, grinning when Keefe blushed.

She was used to Keefe's untucked school uniforms, wrinkled tunics, and loose-fitting pants—which he still somehow always managed to look good in. But now he was all . . . tailored. His fitted jerkin showed broad shoulders Sophie hadn't realized he had, and his pants, cape, and undershirt were all expertly cut and made of thick, expensive fabric. Even Fitz would look sloppy next to him.

"My mom took me shopping," he mumbled. "Said it was time I started dressing like a Sencen. At first I was like, dude, this is *lame*. But then I was like, *but I look good*. And I do, don't

I? Admit it, Foster—you've been checking out the Keefster. And maybe even . . . the keester."

He turned and did some sort of wiggly dance until Sophie tossed a pillow at his head.

"Don't we have a note to leave?" she asked when he scooted across the room to start his dance again.

"I've been waiting for you to lead the way. Unless you'd rather I go first so you can admire the view."

Sophie flung another pillow.

Sandor rolled his eyes at both of them as Keefe chased her down the stairs and out the door and all the way down to the cliffs.

Their laughter echoed off the cave as they tucked the note into place.

"Come and get it!" Keefe shouted, tossing a handful of sand like confetti. Then he stood there waiting, like he expected a dwarf to pop out of the ground any second.

"A watched pot never boils," Sophie told him.

"Wow. That might win the prize for most boring expression ever."

Sophie tossed sand at his head and he chased her back up to the house, earning more eye rolls from Sandor, and amused stares from Edaline.

Sophie spent the rest of the afternoon organizing Edaline's office while Keefe ran down to check the caves every fifteen minutes.

No reply came.

Not until the next morning, when Sophie dragged Sandor down to the beach at the crack of dawn, after another long night with very little sleep.

A tiny black pillbox held the shortest note the Black Swan had ever given her. It simply said:

Okay.

FIFTY-FOUR

ONVINCING THE BLACK SWAN TURNED out to be far easier than convincing Grady to let her go.

He had quite a lot to say about Sophie illegally teleporting to a Forbidden City when she was already in so much trouble. But eventually he agreed, so long as Sandor went with them—a detail he absolutely would not budge on, no matter how many ways Sophie explained the impossibility of disguising a seven-foot-tall goblin from humans.

Edaline finally found the solution, turning one of her lacy capes into a shawl and showing Sandor how to walk hunched over with a makeshift cane. Anyone who got close would surely notice that he was one buffed-out, armadillo-looking grandma.

But from a distance he appeared to be a sweet, albeit rather lumpy looking, little old lady.

Keefe laughed for five straight minutes when he saw him.

Sophie, meanwhile, was battling a major sense of déjà vu.

Not only had she put on the same jeans and yellow shirt with brown stripes that she'd worn on the day Fitz had permanently taken her away, but Keefe had borrowed the dark jacket and jeans Fitz had been wearing.

"Want me to talk like this?" Keefe asked, mimicking Fitz's accent almost perfectly. "Take my hand, Sophie. Let me show you where you truly belong."

"That's *not* what he said," she grumbled. But it wasn't that far off, either. "And just so you know, the mimicking is totally creepy."

"I know, right? My mom does it all the time. You should see the way she mimics my dad. It's almost terrifying."

"That would be."

She shook her hands, trying to shake away the nervous energy as she paced her room and checked the sky. It would be sunset in San Diego in less than half an hour.

"Remember, Foster, *we're* calling the shots this time. No crazy leaps, or midnight flights over the ocean, or drugged cookies. Just us, asking questions and not letting anyone leave until we get some answers."

She nodded, sinking to the floor, not trusting her shaky legs.

"So what is it?" Keefe asked, coming to sit beside her. "I

totally get the nerves and stuff. But . . ."—he brushed a finger across her palm—"what's with all the dread?"

She took out Jolie's mirrored compact, studying the two different Sophies reflected inside.

"The Black Swan knows who I am, Keefe. Not who I was— or who I think I am. Who I really am."

Keefe scooted closer, so close she could see his reflection in the mirrors. "Well, we both know I'm not good at the serious, supportive thing, so I may be a jerk for saying this but . . . when are you going to realize that they can't tell you who you are? Maybe they can tell you a bunch of weird junk about your past and your family—and I get that some of that might be freaky. But if they tell you that your mom is the most open, go-with-the-flow person they've ever known, is that suddenly going to make you stop being so stubborn or keeping so many secrets?"

"I doubt it," Sophie admitted.

"And what if they told you your dad was an even bigger rule breaker than me—not that that's possible. Are you suddenly going to start ditching class and pranking Dame Alina—or, Magnate Leto, or whoever our principal is?"

"No."

"Right. Because our family doesn't decide who we are. *We* decide who we are. Believe me, it drives my parents crazy. And sometimes that's the only thought that gets me through the day."

Sophie closed the compact, tucking it safely in her jeans

444

pocket. "Things have been better with your parents though, haven't they?"

"Yeah. I guess. I don't know." He made his way over to Iggy's cage, rumpling Iggy's orange dreads. "Sometimes it feels like they're starting to accept me for *me*—not turning me into a mini-them. But other times it's like . . ."

"Like?" Sophie prompted.

"Like . . . I've distracted you long enough. The time has come!" He sang the words, fist-pumping the air before dragging her and Sandor outside to the cliffs. "Game faces on, everyone! That goes for you too, grandma. Channel your inner grumpy old lady."

Sandor raised his cane like he was considering clubbing Keefe over the head with it.

"Perfect!" Keefe told him, pulling them closer to the edge. "And hey, I just realized—this is your first time teleporting, isn't it, Gigantor?"

Sandor nodded, staring at the crashing waves below. "I have a feeling I'm not going to enjoy it."

Keefe laughed. "Don't worry—Foster's got this. The jump is the hardest part."

But Keefe was wrong.

The jump was just the beginning.

Mr. Forkle was waiting for them. Sitting in the center of his lawn, looking as puffy and wrinkled as ever while he rearranged the remaining garden gnomes into a circular pattern.

The scene was so familiar, Sophie almost wondered if they'd gone through space *and* time. But then she saw the boarded-up windows and the overgrown grass, and wasn't sure if she was disappointed or relieved.

"You kids," Mr. Forkle grumbled, starting with his favorite phrase. "Late to your own meeting."

He pointed to the sky, where the last rays of sunlight were sinking below the horizon.

"Hey, at least we showed up," Keefe reminded him. "That's more than you can say."

Mr. Forkle studied him, his expression both smug and amused. "You needn't have bothered with the costumes. There are enough obscurers here to erase this place from existence. We're the only ones who know we're here—for now, at least."

"You think the Neverseen will find us?" Sophie asked, glancing up and down the street.

"Neverseen?" Mr. Forkle asked.

"That's the name I found written in runes on the patches of their sleeves."

"Interesting." He moved two of the gnomes outside the circle and craned his neck to study the sky. "And yes, I do expect the rebels to make an appearance. But I also expect them to leave us alone."

"How can you be so sure?" Sandor demanded as he threw off his disguise and straightened to his full height.

"Because"—Mr. Forkle tapped the nose of one of the gnomes and the air shimmered around them—"I just put an impenetrable energy field around us. It'll only last ten minutes, but that should be enough time. Bet you thought I was just a crazy old man, playing with my gnomes."

"Kinda," Keefe admitted.

"So, the gnomes weren't a code?" Sophie asked.

"They were many things, depending on what I needed. Twelve years was a very long time to be separated from my world, and these *ridiculous* statues were all I had to remind me why I was here."

"Why *were* you here?" Sophie asked quietly.

His eyes met hers, sharp and clear—yet somehow impossibly ancient. "*You* are my greatest achievement, Sophie."

There was a softness to the words. A warmth. But the words were still *wrong*.

"That's all I am to you—an achievement?"

"What more would you like?"

She didn't have an answer.

"I know you have questions, Sophie. Do not expect me to give you all the answers. We haven't the time and you haven't the stomach. So here's what I can tell you. I chose this house—this place—these people to protect you, nurture you, keep you safe and hidden and allow you time to become what you needed to be. Of course, I never intended for the rebels—these Neverseen—to find you when they did, but—oh don't sound

447

so surprised," he added when she gasped. "Surely you've figured most of this out already?"

"How could I?"

"Simple deduction. You really think we would set fires in the shape of our sign, just to catch Alden's attention?"

"I guess not," she mumbled. She'd known the Black Swan weren't behind the Everblaze, but hadn't thought much about the first white fires, which had already been burning when Fitz arrived.

Mr. Forkle sighed, filling the air with the scent of dirty feet—a side effect of his ruckleberry disguise. "Somehow the Neverseen knew you were here. They just didn't know precisely where. So they lit the fires to flush you out, taunting us with our own symbol—and framing us in the process. That's when I sent the newspaper article to Alden—the one that led him to you so he could take you away. It was earlier than we'd planned, but I needed to keep you safe, and I thought they'd give up once the eyes of the Council were upon you. But obviously . . ."

"You were wrong," Sophie finished.

"It happens sometimes," he agreed.

"Like our last meeting?" Keefe jumped in. "Or were we really your bait?"

Mr. Forkle became very focused on rearranging his gnomes as he told them, "We saw an opportunity to catch some of our enemy and we took it. And it would've worked if Sophie hadn't seen them too early and had Sandor chase them away."

"Well, maybe if you'd *told us what you were planning*!" Sophie snapped.

"You would've been willing to sit back, pretending nothing was happening while the enemy closed in?"

"I've taken bigger risks, haven't I?" She pointed to the star-shaped scar he'd given her.

"Another of my mistakes," he whispered. "If I'd understood human medicine better . . ."

"It doesn't matter," Sophie said, thrown by the concern in his voice. "My point is, you should've been working with me, not cutting me off, like you have been for the last few weeks."

"We had our reasons." He pulled a small black bottle from his pocket and uncorked the stopper. "We needed to understand how the Neverseen found our ocean base. And we have finally figured out the answer."

"Hey—what are you looking at *me* for?" Keefe asked.

"Both times the Neverseen tracked Sophie down, she was with you."

"What about Paris?" Sophie reminded him. "And the cave? And here? Remember the jogger?"

"Those times were different. They were before we were taking so many precautions. Before we realized how far our enemy was willing to go."

"Uh, that may be—but I didn't betray anyone," Keefe argued.

"I never said you did it intentionally," Mr. Forkle told him as he poured a fine silver dust into his hand. "But that doesn't mean you weren't unwittingly responsible. We disabled both of your registry pendants, and all of Sandor's trackers before our last meeting. But there was one signal we couldn't remove."

He flicked his wrist, showering Keefe with the fine, gritty powder.

Keefe coughed and rubbed his eyes, and Sophie reached forward to help him.

But she froze when she noticed Keefe's hands.

All of his fingers were glowing bright red.

FIFTY-FIVE

BUT . . . MY SKIN'S BEEN MELTED OFF," Keefe argued, staring at his glowing hands like they couldn't possibly belong to him. "Twice."

"Exactly," Mr. Forkle said quietly, "because the homing device is still in your possession. *That's* how the Neverseen have been finding you. Not because of any leak on our end, which was as I'd suspected. But I had to be sure."

He turned to Sophie, pouring more reveldust into his palm. "I'm sorry, but I have to check you, too. And Sandor."

Sophie nodded, holding her breath as he blasted her with the fine powder, then did the same to Sandor. She counted to thirty, wishing with every breath that she wouldn't see the telltale glow. And for once her wish was granted.

Sandor was clear as well.

"Just as I thought," Mr. Forkle said, recapping the vial. "Sandor's methods are far too thorough to keep an ogre device around—even if he can't smell it. Which makes Keefe the perfect target."

"Where is it?" Sandor asked, grabbing Keefe and patting him down.

"You won't find anything," Mr. Forkle warned him. "Otherwise we would've seen a brighter glow. But remember, Keefe is not wearing his regular clothes."

"Regular clothes?" Keefe repeated, still staring at his glowing hands. "I don't have any regular clothes—except my Foxfire uniform, and I wasn't wearing that either of the times we were ambushed."

"So what were you wearing?" Sandor asked.

"It would likely be an accessory," Mr. Forkle added. "Something you always wear, regardless of the outfit. Like a pendant or a nexus—"

"Or a pin," Sophie whispered, afraid to meet Keefe's eyes.

Keefe backed a step away. "No. That . . . there has to be a mistake."

Sophie swallowed, trying to think of anything else it could be.

But the Sencen family crest fit perfectly.

Hadn't his dad only given it to him recently? And now that she thought about it . . . hadn't he given it to him after he found out Keefe was working on something with her?

"No," Keefe said again, shaking his head so hard it looked painful. "My dad's a jerk—but he's not *that*. He wouldn't . . . I mean—these are the people who tried to kill you. And Dex. And *me*. He couldn't . . . could he?"

"There is one way to know for sure," Mr. Forkle said, offering him the vial of reveldust. "But there is one *very* important thing you must keep in mind. If I am right—as I suspect that I am—you cannot let your father know that you are on to him. You cannot let *anyone* know that anything is different—and this goes for you as well," he told Sandor and Sophie. "Not Alden. Not your guardians. No one must know."

"Why?" Sophie asked.

"Because we have a far better chance of Lord Cassius guiding us to the Neverseen's leader if he does not realize he's a suspect."

"How do you know he's not the leader?" Sandor asked, looking ready to perform a one-goblin raid on Candleshade.

"Because their leader is a Pyrokinetic. He left his burns on Sophie's wrists—burns that took me nearly an hour to treat."

"An hour?" Sophie repeated.

She'd figured he'd treated them while she was unconscious on the Paris street, after he'd triggered her new abilities. But she'd never imagined he'd stayed an *hour*.

"I've never seen anything so vile," Mr. Forkle said, his voice suddenly thick. "And I vowed that day to do everything in my power to make sure he pays for his crimes. Which is why I will need you to pretend, Keefe." He pulled a different vial out of his pocket—blue this time, with an atomizer—and spritzed a shimmering mist on Keefe's hands.

Instantly the red glow dimmed, and within a few seconds his skin was back to normal.

"The aromark is still there," Mr. Forkle warned him. "I've only neutralized the reveldust, so no one will know that you've discovered it. You'll need to do the same to your pin—if it does indeed glow red. Can you do that? Can you keep this secret until the optimal time?"

He offered both vials to Keefe.

Keefe backed away, covering his face with his hands and shaking so hard Sophie had to hold him steady.

"My dad's an *Empath*," he whispered. "How am I supposed to do this? How is this even happening?"

"If it's true, you lie to him the same way you lie to any Empath," Mr. Forkle told him. "You use one lie to cover another."

"What lie?" Sophie asked.

"Yes, what lie, indeed?" Mr. Forkle wandered the yard, staring at his swollen feet as they squished in the soggy grass. He'd passed them three times before he said. "We'll use Silveny."

"We'll use Silveny *how*?" Sophie asked, not willing to put the precious alicorn at risk—even for something as important as this.

"She won't actually be involved. We'll just make them think

she is—since we know the Neverseen are interested in her. Actually, this is brilliant." He moved toward Keefe, prying him away from Sophie. "I know I am asking an extremely difficult thing. But this could be the lead we've been waiting for. If you tell your father that the Black Swan have asked you to help move Silveny to a top secret location, it will explain why you seem nervous and distracted *and* give us a perfect way to trap him."

"Trap him?" Keefe sounded like he was going to be sick.

"Yes, trap him, Keefe. And as many of his fellow rebels as we can. We'll make them think we're giving them the opportunity to steal Silveny that they've been waiting for. But the whole situation will be rigged to catch them."

"So Sophie and Keefe get to be your bait again," Sandor interrupted.

"I don't care about that," Sophie jumped in. "I care about Keefe. Look at him!"

Keefe had sunk to a crouch, cradling his head in his hands.

"Could you do what you're asking of him?" she asked Mr. Forkle as she squatted beside Keefe, holding him steady. "Could you betray your own father?"

"I've done far worse," Mr. Forkle whispered. "The right road is rarely the easy road. And no war was ever fought without casualties."

"Is that what this is?" Sophie asked. "A war?"

"Unfortunately, yes. A quiet war, to stop a louder one from raging. You may hate me for asking this of him, but it is the cold reality we all face. We cannot control the actions of others, nor stop them from disappointing us. We can only use the anger and pain to fuel us. To rise above."

The harsh words hardly seemed like the pep talk Keefe needed. And yet, Keefe stood, his jaw set and his eyes dry of tears.

His hand shook as he took the vials Mr. Forkle offered him. But his voice was steady as he said, "I guess it's time to go."

Mr. Forkle grabbed Keefe's hand as he reached for his home crystal. "Go only if you're sure you can handle it."

"I can handle it." Keefe took a deep breath and turned to Sophie. "I'm going to make this right, okay?"

"It's not your fault, Keefe."

"I'm still going to fix it. Whatever he's done—I won't let him get away with it."

"Even though it's your father?" Sandor asked, still looking like he wished he could be the one to drag Lord Cassius away.

"Especially because it's him."

"You'll need to confirm that we're right," Mr. Forkle said as Keefe raised his crystal up to the glow of a streetlight. "If it's true, tell Sophie 'swan song.' She'll pass the message to me and I'll get back in touch with the details of our plan. We'll need to move quickly—no more than a week. Hiding the lie any longer would be impossible." He moved closer, taking Keefe by the shoulders. "This will be the hardest week of your life, but I'm confident you will survive it. I saw you face down the rebels at the entrance to our hideout—you wore a look of absolute determination. You must call on that emotion again. And remember what we're fighting for."

Keefe nodded.

"Wait—what if it's not true?" Sophie jumped in. "Then what does he say?"

"It's true, Sophie," Keefe whispered. "What else could it be?"

"I don't know. But we've been wrong before. What's the code word for 'it's a mistake'?"

"No code word needed," Mr. Forkle decided. "Just call another meeting, since I'm sure there will be much to say."

Keefe shook his head. "That's not going to happen. It's fine, Sophie. I'm sure once this is all over I'm going to need an epic-level freak out. But for now . . . I'm okay."

Mr. Forkle moved one of the gnomes, making the air shimmer again as Keefe gave Sophie a heartbreakingly sad smile and glittered away.

"He's not okay, you know," Sophie told Mr. Forkle, shattering the silence that followed.

"Of course he's not. Are any of us?"

He gathered the gnomes, moving them back to the weed-filled planter and lining them up perfectly straight. Like soldiers.

"Why 'swan song'?" Sophie asked.

She knew what the phrase meant to humans, but she was hoping it meant something different to the elves.

"It's a tradition among our group, going back to our earliest days. We knew the course we'd chosen would involve hardship. So we decided that any time one of us was forced to take a great risk or make a large sacrifice, we would alert the others by declaring it our swan song. That way we all knew to brace for very bad days ahead."

A lump caught in Sophie's throat and she cleared it away to ask, "Have you ever called it?"

"Many times. Many ways."

He moved one gnome, separating it from the others.

"Prentice called his the day before he was captured," he added quietly. "I still haven't figured out how he knew it was coming."

"The Council's never going to approve his healing now. You realize that, right?" Sophie whispered.

"Yes. We've been expecting the same thing. And we'd been working on a plan. But after your incident with King Dimitar"—he muttered something under his breath that started with "you kids"—"we've put that plan on hold. Best to let the dust settle before stirring anything up again. Besides, we have more urgent things to focus on. You're going to have to keep a very close eye on Keefe. The guilt and rage he will experience over the course of the week is going to be life changing. He will need a steady friend."

Sophie nodded.

"Time to go, then."

"Wait!" Sophie called as he pulled out a noticeably blue pathfinder. "What about Jolie?"

"What about her?"

"I . . . I need to know who she was."

"She was Grady and Edaline's daughter."

"No—that's not what I mean." She took a deep breath for courage and shoved the words out. "I need to know who she was *to me*."

"To you?" He stepped closer, leaning down so they were face-to-face. "You think she's your mother."

"Is she?"

He glanced behind him, checking the still-empty street before he told her, "No."

The crushing relief nearly knocked Sophie off her feet.

"Do not bother asking me who your mother is—that is one piece of information I cannot share."

The hard lines of his expression made it clear there would be no arguing with him. But now that she knew she wasn't related to Jolie, she was happy to leave her mother's true identity a mystery.

Still, she wasn't ready to let him leave.

"What did she do for you?" she asked, pulling out the mirrored compact to show him. "I know she was connected to the Black Swan."

He waved the compact away. "I see nothing black. Nor any swan."

"And I see a pretty bird in the sky," Sophie argued, pointing to the constellation pattern. She opened the compact and showed him his reflections. "And a human mirror."

"Fine," he said, glancing over his shoulder again. "I will not tell you any more than this. Jolie volunteered to infiltrate the rebels. She was working *deep* undercover—which was why she owned nothing bearing the sign of the swan."

"Did she learn anything?"

"She must have. We've long assumed they killed her because of it. But she died before sharing her report, and any record must've burned in the fire."

"But—"

"I told you from the beginning that I wasn't going to answer all of your questions. I've already shared far more than I'd planned. It's time to go home."

He leaped away without another word, leaving Sophie and Sandor alone in the dim twilight.

"He's right," Sandor said, when Sophie didn't move. "Without that energy field, we're at risk for ambush."

Sophie nodded, reaching for her home crystal—but she froze as a new thought clicked inside her head.

Jolie was working undercover for the Black Swan. So she would've known about their tradition with 'swan song.'

Maybe she finally had the password Vertina needed.

FIFTY-SIX

"S WAN SONG," SOPHIE WHISPERED, feeling her hopes plummet when Vertina's smile faded. "That isn't the word you needed?"

Vertina sighed. "No, it is."

"Okay," Sophie said slowly. "So . . . aren't you supposed to tell me something?"

"I am."

Seconds ticked by and Sophie lost what little patience she had. "Just tell me the stupid secret, okay?"

"If it's so *stupid*, why should I tell you?"

"BECAUSE I GAVE YOU THE PASSWORD!!!" She backed away, knowing she was dangerously close to tossing Vertina out the window. "Please, Vertina. I don't have time for this."

Keefe could hail her any second and say the words that would change everything—and she'd already wasted ten minutes dodging Grady and Edaline's questions. They were *very* unhappy when she couldn't tell them who the leak was, and if Sandor hadn't assured them that they were keeping the secret for good reason, she would probably still be getting interrogated.

Vertina hung her head. "I'm sorry. This is just harder than I thought. I've been keeping this secret for so long—and if you'd seen her face when she told me . . ."

"I'm only trying to help her," Sophie promised.

Vertina closed her eyes, letting two shiny tears streak down her cheeks. Then she whispered, "The truth lies behind the glass that is not a window."

"The glass that is not a window," Sophie repeated, wishing it didn't have to be a riddle. Clearly the Black Swan had trained Jolie in obnoxiousness.

But she could figure this out! She just needed to think of other glass things . . .

A table?

A goblet?

Or . . .

"Do you mean a mirror?" Sophie asked, digging Jolie's compact out of her desk. "*This* mirror?"

Vertina frowned as she studied it. "I do remember Jolie using that mirror—and I never understood why. One side was so unflattering. But I don't think that's what she meant. I have suspected she meant a mirror. But the way she said it when she told me made me think it was a specific mirror in a specific place."

"Where?" Sophie asked, trying again to pry off the compact's mirrors, just to be safe.

They still wouldn't budge.

"She never told me," Vertina admitted sadly.

"And that's all Jolie said? There was nothing else?"

"That was it."

"Great," Sophie mumbled, shoving the compact into her pocket and heading downstairs.

Every wall in Havenfield was made of some sort of crystal or glass. It could take days to search each piece of it—especially since the mirror she was looking for had to be small enough for no one to notice.

"You don't have to follow me," she told Sandor as he trailed her down the hallway.

But of course he did, stationing himself outside Jolie's room as Sophie slipped inside.

"Please let it be in here," she whispered, snapping her fingers to turn on the lights.

The room looked far more chaotic than she'd remembered—clothes and shoes and books strewn all over the floor, mixed with a maze of half-packed trunks and boxes. She didn't remember it being that messy the last time she'd been in there, but she also realized—with a serious dose of guilt—that she'd never finished packing up Jolie's things.

She would have to get back to that. But right now she had a more important job to tackle. The clue had said the glass was not a window, and maybe Jolie picked that wording to tell her where to start.

She threw back the dusty curtains, revealing the floor-to-ceiling windows. Thin veins of gold divided the glass into square panes, each about the size of her head.

Hundreds of them.

It felt like thousands.

She worked systematically, starting at the bottom and moving her way up and over and checking each. Stupid. Pane. But by the time she reached the other side, she still hadn't found a hidden mirror. And maybe that made sense.

The individual panes were all the same depth. There would be no way to hide anything behind them, unless the mirror stuck out—which would've been way too obvious.

So it had to be one of the walls.

But the walls were all crystal, not glass—weren't they?

Sophie sank to the floor, leaning against the bed and rubbing her eyes to bring some moisture back to them. She was pretty sure she hadn't blinked in over an hour, and she was so tempted to give up and go to bed, try again in the morning when her head was clearer and the light was better.

But she was *so* close.

A vibration in her pocket made her jump, and her stomach turned sour as she pulled out her Imparter.

"Swan song," Keefe whispered, not quite looking at her.

She knew it was lame, but she had to tell him, "I'm sorry."

"Don't be. In fact . . . it almost makes sense. I finally understand everything I've ever felt about my life. I mean, it still sucks. And I have no idea what I'm supposed to do now."

"No one can hear you, right?"

"No. They left me a note. Apparently my mom wanted to go to some fancy restaurant in Atlantis, so he took her and they're still not back. Guess I shouldn't be surprised they weren't sitting at home worrying about me anymore."

"I'm—"

"Please don't say you're sorry again. It makes me want to smash things, and that would be really hard to explain—and not because I'm mad at you," he added. "It's just . . . I don't want *you* to be sorry because one of the people who tried to kill you just so happens to be my dad. Every time I think about it, I want to fling goblin throwing stars at all his favorite things. Which again, would be pretty hard to explain."

"Then don't think about it."

"I won't. I'm going to go drink a couple cups of slumberberry tea and hope it knocks me out until the plan is ready."

"Uh, that's not dangerous, right?"

Half a smile curled his lips. "Nope, it's just tea. My mom makes my dad at least three cups a night. I guess now I know why he has trouble sleeping."

Sophie bit her lip. "I'll hail you as soon as I hear from the Black Swan."

"Thanks. Oh, and . . . Sophie?"

"Yeah?" she asked, surprised he was using her first name.

"Please don't hate me, okay?"

"Keefe, I will never hate you."

"But—"

"No 'buts.' In fact, I remember a pretty smart person telling me that our families don't get to decide who we are. And that goes one step farther. Our parents don't *make* us who we are either. Look at how much you've rebelled against your dad. Deep down, you've always known you didn't want to be him. Now you finally know *why*."

"Yeah, I guess," he mumbled, rubbing his eyes—either from tears or exhaustion, Sophie couldn't tell which.

She hoped it was the latter and told him, "Get some sleep."

He nodded and clicked away.

"I'll go deliver the message," Sandor said, making her drop the Imparter.

"Seriously—how do you sneak around like that on those giant feet?"

"Goblin secret. But the tide is too high for you to join me. Can you stay out of trouble while I'm gone?"

"The only thing I'm in danger of is dying of boredom." She glanced at the endless stretches of crystal and glass, wondering if she was even looking in the right place.

466

Jolie could've hidden the mirror *anywhere*. Maybe even at school . . .

No—that wouldn't make sense. Access to the elite towers was restricted to the elite and Sophie doubted Jolie meant for one of her schoolmates to find it. Why else would she leave the clue at her house? Plus, if she wanted to keep it safe, why hide it somewhere there'd be hundreds of prodigies who could accidentally stumble across it.

No, Jolie *must* have hidden it at Havenfield. And the safest place would be her room.

Sophie just had to search smarter.

She moved to the indent in the carpet where Vertina used to be and placed her feet on the line, facing the same way. Whatever mirror Jolie meant couldn't have been within Vertina's line of sight—otherwise Vertina would've known where to find it. Which meant Sophie could rule out . . .

Most of the places she'd already wasted time checking.

Awesome.

She swallowed her frustration and turned to face where Vertina couldn't see, looking for somewhere that wouldn't draw much attention. One of the corners seemed to have more shadow than light, and there was a strip of space next to the bookshelves, covered mostly by the lace curtains of the nearby window. She tiptoed to the corner—afraid that making a sound would scare the dim possibility away. And maybe it worked, because when she pulled back the dusty lace, she found a narrow row of square glass panes.

The square in the center was a mirror.

"Got you," Sophie whispered, tracing her fingers along the edge.

The mirror felt slightly less flush with the wall than the other panes, and when she pressed the upper right corner, the mirror popped out, swinging on an invisible hinge. Her hands shook as she pushed the door aside, revealing a sliver of a compartment—barely deep enough to pass her fingertips— with a slim lavender journal tucked inside.

The cover felt cold as she traced her finger along the elegant runes drawn in the center, and it took Sophie's mind a second to translate the word:

Reflections.

Jolie had written it using the Black Swan's cipher. And yet, when Sophie turned to the first page she found row after row of carefully shaped runes that formed nothing more than gibberish. Nonsensical words mixed with lines and squiggles and dots and dashes. For page after page after page.

"You've got to be kidding me," Sophie grumbled, flipping the book upside down, like that would somehow fix it.

It didn't.

Still . . . something felt familiar about the runes.

She closed her eyes, hoping a memory was about to trigger.

"What's that?" Edaline asked, making Sophie stumble backward into the bookshelf.

"Sorry, you scared me," Sophie mumbled, trying to hide the journal behind her back. But she knew Edaline had seen it. And when Edaline made her way over she realized she'd left the secret compartment wide open.

"How did you find this?" Edaline whispered, swinging the mirror back and forth on its hinge.

"It's . . . a long story."

"Well, I've got time."

Sophie was tempted to lie—or dart upstairs and lock herself in her room. But . . . Edaline was Jolie's *mother*. So she followed Edaline over to the bed and explained about Prentice's memory, and the mirrored compact, and Vertina's clue, and the gibberish journal.

Edaline didn't speak when she'd finished. Just took the journal and flipped back and forth through the pages.

Flip.

Flip.

Flip.

"Should I not have told you?" Sophie asked, hating the shadows that had crawled under Edaline's eyes.

"No. In fact . . . I think Jolie might have tried to tell me. She came home rather suddenly, not long before the fire. I could tell she was stressed, but she wouldn't tell me why. And one night I found her sitting, pretty much right here, staring at that wall. When I asked if she was okay, she asked me, 'What if someone wasn't who you thought they were?'"

"That's what she told Vertina," Sophie whispered. "I'd thought she'd discovered the leak in the Black Swan. But now we know they don't have a leak, so . . . do you have any idea who she meant?"

Edaline shook her head. "At the time, I'd just figured she was having a fight with her friends. They'd been pulling away from her after she got engaged, and Jolie had been pretending not to notice. But I knew it was breaking her heart. So I told her, 'There will always be people who disappoint us, and it's up to us to decide when to forgive, and when to walk away.'"

"Did she say anything to that?"

"She said 'I love you, Mom.' And I remember being surprised by it. I'd been 'Mother' for a very long time. It was so nice to be 'Mom' again."

There couldn't be a more perfect moment for Sophie to tell Edaline the same thing, finally cross that line and start treating her like a parent, not just a guardian.

But the moment slipped away.

"Was that the last time you saw her?" Sophie asked, hoping the question wasn't too painful.

"No. I saw her the day of the fire. She stopped by out of the blue, and I remember thinking she looked tired—though of course I've since wondered if she also looked afraid. She told me she thought it was time to walk away, and I . . . I thought she meant Brant. I thought the pressure of the bad match had finally gotten to her, and I knew she'd never forgive herself if she gave up just because it was hard. So I told her to never let fear drive her. I told her . . ."

"What?" Sophie asked when she didn't finish.

But Edaline shook her head, handing Sophie the journal as she stood. "Hindsight is a dangerous game to play."

She turned to head for the door. But before she left, she whispered, "I'm not going to try to stop you from finding out what Jolie was into. But I *am* going to tell you what I should have said to her that day. Please be careful. And if whatever you're chasing starts to catch up with you—*run*, don't walk away."

FIFTY-SEVEN

A SCROLL ARRIVED THE NEXT morning, bearing the Council's official seal. Sophie had a horrible, flip-floppy feeling, since the deadline King Dimitar had given the Council was almost up. But when she mustered the courage to break the seal, she found an invitation to an event at Foxfire that evening. As far as Sophie could tell, it appeared to be some sort of hybrid between the inauguration of Magnate Leto and an official Council assembly—which sounded like a terrifying combination. But Grady didn't seem concerned.

"They've always done an inauguration when a new Principal is appointed," he said, pouring himself a cup of some sort of strange red tea. "And the Councillors are always there, just like they are during the Opening Ceremonies. Remember, Foxfire is a noble academy. The Council is a part of their celebrations."

"Right, but, it says"—she picked up the scroll, reading directly from one of the paragraphs—"'Further updates will also be delivered by the Council, and the event will conclude with an important public announcement.' Is that normal?"

"No," Grady admitted. "But . . . this is a strange time for the Council. Both their official amphitheater and their tribunal hall burned in the Everblaze. They also have a brand-new Councillor, a terrified populace demanding answers, King Dimitar threatening war, a city to rebuild, and somewhere in there they also need to inaugurate a new principal. I'm guessing they figured that since we'd all be gathering anyway, they might as well double up and address some of the people's questions."

"I guess," Sophie mumbled, still staring at the scroll.

"You're worried they're going to announce your punishment there, aren't you?" Grady asked.

"Shouldn't I be? I mean . . . doesn't it seem like the perfect place?"

"It does. . . ."

He dragged out the word as he rubbed a crease on his forehead. "Listen, Sophie, I haven't wanted to tell you this, but there's been a bit of drama surrounding your upcoming sentence. A rather vocal group of people have seized upon it as an opportunity to . . . have you expelled."

All the blood drained from her face. "From Foxfire?"

Grady nodded. "They know you were indirectly involved with the fire—and then they watched you almost cause a war with King Dimitar. They're scared, Sophie. And when people are scared, they do crazy, heartless things. Like blame an innocent girl for impossibly complicated situations, and try to keep her away from their children."

Sophie stared at her sleeve, flicking away a piece of lint. "Do you think the Council's going to listen to them?"

"No, I don't. Alden's met with them several times, and he's confident that they have a different punishment in mind."

"And what punishment is that?" she asked, no longer able to breathe.

"Unfortunately I have no idea. They're being extremely tight-lipped, since they need to make sure King Dimitar approves it before the sentence is given. Alden still feels that it will likely involve time at the Sanctuary. But he also warned me that there might be something else in addition, and judging by this invitation, I'm guessing it'll be some sort of public reproval."

"Do I want to know what that means?" she asked, trying not to envision stocks and whips.

"Basically they would deliver your punishment in front of everyone, along with a stern lecture."

"That's . . . it?"

Grady laughed. "And here I thought you'd be panicking."

"Well, I don't *love* the idea of being humiliated in front of my entire school. But compared to being *expelled* . . ."

"It's definitely better," Grady agreed, pulling her in for a hug.

She rested her head against his chest, letting the sound of his steady heartbeat calm her racing pulse.

Then Grady had to ruin the moment by adding, "It's probably going to be a pretty humiliating experience, though, Sophie. People see you as a threat to the peace and safety of our world. If the Council's not going to give them what they want, they're going to have to come down *very* hard on you to prove they have you under control. I promise, everything is going to be okay. But I think we need to prepare for the fact that tonight is going to be . . . a very long night."

The crowd at Foxfire was even larger than Sophie had been expecting.

It leaked out the ornate golden doors to the main amphitheater—where the inauguration was being held—and spilled into the grassy courtyard, crushing the bushes shaped like the different mascots and blocking the path.

A tiny, less-than-nice part of Sophie wished one of the glaring people would accidentally find one of the effluxers and trigger an epic stink blast—especially when she spotted Marella standing with Stina.

There was a pocket of space between them, like neither girl

475

truly wanted to be with the other. But when Marella noticed Sophie watching her, she tossed her hair and turned away.

Sandor kept a loose grip on Sophie's wrist, leading her straight to a security checkpoint outside the main entrance. A dozen elves in bright orange capes were scanning everyone's registry pendants and dividing them into two lines, one leading up to the arena's seats, and one to the floor level. Only noble families were given access to the floor—but not all of them. And as far as Sophie could tell, there seemed to be no reason for the division.

Her family was sent to the floor.

The crowd was thinner there, filled mostly with stern-looking elves dressed in very fancy capes. So Sophie was surprised to recognize a familiar face.

"Dex?" she called, rushing over to his seat in the second row, near the center. He was sitting right behind the seats marked for her, and his whole family was with him—even the triplets. Sophie had never seen Kesler and Juline dressed so fancy—though their capes were still far simpler than the finery that surrounded them. "I didn't know you'd be here."

"Thought I'd be up in the common area, didn't you?" he asked, his wide grin making it clear that he didn't mind if she had. "Not anymore! They stopped us on our way in and told us that because one of my inventions would be featured prominently in the assembly, they wanted me nearby in case they needed any assistance."

"That's awesome," Sophie told him, knowing it was the reaction he was expecting.

But . . . why would the Council want to demonstrate a weapon?

Kesler patted Dex on the back, his pride obvious—though he still looked like he'd rather be back in his lab coat, whipping together some sort of crazy concoction.

"Oh—before I forget," Dex said, glancing over his shoulder as he dug into the pocket of his jeweled blue cape. "I finally had a chance to fix this."

He handed over her iPod, which now had a small silver triangle sticking out of the base. "I still don't get why you need this. But that receiver will pick up pretty much any kind of signal you want. And I made a few tweaks to the way it works, because, well, *man* that thing was slow." He touched the screen, tapped one icon, and instantly the Internet loaded. "That's what you needed, right?"

"Yeah—it's perfect." Sophie shoved it into her pocket before anyone could notice—though Sandor had already seen, and was giving her his *Do you really think this is the time or place to have human technology out in plain sight?* look. "You're the best."

"I know."

She elbowed him, and he laughed.

But he turned serious as he studied the packed audience above them. "I heard the Councillors saying something about an announcement regarding you. Everything okay?"

"I hope so." She said it with a smile, but what little she'd choked down of her dinner turned to prickles in her stomach.

Despite Grady's assurances, she couldn't help worrying that the Council was going to expel her. That wasn't something they would need a unanimous vote for. Only a majority—and she wasn't sure she had *seven* supporters.

She wasn't sure she even knew seven of the Councillor's names.

Still, it had to help that Dame Alina was the newest member to the Council. She'd seen firsthand how well Sophie did at school—surely she'd be able to come to her defense.

"It's time to take your seats," a snooty sounding elf told them, shuffling past in a silver-and-black cape. "The inauguration will begin in a moment."

Sophie had barely settled into her chair next to Edaline—which was also conveniently in front of the steps for the stage—when the bells chimed a slow, tinkling peal, and the Councillors and their bodyguards appeared.

They weren't wearing their usual gowns and capes. Instead, they wore identical silver suitlike garments, with simple, fitted jackets and tailored pants. Their long silver cloaks had hoods, which they all tossed back in unison, revealing matching silver circlets. The female Councillors even had their hair pulled back, making it hard to tell which Councillor was which.

The only one easy to recognize was Councillor Emery, whose dark skin gave him an air of importance as he welcomed everyone to the assembly. He explained that the inauguration would happen first, followed by a brief speech from the Councillors, which would conclude with an announcement—and Sophie was pretty sure he glanced at her when he said the last part.

Sophie reached for Edaline's hand as the Councillors stepped back, leaving room for Magnate Leto to move to the center of the stage. His orange robes were a vivid flame among the muted silver of the Council, and when the floor beneath him lifted to create a pedestal, he looked like a torch—a torch that suddenly had an unearthly green glow as the lights dimmed in the auditorium.

"Foxfire," Sophie whispered, realizing the glow was the same shade as the luminous mushrooms the academy was named after.

No matter how many times the elves explained the "illumination in a darkened world" analogy, she would never stop thinking it was weird to have a school named after glowing fungus.

Councillor Emery's booming voice snapped her out of her spore-related musings, and he unrolled a golden scroll, reading a long, boring oath for Magnate Leto to repeat—most of which Sophie tuned out. All she really caught was the final stanza—and only because Councillor Emery raised his voice to make it echo around the auditorium.

"Do you swear to put the safety and success of your prodigies above all else—even your own life?"

"Yes!" Magnate Leto called, lowering into a deep bow as polite applause filled the arena.

One by one the Councillors dipped their heads, paying their respects to the new principal of Foxfire. And when they reached the last of the twelve, Dame Alina, she stepped forward, holding a narrow scepter with a glowing orange *F* on the end. For a horrible second Sophie thought they were going to brand the *F* onto Magnate Leto's skin, like farmers did to cattle. Instead, Dame Alina pressed the glowing end against the center of the pedestal and turned it like a key, making the room rain with glittering orange sparks.

The sight should've been breathtaking, but it reminded Sophie too much of the Everblaze. And from the squeamish looks on the Council's faces, she clearly wasn't the only one fighting flashbacks.

"That's the key to Foxfire," Edaline whispered as the pedestal lowered and Dame Alina handed the scepter to Magnate Leto.

He dropped to his knees and vowed that the light would never go dark on his watch. Then he pressed the key into the floor and the room flooded with light, so bright Sophie had to rub her stinging eyes.

By the time her vision cleared, the pedestal was gone and Magnate Leto had stepped back to the shadows.

"Under normal circumstances, our festivities would end here," Councillor Emery said as the Councillors moved to center stage. "But we all know our circumstances are hardly normal at the moment. We thank you for your patience and trust, and we're happy to announce that the gnomes have reported to us just this morning that the cleanup in Eternalia is now complete. Every speck of ash and refuse has been washed away—a truly incredible gift these remarkable creatures have given us, and we all owe them a debt of gratitude. In the months ahead we will owe a similar debt to the dwarves for their help rebuilding what we've lost. And we always owe a debt to the goblins for standing at our side, ready to serve and protect. All of these creatures support us—not just because they are generous, compassionate beings—but because they rely on us for something as well. Something that recently we've been failing to deliver." He paused for a second, letting the audience lean forward in their seats, before he told them: *"Peace."*

The word triggered a murmur in the crowd, and Councillor Emery waited for them to fall silent before he continued.

"We did not ask for the role of peacekeepers on this complicated, ever-changing planet. And yet it is the role we were born to take. Our unique gifts and abilities have enabled us to secure stability amongst our world, as well as the five protected kingdoms, for millennia. And despite recent turmoil, our role has not changed. Our rule will not fall to threats, or rebellion. Nor will we stand back and let insubordination go unpunished."

Sophie was pretty sure every eye in the room was on her at

that point, but she didn't scoot down in her chair. Her legs didn't even tremble as she stood at Councillor Emery's command—but her heart pounded so hard it hurt as she climbed the stairs and took center stage.

"We've heard many cries for various punishments for the child you see before you—and I can assure you, we considered each one at great length. It's an extremely complicated issue. On the one hand, many of the actions that have angered you were things Sophie didn't necessarily choose. Others—while wrong—were largely the result of a lack of experience. We all must remember, Sophie Foster is not normal."

Sophie closed her eyes as the words rattled around her mind. She knew they were true. Yet somehow that made them hurt more.

"This child—through no fault of her own—has been given abilities she neither understands nor is able to control. Pair that with a lack of education and experience in our laws, and we have the perfect formula for disaster. But do we blame an out of control cart for crashing? Or do we blame the driver?"

More murmurs and mutterings, many of them clearly blaming her. But Sophie was more freaked out by the realization that she had no idea where Emery was going with this. It didn't sound like the kind of speech that was going to end in *we order Sophie to scoop dinosaur poop at the Sanctuary for the rest of the year.*

"Most of you have heard mention of a Black Swan group

hiding in the shadows," Councillor Emery continued, starting to pace now. "And many of you are aware that they're the very organization responsible for the existence of the child standing before us. Perhaps you've even heard whispers of good deeds they've done to cover their bad. Rumors of future plans meant to save us all. And you probably haven't known how to feel about this information. Neither have we. Such open defiance has never existed in our world, and our inherent desire to believe the best in our people has caused us to hold back, hoping to discover a missing piece that would plant this organization on the side of right. Instead, all we find is wrong."

He turned to stare at Sophie, making it clear he included her in that wrongness, and she wished they'd given her something to hold herself steady. Her wobbly knees couldn't carry her much longer.

"We promised you an announcement tonight," Emery continued, "and it is this. Our vow to you that our primary goal is now to track down the members of this organization and punish them for their illegal actions. And we shall not rest until every last one has been captured."

"What?" Sophie asked, not sure if anyone could hear her over the roar of the crowd.

She couldn't tell if they were cheering or complaining. But she could see Grady on his feet—and Alden moving toward him from his seat a few rows farther back. Their mouths seemed to be saying the same thing she was.

"You're going after the wrong group!"

If Councillor Emery heard them, he ignored it. Instead he called the crowd back to order, holding out his hands as Councillor Liora conjured a small flat black box into them.

"We realize this task we've sworn to will be no easy matter," he said, moving slowly toward Sophie. "We're hunting a group who've become extremely skilled in the art of hiding. Nevertheless, we *will* find them. And in the meantime we will do everything we can to minimize the damage they've done to our world. Which is why we've created this."

He opened the box, pulling out a silver circlet with three flat stones set into the curled pattern. Something about the design looked familiar, but Sophie's mind was spinning too fast to make the connection.

It wasn't until he raised it over her head that she realized what was happening.

Two of the Council's bodyguards rushed to her sides, holding her in place as Councillor Emery clamped the silver band around her forehead.

The circlet was Dex's telepathy restrictor.

The Council was trying to take away her abilities.

FIFTY-EIGHT

SOPHIE COULDN'T THINK THROUGH the pain.

The world had twisted into a smear of color and light—echoing with pounding, pulsing screams. She could feel her body being bumped and jostled, but she couldn't tell what was happening. She wasn't entirely sure if she was still awake—and she hoped she wasn't.

If this was reality, she wasn't sure how to survive it. Except to retreat from the agony.

She pulled her consciousness back, following a faint trail of warmth to the nook in her mind. Soft gray fog curled around her and she buried herself in it, sinking deeper and deeper until the last of the noise faded.

She was safe.

Happy, even.

Content to curl up tight and stay there forever.

But reality came crashing back, flooding her senses with light and sound as someone shook her awake.

"Sophie, can you hear me?" a deep, accented voice asked. "Nod if you can hear me."

Sophie nodded, triggering a chorus of relieved sighs.

Arms wrapped around her then—a tangle so thick, she couldn't tell how many people were holding her. She leaned into them, soaking up their strength and support until she could open her eyes.

Blurry shapes slowly morphed into faces.

Too many faces.

It took her brain a second to work out that some of them lived only in mirrors, and another second after that to recognize Dame Alina's old pyramid-shaped office. In front of her stood Elwin, Tiergan, and Alden, looking stressed and weary as they studied her. Grady and Edaline hovered behind them with tear-stained faces, along with a ghostly pale Magnate Leto. Behind them were all twelve Councillors—none of whom seemed to want to look at her. And cowering behind everyone was a crying, trembling Dex.

"I'm sorry," he mumbled when Sophie met his eyes. "I didn't know—I swear. I thought—"

"There is nothing to apologize for," Councillor Emery

interrupted. "Obeying the order of the Council is never to be regretted."

"In this case it is!" Grady shouted. "You may be able to ban Sandor from this room—but I will defend her when he can't. How could you even *think* of doing this to an innocent child?"

"If she's so innocent," Councillor Emery said calmly, "why did she illegally visit a Forbidden City yesterday?"

"How did you . . . ?" Sophie started to ask, but her voice trailed off when she remembered the registry pendant clamped around her neck.

"Yes, Miss Foster," Councillor Emery said as she reached for her necklace. "We do have ways to keep track of you. We choose not to use such methods very often, to protect our people's freedom. But imagine our disappointment when we checked yours yesterday—during a particularly heated debate regarding your punishment, no less—and found you had visited your former residence. We do not know why you went there, but we can only assume it had something to do with the Black Swan. Which is why we decided on a more *drastic* punishment."

He held out the telepathy restrictor, no longer clamped around her head—which explained why she could think again.

She shrank back in her chair, and Grady and Edaline moved in front of her, shielding her behind them. Alden and Tiergan moved to their sides.

"You're not getting anywhere near her with that," Grady warned.

"The matter has already been decided," Councillor Emery said calmly. "And interfering with the Council's decisions is a treasonous offense."

Grady snorted. "Not if the Council's gone crazy."

"Watch yourself, Lord Ruewen," one of the Councillors Sophie had never heard speak before told him. "We have dwarves on standby, ready to haul any resisters off to Exile. We will not tolerate such disrespect."

"But can you tolerate cruelty?" Alden asked quietly. "You saw how the device affected her. She was practically catatonic."

"And you should see the damage to her cells," Elwin chimed in. "It'll take three serums to heal it."

Sophie tried to swallow, but her mouth had gone dry.

Was her *brain* damaged?

"And that was only from a few minutes with the device," Alden reminded them. "I understand you've never used this technology before, but surely now that you've seen the effect, you realize it's far too dangerous."

"What we *realize* is that it needs some final adjustments. Mr. Dizznee!" Councillor Emery called, his voice ringing off the glass walls. "You told us this gadget might need to be calibrated to the individual, correct?"

Dex stumbled back, scrambling for the door. "I'm not helping you with that."

"The door is being guarded, Mr. Dizznee. And need I remind you that disobeying a direct order from the Council is an exile-able offense?" Councillor Emery asked.

"Before you answer that, Dex, might I also remind you that you are not the only Technopath who can help us with this?" Councillor Alina chimed in quietly. "Surely you'd rather make the needed adjustments yourself?"

"Are you really in support of this, Alina?" Alden asked. "Destroying the abilities of a child—"

"Restricting them," Councillor Alina corrected. "And yes, I am. I find it rather interesting that you all keep referring to her as a child. Have you forgotten that most children Sophie's age have yet to even manifest an ability? The reason for that—one can only assume—is that our genetics know that we are not ready to handle power at such a tender age. The Black Swan broke the laws of nature by triggering Sophie's abilities too early. And don't even get me started on how many they gave her."

"My son manifested at thirteen," Alden reminded her. "And Biana just did as well."

"Yes, and Sophie manifested her telepathy at *five*," Councillor Emery argued back. He sighed, running his hands through his dark hair as he turned to face Sophie, Grady, and Edaline. "It brings us no pleasure having to do this. But Sophie is out of control. Her abilities must be reined in. For the safety of us all."

The rest of the Council nodded in agreement, except Terik and Oralie, and—quite surprisingly—Bronte.

She only had *three* supporters, Sophie realized.

And one of them didn't even like her.

"Perhaps there's another way," Magnate Leto suggested in the silence that followed. "A full-time chaperone, or—"

"The *Council* has already considered all other possibilities," Councillor Emery interrupted, emphasizing the word "Council" to make it clear that Magnate Leto was not a part of it.

If only he'd been elected instead of Dame Alina—though that would still only leave her with four supporters. But four was better than three.

"Now, Mr. Dizznee," Councillor Emery said, holding out the ability restrictor to Dex. "Please don't make this any worse than it already is."

Dex locked his knees and shook his head as thick, sloppy tears streamed down his cheeks.

"It's okay, Dex," Sophie said quietly. "Just do what they're saying."

"How can you say that?" he asked, his voice cracking.

Because it was the only way she could think of to get the people she cared about safely out of that room.

"If Dex can make it so it doesn't hurt," she told Grady and Edaline, "then . . . fine. It only affects my abilities, right?"

"Right," Councillor Alina answered immediately, though Sophie wondered how she could really know. "And it will only be until you're older and mature enough to handle such things—and until the Black Swan's threat is contained."

"The Black Swan is *not* the threat," Alden said firmly.

"We are not getting into that debate," Councillor Emery informed him, grabbing Dex's arm and dragging him forward. "Make the adjustments we need."

"I'll be fine," Sophie promised, when Dex still wouldn't cooperate. "Please, Dex. I could never live with myself if you got exiled for me."

"And how am I supposed to live with *this*?" he whispered.

"Comfortable in the knowledge that you did the right thing," Councillor Emery told him, waving the circlet under Dex's nose.

Sophie could see the emotions warring in Dex's eyes and knew he wasn't ready to agree.

"No one will do a better job making it painless for me," she whispered.

That seemed to be the key.

Slowly, hands shaking, Dex took the circlet from Councillor Emery and stumbled to Sophie's side.

"If this hurts her, you will not like what happens," Grady warned, addressing his threat to the entire group.

"We are well aware of your abilities, Lord Ruewen," Councillor Emery told him. "Don't make us restrict you, as well."

"You'd never get the chance."

All twelve Councillor's arms flew up, their hands lightly smacking each side of their faces.

Judging by the mix of fury and fear in their eyes, Sophie knew they'd been mesmerized into the action.

She grabbed Grady's hand to stop him from going further. "Please don't fight them. It's going to be okay."

Grady's eyes turned glassy. But he nodded and moved to her side, wrapping an arm around her as Edaline did the same.

"I thought I was helping," Dex whispered as he stared at his horrible creation. "I never thought . . ."

"I know," Sophie told him.

"But you tried to warn me. You said I shouldn't—and I still did—and now . . ."

Dex was crying harder by then, and Sophie could only think of one thing that might help.

She pulled him in for a hug.

"You're going to hate me now," he whispered through the sobs.

Sophie promised she wouldn't, hoping it was true. Then she let Dex go, holding his stare as she reminded him that the Councillors were waiting.

Dex's hands shook so hard he nearly dropped the circlet as he closed his eyes. His fingers traced up and down the curled silver wires, bending and kinking them in slightly different ways as beads of sweat trickled down his temples. His whole face was dripping when he finally opened his eyes, letting out a choked sob as he held out the gadget.

"Will that fix it?" Councillor Emery asked, taking the circlet before Dex even answered.

"I don't know," Dex told him, his voice dripping with venom. "Maybe we should test it on *you.*"

Councillor Emery paled at the suggestion, and his voice was wobbly as he told him, "That would be pointless. You were supposed to be customizing it specifically for *Sophie.* So let's see if you have."

"It's okay," Sophie whispered as Grady tried to block him. "Dex made sure it's okay, right?"

Dex's nod wasn't nearly as confident as she would have liked. Still, she clung to Grady and Edaline, promising them everything would be okay as Councillor Emery held the circlet over her head.

"I can't watch," Elwin mumbled, turning away.

Oralie, Terik, and Bronte did the same.

The rest stared in silence as Councillor Emery placed the circlet around her forehead and pressed the stones against each of her temples.

A sour wave rippled through her body. But there was no blinding headache—just a fuzzy sound in the back of her mind, like static.

"Are you okay?" Grady asked, crouching down to get a closer look.

Elwin was already flashing colors around her head and squinting through the light. "Her cells seem okay. A bit sluggish, but no further damage—so *far.*"

"I'm fine," Sophie promised, wishing she had something to

wash down the sour taste. She sucked in slow, deep breaths, relieved when they eased some of the nausea. "Really, I'm okay."

Councillor Emery frowned. "Why can't I get past her blocking? Shouldn't I be able to?"

"Perhaps the device blocks all telepathic activity, even that from the outside," one of the Councillors suggested.

"Perhaps," Councillor Emery said slowly. "But how do we know if the device is actually working?"

"We should test her," Councillor Liora suggested. "Sophie, can you tell me what I'm thinking?"

"And how will that be conclusive?" Councillor Emery asked. "She could just lie."

"Then we'll have Oralie judge her emotions," Councillor Alina suggested.

"No—I will have *no* part in this," Oralie told them in the closest thing to a shout Sophie had ever heard her use.

"Neither will I," Tiergan jumped in.

"Nor I," Alden added.

Councillor Emery rubbed his temples. "Then I suppose we'll have to wait until we have another Empath."

"Or, if I may," Magnate Leto jumped in, "I might not be a Councillor, but I *am* a Telepath, and one of my strengths is knowing if someone has invaded my mind. If Sophie is able to get in, I'll be able to tell."

"And how will we know if *he's* lying?" Councillor Alina asked.

Magnate Leto gave her a cold smile. "If you don't trust me, Emery is welcome to listen to the thoughts in my head."

"No, I suppose that won't be necessary," Councillor Emery said slowly. "And it's likely the best test we'll get."

"Why are you assuming I'm going to lie?" Sophie interrupted. "I've cooperated already, haven't I?"

"Yes. And let's hope you continue to." Councillor Emery told her.

Sophie bit back a venomous reply as she moved shakily to Magnate Leto's side and reached for his temples.

She honestly wasn't sure what she would do if she could hear him, but judging by how fuzzy her head felt, she doubted she would need to decide. Her concentration felt scattered and jumpy, switching from one thought to the next before she could even finish thinking it.

She wondered if this was how people with ADD felt as she closed her eyes, took a deep breath, and tried to stretch out her mind.

It felt a bit like shoving her head into a pool of mud—thick and sloshy and totally murky. But she could still press forward. Just very, *very* slowly.

Bit by bit, inch by inch she crawled deeper into the mire and found . . .

. . . darkness.

And silence.

And pain.

So much pain.

A migraine that was worse than all the ones she'd endured during her years trapped with humans—combined.

She had just started to retreat from the agony when she heard a soft, muffled sound. Not even a whisper. More like a breath. And when she focused what little energy she had left, the sound morphed into a string of faint words:

If you can hear me, Sophie, do not let them know.

FIFTY-NINE

SOPHIE DID THE ONLY THING SHE COULD think of.

She fainted.

Or pretended to, anyway.

She fell into Grady's arms, forcing herself to stay limp as everyone shuffled around her. Only when she heard Elwin talking about a jolting elixir did she slowly groan back to life.

"Sorry. I don't know what happened," she mumbled, realizing with each word how hard her head was throbbing. The buzzing static had turned to a crashing waterfall. "I was trying to concentrate and . . . everything shut down."

Elwin helped her sit up, and when the head rush cleared she stole a quick glance at Magnate Leto.

He nodded—only once. Not really a nod at all.

But clearly he knew she'd heard him. And he was going to protect her secret.

"Here," Elwin said, handing her a bottle of Youth and flashing a yellow orb around her forehead. "You're severely dehydrated."

She downed the bottle in one long gulp. And it helped—a little.

But her brain still felt like the verminion was chewing on it.

Straining to hear that thought had drained every ounce of her strength. She didn't know how she could ever re-create it.

"We should take this contraption off now, before it does any permanent damage," Elwin muttered.

He reached for the band, but Dex grabbed his wrist to stop him. "Once the restrictor's been activated, you can't remove it unless you deactivate it first. That's why they had me take it off the first time."

"Or else what?" Alden asked.

"I'm not sure. It could be anything from partial brain damage to insanity. It's a security feature they asked me to give it, so the person being restricted doesn't have control."

"Great," Sophie grumbled. Leave it to Dex to be *thorough* while sealing her misery.

"I'm so sorry," he told her for what felt like the billionth time. "I'll take it off right now—"

"You'll do nothing of the sort! In fact, your services are no longer needed." Councillor Emery dragged him toward the door. "Know this, Mr. Dizznee: If you make *any* change to the device—or its effect on her—your entire family will be charged with treason."

He shoved Dex into the goblins standing guard, locking him outside before he could respond.

"How do you know the restrictor's not harming her?" Grady demanded. "This is completely untested technology—developed by a thirteen-year-old-boy. You have no idea what effect it's going to have in a few days or weeks."

"We'll monitor her progress closely," Councillor Emery promised. "As I'm certain you will as well. She already keeps Elwin on standby, doesn't she?"

"You dare to make jokes—" Elwin started, but Sophie cut him off.

"I'm kind of queasy, Elwin. Is there anything you can give me?"

The nausea was actually the least of her problems—but she needed to keep Elwin distracted. Enough people she cared about were facing exile already.

Elwin dug through his satchel, handing her at least a dozen elixirs and explaining how to administer them. When he was done, he flashed a green orb around Sophie's face, studying her for a long time before he said, "I almost don't want to say this, but . . . she seems okay. She'll probably need regular supplements, since this puts her under much heavier strain. But her vitals are holding steady."

"Wonderful," Councillor Emery said, so pleased with

himself Sophie wanted to scratch the smile off his face.

"Perhaps Sophie should go home and rest, then," Councillor Terik said quietly. He avoided Sophie's gaze as he added, "It's been a long day for all of us."

"It has," Councillor Emery agreed. "And her punishment is complete, so we can dismiss the assembly without her."

"Wait—people are still here?" Sophie asked.

"Of course," Councillor Alina said, smoothing her hair in one of the mirrors. "They're waiting for the final update."

Sophie could imagine them. Standing there judging her. Laughing at her. And that was only the beginning. *Everyone* knew about this—and if they didn't, her ugly circlet would quickly give her away.

She wasn't The Girl Who Was Taken anymore.

She was *Talentless*.

"I need to go," she told Grady, struggling to her feet. Her legs could barely hold her, but she refused to let anyone carry her out of there.

She would not let the Council think they'd broken her.

She held her head high as Edaline created a path. And the last thing she saw as she stepped into the light was Magnate Leto, giving her a quick wink.

Sophie made it to her bedroom before the tears hit. But once they started, she couldn't stop them.

She didn't even want to.

She collapsed on her bed and burrowed under the covers, wishing she could build a nest and never leave—never have to face the world as the freak-girl with restricted abilities.

It didn't matter that she'd been able to hear Magnate Leto. She'd nearly broken her brain to do it.

But what would she do without her abilities?

No one would want anything to do with her now. Not her friends. Not the Black Swan. Not Grady and Edaline.

And she couldn't blame them.

She didn't want anything to do with herself.

The sobs turned to chokes, bruising her from the inside out until Edaline pulled back the covers and pressed a warm, sweet cup against Sophie's lips.

She knew it was slumberberry tea even before she saw the purple color, and she drank it gladly, downing the whole thing and hoping it knocked her out for a few years—decades—the rest of eternity.

She strangled Ella as warm fluff swelled inside her mind, like her brain was spinning into cotton candy. Still, the softness couldn't erase the sting of the cold metal circlet cutting into her skin, and she tossed and turned and failed to find a comfortable position against her pillow until the drug dragged her away from the pain.

She woke up later and didn't bother opening her eyes. Her neck ached and her forehead was bruised and her pillow was soggy with drool.

Edaline tried to get her to eat something, but she wasn't hungry.

All she wanted was more tea.

She sank back into the cotton mind-candy, ignoring the voices that danced through her fluffy dreams. She couldn't tell if they were real or imagined.

But she heard Elwin worrying about her brain.

Dex apologizing over and over again.

Keefe insisting silver circlets were the hot new trend.

Biana asking if she could help.

Fitz promising he was there if she needed him.

And Grady and Edaline, begging begging begging her to wake.

She knew everyone needed her to be brave.

But *she* needed to stay far, far away. So she dove deeper into her drug-induced haze, wishing she could find her way back to the nook in her mind and stay there forever. She'd been happy there.

Safe.

But all too soon the tea wore off again, and this time when she asked for more, Edaline wouldn't give it to her.

"You're scaring me, Sophie," she whispered, wiping the sticky hair off Sophie's forehead. "Elwin doesn't think the circlet is hurting you—except for the abrasions on your skin, and he's working on a cream for those. But is there something he's missing? Are you sick?"

Sophie pulled the covers over her head.

"It's okay to be angry," Grady said from somewhere in the room. "What the Council has done to you is . . . unspeakable. I resigned my position as Emissary yesterday."

"You did?" Sophie asked.

"Yep. Alden was also ready to resign, but we decided to keep someone on the inside. So he's staying for now. But that might change."

She slid her covers back and opened her eyes, regretting it when blinding light crashed into her brain. She curled up in a ball, rocking through the pain as Grady and Edaline held her as tight as they could.

"I'm so sorry," Edaline whispered. "If I could wear the circlet for you, I would."

"I'd rather make the Councillors run off a cliff."

Grady's voice was so dark, Sophie believed him. Which was exactly what she'd been trying to avoid when she'd agreed to the horrible circlet in the first place.

"Please," she whispered, slowly lifting her heavy head. "Please don't do anything crazy over me. I'm not worth it."

"What?" Grady asked as Edaline pulled her closer again.

"I'm not worth it," Sophie repeated, taking a deep breath to give her the strength to say the rest. "I'm . . . a failed experiment, okay? The Black Swan made me to do something—I don't know *what*, but it doesn't matter now because I'll never be able to do it and the whole thing is a waste. I bet if you asked them they'd say the same thing."

503

"I don't care what the Black Swan created you for," Edaline told her. "I don't care if you dropped out of the sky or floated on the beach in an egg and hatched—you're still my daughter and I will *always* love you. No matter what."

Fresh tears burned Sophie's eyes. "You don't wish you could get rid of me now?"

"Is that really what you think?" Edaline asked.

Sophie hung her head, pointing to her circlet. "Who wants a freak in their family?"

"The freaks are the Councillors who thought this was an acceptable punishment," Grady growled. "But I promise, Sophie, nothing will ever make us not want you in our family. *Nothing*."

"But I keep ruining your lives!"

"No—you made our lives worth living again," Edaline promised. "You are a strong, beautiful, amazing girl, and nothing about this"—she traced a finger across the circlet—"will *ever* change that. You will still be our daughter, and we will still love you because you—"

"Remind you of Jolie?" The words stung her tongue and Sophie wished she could drag them back in. Especially when she saw their stunned faces. "Never mind. I shouldn't have—"

"Yes, you should," Grady said, squeezing her shoulders to stop her from turning away. "Sophie, I—*we*—never meant to compare you to Jolie. Yes, you remind us of her in certain small ways. But only because we love you so, so much. And what we love is *you*. You know that, right?"

A sniffle was the only answer Sophie could come up with.

Edaline brushed a tear off Sophie's cheek. "Please, Sophie. You have to believe us. We want *you. Only* you, okay? And that's never going to change. *Never.*"

Sophie swallowed a sob, feeling the knots tangled inside her loosen as she whispered, "You know what I want?"

"What?" Grady asked.

"A mom and dad."

She said the last words as a test, not sure how they'd feel.

But they felt right. *So* right.

Especially when Grady and Edaline whispered, "That's what we're here for."

"No matter what," Edaline added.

"No matter what," Sophie repeated.

She pulled them close, needing to do this right.

"I love you, Mom," she whispered. "I love you, Dad."

"We love you too," they both told her, their voices dissolving into sobs.

Sophie had no idea how long they sat holding one another, or how much time had passed since the night the Council sentenced her. But she was finally ready to face the next day.

And it was a good thing, because when she showered and dressed and slowly made her way downstairs, Grady and Edaline weren't alone.

Sandor was waiting for her.

So were Fitz and Biana.

And Keefe.

Sophie didn't need to ask why they were there.

She could see the tiny scrolls in their hands.

Each sealed with the sign of the swan.

SIXTY

GIVEN HER RECENT TROUBLES, Sophie would've expected her parents to keep her far, *far* away from the very illegal scrolls that Fitz, Keefe, and Biana were holding. Instead they left them in the living room with mallowmelt and lushberry juice and went upstairs. They *did* tell Sandor to keep an eye on things. But mostly they seemed relieved to see Sophie doing something normal again.

Or maybe they knew she was too useless to be involved anyway. . . .

The Black Swan must've thought the same thing. Apparently they'd given Keefe a note within hours of Sophie's sentencing, instructing him to tell Fitz and Biana about his dad and to wait for a new plan. Replacing one Telepath for another—with a Vanisher as a bonus.

It was hard not to be bitter.

Her friends sat on the couch opposite her, looking anywhere except her forehead.

"You can all stop pretending not to notice it," Sophie mumbled.

She'd managed to cover part of the circlet with her hair, but the bands that crossed her forehead, and the flat beige stone that rested between her brows, were impossible to hide—unless she put a bag over her head. Which she was actually considering.

"Honestly, I think it's pretty," Biana said, earning herself an elbow from Fitz. "What? I know it's a terrible thing. But . . . at least it's not ugly on top of it. Wouldn't that be worse?"

Sophie almost wanted to smile.

Leave it to Biana to consider the fashion sense of an ability-restricting accessory.

"Does it hurt?" Fitz asked after a second.

"Yeah," Keefe told him, before Sophie could lie. "I can feel it from here. And I gotta say, Sophie. I like Dex. But I kinda want to kick him in his special place."

"Me too," Fitz agreed.

"Me three," Sandor added from his post near the front door.

Sophie sighed.

She didn't want to hate Dex. But it was hard when just

concentrating on the conversation felt like it was wringing all the energy out of her brain. She'd already shoved the ring he'd made her deep into the bottom of her drawer—along with her iPod, and anything else he'd given her. And as soon as she had a chance, she was dyeing Iggy back to gray.

Still, Dex wasn't the only one to blame.

"It's my fault too. If I hadn't tried to read King Dimitar's mind . . ."

She couldn't finish the sentence. And she definitely couldn't look at Fitz, remembering the way he'd tried to warn her.

"It's *not* your fault," Fitz promised, leaning closer to her. "The Councillors are being idiots. And if it helps . . . there are lots of people who agree."

Sophie snorted. "I'm sure most of the crowd was cheering."

"There were some," Biana admitted. "But mostly everyone was stunned silent."

"Dude—even *my* dad thought it was messed up," Keefe jumped in. "If that doesn't say something . . ."

His words felt like a slap to the cheek and Sophie hung her head, realizing she was pouting about a circlet when Keefe's whole world was crumbling.

"How's everything going?" she asked quietly.

Keefe shrugged. "My dad doesn't know I know. My mom's asked a couple of times if I'm okay, but I'm sure she just thinks I'm worried about you."

"I still don't think you should be staying there," Fitz said, squeezing the edge of the couch. "What if Lord Cassius figures out that you're on to him?"

"Then he'll see that I'm ready for him." Keefe pulled back his sleeve to reveal a row of goblin throwing stars. The steel in his eyes said he wouldn't hesitate to use them. But there was a quaver in his voice as he added, "I'm keeping close track of his emotions. If I sense anything weird, I'll head to Everglen. But until then, we have to stick to the plan."

"I still don't like it," Fitz mumbled.

"Me either," Biana agreed.

The anger in their tone made Sophie wonder how they'd reacted when Keefe first told them about his dad. After all, they'd known Lord Cassius for *years*.

She was almost glad she hadn't been there.

"Besides," Keefe said, clearing his throat and pulling down his sleeve, "it'll all be over soon anyway. That's why we're here—not that we didn't want to check on you," he told Sophie.

"Right," Biana quickly agreed. "We've actually come by every day. Could you hear us? We couldn't tell."

Sophie's face burned, imagining how ridiculous she probably looked, sulking under her covers. "Sorry. I . . . guess I'm not handling this as well as I should be."

"Uh, there is no 'should be,'" Keefe told her. "I'd be freaking out just as much if it happened to me. Probably more."

"Me too," Biana agreed. "I never could've done what you did."

"What I did?" Sophie repeated.

"I hid in Dame Alina's office—or, I guess it's Magnate Leto's office now—when you were with the Councillors," Biana admitted. "I heard the awful things they said. And I saw how you stopped resisting once they threatened to exile Dex. I don't think I could've ever been that brave."

"Me either," Fitz agreed. "But Sophie's the bravest person I know. What's wrong?" he asked as she turned away to blink back tears. "Is the circlet hurting?"

"No. Well, yeah—it always hurts," Sophie admitted, drying her eyes with her sleeve. "But . . . I'm not brave. I've been feeling sorry for myself for—how many days has it been?"

"Three," Keefe admitted.

"Three days," she mumbled miserably. "So much time wasted. I just . . . I thought no one would want anything to do with me now."

"Why?" they all asked in unison.

She waved her hands around her head, like that explained everything.

Keefe laughed. "You worry about the craziest things, Foster."

"But I'm basically the Council's number one enemy!" she argued.

"So?" Biana asked.

"Yeah, that actually ups your Cool Points," Keefe added.

"And you know what the Council's doing, right?" Fitz asked. "People were judging them for not having frissyn ready to stop the Everblaze, and for not making the healing safe enough in the first place, and for not catching even *one* rebel in all these weeks. So they made you the scapegoat to take the attention off themselves."

"Besides, Foster," Keefe said, waiting for her to look at him, "when are you going to realize that you could wrap yourself in neon green feathers and start walking around roaring like a dinosaur, and we'd still hang out with you? Shoot—I'd join in."

"I would too," Fitz agreed.

"Me too—though I'd want pink feathers," Biana decided.

This time Sophie couldn't help smiling, and somehow it made her head hurt a little less. Enough that she finally felt ready to ask, "So, how much longer are we going to pretend you're not holding scrolls from the Black Swan?"

"We're not pretending," Fitz said after a second. "We just didn't want to upset you."

"Because the Black Swan's plan doesn't include me."

"Actually, they sent us to you." Keefe moved to the empty seat next to her and unrolled his scroll—which contained the longest message the Black Swan had ever used.

In order to guard those who must be protected,
Our plan has changed and been perfected.
A team of three will unite for the trip,
To the Head of the Sky, on the northern tip.

A cave of horrors will set the stage,
Where green boots rest, and never age.
Further plans will await your arrival,
Destroying this note will ensure your survival.
Seek the moonlark to set you on your way,
Then find us at sunrise on the third day.

"Sunrise on the third day?" Sophie asked. "That was today."

"No. They gave these to us this morning. They were hidden in our lockers at Foxfire."

"Foxfire?"

She hadn't realized she'd been missing school. Not that it mattered. Her ability sessions would all have to be replaced, and those were the only subjects she'd been doing well in.

"So you're the moonlark, right?" Keefe asked, like he could feel her mood plummeting. "That's what that line means?"

"I think so," she mumbled.

"Good, because that's pretty much the only thing we could translate," Biana admitted.

"And we aren't fans of that 'cave of horrors' line," Fitz added.

"Yeah, please tell me that's a joke or something, Foster. 'Cause I already did a cave of horrors thing with you a few weeks ago, and it wasn't awesome."

"I'm sure they mean a different cave. But . . . I've never heard of the Head of the Sky or green boots or . . ."

Her voice trailed off as a hazy memory filled her mind—a lecture from one of her old high school science teachers, back when she was living with humans.

"Actually," she said, rereading the note again, "I think they mean Mount Everest. The Head of the Sky is another name humans use for it sometimes—and the Sanctuary's built into the Himalayas, right? So if Silveny's the ruse, it would make sense that the Black Swan would choose there. The northeast ridge has a cave where a climber in green boots froze to death. They call it Green Boots Cave because the body's still there, preserved in the ice."

"Ewwwww—why haven't the humans taken the body away?" Biana asked.

"Because it's way up in the dead zone of the mountain, where the conditions are too treacherous to move it. I remember my teacher telling me there's, like, hundreds of bodies scattered all over Mount Everest."

"That might be the saddest thing I've ever heard," Fitz said quietly. "Why would the Black Swan pick there?"

"Maybe they wanted to creep the Neverseen out," Keefe suggested. "And if so, I'm pretty sure it'll be mission accomplished!"

"But how are you supposed to get there?" Sophie asked. "You can't teleport"—though she realized with a pang that *she* couldn't teleport any more either—"and you can't walk from the entrance to the Sanctuary in less than three days. Even if you could, you'd need a team of Sherpas, and oxygen tanks, and years of training. Climbing Everest is one of the most dangerous things humans do."

"Then why do they do it?" Biana asked.

Sophie had asked her teacher the same thing. And he'd given her the same answer she gave them. "To see if they can."

Biana crinkled her nose. "Humans are weird."

"Maybe," Fitz agreed, "but you gotta admire the bravery it takes to look at a massive mountain, knowing how deadly it is, and think, *You know what? I'm going to climb anyway!*"

"Sounds a bit like our Foster, doesn't it?" Keefe asked. "Maybe that's why she's set a new record for near-death experiences."

"Not anymore," Sophie mumbled.

Now she was just the message translator, sitting in her cushy house while her friends risked their lives for her. "You guys shouldn't do this. It's crazy."

"But it's smart, too," Fitz argued. "Think about it. If it's that dangerous for us—and we have time to prepare—how much worse will it be for the Neverseen when they show up and find themselves at the top of a deadly mountain. I bet that's another reason the Black Swan picked it."

"And my note came with this," Biana added, holding out a tiny black swan charm.

Sophie looked away, wishing she didn't feel so replaced.

But that used to be *her* charm.

"That still won't get you there," she said after a second. "Not without some sort of special light or something."

"Yeah, but they'll probably give it to us that day, just like they did last time," Keefe reminded her.

"Better hope they give you oxygen, too. You won't survive up there without it. And none of your clothes will be warm enough. And even then, you'll still have to deal with the Neverseen—and trap or no, they *will* fight back . . ."

Her voice trailed off when she realized she was technically talking about Keefe's dad.

Keefe patted his sleeve full of weapons again, his face as white as bone. "I have to stop him from hurting anyone again. Fitz and Biana don't have to, but—"

"We're going with you," Biana insisted.

"Yeah, you're not doing this alone," Fitz agreed.

Sophie sighed. "Did the Black Swan have you tell your dad that they're going instead of me?"

"I told him Fitz is coming to handle your telepathic stuff with Silveny. But he doesn't know Biana will be there—and I'm going to make sure it stays that way."

"I'm the secret weapon," Biana said, vanishing again to prove it.

Sophie stared out the windows, watching the sun creep toward the horizon. "It's really hard to sit back and let you guys risk your lives for this."

"Tell me about it," Grady called from the top of the stairs, making everyone jump. "Did you really think I wasn't listening up here?"

"I did," Keefe admitted as Grady came down to join them. "Please—you can't tell anyone about my dad. If he finds out—"

"I know," Grady interrupted, holding out a hand to calm him. "But before I agree, I have to ask—are you *sure* he's with the Neverseen?"

"Yeah," Keefe mumbled, squeezing his Sencen crest pin.

When he didn't elaborate, Sophie explained about the aromark they'd found on Keefe's hands and how the Neverseen kept finding them. Grady's expression turned murderous.

"You can't tell anyone," Keefe reminded him. "We need him to lead us to the others first."

"Right," Grady said, running his hands down his face. "You can't crush the first ant you find. You have to wait for the queen. So I will keep your secret—for now. But I *will* have goblins on standby near Candleshade in case things don't go as planned. And you two need to tell your father," he told Fitz and Biana. "I'm sure he will see the logic behind the Black Swan's strategy—especially with the Council's current uselessness. But he should know what his children are doing, and have the chance to make adjustments to keep you safe. Okay?"

They glanced at each other before they both nodded.

"Good. I'm going to make a few adjustments of my own," Grady added. "First—Sandor's coming with you."

517

Sandor frowned. "But Miss Foster—"

"Will be perfectly safe right here," Grady interrupted. "You should be with everyone on that mountain. And I should mention that this is the only way I'll agree to this plan. Otherwise I *will* find a way to stop you."

Keefe shrugged. "It's fine with me, so long as Gigantor's cool with it."

Sandor surprised him by bowing his head. "It would be my honor, Mr. Sencen."

"Ugh—can we stick with 'Keefe'? I'm not exactly a fan of that name right now."

Sandor nodded.

"Then I guess that settles that," Keefe said, holding out his hands to Fitz and Biana. "I'll need your scrolls. It says to destroy them."

"I can do that," Grady said, removing a silver flint from his pocket.

He lit the scrolls with a purple flame, letting the fire crawl over the paper like glowing moss, until there was nothing but a pile of ash.

"By the way, Keefe," Grady said, dusting the ash off his fingers. "I'm sorry your father is caught up in this. I'm hoping there's been a mistake. But if not, I want you to know that you can come to me with anything. Same goes for all of you," he told Fitz and Biana. "We have enough fighting against us at the moment. If we're going to survive the coming days, we're going to have to trust one another and work together. Can we do that?"

Everyone nodded.

"Good. Then let's all have another piece of mallowmelt. I have a feeling this will be our last peaceful meal for a few days."

SIXTY-ONE

SOPHIE RESISTED THE SLUMBERBERRY tea before bed, and without it—and without a way to reach Silveny—she found sleep impossible. She finally crawled out of bed and spent the rest of the night curled up on the floor near her window, staring at the stars.

They looked different, now that she'd seen how deadly their fire could be.

She wondered if the Council felt the same. Did they stay awake all night, regretting holding Fintan's healing in a room with a glass ceiling?

They should.

So why had they chosen that tower?

Did they fear some sort of rescue by the dwarves who'd gone missing if they kept him underground?

Or was there a darker, more sinister reason?

Doubt was such a curious thing. Like lenses over her eyes, it blurred the lines between shadow and light, making everything murky and gray. Anything could mean anything. Or it could simply mean nothing at all.

She knew only that the Council was capable of cold, unkind things, and now she was powerless to do anything about it.

Or was she?

She wasn't ready to face Foxfire yet, and when she checked Grady's office she found a runic dictionary thicker than her head. Her arms ached as she pulled it down and carried the heavy volume to her room, but it was worth the strain. Whatever code Jolie used in her journal had to have a pattern or a key. If she could figure out how it worked, she would be able to translate the pages.

Her circlet slowed her progress. Every few lines her concentration started to stray—and she was fairly certain her photographic memory wasn't working with the precision she was used to. But it felt good to do something productive. Even if it didn't seem to be helping.

Whenever she compared Jolie's markings against the runic alphabets in the dictionary, she couldn't find a match. In fact, the more she studied them, the more the writing looked unnatural—like Jolie had tried to copy something she'd been looking at, and sometimes her hand had failed her. Marks were scribbled on top of themselves, and many of the lines were bunched so close together that Sophie couldn't tell which rune they were connected to.

And yet, the whole mess still felt familiar.

Her eyes were starting to blur when Sandor announced that she had a visitor, and Dex shuffled nervously into her room.

"I wasn't sure if you'd see me," he mumbled.

"I thought you were Fitz."

She knew she was being cruel, but she couldn't stop herself.

Dex didn't rise to her bait. He just stared at the carpet, looking so sad and lost she had to tell him, "Sorry."

When he looked up there were tears in his eyes. "I'll take it off right now, Sophie. I don't care if they exile me."

"Yes you do. And you know it won't be just you. I can't let that happen."

"Then what should I do? Want me to wear one too? I will. I already started building it."

He reached into his Foxfire satchel and pulled out a dull metal circlet with a spikey pattern instead of swirls.

Sophie grabbed it from him and ran over to Sandor, who crushed it into a ball of mangled metal with his giant goblin hands.

"I know what you can do," Sophie said as she took the ruined circlet and handed it back to Dex. "You can never build another one—and stop making weapons for the Council!"

"I already did. I told them I wouldn't build them another thing."

"What did they say?"

He stared at the crushed ball, tracing his fingers over the individual bits of metal, like they were itching to repair it. "That they need my help to track down the Black Swan. And that even though things have calmed down with King Dimitar, that we still should be prepared from now on. They told me I could have some time to reconsider. But I won't. I don't trust them anymore. I never *really* did. I just . . ." He sighed, shoving the ball of scrap into his satchel. "I just liked that I mattered, you know? All my life I've been treated like a waste of a birth fund. And then suddenly I had Councillors visiting my house to talk to *me*, telling me how amazingly talented I was. And I wanted to impress them. I know that's no excuse. But I was just trying to make the Dizznee name something people respected. So the triplets wouldn't have to go though what I went through."

Sophie sighed. "I know, Dex. I do understand. And I don't *want* to be mad at you. But I am. And I probably will be for a while. Can you give me some time?"

He nodded sadly.

"But can I have one favor?" he asked. "No, favor isn't the right word. I know I don't deserve a *favor*." He stepped closer, pointing to her bare finger. "I totally get why you took your panic switch off—and I know the last thing you want to do is call for me. But . . . what if the rebels come after you again? You can't inflict or call anyone telepathically or teleport away, and I couldn't live with myself if anything happened."

"She has me," Sandor reminded him.

"I know. But *please*, Sophie. Let me do *something* to keep you safe."

His eyes glistened with tears, and Sophie felt her eyes burn too.

Dex was the boy who'd tackled the kidnappers so she could try to get away. He'd suffered in silence as they burned him over and over because he didn't want them to do it to her. He was her first friend—her best friend—and he just wanted to keep her safe.

So even though she was still angry with him, she dug out his ring and slipped it on her finger—and she stuffed her iPod back into her pocket, too.

"Thanks," he mumbled, turning away and wiping his eyes. "And remember, if you need *anything*, all you have to do is press the center stone and it will call for me."

Sophie nodded.

She had no intention of ever using the button. But it was nice to have Dex back on her side.

He left her then, and she went back to the mind-numbing task of studying runes. She'd only made it through a few more pages when Edaline peeked her head through the doorway, letting her know she had another visitor waiting for her in the living room.

She expected to find Fitz, Keefe, or Biana with news of the Black Swan. Instead, she found Magnate Leto standing under the crystal chandelier. He looked strange in his orange cape and tunic. Less intimidating than the silver clothes he used to wear as Beacon. Or maybe she just trusted him now.

"I can't stay long, I'm afraid," he told her as she offered him a seat on the couch. "I have a number of things still to arrange. But I wanted to stop by when I saw you were absent again today—and not to pressure you. I understand you might need further time to adjust. However, your sessions are waiting for you whenever you're ready to return. *All* of them."

"Even my ability sessions?" Sophie asked.

"Of course."

"But . . . doesn't *this*"—she pointed to her circlet—"make them kind of impossible?"

"Ah, I was under the impression that nothing was *impossible*." He tapped his lips, making it clear her secret was safe. "But even if I'm mistaken in that regard," he added, "all of your Mentors still see value in your sessions. I know Tiergan is *very* much looking forward to ensuring your thorough understanding of the rules of telepathy."

"What about Bronte and Lady Cadence?" Sophie had to ask.

"Lady Cadence assures me that there are tricks for successful mimicking that go beyond simply being a Polyglot. And Councillor Bronte actually came to *me*, insisting your session not be cancelled. I almost didn't allow it, given his role in your current *predicament.* But I told him I would leave the decision up to you. So he asked me to give you a message. Repeated it four times to ensure I remembered it."

Magnate Leto's eye roll told her how he felt about that.

"He said, 'It takes a special person to see darkness inside of someone and not condemn them.' Any idea what he means?"

"Not really," Sophie admitted.

Unless Bronte was referring to their rather dramatic last session.

But she *had* condemned him. She'd been ready to have Keefe go lie detector on him to find out if he was the leak in the Council. Good thing they hadn't done that. Now Bronte was one of the only Councillors still on her side—even if she did still think he was hiding *something.*

"Was that his whole message?" she asked.

"No, there was one other part. He said, 'Inflicting comes from the heart, not the head.'"

"Wait. Does that mean he thinks I can still—"

Magnate Leto smiled. "So should I assume you'll leave your schedule as is?"

"I guess," Sophie mumbled, hardly believing that she was voluntarily keeping her session with Bronte.

But the thought of taking the ability back sent prickles of hope flaring in the back of her mind, clearing some of the clouds choking her concentration. Especially when Magnate Leto squeezed her shoulder and told her, "Take the time you need to adjust to your new situation. But know that Foxfire is waiting for you. We need our star prodigy back."

"I'm not a star," she told him as he pulled a slender pathfinder from his sleeve.

"That's not what I've seen. I have it on good authority that nothing can stop you from being who we need you to be."

Then he was gone, leaving her with renewed energy as she returned to her room and focused on Jolie's journal.

Her thoughts were still slower, and her headache couldn't dull completely. But this time she felt confidence—and the confidence made her realize she was on the wrong track completely.

Jolie had wanted the Black Swan to have this journal, otherwise "swan song" wouldn't have been part of the key. So she had to have left a clue to tell them how to read it. And the clue had to be hidden in the only runes written in the Black Swan's cipher.

"Reflections," Sophie whispered, tracing her fingers over the careful lines and squiggles.

What was Jolie trying to tell her? To reflect on something inside the journal?

But how could she do that if she couldn't even read it? What would she use to . . .

Sophie dropped the journal, not sure if she wanted to kick herself or jump up and down.

She decided to see if she was right before she made her decision.

She'd been reading the title like it meant "musings" or "observations." But what if Jolie meant it much more literally?

"Please please please," Sophie whispered, holding the human mirror in Jolie's blue compact up to the first page.

If Sophie was right, the letters should inverse in the reflection and . . .

She had one second to celebrate as the squiggly lines morphed into words she could finally understand.

Then she read the first sentence.

If you found this journal, it's too late to stop him.

SIXTY-TWO

WHO?" SOPHIE SHOUTED AS she squinted at the page.

Jolie didn't seem ready to tell her.

In fact, the first sentence must have been added later, because after that it switched to an account of why Jolie had joined the Black Swan in the first place.

Translating the runes was tedious, and forced Sophie to work at a glacial pace. Jolie must've been copying down a reflection of an original entry, and her writing was sloppy and nearly impossible to read. Still, when Sophie took it one letter at a time, she was able to piece together the words to Jolie's story.

Prentice had recruited her for the Black Swan toward

the end of her first year in the elite. He'd been the Beacon of the Golden Tower, and overheard her tell a friend that the old ways didn't apply to the present day. She'd meant it in regards to matchmaking, but Prentice had spent the next weeks revealing why she should apply it to the entire Council.

At first she'd resisted such traitorous statements, but then he'd shown her a scroll written in an ogre's hand. The message made it clear that some sort of information exchange had been occurring between the ogres and a small band of elves. But when Prentice had shown it to the Council, the matter had been ruled a "misunderstanding" and dismissed without investigation. Same with several other disturbing bits of intelligence the Black Swan had uncovered. Which was why they'd formed their organization. Someone needed to start acting, before it was too late.

Still, Jolie refused his offer, arguing that her life was complicated enough already. But they wouldn't let her walk away. Strangers would bump into her in the halls, whispering things like "The fall is never seen before the rising" and "The bold and brave are never seen." Later she'd find bits of paper shoved into her pockets with times and dates for her to meet.

She never went, and eventually confronted Prentice, demanding the Black Swan leave her alone. But the Black Swan had nothing to do with those messages.

The rebels were trying to recruit her too.

That was when she decided to join them as a double agent.

Prentice warned her it was too dangerous, but Jolie refused to be persuaded. She swore fealty to the Black Swan and trained in their basic methods. But the next time she found a note shoved into her pocket, she followed the instructions to find the rebels.

The next three pages were a detailed account of all the different notes and clues and hoops the rebels made Jolie jump through, trying to decide if they could trust her. She'd been to more than a dozen of their "meetings"—which were nothing more than her finding another note they'd left her—before she even learned they called themselves the Neverseen. And for months after, they continued to live up to the name.

She'd find random messages, or hear whispers—but never meet an actual member. She was starting to think the whole thing was just shadows and games when—

"Hey, Sophie?" Edaline asked, nearly giving Sophie a heart attack.

She gave a small smile as she set a bowl of pink soup and a plate of black-and-white speckled cubes on the floor next to Sophie. "Looks like you found a way to translate that."

Sophie nodded. "I'm writing a version you can read when I'm finished—not that I'm learning much."

Fascinating as Jolie's history was, she hadn't given any actual answers. And it wasn't like Sophie could skim ahead.

The confusing runes made it way too easy to miss something crucial.

"What is this stuff?" Sophie asked, pushing the slimy cubes around the plate.

"They're not the best tasting, I'll admit," Edaline warned her. "I tried some as I was slicing them and they're rather sour. It's a fruit called clarifava. The gnomes gave it to me, because it's supposed to help the body resist the influence of technology. Honestly, I have no idea how that works. But I know that gnomes believe anything beyond nature is corrupting. And when they heard about your circlet they insisted you eat a serving every night. Claimed it would clear your head and sharpen your body's defenses. So I thought I'd leave it up to you if you wanted to try it."

"It can't hurt, right?" Sophie decided—though she regretted the decision when the first bite zinged the glands near her ears.

"Rather sour" was a bit of an understatement.

Still, she forced herself to finish the plate, and by the time she'd choked it all down, she did feel a little better. It could've been the placebo effect, but her headache seemed like it had dulled around the edges.

"I actually think it helped," she said, shoving aside her soup so she could get back to work. "Can you thank the gnomes for me the next time you see them?"

Edaline pushed her soup back to her. "I will. But you still

have to eat some actual dinner, Sophie. The journal can wait ten more minutes."

Sophie scowled, but didn't argue, devouring the still-too-hot soup so fast, she was pretty sure she burned off all her taste buds.

"Okay?" she asked, showing Edaline the mostly empty bowl.

"I suppose." She snapped her fingers, making the bowl disappear, then again to bring a plate of custard bursts. "I made them with caramelized sugar this time, and I have to say, it might be my best batch ever. I'll have to remember it the next time I bring them to Brant."

"Can I get in on those?" Grady asked, helping himself to two as he joined them. "What? I need one for each hand!"

Sophie smiled—and totally copied him.

And Edaline was right, they were the best custard bursts she'd made. Rich and creamy, like the world's best crème brûlée had been stuffed inside the thin sugary shell. She could've eaten the whole plate—or, she could have until Grady killed the mood.

"A package just arrived for Sandor from the Black Swan," he said quietly. "They gave him a heavy white cloak and some sort of silver gadget to help him breathe at the high altitude."

Sophie fiddled with the flowers on her carpet, not looking at Grady as she asked, "Did they tell him any more about their plan?"

"Actually they were surprisingly specific. I still had to read between the rhyming lines, but it sounds like they want everyone to meet at Kenric's Wanderling at sunrise, where they'll find whatever they need to leap to that awful cave you told them about."

"And then?"

"Then they'll find a hidden door that the Neverseen should think is a secret path to the Sanctuary. But it actually dead-ends in a small cavern, where they'll wait while the Neverseen set up whatever ambush they're planning. Then the Black Swan's dwarves will ambush *them*. And you don't have to worry about Silveny. Somehow they've convinced Jurek to secure both her and Greyfell for the night with unbreakable chains. And Keefe, Fitz, and Biana will never leave the cavern. All the fighting will be done by the Black Swan."

"Is that it?" Sophie asked, wondering if she was missing something. "That sounds so . . . simple."

"Simple plans are always the best."

"Maybe. But . . . so . . . Fitz, Biana, and Keefe are just going to sit in a cave and hide while the Black Swan attacks? Why do they even need to be there?"

"Because the Black Swan needs the Neverseen to see another easy, unsuspecting target and have their guard down. It sounds like they're basically re-creating the same scenario that happened in the cave you and Keefe visited. Only this time you guys know they're coming. And that is the only difference that matters."

"I guess," she agreed, not sure why it felt so disappointing.

She should be glad that her friends were going to be safe. But somehow it felt wrong to catch the bad guys so easily. For all their notes and theatrics, she'd expected more from the Black Swan than dwarves popping out of the snow.

"They're going to be okay," Grady promised, misunderstanding her frown. "Sandor will make sure of it. And if their Pyrokinetic is with them . . ."

He didn't finish the sentence. But the look he shared with Sandor made it clear an arrangement had been made between them. A deadly one.

"Are you okay with this?" Edaline asked, reaching for Sophie's hand. "I know it can be hard to sit on the sidelines."

"It's weird," Sophie admitted. "But . . . I have stuff to keep me busy."

She tensed when she remembered Grady was in the room.

He patted her on the head. "Edaline does tell me things, Sophie. Is there anything *you* want to tell me?"

Sophie pointed to the tiny runes she was translating. "I'm hopefully getting close. But so far it's just a long, rambling story."

Edaline sighed. "That sounds like Jolie."

Grady closed his eyes, his voice thick as he whispered, "I want to know *everything* you find."

"You will, I promise."

He nodded, and the silence that followed felt heavy. None

of them seemed strong enough to break it, so Edaline finally led Grady out of the room, letting Sophie get back to translating.

She worried she was going cross-eyed as she worked through Jolie's description of the first time she talked to the Neverseen. It was a woman—though Jolie could only hear her voice through a crack in the wall. The woman told her they could fix her bad match and have Brant's status as Talentless erased. The changes would take time, but she promised they *would* happen if Jolie swore fealty to their cause.

Jolie agreed.

She told herself it was part of her plan to infiltrate their group. But as she followed the Neverseen's directions to a forest in a Forbidden territory, her doubts took hold. Her only proof that the Neverseen were the villains came from the Black Swan. How did she know she hadn't been misled? She'd almost convinced herself that the Neverseen were fighting for the same cause. But then she reached the designated clearing.

Figures hidden under heavy black cloaks surrounded her in the dark, and one—a male voice that felt somehow familiar—told her she must prove her commitment before she could join. He raised an unlit torch, and with the slightest flick of his wrist, the end ignited, erupting into a blaze of white flame that smelled like burning sugar.

Sophie's nose tingled, remembering the white fires that

had torn through San Diego. The flames had smelled exactly the same. Which meant Jolie hadn't just met the leader of the Neverseen.

She'd met her killer.

The torchbearer told her that joining their ranks meant accepting their enemies. And enemies had to be destroyed. Then he handed her the torch and pointed to the woods, which bordered some sort of human nuclear facility, poisoning the earth with its toxic chemicals. "Nothing so vile should be allowed to continue," he told her, ordering her to spark the first flame.

She tried to hand the torch back, but he gave her a speech about protecting their planet and taking back what was rightfully theirs. Told her the war was coming whether she wanted it or not and begged her to join the side that would win. When she still tried to push past him, he grabbed her wrist, searing her with his fiery hands. She screamed from the pain, but he didn't let go, ordering one of the cloaked figures to wash Jolie's recent memories clean.

Before they could wipe her mind, Jolie used her home crystal to leap away.

She hid at Havenfield for the next few days, afraid the Neverseen were waiting for her.

But there was another reason to hide. One that was far more terrifying.

She'd figured out why his voice had sounded familiar. He . . .

The next several lines were scratched through so thoroughly, Sophie couldn't pick out even a single letter. And when the legible runes picked back up, the tone of Jolie's narrative had changed.

It wasn't a story anymore.

It was a plea.

You have to remember how angry he is.

How lost he feels.

He just wants the life that's been stolen away from him.

"But who?" Sophie asked, wishing she could reach through the journal and shake Jolie.

Why was she protecting him?

She kept going on and on about the burden that the ban on pyrokinesis had placed on him. Branding him Talentless when he had an ability that should have qualified. Forbidding him from ever satisfying his insatiable craving for flame. Apparently he'd fought as long as he could, but the struggle had been too great. And when he'd turned to Fintan for advice, Fintan gave him secret pyrokinesis lessons instead, opening his mind to new longings, new possibilities.

The power fueled him and haunted him, changing him into someone Jolie didn't recognize. But she still wouldn't say who he was—and the pages in the journal were quickly running out.

"Please tell me you put his name in here," Sophie begged as she turned to the last page.

The final paragraphs gave her no answers. Just hasty scribbles about how he deserved another chance.

Jolie was planning to go to him one last time and try to make him see reason. And if she failed . . .

"You have to be kidding me!" Sophie shouted when the final sentence ended.

Did Jolie really make a special compartment in her wall, and give Vertina a password, and record the message backward so only someone with a special mirror could read it—and even then, only if they had a tremendous amount of patience— AND THEN NOT GIVE HIS NAME?

Sophie stood, needing to move—or maybe kick something— to clear her head.

Could she have mistranslated? Should she go back through and double check?

She picked up the journal and mirror, wondering if her eyes could really handle another marathon translating session, when Grady peeked his head through her doorway.

"Everything okay in here?" he asked. "I was on my way up to let you know Sandor had left, and I thought I heard you yelling."

"Sandor left?" Sophie glanced out her windows, stunned to see purple-blue streaks announcing the coming sunrise.

"A few minutes ago," Grady agreed. "But somehow I don't think that's what you were shouting about. Was it something in there?" he asked, pointing to the purple journal she was clutching with a death grip. He took a deep breath before he asked, "Did you find something bad?"

"Honestly? I didn't find anything. After all I had to go through to get this thing, it's just a long story that tells me nothing."

Grady's shoulders relaxed. "That's how Jolie's stories always ended. She would act like she'd revealed this huge thing, and most of the time I'd be thinking, *That's it?* But after a while I realized that what she'd told me was big—for her. She wasn't big on sharing secrets. I think that's why the bad match was so upsetting for her. Suddenly everyone knew way more about her personal life than she wanted. Which was ironically how I knew she truly loved Brant. No matter how hard it got, she always stood beside him."

He smiled at the memory, because for him it was sweet.

But Sophie felt like she was back in that burning tower, watching the world bubble and melt around her.

The mirror slipped from her hand, hitting the carpet with a soft thud.

"Are you okay?" Grady asked.

Sophie shook her head, unable to form an actual reply.

She wasn't sure she would ever be able to speak again—and she almost hoped that was true, so she would never have to tell Grady the truth.

She rubbed her wrist, remembering the burns her kidnapper had given her. But she could remember a different burn too, one she hadn't even thought was a burn, even though it had needed burn ointment to treat it.

The wound Brant had given her.

"He's a Pyrokinetic," she whispered, knowing the words were true even though she desperately didn't want them to be.

Because if she was right, then . . . Brant hadn't just been with Jolie the day she'd died.

He'd set the fire that killed her.

SIXTY-THREE

SOPHIE BURIED HER HEAD IN HER HANDS, trying to think of any reason she could be wrong.

She'd visited Brant—talked to him.

And he'd creeped her out both times.

He'd even told her, "I've seen you before," the first time she met him.

Now she finally knew where.

But his voice! She remembered her kidnapper's voice—and he hadn't sounded like Brant.

Except . . . Brant had been sick when she'd visited.

Or he was trying to disguise it.

He'd even stopped her from probing his memories—was that because he was afraid of what she'd find?

"No," she whispered, repeating it over and over, like if she just said it enough times it would suddenly be true.

"Okay, I've been pretty patient," Grady said, taking her hands and waiting for her to look at him. "But you're going to have to tell me what's going on."

She knew he was right—but this was too huge.

Too life changing.

It would shred his heart into itty-bitty pieces.

"Please tell me, Sophie. I need to know."

"I know," she whispered, smearing away tears.

But she still couldn't look at him.

"Who is the Pyrokinetic? Just say it really fast."

She tightened her grip on him, knowing they'd both need something to hold on to if she was going to do this.

Grady curled his fingers around hers and she took deep breath, choking down the bile in her throat as she whispered, "Brant."

Grady went very, very still.

It felt like time had stopped—like the entire universe was resting on the edge of nothingness, ready to topple over any second.

But Grady's voice was soft—barely even audible—as he let go of her and said, "I have to go."

"Where?" Sophie asked, stumbling into her nearest pair of shoes as she ran after him.

She wasn't surprised that he went up the stairs instead

of down, nor when he stepped under the crystals of the Leapmaster and called for Brant's house.

But she couldn't let him go.

"You can't do this, Grady," she begged, running to his side.

"Believe me, I can."

He moved to step into the light—but Sophie grabbed his arm, dragging him back.

"I might be wrong."

"Are you?" he asked.

She rubbed her wrist, remembering the sting of Brant's last burn. And she replayed the memory she'd seen in his mind of the fire—the way the flames had exploded so strongly. So suddenly. Why had Brant been knocked back to safety, while Jolie had been surrounded?

It only made sense if *he* sparked the fire.

"It's true," she whispered.

"Then let me go."

"But he probably won't even be there," she reminded him. "I'm sure he'll be with the others on Mount Everest."

"Maybe," Grady agreed. "But I'll be waiting for him in case he gets away."

When she still didn't let go, his expression became dull and rigid—like he'd turned to stone. "Don't make me force you to let go, Sophie."

She realized what he meant and dropped his hand.

"Don't tell Edaline," he whispered.

She lunged for him as he stepped into the light, not entirely sure what she was doing. She had just enough time to hope Brant wouldn't be there. Then the force of the light ripped them away.

"You shouldn't have done that!" Grady shouted as they reappeared on the rocky ground of the cold, bleak cliff. "Go home now!"

"Not without you!"

"Trust me, Sophie, you don't want to be here for this."

She shivered as she turned to face Brant's square, windowless house.

The house Grady and Edaline had built to accommodate his every need.

The house they'd visited every year. Bringing him his favorite cookies. Treating him like a *son*.

"Sixteen years," Grady said, picking up a stone and hurling it at the wall.

It crashed with a thunderous *CLANG!* and shattered to a dozen pieces.

Sophie froze, waiting for Brant to slam open the door and confront them.

But the door stayed sealed and the house remained eerily silent. Nothing but the roar of the icy wind and the crashes and bangs as Grady threw stone after stone after stone.

Finally, out of breath and out of stones, he turned away to

dry his tears with his sleeve.

Sophie strangled him with a hug, hoping if she held him tight enough she could keep him together.

"All this time," he whispered. "I thought he was broken by his *grief*."

"Maybe he was."

She could still see Brant cowering in the corner, cradling Jolie's pin in his hands. And he'd written her hundreds and hundreds of love poems and letters.

"What if it was an accident?" she asked quietly. She knew better than anyone how unstable Pyrokinetics could be. And he'd ended up burning himself. "What if he lost control of his temper and the fire just . . . happened?"

"I love this about you, Sophie," Grady said, brushing his fingers over her head—careful to avoid her circlet. "You always hope for the best."

"But what if I'm right?"

"Even if you are—and I don't think that's the case—how was what he did to *you* an *accident*?" He pulled away, taking her hands and tracing his fingers over her wrists.

Wrists that had taken Mr. Forkle over an hour to heal.

"Maybe—"

"Well, I guess this means no more custard bursts," a bitter voice said behind them.

Grady's grip was like a vise as he pulled Sophie behind him and turned to face Brant.

Brant leaned against the metal door, looking perfectly at ease in his strange yellow-orange robe, like he'd known this day would come—and had been preparing for it.

"I guess there's no need to pretend anymore, is there?" he asked, switching to the hollow, raspy voice Sophie would recognize anywhere. His scarred lips curled with the hint of a smile as he met her eyes. "What? Not happy to see me again? And here I thought you were working so hard to find me."

"Actually, I was working to stop you," she told him.

"Hmm—and that hasn't gone very well either, has it?" He traced his fingers across his forehead, miming her circlet. "I must say, that contraption is the only good decision the Council's ever made. Well, that, and having you heal Fintan. Both worked out very well for me."

His grin made Sophie want to vomit.

"Watch yourself, Brant!" Grady warned him.

"Why? So I can wait another sixteen years for you to figure out what's going on? Tell me this—what do you think I do all day? Sit in this cold box of a house, staring at the walls, waiting for my annual visit? Actually, I get out all the time. It's amazing how much a little ash helps me slip past goblins."

Sophie sucked in a breath. "You were the intruder who left that footprint in the pastures—and you've been to the Sanctuary, haven't you?"

His smug smile was the only answer he gave.

"What do you want with Silveny?" she demanded, wishing Grady hadn't used up all the rocks to throw at him.

"A creature the Council will do *anything* to keep alive?" Brant asked. "Whatever would I do with that?"

Before Sophie could reply, Brant's fist flew up, punching himself in the face. He stumbled backward, crashing into the wall—and when he righted himself there were red streams dripping down his scarred chin.

"I wouldn't do that again if I were you," he warned Grady.

"Or else what?" Grady asked, making Brant elbow himself in the stomach so hard he doubled over. "You're not fooling anyone, Brant. I've seen the madness you're hiding beneath the surface. I've watched you clawing at the walls and slithering on your belly and collapsed in a puddle of your own drool."

Brant's teeth were smeared with red as he smiled. "Or maybe I just wanted to see if you'd mop up my spit!"

That earned him two more self-punches to the face, but the pain only made him laugh.

"Does that make you feel better, Grady?"

"*Nothing* will ever make me feel better!" Grady snarled. "You've stolen everything—"

"EVERYTHING WAS STOLEN FROM ME!" The outburst left Brant panting for breath, and he clutched his chest, staring at the pale, empty sky. "All I ever wanted was to take my rightful place in society. But the Council wouldn't let me. Because they were too scared of this."

He snapped his fingers and red-orange flames sparked across his hand, crawling over his skin.

"Look at you both cower!" he said as held his palm out to them. "Can't you see the beauty of it? This is a *gift*."

"Fire destroys everything it touches," Sophie reminded him as she watched the flames flicker and dance.

"Not me." He waved his hand, showing how the skin wasn't melting.

"Yes it did. I saw the letters you wrote Jolie. I know how much you loved her."

"I did." He curled his fingers into a fist, snuffing out the flames. "But the Council and the Black Swan poisoned her against me."

"She wasn't against you," Sophie told him. "I read her journal. She defended you—even at the end, when she knew what you were."

"What I am," Brant said calmly, "is a *visionary*!"

"No—you're a murderer!" Grady shouted. "And I won't let you get away with it anymore."

"I'd like to see you stop me."

Before Sophie could blink, Brant curled his fingers at the sky and hissed some sort of word, drawing down a basketball-size sphere of Everblaze.

"Enough," Grady told him, his voice unnaturally calm as Brant froze like someone had just hit the pause button.

The Everblaze hovered above Brant's palm like a tiny

burning star, bathing him in the flickering neon yellow glow.

"Put it out," Grady demanded.

Brant managed a crooked smirk back at him. "I'd like to see you make me."

"Oh, I can."

Brant's smirk morphed into horror as his free arm rose in a slow, deliberate motion and shoved his hand into the center of the ball of Everblaze.

"Stop!" Sophie shouted as Brant screamed.

"He can stop it himself," Grady told her. "He just has to put out the flame."

"Never," Brant spit through gritted teeth.

"THEN YOU CAN BURN!"

Brant's screams grew louder and Sophie covered her ears—but she could still hear the agonizing wails echoing off the rock face. And the rotten, sickeningly sweet smell of burning flesh was inescapable.

"Please, Grady," Sophie begged.

But Grady didn't so much as flinch.

It wasn't until she squeezed his arm and whispered, "Jolie wouldn't want this," that he lowered his head and Brant's screams faded into muffled whimpers.

"You should go, Sophie," Grady told her as his whole body started to shake.

"Not without you."

"I have to finish this first."

"How?" she asked him. "If you don't stop now, you'll end up just like him."

"Listen to her," Brant mumbled, slowly pulling himself to his feet. Sophie avoided looking at his hand—not wanting to see the damage the Everblaze had done. "She's such a smart little weapon."

"I'm not a weapon!" Sophie snapped.

"Not anymore," Brant agreed, whipping his arm and launching the Everblaze at her head.

Sophie dropped to her stomach, feeling the edges of her hair singe from the heat as the fireball streaked above her—missing her by inches.

She covered her face, preparing for a second attack, but Brant had gone quiet.

Everything was silent—except the tongues of yellow flame licking across the jagged rock wall behind her, spreading into a wild blaze.

"Grady?" Sophie shouted, realizing he was no longer beside her.

She pulled herself to her feet, squinting through the thick smoke to spot two figures standing near the edge of the cliff.

"Stop!" Sophie screamed, racing to Grady's side.

He froze her before she could reach him, stopping her mid-lunge, like she'd been grabbed by an alien tractor beam. "You don't want to do this, Dad."

"No," he agreed. "But I have to. It's the only way to keep you safe."

Brant inched another step forward, sending a shower of pebbles toppling over the edge.

"Stop!" Sophie screamed again. "Just let the Council take him away."

"So he can end up like Fintan? They'll never do what needs to be done. And he'll find a way to burn again."

"I can burn now!" Brant hissed a command and Everblaze snaked to his side, swirling into a massive fireball above them. "Let me go or I'll make it rain on all of us."

"You'll never get the chance," Grady promised.

"Oh, I will." The fireball sank lower, making Grady duck. "Just give me a reason, Grady, and we all go up in flames—and moving Sophie counts," he added, dropping the fire lower still, forcing Grady to duck. "If she goes, we all go. Or you can admit you've lost and let me go free."

"I can make you *want* to surrender," Grady snapped back.

"Can you?" He laughed as Grady gasped and rubbed his head. "Looks like you can't. Guess that's an advantage to having a few cracks in the old brain."

"I will *never* let you go, Brant."

"Well, then you can sacrifice another daughter. The choice is up to you."

No—Sophie realized. It was up to her.

If she let Grady kill Brant she'd lose him in the process,

and that was a risk she wasn't willing to take. She had to make him change his mind, and she was pretty sure she knew how—assuming Bronte was right about the heart being the secret to inflicting.

She closed her eyes, trying to tune out the chaos and focus on her memories of love. Her brain didn't want to focus, but she let her heart swell with feelings, the warm burst when Grady and Edaline had told her they loved her, the trust and faith she'd felt the day they adopted her, and the sweet relief of the moment she'd first called them Mom and Dad. She felt her love for her human family, too, all the smiles and kisses and late-night back rubs to help her sleep. She could feel the last hug she gave them before she said goodbye forever. And the gentle strength of Fitz's shoulder as he'd held her and let her cry and promised her everything would be okay. She could feel herself clinging to Dex as they escaped together, and the pride and gratitude she'd felt as she watched Keefe fight to protect her outside the dark, treacherous cave. She even felt the calm respect for Biana, who always came back, no matter how much they'd fought, and the comfort and happiness Silveny and Iggy had brought into her life.

Each feeling rushed through her like a summer breeze, and she swirled them together, letting them spin into a mental storm. The energy was wild and unruly, but powerful.

So powerful.

It was the most powerful force she'd ever felt. And as it surged inside her mind, she knew nothing could hold it back—certainly not a silly circle of metal.

She took a deep breath, readying her body to grab Grady as soon as his mesmer was lifted. Then she opened her eyes and shoved the warm energy out of her mind.

Grady groaned as the wave hit him, and Sophie tackled him, rolling him away as the fireball crashed down beside them.

She lost sight of Brant in the wall of flames, but she had bigger problems to worry about. Grady had gone limp in her arms, and his cloak was already burning.

She tore off the flaming fabric and tossed it away, then grabbed Grady's arms and dragged him as fast as she could move him. The Everblaze was spreading, but the winds were in her favor, and she dropped him behind a giant boulder, checking his pulse and making sure he was still breathing.

"You should've let him kill me."

Sophie spun around to find Brant standing behind her, his blood-streaked face as wild as the fire behind him.

One of his hands was gone. The singed stump was wrapped in orange cloth he'd torn from his robe. The other hand controlled another burning sphere of Everblaze.

His scarred, bloody lip curled with a smile as he told her, "Now I get to finish this."

SIXTY-FOUR

IS THAT REALLY WHAT YOU WANT?" SOPHIE shouted as Brant raised his arm to hurl the Everblaze. "Your own parents abandoned you—but Grady never did. Is this how you repay him?"

"It's how he repaid me," he said, showing her his blackened stump. "But maybe I should let him live. Then he can wake up every day knowing he lay there useless as I killed another of his daughters."

Sophie's hands curled into fists, feeling cold metal bite into her fingers.

Her ring.

She pressed the panic switch, not sure how Dex was going to help her—if he could even find her. But she was too drained to inflict again. Calling for help was the only play she had left.

Well, she did have one other—but it might be the stupidest thing she'd ever done.

"You don't want to kill me," she whispered, taking a slow step away from Grady to keep him safer.

"No, I really think I do."

"You don't. If you did, I'd already be dead. You had plenty of chances when I was your hostage."

"I had orders not to kill you."

"Orders?" Sophie asked, stunned to realize Brant *wasn't* the leader. "From Fintan? Or was it the ogres?"

"Nice try. And stop trying to distract me—it won't save your life."

"Then what are you waiting for?" Sophie asked, hoping she was right about why he was hesitating.

She held out her arms, fighting the urge to cower and close her eyes.

Brant didn't move.

"You can't, can you?" she asked, lowering her arms back to her sides. She took a shaky breath as she asked, "It's because I remind you of her, isn't it?"

"No!" Brant shouted, but his face said otherwise.

And for once Sophie was glad she reminded someone of Jolie.

"I know you didn't mean to kill her, Brant. It was a horrible, tragic accident. Don't make the same mistake again. Let me live this time—like you wish you could've done for her."

For a long second Brant looked tempted.

Then he whipped back his arm and screamed, "If she doesn't get to live—no one does!"

"That's what you think!" Dex shouted, charging out of the smoke and tackling Brant before he could launch his attack.

They rolled across the uneven ground as the fireball crashed behind them, igniting the rocky soil and forming another fire line.

"Dex, get out of there!" Sophie screamed as she grabbed Grady and tried to shake him awake.

Whatever she'd done with the Inflicting had really knocked him out, leaving her no choice but to drag him as far from the fire as she could—which was only another hundred feet. Then she reached the sheer edge of a cliff.

"I'm serious, Dex, we have to go—now!"

"Do you?" Brant asked, parting the wall of Everblaze so he could walk through—and dragging Dex by the throat with his good hand. "Lovely gift you've brought me. A chance to take care of *both* the kids that got away. Remember me, boy?" he asked as his hand turned red-hot, searing Dex's neck.

Dex eyes watered and his body shook from the pain, but he didn't scream.

"So here we are again, Sophie," Brant said, shoving Dex in

front of him. "What is this—the third time today? Are you as weary of the games as I am?"

"No—I just got here," Dex answered for her. "Let's keep playing."

Brant rewarded him by burning Dex's cheek, leaving a finger-shaped blister.

"Ready to lie down and die yet?" Brant asked him.

"Not even close." Dex shifted his feet to steady his balance. Then he spun around and punched Brant.

It was a solid punch—square in the jaw. Still, Sophie was surprised when Brant toppled backward, rolling head over feet into the neon yellow flames.

"Grab his arms!" Sophie shouted, hardly believing she was saving Brant as she ran to the fire line and tried to drag him free.

Dex stumbled over, and together they pulled Brant's thrashing body from the flames. He wasn't as scorched as Sophie thought he would be—but he didn't look good. His skin was covered in blisters and boils and he could barely breathe from all the coughing and wheezing.

So the last thing Sophie expected him to say was, "Will one of you hand me the leaping crystal from my inner pocket? My arms are a bit immobilized at the moment."

Dex snorted. "Like we're going to do that."

Brant laughed, the same breathy, haunting laugh that had filled Sophie's nightmares for weeks. "I think you will. I have information you need—and there's only one way I'll share it."

"There's nothing we need to know that badly," Sophie promised. She was dying to find out if he knew about the ogres or the missing dwarves—but that information could wait.

"Even if it's about your friends?" Brant asked. "The ones who think they're setting up an ambush for us today—if you're wondering who I mean."

"How do you know about that?" Sophie shouted, pressing him harder into the ground.

Brant coughed and wheezed in her face as he told her, "First, give me the crystal."

"He's just saying that so you'll let him go," Dex argued as Sophie bit her lip.

"Yes, but it's also the truth," Brant promised. "And if you hurry, you might still have time to save them. But only if you let. Me. Go."

"You can't trust him," Dex warned her, and Sophie knew he was right.

But the fact that Brant even knew about the ambush proved he knew *something*—and she couldn't waste any more time thinking about it. The ambush was happening *now*, and the Everblaze was closing in around them.

"Pin his wrists," she ordered Dex, making sure Brant couldn't grab her or toss her into the flames as she peeled back the scorched fabric over his chest, revealing a tattered pocket with a slim wand crowned with a green crystal.

"You could've used this the second we got here," she realized, studying the strange pathfinder, wondering where the crystal led. "But you stayed to face us."

"I wanted revenge," he growled, triggering another round of coughs and hacking.

"And it cost you your hand." She leaned closer, so her face was directly over his. "I *will* find you again—and next time you won't get away."

He coughed a wheezy laugh. "Where I'm going you'll never be able to follow. Now. My crystal?"

Dex tightened his hold on Brant's wrists as Sophie placed the pathfinder in his blistered palm. Before she let go, she ordered, "Tell me what you know about the ambush."

Brant coughed again, and a thin stream of blood trickled from the corner of his mouth. "We're on to your friends' little plan. They're going to cower in their secret cave while the dwarves attack, right?"

"How do you know that?" Sophie demanded.

"We have many ways. Just like we have many dwarves hiding in the mountain—far more than the Black Swan will be bringing. And they have orders to kill everyone waiting for them."

The words were still on his lips when he bucked his body, throwing Sophie and Dex backward. He groaned in agony as he raised the crystal to create a faint path. But his lips were smiling as he rolled into the light, vanishing in a vivid green flash.

"Come on," Dex said as he offered Sophie a helping hand. "We have to get Grady out of here."

"No—I have to go warn the others."

"Then I'm going with you. We'll drop Grady at home and then—"

"There's no time. You heard him—we might already be too late."

"Okay . . . then . . . tell me where to find them and I'll go while you—"

"I'll have to teleport there—if I can even remember what the cave looks like. I don't know if I ever saw a picture of it and I—wait."

She patted her pockets, never so happy to feel her iPod. And when she touched the screen it sprang instantly to life.

"Green Boots Cave," she whispered as she punched the letters into a search and dozens of pictures of the disturbing scene scrolled across her screen.

"This is all I need. I'll teleport there while you take Grady home—actually, no, go to Everglen and tell Alden . . . what?" she asked when she caught the look on Dex's face.

She realized what she was forgetting before he even said it.

"Right. I can't teleport."

Dex reached for her forehead, but Sophie backed away.

"You can't, Dex—they'll know."

"You have to go, right?"

She gave herself five seconds to accept that it was the only way. Then she nodded.

Dex nodded too, closing his eyes and whispering something she couldn't understand as he reached up and pulled the circlet off her head.

Instantly her headache vanished and the world clicked into focus. Her mind raced through a dozen different thoughts and sensations, like her brain was stretching its weary muscles after being closed in.

"You okay?" Dex asked as she rubbed her temples.

"It's like I can *think* again."

"I'm so sorry."

She smiled sadly. "I have to go."

"Wait!" he said, pulling a wide black cuff off his wrist. "I know you probably don't want any more of my gadgets, but did you see how far Brant flew when I punched him?" He flipped the cuff over to show her three silver rimmed slits. "These release an extra burst of air to thrust your arm forward a lot faster. I think you should wear it. Just in case."

She didn't know what to say as he gently clasped it around her right wrist, just above her nexus. So she threw her arms around him, holding on with all the strength she had. "Thank you, Dex. Take Grady to Everglen, and make sure Edaline's safe too. I'll be back as soon as I can."

She gave herself one quick breath before she let him go.

Then she ran to the end of the cliff, turning back to wave goodbye.

She caught a quick glimpse of Dex tossing her circlet into the glowing flames of the Everblaze.

Then she closed her eyes and jumped off the edge.

SIXTY-FIVE

A SHEARING WIND NEARLY KNOCKED Sophie over as she landed in a snowdrift on the narrow ledge of a vertical incline. She had about a second to celebrate that her teleporting had worked and she'd made it to Everest. Then reality kicked in.

She hadn't considered the toll it would take on her body to drop into such an extreme environment with no oxygen, or coat, or boots, or *anything* she needed to survive. Within seconds, her blood started to freeze in her veins, making her brain throb and her whole body shake as she lost feeling in her fingers and toes. She could vaguely see the rigid shape of a corpse in green boots amid the blinding white surrounding her, but her head was spinning and her chest was heaving and she was fairly certain she was dying—if she wasn't dead already.

She stumbled forward, and the motion made her want to vomit. Her limbs felt like they were dragging anchors, and all her instincts begged her to curl up in a ball and never move again. Only sheer desperation propelled her into the cave, which mercifully gave her a slight break from the relentless wind.

But it was empty.

It was just her and Green Boots—a fact she was trying very hard to *not* think about.

She trudged to the rock face, searching for any sign of the door that was supposed to be there. But all she found was solid ice.

Panic took over and she pounded on the walls, screaming for Fitz or Keefe or Biana or Dex or Alden or Grady—she couldn't remember who was supposed to be there anymore. She could barely remember her name. And she knew she was there for something important, but she couldn't remember what it was.

At least she wasn't shivering anymore.

In fact, she felt . . . hot.

Scorching.

Her tunic was suddenly smothering her, and she thrashed and flailed, trying to make her numb fingers rip off the suffocating fabric. Before she managed it, strong arms dragged her into a dim cavern, which sealed closed behind her.

She fought and squirmed as something metal was shoved over her nose, but the muscled arms held her in place as a gruff voice said, "Breathe, Sophie."

Sophie.

Her name was Sophie.

Her shoulders relaxed and she inhaled a deep breath of warm, sweet air.

Then another.

And another.

Her head felt like it was filled with gray, sloshy soup, but she could feel tingles in her toes and fingers as her frozen body started to thaw.

"Better?" the voice asked, pulling the cold metal away from her nose.

When she opened her eyes, she found Mr. Forkle leaning over her in a small, low-ceilinged cave. A bubble of warmth, and—strangely—normal air, deep in the mountain.

"Atmosphere stabilizer," Mr. Forkle said, holding up a triangular gadget, like he knew what she'd been thinking. "Only works in small spaces. Think you're capable of swallowing something?"

Sophie nodded, even though her tongue had frozen to the roof of her mouth.

He tipped her head back and poured a small vial of yellow-orange liquid through her lips. The salty serum thawed her tongue enough to let her swallow, and the medicine turned warm as it rushed through her veins, defrosting her from the inside out.

"Better?" Mr. Forkle asked.

"Yes, thank you."

"Good. Now. *What were you thinking?*" he shouted. "Five more minutes and I might not have been able to save you!"

"Uh, this is Foster we're talking about. Are we really surprised?" Keefe smirked when she sat up enough to find him in the tiny cave. "What—had it been too long since your last brush with death?"

"Judging by the state of her clothes, I'd say her last brush with death was only moments ago," Mr. Forkle said quietly.

"Her circlet's gone too," Fitz said behind her.

Sophie reached up to feel her forehead, stunned to realize he was right. She traced her fingers where the metal had rubbed her skin raw, and felt her memories rush back.

"They know we're here!" she shouted, jumping to her feet—and then immediately collapsing from a head rush.

"Yeah, that's the point, remember?" Keefe told her, pointing to the Sencen Crest pinned to his long white cloak. "Everyone's in position."

"No—I mean they know it's a trap. They have a whole army of dwarves waiting for us."

"Are you sure?" Mr. Forkle asked as Sandor rushed to a hairline crack in the wall and pressed his nose against it.

"I detect nothing," he announced after several deep breaths.

"But your senses can be tricked, right?" Sophie reminded him. "Brant told me they're here."

Sandor froze. "Brant? As in . . . ?"

Sophie nodded. "He's part of the Neverseen. He's the Pyrokinetic who burned me—and killed Jolie. Grady went to confront him and it turned into this huge fight and Brant called down Everblaze and—"

"Everblaze?" Mr. Forkle interrupted, rubbing his temples when Sophie nodded.

Sandor knelt beside Sophie to check her more closely. "Was anyone hurt?"

"Grady passed out after I inflicted on him, but Dex is taking him to Elwin. I didn't mean to do it, but he'd already made Brant burn his hand off—"

"Whooooooooaaaaaaa," Keefe whispered. "Grady's hard-core."

Fitz elbowed him.

But Sophie nodded. "He really lost it. He was going to make Brant jump off a cliff, until I stopped him—but then the Everblaze went everywhere, and Brant almost caught me, so I called for Dex, and we almost had him trapped—but then Brant said he'd tell me what he knew about the ambush if I let him go, and I had to make sure you guys were okay—"

"You let Brant go?" Sandor asked, clearly not thrilled with her decision.

She wasn't a fan of it either. But . . .

"He knew what the Neverseen were planning, and he wouldn't tell me unless I gave him his green pathfinder."

"Green?" Mr. Forkle sighed when Sophie nodded. "Green crystals go to the ogre cities."

Sandor swore under his breath, and Sophie was tempted to do the same. Now she knew why Brant said she wouldn't be able to follow him. And clearly the Neverseen really were working with the ogres.

"Uh . . . is anyone else as confused as I am?" Biana asked, reappearing in the shadows.

"Yes," Mr. Forkle admitted. "But it will be easier if I *see* it," he explained as he reached for Sophie's temples.

Sophie forced herself to relax as Mr. Forkle pressed two fingers on each side of her head and closed his eyes. Two hundred and twenty-nine seconds passed before he released her, his swollen face paler than she'd ever seen.

"I want you to know that you made the right decision letting Brant go," he said quietly. "You may have saved us all—though we have a hard fight ahead of us."

He stood and stomped his heavy leg against the ground in a strange pattern of beats and pauses.

One by one, dwarves popped out of the hard soil, shaking bits of frozen earth out of their shaggy fur and gathering around him.

"We are far more outnumbered than we realized," he told them when all ten had crowded into the cramped space.

"Also . . . it appears you'll be forced to fight your own kind—if anyone is uncomfortable with that, you're free to leave now with no judgment on our part."

None moved.

"Thank you, my friends. Your support will not be forgotten."

He called Sandor to his side and the dwarves huddled around him, talking strategy. Sophie tried to listen from the fringes—and tried to understand the strange diagram Sandor scratched in the ground with his blade—but most of it made zero sense.

"Where should I be?" she asked, when Mr. Forkle opened it up to questions.

"Home," Sandor answered immediately.

"He's right," Mr. Forkle told her. "Though, I fear they might have something planned for you at Havenfield, knowing you're separated from your bodyguard. Perhaps Fitz and Biana could take you and Keefe to Everglen—"

"I'm not going anywhere," Sophie interrupted.

"Me either," Keefe agreed.

"Neither are we," Fitz and Biana added.

Mr. Forkle shook his head. "Sophie, you aren't even properly dressed. You'd be crippled by frostbite and altitude sickness in a matter of minutes."

"Maybe," Sophie reluctantly agreed. "But I can inflict from here. I'd only need the door left open enough to see where everyone is."

"And I can cover her," Fitz offered. "And share part of my cloak."

"Me too," Biana added.

"I'm still going after my dad," Keefe said quietly.

"I know," Sophie told him, knowing why he needed to, but wondering how he was really going to be able to face down his dad.

"You kids are forgetting that none of you were meant to fight," Mr. Forkle interrupted them.

"But I have my abilities back now," Sophie argued.

"And I took this from my dad's office," Fitz said, holding up a silver melder.

"And I'm the secret weapon," Biana added, turning invisible.

"I . . . don't have anything fancy," Keefe mumbled, patting his arm, which seemed to be missing his throwing stars. "But there's no way you're taking on my dad without me."

"If I have to tie you in this cave, I will," Sandor warned them.

"So the dwarves can find us totally defenseless if they get past you?" Sophie asked.

Sandor grabbed three throwing stars from a pocket near his ankle and whipped them at her, each one thwacking the wall in a perfectly straight line, just above Sophie's head. "They *won't* get past me."

"The simple truth," Mr. Forkle added, before anyone could argue, "is that you are far more valuable than any of us—and I don't just mean Sophie. She's *incredibly* important. But she has always needed the strength and support of her friends. I was willing to keep you here when I thought this was a simple ambush. Now that I know it's not, you *will* head to safety. And if you try to resist, you will discover that I have many ways to ensure my demands are obeyed."

"But—"

"That is the end of the matter!"

He glared at them, daring them to argue.

"Good," Mr. Forkle said when they didn't. "But before you go, there's something I must teach Fitz, in case another opportunity does not present itself."

He waved Fitz over to where Sophie was standing.

"Place your hands on Sophie's temples. I'm going to show you how to slip past her blocking."

"WHAT?!" Fitz, Sophie, Keefe, and Biana all asked at the same time—though Keefe was the loudest.

"Are you okay with that?" Fitz asked.

Sophie didn't hesitate before she nodded. It would be weird, but . . . "I trust you."

Keefe grumbled something about Telepaths as Fitz reached for Sophie's temples and Mr. Forkle pressed his hands against Fitz's.

"Do you feel the trail of warmth I'm leaving?" Mr. Forkle asked him.

"Yeah—wow, that's crazy. How are you doing that?" Fitz asked.

"Focus, Fitz. I need you to memorize the path so that you can find it on your own."

"Right," Fitz mumbled, his brow furrowing with concentration.

Sophie tried to feel what they were feeling, but she couldn't detect even a trace of their presence.

"There," Mr. Forkle announced, making Sophie jump. "Did you see that?"

"I think so. But I don't understand what you did."

"It's a point of trust. Transmit the right thing and her guard will lower."

"What do I transmit?"

"It varies person to person. What makes her trust me will not work for you."

"Just so you guys know, this is *super* weird to watch," Keefe told them, earning himself a shout of "Silence!" from Mr. Forkle.

But Sophie had to agree. She'd never expected to have an audience while the elf who created her taught someone how to slip past her mental defenses. Especially when Fitz leaned closer and whispered, "What do I say?"

"How do I know? I don't even know what *he* says!" she told him.

"She's right. It's her subconscious you're reaching," Mr. Forkle explained. "Her conscious mind cannot help."

Fitz sighed, his eyes wandering over Sophie's face like he expected the answer to be scrawled across her lips. Maybe it was, because a few seconds later he pumped his fist and shouted, "I'm in! And whoa—it's . . . overwhelming."

"Yes," Mr. Forkle agreed. "Photographic memories can be. We're running out of time, so I'm afraid you can't explore. But are you following the warmth?"

Fitz nodded. Then his eyes widened.

"Yes," Mr. Forkle told him, before Fitz could speak. "Remember this place. You may need it. Possibly soon."

"What?" Sophie asked.

"Don't tell her," Mr. Forkle ordered Fitz. "She is not yet ready to know."

"Are you kidding me?" Sophie shouted. "It's *my* brain."

"Yes, and I'm doing everything I can to protect it. Come on, Fitz, that's enough for today."

He pulled Fitz back and Fitz shook his head, rubbing his temples.

"You okay?" Keefe asked, and Sophie wasn't sure if he was asking her or Fitz.

Their answers were both the same. "I think so."

Though Fitz sounded far less sure.

"And now it's time to go," Mr. Forkle said, fishing out a glowing purple vial and handing it to Biana. "You still have the charm?"

Rumbling above them drowned out her answer, and everyone ducked and covered their heads as rock and ice rained down.

"Is it an avalanche?" Sophie shouted, realizing that if it *was*, screaming probably wasn't the best idea.

But it wasn't an avalanche—or not a natural one, at least.

It was two gorilla-size arms punching through the rocky ceiling.

They grabbed Sophie by the shoulders and pulled her back through the roof before she had a chance to scream.

SIXTY-SIX

SOPHIE'S BODY STARTED TO SHAKE—
but not from the arctic air.

She barely felt the wind or the snow or the sharp jostling of what she assumed was an ogre carrying her. The world grew dim as the blackness clouded her mind, and red rimmed the edges of her vision as the fear and fury boiled into a frenzy.

She let the rage stew as long as she could bear it. Then she shoved the bitterness out of her head, spreading the pain and wrath as far as it could travel.

Her captor grunted and dropped her. But when she sank into the ice, the cold bored into her bones, breaking her concentration and leaving her numb and useless. She lay there shivering, knowing she should run, but her head was spinning spinning spinning. The air was so thin, it felt like she wasn't even breathing. And she was so tired. Maybe if she just closed her eyes . . .

Thick hands hoisted her up and she tried to thrash, but her muscles were too weak. She barely managed a raspy scream before cold metal was shoved over her nose and . . .

She could breathe.

She gulped the sweet, soft air as a heavy white cloak wrapped around her shoulders, shielding her from the icy wind.

"I've got you," a high, squeaky voice promised, and it took her a second to realize it was Sandor. He hefted her over his shoulder and she tightened her grip as Sandor started to slide down the steep embankment.

They'd only gone a few feet when something yanked Sandor backward.

Sophie slipped from his arms, tumbling through the snow, trailed by howls and snarls and growls and whimpers. She couldn't tell which massive body was Sandor's in the glimpses she caught through the blasting snow. But she could tell he was battling an ogre. And when an agonizing screech splattered red among the pristine white, she scrambled toward the collapsed body, promising she would never give Sandor a hard time again if it would just not be him.

A blur of gray muscle yanked her away and it took her a second to recognize the familiar flat-nosed face.

"You're not dead!" she cried, feeling her tears freeze before they could fall.

"Neither is he." Sandor grunted as he shifted her weight onto his other shoulder.

That's when she felt the warm wetness seeping from his chest. "You're bleeding!"

"These conditions have slowed my reflexes. Especially without the Purifier."

Sophie reached for the oxygen mask he'd given her, but he grabbed her hand, smearing her palm with blood.

"Sorry," he murmured, wiping her hand on a clean part of his chest. "You need that far more than me. I can breathe relatively naturally up here. It just makes everything foggy. That's what cost me my sword."

"Where's everyone else?" Sophie asked, trying to see through the whiteout around them.

"I do not know. Their dwarves came up through the ground as I chased after you. But I'm hoping your friends are still waiting near the outcropping. Is your head clear enough to teleport?"

"I think so," she said, sucking in another breath. "But I'm not leaving."

"Yes, you are! And don't even think about—"

A wall of muscle slammed them from behind, sending Sandor crashing on top of her. The thick snow saved Sophie from the bulk of his crushing weight, but the fall still knocked the wind out of her, leaving her coughing and wheezing as Sandor pushed himself to his feet. He'd barely gone two steps before the massive ogre tackled him again, tearing at Sandor's neck and chest with his pointed teeth as they tumbled over the ground.

"You're going over, flat nose," the ogre shouted as he shoved Sandor toward the edge.

"If I do, you're coming with me." Sandor widened his stance, holding his bleeding arms at the ready.

"Deal!"

The ogre launched himself at Sandor with all of his strength, the collision so loud it knocked Sandor back another step.

They wobbled once, twice, then toppled off the cliff.

"NO!!!" Sophie screamed, sprinting to where they'd fallen.

The drop had to be at least a thousand feet.

And all she could see at the bottom was red.

SIXTY-SEVEN

ANDOR!" SOPHIE SCREAMED, HER chest heaving with sobs as she searched for a way to climb down the embankment.

She glanced over the edge, wondering if she could see enough details to teleport down to him, when a deep voice spoke behind her.

"Surrender, Sophie, and no one else has to die."

She spun around, feeling her whole body shake with rage as three black-cloaked figures stepped through the blinding white swells. Glints of silver flashed in their hands, and Sophie realized they each carried a melder.

She pooled her fear and fury, spinning it into an angry swarm in her mind. But before she could inflict any of it, a sharp blast of pain flared in her chest, dropping her like a stone.

"She was trying to inflict," a familiar voice shouted as the other two figures accused him of violating their orders. "Besides, all he said was to bring her in alive. He didn't say anything about untouched."

Sophie tried to move—tried to scream—but the melder had paralyzed her from head to toe, forcing her to lie still and watch as the figures drew closer.

The one who'd shot her leaned over the edge and laughed. "Looks like we don't have to worry about her bodyguard."

Sophie raged inside her mind as the others shared in his laughter. She tried to channel the energy into a force she could blast them with. But the melder must've done something to her heart. No matter how hard she concentrated, she couldn't find the force she needed to launch any emotions.

"Let's go," one of the other figures said as he crouched in front of Sophie and waved a hand in front of her face. "Think she's stunned enough?"

"Might as well be safe," the one who'd shot her told him, blasting Sophie again.

Lightning seared through Sophie's veins and the iron taste of blood coated her tongue. She stared at the dark spaces where the figures faces hid behind their cloaks, vowing to make them pay the next time she got the chance.

But for the moment, all she could do was endure the agony

and try not to wonder how much worse the pain had been for Dex when they'd blasted him three times on the streets of Paris.

"That should do it," the third figure—who'd yet to speak—decided. "Grab her and let's get out of here."

"What about the boy?" the one in front of Sophie asked.

"Which boy? The Vacker one? He'd only be an asset to the girl."

"No—the boy who led us here. He can't be allowed to go home."

"Why?" Keefe shouted, stepping through the wall of wind and snow, looking like a ghost in his white hooded cloak and boots. Fitz flanked him, pointing his melder at the figure closest to Sophie, as Keefe asked, "Afraid I'll tell Mom?"

The figure stood, his laugh so cold Sophie shivered inside. "Trust me," he told Keefe. "Your mother is not my concern."

His voice was clearer now, and Sophie recognized it as Lord Cassius. Keefe must've noticed it too, because he looked like he'd been punched in the stomach.

"Is this really what you do?" Keefe asked, choking slightly when he pointed to Sophie's paralyzed form. "Is *that* the Sencen legacy?"

"No, it's a necessary sacrifice for a larger plan."

"I hate you!" Keefe screamed, grabbing a chunk of ice and flinging it at his father's head.

Lord Cassius stepped to the side and the ice breezed past him, plummeting over the edge and falling so far, Sophie couldn't hear it crash.

Sandor had fallen the same way. . . .

She shook the heartbreaking thought away, forcing herself to focus.

Lord Cassius was stomping the snow off his boots as he told Keefe, "You hate, only because you do not understand. I am building you a better world. Someday you'll thank me."

"I will *never* thank you," Keefe told him, backing a step away. "I will never speak to you again."

"Well, then it's going to be a very quiet day. Gethen—grab the girl," Lord Cassius ordered, pointing to the figure who'd shot Sophie. "We'll take all three of them."

"Don't come any nearer," Fitz warned him, pointing his melder at Gethen's head.

Gethen laughed and aimed his melder at Sophie. "Shoot me and I'll shoot her again—and she's already taken several blasts. How many more do you think that freaky little mind of hers can handle?"

"Sophie can handle anything!" Keefe shouted, hurling another chunk of ice and smashing Gethen's arm so hard it knocked the melder out of his hand.

Gethen scrambled to retrieve it but Fitz blasted him in the chest, dropping him to the snow like a lump of coal before Fitz dove for the melder and tossed it to Keefe.

Fitz spun to check on Sophie as she watched Keefe stalk closer to his father.

"I knew all that bramble practice would come in handy,"

Keefe told him. "And you said it was a foolish game."

Lord Cassius laughed. "Put it down, son."

"I'm not your son!"

"Yes you are—and you always will be. And regardless of what you may think, I don't want to hurt you."

"Funny—I will have *no* problem blasting the snot out of you."

"Then let's take stock of your situation, shall we? We have your dwarves outnumbered three to one. Your bodyguard is dead—"

"Sandor?" Fitz and Keefe both asked.

"Yes. Poor oaf took a dive off that cliff—and last I checked goblins can't force-shift like ogres. So . . ." He raised his hand, miming a diving motion that ended in a splatter.

Sophie was glad she couldn't move, because she would have tossed him over the edge.

"And last we saw, your puffy leader was pinned down by at least a dozen of our dwarves," Lord Cassius added. "I'm sure they'll be delivering him to us any minute now. So it's over. Set down your weapons and we'll bring you in with no further injuries."

"No, I don't think we will," Keefe said, taking a slow step toward Sophie. "Because I think *you* forgot to take stock of *your* situation."

"Three scrawny kids—one of whom is currently paralyzed,"

Lord Cassius started—but Keefe shook his head.

"Not three. *Four*."

"NOW!" Fitz shouted as Biana appeared and tackled Keefe's father.

Fitz dropped the other figure with a melder blast and Keefe took over the fight with his dad. Biana ran to Sophie's side and pulled her away from the ledge, twisting her into a sitting position so she could place her fingers at the base of Sophie's skull. "This is going to hurt, but it'll pull you out of the daze. My dad taught me, just in case."

Sophie couldn't nod, but she held her breath, bracing for the worst as Biana dug her fingers into the tender skin, right where Sophie's neck met her skull.

Pain surged immediately—like Biana had awoken some sort of beast and let it tear around inside her—and when she loosened her grip, Sophie fell to her side, coughing and thrashing and wondering if she was going to be sick.

Biana helped her to her feet, wrapping Sophie's shaky arm across her shoulders and pulling her back toward Fitz.

"No . . . we . . . Sandor," Sophie said, between gasping breaths. "He might be . . . need to check."

"We will," Biana promised as they came up alongside Fitz. "As soon as Keefe's ready. How's he doing?" she asked Fitz.

Fitz could only shake his head and point.

A sheet of white blocked most of the view, but she could

vaguely discern two cloaked figures scaling another incline, one in black, the other nearly invisible in white.

Sophie, Fitz, and Biana climbed after them.

Chunks of snow slipped under Sophie's feet and she wished she had the heavy boots Fitz and Biana were wearing. Their progress was painfully slow until Fitz found icy ropes they could hold on to. He stayed behind her to catch her if she slipped, and they pulled themselves up, stopping at a new ledge that stretched to a relatively flat area.

The whiteout barely let them see five feet in any direction, but they shoved blindly forward until Biana grabbed their arms and pointed to a smear of black among the white.

A few more steps and they could see Keefe and his father, standing in the winds. They weren't fighting. They were just . . . staring. And when Sophie moved closer, she understood why.

The wind—or maybe Keefe—must've thrown back his father's hood.

But it wasn't his father facing him.

It was Lady Gisela.

Keefe's *mom.*

586

SIXTY-EIGHT

I DON'T UNDERSTAND," SOPHIE SAID, VOICING
the thought she was pretty sure they all were having.
"She sounded like Lord Cassius."

And then she remembered: *Keefe's mom can mimic.*

"You?" Keefe pointed to the Sencen crest on his cape. "But
Dad was the one who gave this to me."

"And *I'm* the one who gave it to him. Honestly, Keefe"—
she stomped her feet, shaking the snow off her heavy boots,
even though they immediately sank back into the snowdrift—
"Don't you know your father at all? He never set so much as
a hair out of place, especially if it risked all those honors he's
gotten from the Council."

"But, Dad's—"

"A jerk?" Lady Gisela finished for him. "Yes, he is. And your hating him has been hugely helpful to me. Every time I slipped and let any emotions that might've given me away show through, I could just blame it on your latest mess. In fact, when I return home tonight, all he'll feel is a mother distraught over her son's tragic disappearance."

"You monster!" Biana shouted, accidentally revealing that she'd moved dangerously close to Lady Gisela.

Lady Gisela grabbed Biana's cloak and pressed her melder against Biana's head. "I wouldn't move, if I were you. A blast this close will likely cause permanent damage."

"Go ahead," Biana told her, her voice surprisingly steady.

"You can drop the mock bravery, my dear. There are safer ways to impress my son. Just ask that one."

"SHUT UP!" Keefe screamed as Lady Gisela tilted her head toward Sophie.

"Yes, you're right," his mom agreed. "I'm cold. And the altitude remedy the ogres gave me is triggering a headache." She pointed her melder at Keefe again. "This is your last chance to spare your friends unnecessary pain. Throw down your weapons and come with me."

"Uh—in case you didn't notice, there's four of us and only one of you," Keefe reminded her.

"That's my Keefe. Always missing the obvious."

She covered her face with her hood and stomped her foot

again. And when the ground rumbled, Sophie realized what she was doing.

"She's calling her dwarves!" she shouted, but she was too late.

A dozen furry bodies launched out of the snow and surrounded them.

"Any ideas?" Fitz asked, backing up as the dwarves circled closer.

"I'm thinking." Sophie wasn't sure if she could inflict without taking her friends down in the frenzy—and with the ice clawing up her poorly-dressed legs and feet, she didn't think she could concentrate hard enough to affect such a large group anyway.

"I'll give you until the count of three to throw down your weapons and lie in the snow," Lady Gisela called.

"Never," Keefe shouted. "Guys, leap out of here!"

"Not without you!" Sophie shouted back.

"One," Lady Gisela counted. "And you'll never create a strong enough beam of light in this storm."

Sophie glanced at the flurries around them, hating that Keefe's mom was right. Especially when she counted, "Two."

"Three!" Mr. Forkle shouted, belly flopping onto four of the dwarves closest to Fitz and Sophie, crushing them with his massive girth.

A handful of the Black Swan's dwarves popped out of the ground and dove into the fray, and Lady Gisela dropped Biana and turned to run away. But Keefe tackled her, sending them toppling through the wall of wind and vanishing into the white nothing.

Sophie, Fitz, and Biana chased after them—or tried to, anyway. The snow was waist deep, and they were climbing uphill again, so it felt like they were dragging heavy chains.

"He's over there!" Biana shouted, pointing to a flash of black, before it was swallowed again by the blinding white.

They picked up their pace, pushing their bodies so hard they could barely breathe. But by the time they reached them, it was still too late.

Keefe lay facedown in the snow, pinned under his mom's foot, with her melder pointed at his head.

Sophie had barely screamed, "LET HIM GO!" when Biana pounced, slamming into Lady Gisela and sending them tumbling down the incline.

Keefe scrambled to his feet and chased after them, joining Sophie and Fitz on the way.

"Did you know Biana could fight like that?" Sophie asked as Keefe's mom tried to stop their tumbling, and Biana shoved her shoulders and sent them both toppling again.

"Actually, yeah," Keefe admitted. "She's thrown me down a hill during base quest several times."

"Me too." Fitz agreed.

Sophie smiled, trying to picture them—but it quickly faded when she realized how close Biana was getting to the edge.

"BIANA, STOP!" Sophie, Fitz, and Keefe all shouted, but

Biana either couldn't slow or didn't hear them.

They were seconds away from dropping off the edge when Lady Gisela grabbed Biana's arms and swung them both into a drift of snow so deep, it seemed to swallow them.

"It's over, Mom," Keefe called as she struggled to her feet. He pointed his melder at her heart as she raised her foot to stomp for her dwarves. "I will drop you with this if I have to."

She shook the snow out of her hair and stomped her boot anyway.

No dwarves jumped out and attacked them.

"Well, I guess they're busy," Lady Gisela said, glancing at the cliff behind her.

"There's nowhere to go, Mom. Just give up and come with me." He raised the melder at her head. "I don't want to use this—but I will."

"I know." She smiled at him then, but it was a sad smile.

A broken smile.

"I'm not going back with you," she told him.

"You don't have a choice."

"Oh, there's always a choice."

Her smile faded as she turned to look at the ledge again, and Sophie realized what she was thinking a second too late.

She screamed almost as loud as Keefe when Lady Gisela launched herself backward. And they all watched in horror as she plummeted off the edge of the cliff.

SIXTY-NINE

KEEFE SANK TO HIS KNEES AND FITZ
and Biana gathered around him.

Sophie leaned over the edge, trying to squint through the swirling snow.

"I can't see anything," she said quietly, knowing Keefe would need to know for sure.

I'll have to teleport down there and look, she transmitted to Fitz.

"Not alone, you won't," Fitz told her. "I'm going with you."

"Me too," Keefe said, struggling to his feet. Clearly her secret communication hadn't fooled him.

"I'm *going*," he insisted.

His voice was shakier than his legs, but his eyes were determined.

"Okay," she relented, offering him her hand.

He twined their fingers together as Fitz took her other hand and Biana held on to Fitz. Then she pictured what she'd seen of the spot where Sandor had fallen, waiting until the image felt clear in her mind before she ordered everyone to hold on tight and pulled them off the cliff.

They landed in a pile of slushy snow.

Red slushy snow.

Sophie scrambled back, nearly tripping over the body as she tried to get away.

But it wasn't Keefe's mom.

"Sandor!"

Sophie dropped to her knees beside him, begging him to open his eyes.

He didn't.

But his injuries didn't look nearly as bad as she would've expected. There was a gash on his forehead and another on his chin. But most of the blood seemed to have come from the deep scratches on his chest and neck. His legs and arms looked like they were bent the wrong way, but his spine seemed straight. And when she pressed her ear against his chest, she could feel the rise and fall of shallow breaths.

"He's alive! Though only barely. We have to get him to Elwin. Fitz, if you take his feet, I can get his arms, and if we all hold on to him as we fall I should be able to get us all . . ."

Her voice trailed off when she met Keefe's eyes.

"I don't see my mom," he whispered. "Do you?"

Sophie turned to the wider part of the ledge, which was solid white, except for a few dark rocks.

No red anywhere.

"We all watched her jump, right?" Keefe asked.

He craned his neck, probably checking to see if there was another ledge above them that could've caught her. Sophie did the same, and it was hard to tell with the limited visibility.

"But Sandor's here," Fitz said quietly. "So she'd have to be, wouldn't she?"

"Where's the ogre, though?" Sophie asked.

She went back to Sandor, using the last of her strength to roll him to his side.

All she found underneath him was more red snow.

"An ogre knocked Sandor off the ledge and they went over together," she explained. "So where's the ogre?"

"My guess is he force-shifted," Mr. Forkle said, limping toward them from a snowdrift Sophie was sure had been empty a second earlier.

"How did you . . . ?" she started to ask, but Mr. Forkle waved the question away.

"Your mother *jumped* off the edge, right?" he asked Keefe. "You didn't push her?"

Keefe nodded blankly.

"Then I'm sure she tried to force-shift. It's a method of ogre transportation I'd thought was simply a rumor—something about a special device they use that helps them shift the force of gravity to launch themselves to safety."

Keefe sounded both hopeful and horrified as he asked, "So . . . she's alive?"

"It would appear so. Though I'm only assuming she knew about phase-shifting."

"She did," Sophie told him.

Mr. Forkle nodded. "I think it's best if you all go. Get somewhere safe. I'll clean up here."

"How many did we lose?" Sophie forced herself to ask.

"Three dwarves, so far. But there might be a fourth." He wiped his face, and Sophie wondered if he was drying tears or clearing the frost off his cheeks.

"But . . . that's better than I'd feared, honestly," he said after a second. "And it wasn't all for naught this time."

He stomped his foot and two limping dwarves slowly emerged from the snow, dragging a black-cloaked figure.

"You caught one?" Sophie asked.

"Actually, I believe you three caught this one. We found him paralyzed from a melder blast up above. I only woke him up a few minutes ago, and, well, he's less than pleased to be our guest. But we have lots of getting to know each other to do, don't we?"

The figure responded only with a curse, and Sophie watched him thrash against his silver bonds.

"Can I see his face?" she asked.

"Quickly," Mr. Forkle agreed.

She held her breath as she stepped closer, giving herself three seconds to steady her nerves before she swept the hood back.

Her mouth fell open.

"This was the jogger who came to my house and tried to grab me!"

"Yes, I remember," Mr. Forkle murmured. "It took all of my mental energy to hold him back from snatching you off the street that day. And if I hadn't known Fitz would be coming for you momentarily, I would've had to take you into hiding."

"Whoa," Fitz whispered. "I forgot about that."

"I didn't." Sophie stalked closer, remembering the way he'd slung Dex over his shoulder on the bridge in Paris, ready to dispose of him like trash. "What are you going to do to him?"

"Whatever we must to find out what he knows."

"It won't work," the rebel snarled. "I've trained for this."

"So have we."

"Your name's Gethen, isn't it?" Sophie asked, smiling when he flinched. "I heard Lady Gisela call him that. But wait—Fitz paralyzed two people, not just one. Where's the other one?"

"We followed his tracks to the edge of the cliff, so I'm assuming he woke up and force-shifted like Lady Gisela did."

"And you're sure she's alive?" Keefe interrupted.

"Worried about your mommy?" Gethen asked, laughing

when Keefe spun toward him. "Don't worry, we take good care of her. Way better than you or your dad ever has."

Fitz grabbed Keefe before he could lunge for Gethen's throat. "He's not worth it."

"No—you're not worth it." Gethen snarled. "I'll be free by the end of the night. We have an army of ogres on our side. Do you really think—"

The sound of crunching bone cut him off and his head snapped back so hard it left him bleeding and unconscious.

"Sorry," Sophie mumbled, staring at her fist in wonder. She stretched her sore fingers, testing to make sure none were broken.

"Everyone else saw that, right?" Keefe asked, turning to Sophie. "I'm kinda freaking out here, so . . . I didn't imagine that, did I? Foster just beat the snot out of him with one punch?"

Fitz and Biana nodded.

Sophie pointed to the cuff on her wrist. "I had a little help from Dex."

"In more ways than one, I suspect," Mr. Forkle said, pointing to where her circlet used to be.

"About that—"

"Later," Mr. Forkle told her. "Right now you need to get Sandor to Everglen, and I need to get Gethen somewhere he'll feel . . . a bit more like talking."

"Wait!" Sophie called as the dwarves started to tunnel away. "When will I see you again?"

Mr. Forkle moved closer, taking her by the shoulders and staring deeply into her eyes. "That will depend on you."

"Me?" she repeated.

"Yes. You have a choice to make. But first, you must take care of your friends."

SEVENTY

ELWIN WAS WAITING FOR THEM AT Everglen when they arrived. Dex had called him to help with Grady—who'd thankfully only needed a few elixirs to clear his head before he was back to normal.

Well . . . normal health-wise, at least.

Mentally would be a much longer recovery, but Sophie supposed that was to be expected after the betrayal he'd endured.

She hadn't had a chance to talk to him—or Edaline—since she'd arrived.

There'd been too much chaos getting Sandor's massive body inside and helping Elwin adjust his treatments for goblin physiology. Elwin expected Sandor to make a full recovery—

but he'd be off his feet for a month. He'd broken most of his bones in the fall, and would need to stay sedated for the rest of the week. But all things considered, he was incredibly lucky.

Sophie had wanted to stay by his side until he woke up, but Elwin insisted on treating her for frostbite and altitude sickness and smoke inhalation and a dozen other maladies her adventures had given her. And he didn't ask about her missing circlet as he rubbed a healing balm on the abrasions on her forehead, but he gave her a huge hug when he was finished.

Sophie hugged him back, feeling her eyes burn with tears. She was starting to realize what choice Mr. Forkle had meant before she'd left Mount Everest. And she had no idea if she was brave enough to make it.

Alden had insisted everyone stay within Everglen's protective gates—even Dex, who looked extra nervous in the grand, glittering halls, regardless of how many ways Della tried to make him comfortable.

Sophie was given the same bedroom she'd slept in twice before, once on her first night in the elvin world, and the other after she'd first been rescued from the kidnappers. But she knew this night would be her scariest night yet.

She sat awake long after Grady and Edaline brought her Ella to help her sleep, trying not to remember the heartbreak she'd seen etched into their faces. It wasn't her fault they looked so lost and devastated—but it would be soon, if she did what the Black Swan had asked.

But did she really have another option?

"Can't sleep either?" Keefe asked, peeking through the crack in her doorway. He fidgeted with the sleeves of the blue pajamas he'd borrowed from Fitz as he sat on the edge of her bed. "Please don't ask how I'm doing. That's all anyone's said to me since I got here, and they keep tilting their heads and puckering their brows and it makes me want to punch them—and I really don't want to punch you. Especially since I'm pretty sure you could knock me across the room."

Sophie smiled at the cuff still on her wrist. She knew she should give it back to Dex, but she had a feeling she was going to need it.

A lot.

"So when do you leave?" Keefe asked, like he knew what she'd been thinking.

"Ugh—I swear, for an Empath, you act more like a Telepath."

"That's because I'd be an awesome Telepath. And I can guarantee, if I snuck into your head and saw secret things, I would tell you what they are. Most of them, at least. Okay, maybe just the part about you being completely lost without me and needing me to come with you when you leave."

Sophie reached for an itchy eyelash, but stopped herself on the way. If she was going to do this, she needed to learn to be brave.

"I don't even know if I'm going," she mumbled.

"Yes, you do. I mean, you're also scared and stressed and

stuff. But I can feel your resolve. Shoot—I could feel it down the hall. Which is why I had to come in and bug you. Because I want in—and before you say anything, you should know I'm not really giving you a choice in this. I'll follow you if I have to, but I'd rather not have to be creepy like that."

"Keefe—"

He took her hand, waiting for her to meet his eyes. "Don't make me beg, Sophie."

"Keefe, if I do this, I don't know when I'll be able to come home."

"Sounds perfect. Is now too soon to leave?"

"If you don't want to stay with your father, I'm sure you could stay here."

"Probably. But then I'd still have to see him." He picked at a thread on the end of his sleeve, unraveling the perfect seam. "Who knew he'd turn out to be the 'good' parent? Didn't see that one coming."

"Keefe—"

"Whatever you're going to say, I'm sure I've already thought it. I've been replaying the last few years of my life—and you know what I keep focusing on? That wound you spotted on my mom's arm. The one you were worried my dad gave her? Turns out *I* gave it to her. I hit her with a goblin throwing star during that battle on the cliff, right after she clocked me in the head with a rock and knocked the melder out of my hand. And the thing is . . . I wasn't wearing a disguise like she was. She knew it was me. And she still attacked me."

"But she did stop Biana from falling off the edge of that cliff," Sophie reminded him. "She didn't have to do that."

"She also pressed a melder to Biana's brain and threatened to pull the trigger. She didn't have to do *that,* either."

"I guess that's true," Sophie admitted.

Honestly, Lady Gisela scared her way more than Brant did.

At least Brant had a *reason* for being broken and crazy.

Nothing would ever excuse the horrible things he'd done, but Sophie could understand why he'd joined the rebels in the first place. She knew better than anyone what it felt like to have her abilities stripped away, and the hard choices that had to be made.

"So when do you want to leave?" Keefe asked, sensing her mood shift.

Sophie threw up her hands. "I don't even know where I'm going!"

"I do," Fitz said, leaning in through her doorway. "One of the things Mr. Forkle showed me was the rest of that memory I found earlier—that window in Italy?"

He plopped next to Keefe on the bed, wearing the exact same pajamas, only his fit better.

Under normal circumstances, Sophie might've teased them about being twins. But given everything that had happened, all she asked was, "Did you find out where it is?"

"Yeah. I guess it's in a city called Florence. Or was it Firenze?"

"They're the same place," Sophie explained. "Firenze is Florence in Italian. But that's a huge city. Did it tell you any more information than that?"

Fitz nodded smugly. "But I'm not telling you until you say I can go with you."

"And me!" Biana added, appearing in the corner of the room—making Sophie wonder how long she'd been there.

Sophie got up to pace, realizing only after she did that she was wearing a long pink nightgown Biana had loaned her, covered in sparkly unicorns. It might not have been so bad if Biana weren't wearing a simple black tunic and stretch pants with red fluffy slippers.

"Guys, this isn't some, like, fun adventure I'm going on," she told them, crossing her arms and trying to look serious. "It's not even like the other stuff you've helped me with. We're talking about running away to find the Black Swan!"

"We are?" Dex asked from the doorway. "Guess it's a good thing I came upstairs, then, because I definitely want in on that."

Dex was *also* wearing a pair of Fitz's blue pajamas, though he'd had to cuff the pants and the sleeves several times to make them fit. The extra fabric swished as he made his way to where Fitz and Keefe were sitting and dropped down beside them.

"So where were we?" he asked.

"I'm pretty sure this is the part where Sophie goes on and

604

on and *on* about all the reasons why she's not going to let us go and we have to wear her down bit by bit," Fitz told him.

"You're not wearing me down!" Sophie insisted.

"She's cute when she's in denial, isn't she?" Keefe asked. "Especially covered in sparkly unicorns."

Sophie rubbed her head, wondering if it would be easier to hide in the bathroom until she was ready to leave. "You guys have to understand—if I do this, I'll be a fugitive. Not only will I be going to live with the group the Council has basically made their Public Enemy Number One—"

"The group we all illegally went to help this morning?" Fitz asked, grinning at her when she was forced to nod. "Just making sure. Carry on."

Sophie rolled her eyes. "Not only will I be going to live with the group the Council has basically made their Public Enemy Number One, but I'll be doing it without the circlet they ordered me to wear—"

"You mean the circlet I illegally helped you remove and then threw into the Everblaze to destroy?" Dex asked.

"I see what you guys are trying to do," Sophie told them. "And yeah, you're probably going to be in trouble. But that's not the same as leaving everything you know behind. If I do this, I don't know when I'll be able to come back. Is that really what you want?"

"Yes," Keefe answered immediately.

"Yeah, I know," Sophie told him, turning to Fitz, Biana, and

Dex. "But what about you guys? Do you really want to leave your families, not knowing when you'll see them again? Do you have any idea what that'll do to them?"

"You have a family too," Biana reminded her.

"I know." And the stabbing guilt she'd been trying to ignore jabbed her heart like a hot poker. "But *I* don't have a choice here."

"Neither do we," Fitz told her. "Like it or not, we're all involved, Sophie. So you can let us come with you and we can solve this mess a lot faster together. Or you can be stubborn and try to sneak away and we'll just follow you. In fact, we'll beat you there, because—let's not forget—I already know where you need to go, and you don't."

"Can I say something?" Alden said from the doorway, making them all jump.

They jumped again when they realized he wasn't alone. Della, Grady, and Edaline all followed him into the room as Sophie sat beside her friends, bracing for the lecture of the century.

Instead Alden told them, "I think the five of you should go."

"What?" they all asked in unison.

"To the Black Swan," Alden clarified. "I think you should go."

Fitz was the first to recover, clearing his throat and asking, "You do?"

"Yes. Mind you, it's not what I *want*. What I want is to lock all of you in your various bedrooms to keep you safe. But when

I embarked on my search to find Sophie—which was technically an illegal operation, by the way—I knew I was wading into dangerous waters. And yet I still did it, and even involved my son"—he smiled sadly at Fitz—"because of one simple fact: I knew it was right."

He paused to look at each of them in turn before he continued.

"The Council was *wrong* when they sentenced you to wear that circlet, Sophie. Just like they were wrong to target the Black Swan. And to ignore the warning signs from the ogres. And I fear they're going to get far worse when news of these recent adventures finds them. Which means—much as it pains me to admit—locking you in your bedrooms isn't going to keep any of you safe right now. The best place you can be is with the group the Council has been failing to find for decades. And you have a much better chance of making it there safely if you go together. So I think you should leave. Tonight. In fact, the gnomes are already gathering a few things you might need for your journey. You should be ready to depart within the hour."

"Seriously?" Biana asked, clapping her hands and clearly seeming way too giddy for the occasion.

Sophie turned to Grady and Edaline, who were both wiping tears from their cheeks. "You guys are really okay with this?"

"Yes and no," Grady said, holding out his arms for a hug.

Sophie crossed the room and sank into them, tearing up when she felt Edaline's fingers stroking her hair, lingering on the crown of her head where the circlet had been.

"Havenfield won't be the same without you," Grady said softly, "and it will *always* be ready for you to come home. But I have to agree with Alden. The safest place for you right now is with a group who knows how to hide. Dex's parents agree as well. I met with them while Sandor was getting treated."

Sophie glanced at Dex, and he nodded.

"But . . . will you guys be okay?" Sophie whispered, turning back to Grady and Edaline. "After . . . you know . . . you won't need me?"

"We'll always need you," Edaline said quietly. "But that's the point. What we need more than anything is for you to be safe. And I knew you wouldn't believe me. That's why I've already packed your things."

She pointed to a purple backpack stashed by the door.

The same purple backpack Sophie had shown up with after she left her human family.

It was crammed a lot fuller this time. But it still seemed impossibly small.

Was that really all she'd have to help her for the next stage of her journey?

No.

She turned to study the faces of her friends—the faces that had been with her through everything. She'd fought so hard to protect them that she hadn't really considered how much they'd protected *her*.

Individually they were vulnerable. But together, they were a *team*.

"You guys are sure you want to do this?" Sophie asked, needing to check one last time. "There's no going back from here."

Keefe smirked. "Uh, how many times do I have to tell you: *Bring it on, Foster.* I'm ready."

"Me too," Fitz promised, nodding quickly at his dad.

"Me three," Biana agreed.

"So the real question," Dex said, flashing his dimpled grin, "is, are *you* sure you want to do this?"

"Yes," Sophie told him, not needing any deep breaths or counted seconds before she decided.

She *was* ready.

So all she had left to say was, "Let's go join the Black Swan!"

ACKNOWLEDGMENTS

Yay, you made it to the end—and you're still reading! That makes me *ever* so happy. So I want to start by thanking you, dear reader, for coming along with Sophie and her friends on their incredible journey through the Lost Cities. Thank you for reading, for telling your friends, for following me online, and for all of the amazing e-mails and fan art that you take the time to send me. *You* make this job worth doing.

reaches through the pages to hug you

I would also never survive this crazy, confusing business without an army of brilliant people at my side.

Laura Rennert, I can't thank you enough for your unfailing

belief in both me, and this series, and for handling all of the complicated agent-y things so I don't have to deal with them. I also want to thank the entire team at Andrea Brown Literary, as well as Taryn Fagerness for her untiring efforts to bring KEEPER to readers all around the world. And to my foreign publishers, thank you for taking a chance on these books, and for all of the time and energy you put into translating them for your readers.

Liesa Abrams Mignogna, thank you for rolling with every twist these stories throw at me, and for always pushing me to make the books the best they can be. I also want to thank everyone at Simon & Schuster for the support they give this series, especially Mara Anastas, Mary Marotta, Lauren Forte, Fiona Simpson, Alyson Heller, Emma Sector, Carolyn Swerdloff. Julie Christopher, Lucille Rettino, Paul Crichton, Michelle Fadlalla, Venessa Carson, Anthony Parisi, Ebony LaDelle, Matt Pantoliano, Michael Strother, Amy Bartram, Jeanine Henderson, Mike Rosamilia, Siena Konscol, and the entire sales team. Plus a tremendous thank you to Karin Paprocki for yet another breathtaking cover design, and to Jason Chan for his seriously stunning artwork.

Thank you, Kari Olson, for the peptalks, honest opinions, and lightning-fast critiques—plus your ever-loyal support for all things related to Keefe. And thank you, Sara McClung, for squeezing in a second read among all the hectic, new-mom things, and Sarah Wylie for loving the draft so much, you're now contemplating a switch to Team Fitz. (I know how much it pained you to admit that.)

Every author also needs a network of writer-friends to lean on and laugh with, and I'm lucky to say I have some of the best. Thank you, Heather Brewer, MG Buerhlen, Lisa Cannon, Christa Desir, Debra Driza, Kirsten Hubbard, Nikki Katz, Lisa Mantchev, Andrea Ortega, Cindy Pon, CJ Redwine, James Riley, Amy Tintera, Kasie West, Natalie Whipple, and Kiersten White, plus the wonderful ladies of Friday the Thirteeners. I also must thank Margaret Peterson Haddix for joining me for some very hectic touring in the Midwest, and for braving a midnight Walmart bathroom stop somewhere between Minneapolis and Milwaukee. (Oh, the glamorous lives we authors lead.)

I will never be able to properly express my gratitude to the teachers, librarians, bloggers, and booksellers who have gotten behind these books and helped get them in the hands of readers, especially Alyson Beecher, Katie Bartow, Maryelizabeth Hart, Faith Hochhalter, Katie Laird, Kim Laird, Brandi Stewart, Andrea Vuleta, and so many others. I wish I had the space to thank you all individually, but since I don't (this book is rather thick, after all), I hope you all know how much I truly appreciate each and every one of you, and if I haven't had a chance to meet you in person yet, I hope our paths cross soon.

To my parents, thank you for telling pretty much every person you meet that they need to read these books (regardless of whether or not they have kids), and to all my friends and family, thank you for the unending amount of slack you cut me as I battle through my crazy deadlines. And thank you for not judging me for getting *another* cat. They make the best writing buddies. Plus, I needed an orange one.☺

Turn the page for a sneak peek at

KEEPER OF THE LOST CITIES

Book 4: NEVERSEEN

W

E HAVE TO GO," FITZ SAID, bursting through the doors of Everglen's upstairs guest room.

He found Sophie sitting alone on the edge of the giant canopy bed, already dressed in some of her old human clothes.

"I thought we were waiting another hour?" she asked, glancing out the window at the endless black sky.

"We can't. The Council is already convening to vote on our punishments."

Sophie took a slow breath, letting the words pulse through her veins, steeling her nerves as she reached for her purple backpack. It was the same bag she'd used when she'd left her human life nearly a year earlier. And now she would use it again to leave the Lost Cities.

"Is everyone ready?" she asked, proud of her voice for not shaking. She also resisted the urge to tug out an itchy eyelash.

This was not a time for nervous habits.

It was time to be brave.

The Council had vowed to capture and punish anyone associated with the Black Swan—the mysterious organization responsible for Sophie's existence. But Sophie and her friends knew the real villains were a group called the Neverseen. Fitz, Keefe, and Biana had even tried to help the Black Swan capture the rebels on Mount Everest. But the Neverseen guessed their plan and turned the mission into an ambush. Sophie had discovered the trap in time to warn her friends, and they'd escaped with their lives—and managed to capture one prisoner. But they'd each broken numerous laws in the process.

Their safest option now was to flee to the Black Swan and go into hiding. But Sophie had mixed feelings about getting up close and personal with her creators. The Black Swan had tweaked her genes to enhance her abilities as part of their Project Moonlark—but they'd never given her any clue as to *why*. They'd also never told her who her genetic parents were, and Sophie had no idea if she'd finally have to meet them.

"'Bout time you got here," Keefe said as Sophie followed Fitz down the twisting silver staircase. He stood next to Dex in Everglen's glittering round foyer, both of them looking very human in hoodies and dark jeans.

Keefe flashed his famous smirk and patted his carefully mussed blond hair, but Sophie could see the sadness clouding his sky-blue eyes. During their confrontation with the Neverseen, Keefe had discovered that his mother was one of their leaders. She'd even attacked her own son, before fleeing to the ogre's capital and abandoning her family.

"Hey, no worrying about me, Foster," Keefe said, fanning the space between them. He was one of the few Empaths who could feel Sophie's emotions rippling through the air.

"I'm worried about *all* of you," she told him. "You're all risking your lives because of me."

"Eh, what else is new?" Dex asked, flashing his dimpled grin. "And will you relax? We've got this! Though I'm not sure about my shoes." He pointed to his soft brown boots, which were a typical elvin style. "All the human ones Fitz had were too big for my feet."

"I doubt anyone will notice," Sophie told him. "But I guess it depends on how long we'll be around humans. How far away is the hideout after we get to Florence?"

Fitz smiled his movie-ready smile. "You'll see."

The Black Swan had taught Fitz how to sneak past Sophie's mental blocking and view the secret information hidden in her brain. But for some reason he wouldn't share what he'd learned.

So all Sophie knew was that they were headed to a round window somewhere in the famous Italian city.

"Hey," Fitz said, leaning closer, "you trust me, don't you?"

Sophie's traitorous heart still fluttered, despite her current annoyance. She *did* trust Fitz. Probably more than anyone. But having him keep secrets from her was seriously annoying. She was tempted to use her telepathy to steal the information straight from his head. But she'd broken that rule enough times already, and the consequences definitely weren't worth it.

"What is *with* these clothes?" Biana interrupted, appearing out of thin air next to Keefe.

Biana was a Vanisher, like her mother, though she was still getting used to the ability. Only one of her legs reappeared, and she had to hop up and down to get the other to show up. She wore a sweatshirt three sizes too big and faded, baggy jeans.

"At least I get to wear *my* shoes," she said, lifting her pant leg to reveal purple flats with diamond-studded toes. "But why do we only have boy stuff?"

"Because I'm a boy," Fitz reminded her. "Besides, this isn't a fashion contest."

"And if it was, I'd totally win. Right, Foster?" Keefe asked.

Sophie actually would've given the prize to Fitz—his blue scarf worked perfectly with his dark hair and teal eyes. And his fitted gray coat made him look taller, with broader shoulders and—

"Oh please." Keefe shoved his way between them. "Fitz's

human clothes are a huge snoozefest. Check out what Dex and I found in Alvar's closet!"

They both unzipped their hoodies, revealing T-shirts with logos underneath.

"I have no idea what this means, but it's crazy-awesome, right?" Keefe asked, pointing to the black and yellow oval on his shirt.

"It's from *Batman*," Sophie said—then regretted the words. Of course Keefe demanded she explain the awesomeness of the Dark Knight.

"I'm wearing this shirt forever, guys," he decided. "Also, I want a Batmobile! Dex, can you make that happen?"

Sophie wouldn't have been surprised if Dex actually could build one. As a Technopath, he worked miracles with technology and gadgets. He'd made all kinds of cool things for Sophie, including the slightly lopsided ring she wore—a special panic switch that had saved her life during her fight with one of her kidnappers.

"What's my shirt from?" Dex asked, pointing to the logo with interlocking yellow W's.

Sophie didn't have the heart to tell him it was the symbol for Wonder Woman.

"Why does Alvar have human stuff?" she asked. "I thought he worked with the ogres."

"He does," Fitz replied. "Or he did before you almost started a war with them."

Fitz said the words in a light, teasing way, but the truth behind them weighed heavy on Sophie's shoulders. They'd be in a *lot* less trouble if she hadn't ignored the rules of telepathy and tried to read the ogre king's mind. She'd known it was a dangerous risk, but she'd been desperate to know why the ogres had snuck into the Sanctuary and hidden one of their homing devices in Silveny's tail. The rare female alicorn wasn't just essential for the survival of her species. She was one of Sophie's closest friends. If only Sophie had known that ogres' minds could detect Telepaths—even genetically enhanced Telepaths like her. She hadn't learned anything useful, *and* she'd nearly voided the elvin-ogre treaty and started a war.

"But that still doesn't explain why Alvar has human stuff," Sophie reminded Fitz. "Ogres hate humans even more than elves do."

"They do," Fitz agreed. "But these clothes are from years ago, back when Alvar used to go out looking for you."

"He did?" Sophie asked. "I thought that was your job."

Fitz was the one who'd found her on her class field trip about a year earlier, and brought her to the Lost Cities.

It was the best thing that ever happened to her.

Also the hardest.

Fitz smiled sadly, probably remembering the same thing: the moment she'd had to say goodbye to her human family. He was the only one who really understood what she'd lost that day, and she couldn't have gotten through it without him.

"I started searching for you when I was six," he told her. "After Alvar started his elite levels and wasn't able to sneak away from Foxfire anymore. But my dad searched for you for twelve years, remember? I couldn't go on secret missions when I was a toddler."

"What a slacker," Keefe interrupted. "I totally could've pulled that off. But then again, I'm Batman, so"—he draped an arm over Sophie's shoulders—"I could be your hero any day."

Dex pretended to gag, while Biana stared at Keefe's arm around Sophie.

"Aren't we supposed to be leaving?" they both asked at the same time.

Sophie had barely managed to slip out of Keefe's hold when Alden called "Wait!" from the top of the stairs. His elegant cape swished as he rushed down to catch them. "You can't leave wearing your registry pendants."

Sophie grasped the choker clasped around her neck, hardly believing she'd overlooked that incredibly important detail. The pendants were special tracking devices from the Council. She wondered what other important things she might be forgetting. . . .

Alden pulled out a pair of sharp black pliers and said, "Let's start with Fitz." He spoke with the same crisp accent as his children, but his voice sounded weak and wobbly.

Fitz flinched as Alden cut the thick cord and the crystal pendant clattered to the floor.

"Whoa. This just got real," Keefe whispered.

"Yeah, it did." Fitz traced his fingers across his now bare neck.

"Are you okay?" Alden asked Biana, who was clutching her pendant in a white-knuckled fist.

"I'm fine," Biana whispered, lifting her long dark hair to expose her necklace.

Alden hesitated only a second before he sliced through the silver band. Her pendant landed next to Fitz's, followed by Keefe's.

"Yours will be trickier to remove," Alden reminded Dex and Sophie.

The Council had added extra security measures to theirs after the Neverseen kidnapped them and used their pendants to convince everyone Sophie and Dex were dead. Both of them even had trees in the Wanderling Woods—the elves' equivalent of a graveyard—from the funerals their families had thrown for them.

Alden's brow beaded with sweat as he pried at the thick metal, but eventually the cords broke free. "I'll need to remove your nexuses, as well," he said, pulling out a small flat disk the size of a dime.

Sophie sighed.

Another very important detail she'd overlooked . . .

A nexus was a safety device meant to hold their bodies together during light leaps, but the force field it created could be tracked.

"I guess I didn't plan this running-away thing very well, did I?" Sophie mumbled.

"It's not the kind of thing one can plan for," Alden reassured her. "And do not expect yourself to think of *everything*. You're part of a team now. Everyone works together and helps."

The words would've been a lot more comforting if her "team" hadn't forgotten the same important things—though Fitz, Keefe, and Biana were already nexus-free. Their concentration strength had reached the required level. Dex was almost there too. The meter on his wide blue cuff had less than a quarter of the way to go.

When Alden pressed the tiny disk against it, the level surged to full.

"I've been tempted to do that myself," Dex admitted as he slipped the nexus off his wrist. "But I didn't want to get in trouble for cheating."

"Wise choice," Alden agreed. "Having the ability to do something does not mean it's the safest course of action. It also does not give us permission to break the law."

"It does when the law is stupid," Keefe argued.

"I wish I could disagree. But look at where we are." Alden gathered their fallen pendants and tucked them into his cape pockets along with Dex's nexus. "There was a time when I believed in the infallibility of our world. But now . . . we must rely on our own moral compass. Right here"—he pressed his hand to his heart—"we know what is necessary and true. You all must hold to that and let it guide you through what lies ahead. But I've let myself get sidetracked. Sophie, let's take care of those nexuses."

Thanks to Elwin, her overprotective physician, Sophie had to wear one on each wrist. He'd also locked her nexuses so they couldn't unlatch, even though both of her meters were full. She'd faded several times during leaps—one of which had nearly killed her. But that was before the Black Swan enhanced her concentration and healed her abilities.

Still, Sophie reached for the Fade Fuel she wore around her neck in case of emergencies. It hung next to her allergy remedy, both vials tucked safely under her T-shirt. She hadn't needed either elixir in weeks, but she still felt better having them. Especially as Alden produced a twisted silver key and unlocked each of her nexuses.

She stopped him as he examined her third black cuff. "That's one of Dex's inventions."

"I call it the Sucker Punch," Dex said proudly. "It releases a burst of air when you swing your arm, so you can punch way harder than normal."

"Very clever," Alden told him. "And a good thing for you to have. Though, Dex, I'm hoping you've learned the dangers of inventing new weapons."

Dex's shoulders drooped as he promised that he had. Dex had built the painful ability-restricting circlet that the Council had forced Sophie to wear, not realizing it would be her punishment for what happened with the ogre king.

She nudged him with her elbow and smiled to remind him that she'd forgiven him. But he kept his eyes fixed on the floor.

"I think that takes care of everything," Alden said. "Though you all must remember to look out for one another. Fitz and Biana, share your concentration with Dex when you're leaping. And Keefe, I want you to help Sophie."

"Oh, I *will*," Keefe promised with a wink.

"We *all* will," Fitz corrected.

"Hey, I can take care of myself," Sophie argued. "I'm the one bringing us to Florence, remember?"

The blue leaping crystals all led to the same place in each Forbidden City, which would make it easier for someone to follow them. So they'd be teleporting to Italy, an ability only Sophie had, thanks to a surprise side effect of the way the Black Swan altered her DNA.

"All of you can take care of yourselves," Alden said quietly. "But you are stronger when you work together. You must also have a leader to keep the team organized, so Fitz, since you're the eldest, I'm putting you in charge."

"Hey, wait a minute," Keefe argued. "He's only older by a few months."

"Uh, by 'few,' you mean *eleven*," Fitz corrected.

Dex snorted. "Dude, you guys are *old.*"

He glanced smugly at Sophie, and she blushed, hating that she'd been thinking the same thing.

Well . . . she didn't think Fitz and Keefe were *old*. But they were definitely older than her.

She'd guessed that Keefe was fourteen, which would make Fitz at least fifteen—but they could be even older than that. . . .

It was hard to keep track of age in the Lost Cities. The elves didn't really pay attention to it, thanks to their indefinite lifespan. In fact, Sophie had no idea how old any of her friends actually were. No one ever mentioned their birthdays. Maybe that meant Sophie wasn't supposed to care about age either—but she was very aware that she was only thirteen and a half, and the difference between her and the boys felt *huge*.

"Hey, I'm the one who knows where we're going," Fitz said. "So I'm in charge, and . . . I guess we should probably head out. Though, wait—what about Mom? Shouldn't we say goodbye?"

Alden glanced at Biana. "Your mother has to take care of something at the moment. But she told me to tell you she'll see you soon."

Fitz didn't look very satisfied by that answer. But he didn't argue either.

Alden turned to Sophie, not quite meeting her eyes. "I . . . offered Grady and Edaline a sedative a few minutes ago and they decided to take it. We feared what would happen when they actually had to watch you leave. So they told me to tell you they love you, and that they left a note for you in your backpack."

The lump in Sophie's throat made it hurt for her to nod, but she forced herself to do it. Grady and Edaline were her adoptive family, and she hated leaving without seeing them. But she doubted they were strong enough to handle another tearful goodbye, given everything that had happened.

They'd lived in a deep fog of depression ever since they'd lost their only daughter, Jolie, to a fire seventeen years earlier. And now Sophie had discovered that Brant, Jolie's former fiancé—who Grady and Edaline had been caring for as if he were part of their family—had been the one to set the fire that killed her. Brant had been hiding that he was a Pyrokinetic—the elves' only forbidden talent—and joined the Neverseen because he hated living as a Talentless. But when Jolie discovered his betrayal and tried to convince him to change his ways, he lost his temper and sparked the flames that accidentally took her life.

The guilt and grief had shattered Brant's sanity and left him dangerously unstable. He'd even tried to kill Grady and Sophie when they went to confront him. Grady had been so furious, he'd used his ability as a Mesmer to make Brant burn off his own hand. Sophie had barely managed to stop Grady before he went too far and ruined his own sanity. She'd also had to let Brant escape in order to get the information she needed to save her friends.

"All right, we've lost enough time," Alden said, pulling the five of them close for a hug. "Remember, this is not goodbye forever. It is simply goodbye for now."

Sophie felt tears slip down her cheeks as Fitz asked, "Do you want us to let you know when we get there?"

"No, I cannot know anything about what you're doing. None of us can."

"Do you think the Council will order memory breaks?" Sophie whispered.

"No, the Council will not sink to that level. Plus they know we are too prominent and powerful. It is simply wise to be cautious. I promise, there's no reason to worry."

Sophie sighed.

No reason to worry were Alden's favorite words. And she'd learned to never believe them.

"Come on," Biana said, pulling open Everglen's shimmering doors.

They tromped down the shadowy path in silence.

"I never thought I'd say this," Keefe said, "but I really miss having Gigantor tagging along with us."

Sophie nodded, wishing her seven-foot-tall goblin bodyguard were healthy enough to join them. Sandor had been thrown off an icy cliff during the ambush on Mount Everest and broken pretty much every bone in his body. Elwin had assured her that he'd be okay, but Sandor had a long road to recovery before him.

Not as long as the road we're about to travel, Sophie thought as she spotted Everglen's enormous gates through the gloomy night. The glowing yellow bars absorbed all passing light, preventing anyone from leaping inside.

"Time to run," Alden whispered.

Teleporting only worked when they were free-falling, and the bluffs they needed to jump off were beyond Everglen's protection.

Fitz wiped his eyes. "Tell Mom we love her, okay?"

"We love you, too, Dad," Biana added.

"And don't let the Councillors anywhere near my family," Dex begged.

"You have my word," Alden promised. "And I won't let them near Grady and Edaline, either."

Sophie nodded, her mind racing with a million things she wanted to say. But only one really mattered. "Don't let Grady go after Brant."

Alden took her hands. "I won't."

Everyone looked at Keefe.

"Tell my dad . . . that I've been hiding his favorite cape in a closet on the twenty-ninth floor. But don't tell him the door is rigged with a flask of gulon gas. Let him find that one out on his own."

"Is that really all you want to say, Keefe?" Alden asked.

Keefe shrugged. "What else is there?"

Alden wrapped Keefe in a hug and whispered something in Keefe's ear. Whatever it was made Keefe's eyes water.

Sophie's eyes did the same as Alden pulled the lever and opened the gates.

The five friends stared at the towering forest and locked hands.

Slowly, together they took the first step into the darkness. They'd just crossed the threshold when a cloaked figure stepped out of the shadows—not a black cloak, like the Neverseen wore.

A diamond-encrusted silver cloak.

The style worn by the Councillors.